TELL TALE

SAM HAYES

LARGE PRINT

Oxford

Copyright © Sam Hayes, 2009

First published in Great Britain 2009
by
Headline Publishing Group

Published in Large Print 2010 by ISIS Publishing Ltd.,
7 Centremead, Osney Mead, Oxford OX2 0ES
by arrangement with
Headline Publishing Group
an Hachette UK Company

All rights reserved

The moral right of the author has been asserted

British Library Cataloguing in Publication Data
Hayes, Sam.
    Tell tale.
    1. Suspense fiction.
    2. Large type books.
    I. Title
    823.9'2–dc22

        ISBN 978–0–7531–8636–7 (hb)
        ISBN 978–0–7531–8637–4 (pb)

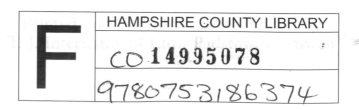
F

HAMPSHIRE COUNTY LIBRARY

CO 14995078

9780753186374

For Ben, my son, my friend.
With all my love.

Acknowledgements

Sincerest thanks to Anna and Sherise for your much-valued input, friendship and dedication to my books. As ever, grateful thanks indeed to the entire team at Headline — on both sides of the planet.

Thanks in abundance to my beautiful niece from Brisbane, Emma Dean (dot com), whose music is inspiration and medication when I need some help — and of course to Tony Dean and the rest of the band.

Terry, Ben, Polly and Lucy . . . love forever. A special mention to the Southfield girls and finally, as ever, to Sandra. Keep the magic alive.

Prologue

The tide is high — a dizzying swell several hundred feet below. She grips the suicide wires, overbalancing as her billowing skirt blows free from the lock of her unsteady knees. She knows that any moment now, officials will be running towards her, trying to coax her down as they have done for dozens before her. She must be gone before then, but not until they have witnessed her jump. The driver of a passing car hoots and waves, as if urging her on.

It will take three seconds to die.

She looks down, focusing on the water beneath. Her mouth is dry and her throat collapses when she swallows. She remembers what he said: *feet first . . . ballerina toes . . . arms locked . . . a tilted entry*. Her hair is tied back but a loose strand whips against her cheek.

"Look for the bubbles," she whispers. Her final words.

It's pitch black down there, he'd said with a smile. Follow the bubbles to the surface. Then swim for your life, he told her, laughing now, if you were really going to do it. No one would, though, he said. Not without equipment.

She loosens her skirt — not really a skirt, but swathes of special material. Beneath it, her wetsuit clings to her shaking body. She slips the nose-clip either side of her nostrils, which are flared with fear, and alters her grip on the bridge. The lattice railings are cold and sharp in her hands as she turns into her final position. The river below is as far away as another planet, another life.

She glances along the bridge's pedestrian path. A woman stands frozen about fifty feet away, her hand clamped over her mouth, stifling a scream. Behind her, an overweight bridge official runs with an ungainly gait towards her perch. The sky hangs heavy with churning storm clouds, and a dozen gulls glide through the squall with ease. A white plumber's van slows but then accelerates again, while a small red car stops completely. She notices all these things as she takes one tiny step into the void.

Three seconds to die, yet it takes the rest of her life.

Slowly, slowly, she has time to think. Her bare toes stretch to painful points, while her fingers lock above her head. The wind rushes through her, cleansing, eradicating, restoring, saving. She smiles. A grimace of what is about to come — not on impact, but what will happen after that.

Her sand-coloured skirt billows and ripples but then settles into a tight circle of drag a second and a half before her toes cut the surface of the river. She tries to tilt backwards but the force prevents a clean angle. Inch by inch, her body enters another world. Her feet, her

2

ankles, her knees, legs, thighs, are engulfed by the concrete-hard water. Her body, her chest, her shoulders and neck are consumed by the flow. Then, as her eyes instinctively close, her head submerges. Everything is silent. Everything is black. Everything is slow motion.

Finally, she is able to move her heavy limbs, not certain they are still attached to her body. She untangles herself from the skirt and, as she reaches for it, it billows away in the current like a freed jellyfish. Then all she can see are the tangled swathes of her hair and a silver trail fizzing through the murk.

Follow the bubbles, she thinks through a waterlogged mind, not knowing which way is up.

Cupped into paddles, her hands pull her towards the surface. Her chest burns and her legs will barely move. She pushes onwards, desperate for a glimpse of light; desperate for a glimpse of the afterlife.

CHAPTER
ONE

Nina Kennedy kicked off her heels and pummelled her sore feet. "Fetch me a couple of headache pills, sweetheart." She closed her eyes.

"Here you go, Mum." Josie delivered the tablets with a glass of water. "Are you OK?"

Nina grinned through the pain. "I certainly am." She massaged her forehead. The day had been long, an endurance test, but she'd loved every minute of it. "My feet may be numb, and my head feels as if it's been split in two, but it was certainly worth it." Nina hugged her daughter. "That presentation did the trick."

"You mean . . . you got the contract?" Josie blinked repeatedly — a tic that had plagued her for years — and hardly dared to breathe. She pulled her long hair back off her face, exposing a lean face stuck somewhere between child and woman.

"I sure did. Chameleon FX is now the official make-up and effects provider for Charterhouse Productions' next three films."

Josie was silent for a moment. Her lips rolled inwards as she took in the news. "At Pinewood?" She had to check.

Nina nodded and swallowed the tablets. "We start with *Grave*. Shooting begins in two weeks. You can come on set with me while it's still the school holidays." Nina bent her arms out of her jacket and chucked it on the back of the chair. Her daughter was obsessed with acting. It was a healthy release; a way to express her teenage angst and emotions. Better than smoking or drugs, Nina concluded.

Josie didn't say a word. Her eyes grew wide and her cheeks swelled as if they were about to burst. She ran out of the room. Seconds later, Nina heard the verbal explosion as her daughter telephoned all her friends to spread the news. *Her mum was going to be doing make-up on famous people.*

Nina went into the kitchen to unpack the groceries she'd picked up on the way home. She poured herself a glass of wine and sat at the kitchen table, wondering if the grin on her face was really as big as it felt.

Mick didn't know about her success yet. She would tell him as soon as he came back inside. It was the biggest contract to date for Chameleon. She usually worked on theatre productions, model shoots, commercials, and she'd done some TV. There had been a few feature films, although she'd only ever assisted and that was a while ago. Making Chameleon's name stand out in what was a very competitive business was Nina's greatest ambition. It was a chance to showcase her talents — changing actors into characters; making fantasy from reality. It was all about transformation, and that was what Nina did best.

"It's going to mean horrifically early starts. I have to be on set by seven." An hour later, Nina was serving dinner. She'd pulled together a bean salad, some lamb with couscous. Mick had finished work for the day, lured back up to the house by hunger. "We'll manage, won't we?"

"You know we will," Mick replied. He stared hard at his wife, thrilled by her news. He chewed, thinking. "No need to worry about things here." He flashed a fond look at his daughter and spooned some beans on to her plate. "What do you reckon, Pumpkin? Think we'll survive?"

Josie shrugged, holding up her hands at the quantity of beans her father was serving. She hated it when he called her that. And he always gave her too much food, as if he wanted to fatten her up. Josie didn't care if her mum stayed out all night, as long as she got to hang around Pinewood. She'd wanted to be an actress ever since her mother first dropped her at Saturday drama school aged five. She was never happier than when she was pretending to be someone else.

"Really, you deserve everything that comes your way," Mick said, halting Nina's hand with his. He tightened his grip around her wrist. "I'm proud of you. So proud." He leaned forward and spotted a kiss on her neck. Everything was coming together, just as they had always planned.

Later, when Josie had gone to her room, Nina and Mick sat outside. The evening air was warm and smelled of jasmine, undercut by the scent of salt and mudflats fanned in from the estuary low tide. Nina breathed in deeply. It wasn't quite dark. She laughed into the twilight as her heart skipped a contented beat in her chest. "We did it, you know." She couldn't wait to telephone Laura in the morning. She would be thrilled at the news.

"Did what?" Mick was pensive. He'd been distracted by work for several weeks. He tracked a plane as it headed out to sea. But the grin that appeared on his face told Nina he knew exactly what she meant. He just wanted to hear her say it.

"All this." Nina leaned back and looked at their house. The nineteen thirties semi-detached wasn't a palace — it was modernised and comfortable — but felt pretty close to it. "Owning our own place, for a start."

"Apart from the mortgage," Mick said, rolling his eyes.

"We have a beautiful daughter."

"I'm with you on that one." Mick was a devoted father, quite unlike many of Josie's friends' dads, who perhaps saw their kids at an occasional family meal, a birthday gathering, or when a reprimand was due.

"And I have a gorgeous, handsome, talented husband," Nina continued with her list, trying to prevent the smile, knowing what was coming.

"Well, I'm definitely in agreement there." Mick put down his wine. A candle flickered on the table between them. "Come here." He reached out his arms. She knew not obeying was pointless. Mick always got his way with her.

"Plus we mustn't forget your recent good news." Nina finished her wine and stood up. "I won't have it overshadowed by mine." She straddled her husband's legs. The wooden chair creaked as she lowered herself to sit on his lap. "Things are finally going well for us. I'm so happy, Mick." She stared into his eyes, attempting to fathom what lay within the mystery of them. She was more in love than ever.

"Things finally went well for me the minute I met you." Mick wove his fingers through the mass of his wife's hair. He tugged on her neck and brought her face towards his. They kissed. Nina sighed from deep inside, a special reserve, as if she had a secret stash of love reserved especially for him. Mick withdrew but kept their lips near. "There's something I want to show you."

"Oh?" Nina leaned back and stood up when she felt Mick shifting beneath her. "What is it?" Pinwheels of excitement spun through her. That was the thing with Mick — he made her feel so alive. Some of her friends had complained that their marriages needed a kickstart after only a couple of years. Infidelity, boredom, incompatibility, work pressures had all added to the downfall of wedded bliss. Not so in the Kennedy household.

It made Nina feel almost guilty confessing that her husband was passionate, spontaneous, and that he still adored her. She remembered telling all this to Laura when they'd opened a second bottle of wine one night. Nina hadn't meant to brag or send Laura into a flat spin about her own marriage. But Mick had a knack of

9

injecting freshness and excitement into their lives. She just couldn't keep to herself how she felt.

"I wasn't going to show you until it was finished, but I can't wait any longer," Mick said solemnly.

"I'm intrigued, Mr Kennedy." Nina felt herself being pulled by the hand and led down the garden towards the studio. Mick had had the wooden cabin built when they moved into the house five years ago. It was practically a second home for him now.

They stopped halfway across the lawn. Suddenly, everything went dark. "Hey, what's going on?" Nina could smell nicotine on her husband's fingers as they blanketed her eyes. She felt a moment's apprehension, but then laughed.

"Come into my dark abode," he growled playfully. "I want to do despicable things to you."

Nina giggled and allowed herself to be led blindfolded across the grass. She felt a twig crunch underfoot and noticed the sickly-sweet scent of the tea rose she had recently planted as they brushed past the border. "Mick Kennedy, you are a wicked, evil man, but I love you." This was the perfect ending to a significant day. She heard his breathing as he unfastened the door. He always kept the key on him, protective of the studio's precious contents.

Inside, Nina breathed in Mick's cologne and the scent of his work. Her eyes were still clamped shut as he closed the door. She heard him flick on the light. "What is it, Mick?" It was a thrill to have his warm fingers blinding her. "I'm dying here. *Please* tell me."

Light suddenly flooded Nina's pupils as he released her. She squinted.

"Well?" Mick stepped over to a huge canvas and spread out his hands. "What do you think?"

Nina's breath caught in her chest, trapped between ribs that had frozen in place. Finally, she said, "It's amazing. *Beautiful*." Tears welled in her eyes as she focused on a nude, life-size painting of herself. "I absolutely love it. But why did you paint *me*?"

"So I can see you while I'm working. Every bit of you." He half smiled, half pouted. Nina's heart raced in her chest. "Now that I have the deal with the Marley Gallery in London, I'm going to be flat out supplying them." He sighed. Perhaps, Nina thought, from the extra workload. He'd been so stressed recently. "You can keep me company in the wee hours." He was pleased she approved.

"It's so . . . so real." Nina blushed as she walked up to the painting. She followed every contour and line. One limb led to another; swirls of her long hair drew the eye to remote parts of her body. Vaguely abstract like most of Mick's works, yet real with exquisite clarity, Mick had captured a side of her she had long forgotten existed — a woman, a youngster, the child within.

"Couldn't you spare any paint to give me clothes?" She stepped up to her husband and wrapped her arms around his neck. Their previous kiss still lingered in the pit of her belly.

"This is how I see you. Free, lovely, naked. As vulnerable as when you were born."

"At least you've given me a scarf." Nina pointed at the long stretch of fabric that Mick had painted tied round her wrist. It was loosely bound to the other one. "It's pretty. I'd like a scarf like that." Deep purple and red chiffon brushed her skin. "But don't you think I look too thin?" She was becoming self-conscious.

"It's how you are," Mick said, unscrewing the lids of several tubes of paint. He didn't take criticism well.

"No, really. I'm a little heavier than you've made me." Nina studied the layers of paint that made up her body. Sometimes Mick used a palette knife. Sometimes he used a sable brush with only a couple of fine hairs.

"Prove it." Mick's eyes simmered blue-black.

For a second, Nina thought he was angry at her comments. Then she raised her eyebrows and unfastened the top buttons of her blouse. "You realise that you're going to have to inspect every inch of me to make sure the likeness is good."

Mick grinned before he made his move. With one hand he locked his wife's wrists together and with the other he stripped her naked. No one heard their noise or knew of the passion that flared between them as they lay down beneath the painting; no one else felt their happiness.

When Nina stumbled back across the garden, it was dark. She blew out the candle left burning on the rear deck. Mick, who often worked at night, stayed in the floodlit studio to paint.

In the bathroom, Nina studied herself in the mirror. She nodded slowly. The likeness of the painting was a good one. In bed, she stared at the ceiling, smiling her way into a peaceful sleep.

CHAPTER
TWO

I'm staring up at the huge gates with the car engine ticking over. The wrought iron is painted black, with twitch grass fringing the trunk-like wooden posts. There's a security keypad to one side. The pass code was included in my new employee's pack. I punch in four seven one six.

The iron gates creak and part in the middle. I edge the car forward, keen to get in. I check the rear-view mirror. The gates close, sealing me inside the grounds. I drive on, swallowing away the nerves that have been brewing in my throat the last few days.

The drive is tree-lined, with branches spreading like out-stretched arthritic arms, forming a mottled canopy. Beech and oak stand sentry as I pass beneath. I keep my eyes fixed firmly ahead.

The drive yawns into a wide courtyard with a Victorian mansion sitting squarely between the stables and a modern building beside it. As I approach, I read "Science Block" on the ugly modern bricks.

I park my car and crunch across the gravel, carrying my suitcase to the main front entrance. It was raining earlier and the air smells sickly-sweet from the hanging

14

baskets and tubs of dazzling flowers clustered around the entrance.

I take a deep breath and step inside.

"Hello. I'm Frankie Gerrard," I announce as cheerfully as I can manage. "Francesca," I add when the school receptionist appears puzzled.

"Ah, yes, of course." She smiles at me. "We've been expecting you." She comes out from behind the desk and hooks a hand under my elbow. "Welcome to Roecliffe. Come on, I'll show you to your room and then you can meet everyone."

"Thank you," I say. She tells me her name but I immediately forget it.

"That's the dining hall," she says as we pass by. I glance inside. My heels click on the tiled floor. I never usually wear heels. "And that's the library in there. See all the trophies that our girls have won? We're a very sporty school," she says proudly. I follow her gaze.

"Impressive," I say, hurrying to keep up.

We pass along a long corridor, up several flights of stairs that take us to the summit of the hundred-and-fifty-year-old building, down a few more creaky steps, along another passageway, and we finally arrive.

The receptionist unlocks a low door. "You'll be comfortable in here." We step inside and she gives me an old key. It has a red ribbon attached with my name on a paper tag. "In case you lose it," she says. "The bathroom is at the end of the hall. Let me know if there's anything you need."

"It's all lovely," I say, smiling. I let my small suitcase drop to the floor. It topples over as if it's already settled in.

"I'll leave you to unpack then. There's a pre-term staff meeting at three. A cup of tea and a chance to get to know everyone." She's still a little wary of me, the way her eyes dance over my face. "You're not the only one that's starting this term. There's a new games teacher, and a French teacher over from Paris for a year."

She's trying to make me feel better. "Thank you." I hold open the door. "See you later then." I force a smile.

I lock the door after she's gone.

I sit on the single bed. Iron frame, sagging mattress, faded quilt. "Well," I say to test the sound of my new room. I close my eyes and listen to the silence of my new life.

CHAPTER
THREE

The most important thing my daddy ever told me was that my name meant *bird*. It was from the Latin, he said, and my mother had chosen it before she died. For the next ten years, he had me believing that I might one day wake up with wings and be able to fly away.

"Ava," he'd said. "My skinny little bird."

The smell of exhaust mixed with the tang of his smoky skin as I hung on to his neck stayed with me all those years. The hum of his big car when I saw it cruise out of sight rattled in my head, making me think he was somehow close when really he couldn't have been further away.

"Next week then, Ava. I'll come back to see you next week."

But he didn't.

Until that day, he'd been true to his word and visited me every Sunday for nearly two months. Since the day he announced he couldn't cope.

"But *I* can cope," I'd tried to convince him, aged eight. "I'm good at coping." But it wasn't enough to prevent my dad calling someone — I never knew who exactly — and that someone coming to our shabby terraced house and taking me away.

"Now, Ava, don't make a fuss," my dad had said. I hooked my fingers on to the door frame and scowled. "I'll visit you on Sunday."

"This Sunday?" I asked. He nodded. He tweaked his moustache. "And will you come the Sunday after that?" He nodded again. "And the one after that?" I asked a thousand times more until my father peeled my fingers off the wood and shoved me out of the door. I dragged my suitcase behind me, climbed silently into the waiting car, and was driven off to the children's home.

So on Sundays, I sat on the stone window seat near the entrance of the home. It was my special place to wait for my dad. To pass the time, I imagined life as it used to be — just him and me, perhaps curled up on the grubby sofa, the chant of a football match on the television, the stink of the beer as it dried on Dad's shirt. I'd watch the rise and fall of his chest as he slept, and count the wheeze of his breaths. If it ever slowed or fell out of its drunken rhythm, I pummelled him until he stirred.

Other times — times that didn't happen very often — I would help him work in the garden. The sun sliced into my eyes, making me screw up my face as I watched my dad wield the spade at the end of our small patch. I stood picking dirt out of my nails, wondering what the point was. The potatoes were always left to rot in the ground.

Every year, Dad said he was going to grow his own vegetables. "We'll have a right feast, me and you. Our own sprouts at Christmas." But every year, William Fergus Atwood only got as far as hacking down a few waist-height weeds, or perhaps digging a couple of square feet of the heavy clay soil before he succumbed to the bottle.

Some days, I went to school. I liked it there but couldn't always go. Often I didn't have any clean clothes to put on. Not even a T-shirt. I picked through garments that had gathered under my bed and piled in the corners of my tiny bedroom as if they'd been blown there on a desert wind. Stripes and patchworks that I once remembered colourful had turned to a sombre version of their original hues from weeks' worth of stains, forcing me to stay in my knickers and vest.

I slouched about the house, driving my dad nuts by playing games with stuff that wasn't mine. I fiddled with his precious demijohns, watching the bubbles blip at their necks as the wine fought for life. I tangled his fishing line and spilled his tobacco while I crunched breakfast cereal from the box. I emptied out the eggs from their tray and made nests for imaginary chicks that would never hatch.

Occasionally, a lady from the council came to tidy, to cook meals, and clean up the mess down my dad's front while he snored. She stalked slowly around our little house as if she hardly dared enter the poky rooms. She muttered as she worked, using the tips of her fingers to move our things about. Afterwards, things were better for a time. It made me happy. I could put on clean clothes again and go back to lessons. I was learning to read and I loved painting pictures.

But other times, even when there were clothes to put on, I didn't make it down the road to join the other children on their way to school. Often Dad was slumped on the floor blocking the front door. The walk back from the pub the night before finished him off and it was as much as he could do to unlock the door. His body was a dead weight filled with several days' worth of drink.

"Dad, get up," I would call out. "Go to bed." I yanked at his hair. I tried to roll him, to pull him, and I prodded him with my foot until he growled and heaved himself a couple of feet so that I could prise the door open six inches. That's all it took for me to slip out into the fresh morning air and join the procession of other kids on their way to school.

When Dad didn't budge and I couldn't squeeze through the door, I would rest my chin in my hands with my elbows pressed on to the window sill. I'd watch my friends trotting past the house with their lunch packs and smiles. I'd tried in vain to open the windows to climb out. The downstairs ones were all glued up with paint and the back door was so warped from age and damp that only Dad could open it with two fists and his boot. On those passing-out days, as I called them, I was a prisoner.

"Like now," I thought, drumming my fingers on the grand stone mullion — a far cry from Wesley Terrace — waiting for the sight of my dad's car to appear at the turn of the drive. Not many cars ever came down the long drive to Roecliffe Children's Home. It was as if we'd been forgotten by the rest of the world. Delivery trucks sometimes dropped off sacks of potatoes and carrots, and occasionally the repair man came to bang around in the boiler room. The older kids said that this wasn't all he came for, but I didn't know what they meant. And sometimes, although I'd never seen one, a bus came to take the children on a trip out. I didn't want to be in the home long enough to find out if this was true or not.

But when a vehicle did burst from within the cluster of trees at the end of the drive, the news quickly spread and everyone gathered round the window to see who it was. Me, I stuck fast on my special seat; wouldn't budge in case it was Dad. I wanted to wave him all the way in.

I loved my dad, even though he wasn't like other dads. Since he lost my mum, I think he'd lost his mind.

My forehead rested on the cool glass. A part of me wished my skull would crack right through the panes. I imagined the blood fingering down my face, spilling either side of my nose and around my mouth. I thought of the panic as the carers dabbed my skin with wet cloth and scolded me for being so stupid. I pressed as hard as I dared on the glass, but then jumped out of my skin. A hand dropped on to my shoulder.

"Haven't you got anything better to do?" I turned and saw a man I didn't recognise staring down at me. The sight of his mottled face set upon a trunk-like body froze me solid. His arms stuck out like branches, while the lines carved in his face reminded me of brittle twigs against an angry sky. The blood drained from my head; my heart thudded in fear. I wanted to go home. I wanted my dad.

21

I shook my head from side to side, trying to answer but nothing came out of my mouth. I'd not been living at the home long, but I couldn't stop thinking of those horrid stories, the stupid lies that flew from one grubby mouth to another. I screwed up my eyes to block it all out. My lips clamped together to stifle the scream that was brewing.

"Then you'd better come and help me," he growled when I remained silent. I dared to peek out of one eye and saw something knotty and veined sitting at the man's craw, as if he'd swallowed a bunch of rotten grapes and they were sticking out through his baggy skin.

He nipped a hand round my arm and pulled me off the window seat. "The devil makes work," he muttered, walking off down the long hall, towing me as if I were a stray puppy.

The stories flew through my mind like the wind flipping through the leaves of an old book. Memories of the other kids' nightly tales were interlaced with the oblivion of sleep and nasty tablets. Perhaps I'd imagined it all. But the goings-on somehow found their way into our everyday lives as if they were perfectly normal — as normal as if we'd been told to shake out fresh sheets on the washing line, or sweep the floor, or lay the fire in the grate.

Reluctantly, I followed the stranger down the dark corridors of the home. As we walked on, new rooms suddenly telescoped out of others. "Where are we going?" I plucked up the courage to ask, but the man ignored me.

Wide-eyed and stiff-limbed, my mouth hung open, fixed in a silent scream. My feet stubbed the floorboards in unwilling steps as the strength of the man outweighed my meagre protests. We stopped outside a door. The horrid man knocked and went straight in.

A light so bright I thought the sun had somehow got in there made me screw up my eyes. I couldn't see anything at all apart from the black silhouette of another man sitting behind a desk. Half from fear, half from the pain burning my eyes, I pressed my forearm across my brow. I prayed it would all go away.

"Not her." the man behind the desk said in a voice that made me believe we'd stepped into hell. "There's a father. Get another one."

CHAPTER
FOUR

"Miss Gerr-ard," the man says, drawing out the syllables. "I'm Mr Palmer, the headmaster." His skin is waxy and moist, and brushes limply against mine for a second as we shake hands. There is a sugar-dusting of dandruff on one shoulder of his dark suit.

"Please, call me Frankie," I tell him.

"Are you settling in? How do you like Roecliffe? Matron told me all about you."

I open my mouth to speak.

"She's only been here an hour, Geoff. Give her a chance," the receptionist interrupts, handing me tea and leading me away. "Come and talk to Sylvia, dear. Trust me, Geoff'll bore you for hours with stories about this and that. He knows everything there is to know about this place, and he seems to think everyone wants to hear about it." She grins knowingly.

I offer a bemused smile and follow her through the dozens of staff milling about. I feel way out of my depth.

"Hello, Bernice," Sylvia says fondly, kissing the receptionist on both cheeks. "How was your holiday?"

Sylvia, the matron, interviewed me on the telephone two days ago. It was all such a rush. I'd seen the position advertised on the school's website last week. There were several jobs available, but the others were for teaching posts and I'm not qualified for those. It almost makes me giddy, thinking about the last few days.

It took all my courage to call about the job. Matron confessed on the phone that she was desperate for help. Term was about to start. There had been a girl lined up to fill the post, but she'd pulled out at the last minute without explanation. After Sylvia learned that I'd spent several years working with teenagers, she offered me the job there and then.

I sip my tea, patiently listening to Sylvia and Bernice chatting about the long summer break. Sylvia doesn't look much like a school matron.

"Hello again," I say, when she finally gives me her attention. She grips both my hands, squeezing hard. "Reporting for duty," I add with a forced laugh. Despite her jumpy disposition, I like Sylvia. She gave me a chance. She makes me feel as if I might one day belong.

"Frankie, it's lovely to have you here at Roecliffe Hall. I'm so pleased you accepted the position. Is your room all right?" She stands on tiptoe to deliver a brief kiss to my cheek. "Anything you need, just shout. I'm determined not to lose you like all the others."

"It's all fine," I tell her. "I'm very . . . happy to be here. I have a lovely view right across the grounds from my room." I wonder what she means, about losing the others.

"You just wait until autumn. The trees are dazzling."

"I can imagine," I say. "When do the pupils arrive?" I picture meeting the girls, seeing their earnest faces, their lips bubbling with holiday banter, their eyes brimming with tears, excitement as their parents leave, as another term starts.

"Between seven and nine. We have a few hours to prepare for the hormonal onslaught." Sylvia laughs.

"Oh gosh." I laugh inappropriately, loudly. My hand spreads across my mouth.

"What's so funny then?" A sandy-haired man steps sideways and nudges Sylvia. "Aren't you going to introduce me?"

"Frankie, meet Adam. Adam's history."

"It's true. I live in the past," he says pleasantly. I detect a slight accent. South African perhaps?

"That's not very healthy," I joke, for the sake of something to say.

"Frankie's my new house assistant," Sylvia continues. "She wanted a live-in job, and I desperately needed help since that girl let me down. Where is it you said you came from, Frankie?"

"Down south," I say vaguely, trying to deflect Adam's interested gaze. He is tall and his body leans casually as if an imaginary wall were propping him up. The delicate cup and saucer look ridiculous in his large hands. He is wearing a striped shirt loose over black jeans; tousled hair over tanned skin. He looks more like a surfer than a teacher.

"Ah," he says slowly. His grin sits broken over the jut of his chin. "From the south, like me then. And I expect you'll be living very much in the present looking after all the girls." He sips his tea, not taking his eyes off me. "Loud music, the internet, electronic games, make-up, boys, and tears. Good luck." He has eyes that are so blue they make the rest of his face look insignificant. It's only when I draw away from him that I see he has a laptop tucked under one arm.

Sylvia is talking to someone else. "What are the girls like?" I ask him. It's that or stand there in awkward silence.

Adam glances at my cheek. His mouth opens and shuts several times before speaking. I blush. "They . . . they're a nice bunch generally. Some can be a bit spoilt and demanding." He's still staring.

"Perhaps they have problems at home." I dig my nails into my thigh. I feel so awkward.

"Privileged, I think is the word you're looking for. And you're hurt." Adam frowns, making me flinch as if he's about to touch my face. I step backwards.

The headmaster taps his teaspoon on his cup, saving me from having to explain.

"I'm fine," I whisper when Adam refuses to stop staring. "Just a graze."

I turn my back on him and concentrate on what the headmaster has to say. In a few words, he cheerfully prepares us for the start of term; reminds us of the responsibilities we have to the three hundred and fifty-seven girls attending Roecliffe Hall; encourages us to give a moment's prayer for another successful and happy school year. When everyone bows their heads, I hold mine high. I blink back hot tears. In my experience, prayers don't work.

The girls arrived around seven — battalions of noise and belongings. From the small leaded window of my room, I watched the procession of cars on the drive below. My breath clouded the old glass as expensive vehicles deposited their children at school after the long summer break — some departing with no more than a cursory wave goodbye once the boot contents had been unloaded.

It made my throat go tight.

"Sylvia, do you mind if I quickly make a phone call?" We were ushering girls to the correct dorms and helping the new pupils.

She shooed me away with a grin. "Run for your life, if I were you."

The cacophony of schoolgirl clatter diminished as I tunnelled down the corridor to where I'd spotted the payphone earlier. I didn't have a mobile phone. Underneath the Perspex hood, names and numbers were jotted on the wall, along with general graffiti scribed in nail polish, Tippex and compass points.

I fished fifty pence from my pocket. I pushed it into the slot and listened to the dial tone for several minutes before hanging up. The coin dropped out. With the receiver replaced, I dialled the number anyway without credit. No harm.

"Everything OK, Miss Gerrard?" The headmaster slowed as he walked past. In the dim light, his face appeared carved, made from weathered wood. Seeing him down the dark corridor made my skin prickle.

I put the coin back in my pocket. "Everything's fine, thank you," I replied, but he hadn't stopped to listen.

The next morning at breakfast, Adam sits down next to me at the refectory table. All the other spaces are taken. He nods a greeting at me and the other staff around us, and then opens up his laptop. He taps away at the keys, punctuating his work with bites of toast and jam. He asks a woman I don't know to pass the teapot.

"How was your first night?" He glances up from the screen, able to think, type, eat and talk without getting in a bother.

"I was only woken four times. Three weepies and a vomit." I take a large sip of my coffee. None of the other staff bothered me with much more than a good morning.

Adam stops, toast halfway to his mouth. He drops it on to his plate and then types again for a minute or two. I can't see what's on the screen. Rays of coloured sun burst through the stained-glass window, highlighting the edges of his hair.

"Bad luck then," he says as if he's just remembered we were talking.

"Not a bad night, considering," I reply vaguely. Truth is, even if the girls hadn't woken me, I don't think I would have slept.

"So." Adam turns to face me, snapping his laptop shut. "What does your first day at Roecliffe hold?" I still can't quite place the accent. He picks up his tea and hugs the mug.

I sigh, hoping a bell will ring, prompting a scramble for class. "I have to make sure the girls have unpacked everything in their trunks. Then there's the beds, the

29

dirty clothes, make-up, sweet wrappers, tissues, and general rubbish that can be found in teenage girls' rooms. I have to do a drug search, sort out last term's lost property, make sure they all eat lunch — I have a list of the anorexics — after which, I have a house staff meeting to discuss the laundry procedure and —"

"Oh, OK," Adam laughs. "You're obviously an expert on this. Where did you say you'd worked before?" He waits for my reply.

It's as if the breakfast bustle in the dining room suddenly stops; as if everyone wants to hear my answer.

"Frankie, are you OK?" Adam frowns.

I nod. The noise of the dining hall returns. "I just feel a little faint." It's the truth. "But I'll be fine." I don't want to be rude. I just want him to go away, to get on with his lessons while I get on with my duties.

Adam scissors his legs free from the school bench and clatters his mug on to his plate. He appears to have taken the hint. "See you later, perhaps." He looks me up and down before leaving.

Seconds later, the bell rings. I sit perfectly still while dozens of feet hammer the wooden floor around me, shaking me to the core, punching it all home. The stampede of pupils and staff, the ordered panic as the day begins, the hundreds of lives that are being shaped within this building transport me back lifetimes. To a place I never thought I'd return.

CHAPTER
FIVE

Nina smudged a line of kohl under Josie's eyes. Josie scowled. "That's enough or I'll be late."

"Let me just highlight your brow bone." Nina peered over the top of her glasses and stroked a shimmering powder above her daughter's eyes. "So pretty," she said, stamping a kiss on Josie's forehead.

"No I'm not." Josie meant it. She hated it when anyone complimented her looks.

"You go and have a wonderful time but no —"

"No alcohol, drugs or sex, right?"

"I was going to say no wiping off my hard work in the loos, but none of those things either, young lady. What time is Natalie's mum dropping you back?"

"Midnight?"

"Try ten thirty. It's what we already arranged. I just want to make sure you have it fixed in your mind so you don't keep Laura waiting."

"Oh, Mum." Josie adjusted the belt on her hips and slung a bag over her shoulder. She kissed her mother.

"Oh, *Josie*." Nina grinned. "Go on, or you'll be late for the concert."

Josie skipped out of her bedroom but was back in a second. She wiggled the mouse beside her computer.

From the doorway, Nina caught a flash of something on the screen before Josie clicked on a button and exited the window.

"What was that?"

"Just a silly online game I was playing." Josie gave her mum a look that told her if she took it further, it would ruin the pleasant hour they'd just spent rummaging through clothes and make-up. Nina heeded the silent warning, glancing back at the computer as she left the room.

An impatient honk sounded through the front door. "Dad's in the car already."

Josie hesitated.

"Go! He's waiting." Nina guided her daughter out of the door. "Enjoy the concert." She touched a whisper of a kiss on Josie's head and watched as the two most important people in her life drove away.

Mick had blown into Nina's life on a storm. The unseasonal summer winds had closed shipping channels in the estuary, and high-sided vehicles were banned from tall bridges. Warm rain lashed against the side of the crew van, and the wind buffeted it so that it rocked on its wheels. They had to shout to be heard above the noise.

"I'm nearly done." Inside the van, Nina dabbed at the reporter's cheeks with a make-up sponge. She was nervous. She'd seen him on the telly before and now here she was, streaking foundation across his nose.

"Don't see the bloody point," he growled, sounding quite different to the slick reporter she was used to seeing on TV. "It's going to get washed off as soon as I step out there. What fool would be out in this weather, let alone go out to sea?"

"The fool that you're about to interview," the research assistant said, clutching a clipboard. "Nina, we've only got one minute."

Nina nodded. She worked quickly. It was her first proper job since leaving college. She'd done a few weeks' work experience during her training and had subsequently applied for a permanent position at the news station when she'd qualified. The people were interesting, the pay was terrible, but she was doing what she loved, what she was good at. Changing people's appearances.

"All done," Nina said, snapping the cap back on the make-up bottle. "Oh, wait." She swiped a soft brush across the impatient reporter's forehead. "There you go."

The door of the van slid open and a gust of wind stirred a mini tornado inside. The reporter was met by a film crew who were to shoot a short interview with a man who had saved a dog from the rough seas earlier that day. He in turn had needed rescuing, and the lifeboat had been called. Nina thought that this man could use some foundation as well. His cheeks were scarlet.

She followed the team across the car park to the harbour wall, staggering as the wind blew her sideways. Her waterproof jacket billowed out like a loose spinnaker and she held her make-up bag close. Any touch-ups would be pointless in these conditions. She watched as the team set to work, interviewing the foolhardy man about his antics.

"News must be in short supply," she said but her words were blown away. The wind whipped against her neck and her lips tasted salty. The entire crew looked fed up as they battled the weather to get their story. "I'll be over here," Nina yelled but no one heard. Desperate for cover, Nina approached a wooden shelter that faced out to sea. She couldn't stand the wind any longer.

"Oh," she exclaimed as dozens of sheets of paper suddenly tumbled out of the shelter and blew around her feet. One wet piece wrapped round her ankle like an army gaiter. "Oh no," she cried, looking down. Grey and blue paint had smeared all over her black work trousers.

"That's amazing," said a deep voice. "The colours are absolutely perfect."

Nina looked up and squinted through the drizzle. Unlike hers, this voice didn't seem to end up out at sea on the gale. A man had emerged from the shelter holding a paintbrush. She eyed him suspiciously.

"The paint on your leg. It's incredible."

"It is?" Nina pulled the paper from her leg, but it started to tear. "Oh, I'm so sorry," she said, but he didn't hear. He was crouching, studying Nina's trousers.

"See how the ultramarine has combined with the viridian? The bleeding? The feathering?" The man squinted at her hem. "It's what I've been trying to achieve all day. And here you are, a casual stroller, and suddenly my vision appears on your leg." He stood up.

"I'm not a casual stroller as such." Nina's hair flapped around her face. The strands whipped at her eyes, making what she was seeing all the more surreal. "I was trying to find somewhere out of the wind to wait while the crew get their take. I have to be on hand." She pointed to the news station van and raised her make-up bag. In doing so, the painting tore in the wind and one half escaped her fingers, flapping towards the sea. "Oh no!"

"It doesn't matter. It's not a patch on this." He bent down again and trailed a finger lightly over Nina's leg. "Inspiration eternal." He was mesmerised.

"It's no problem, honestly. It'll wash out." She stared down at the man's head. His hair wasn't grey, rather charcoal — an unusual colour — and Nina thought it matched the weather.

"No, no, don't wash it out. I tell you what," and he stood up, his face close to Nina's. "Let me buy them from you. I want to buy your trousers."

Nina laughed and, at the same time, a gust of wind toppled her sideways. Her white teeth flashed amusement in the storm. "You can't buy my trousers," she said. "You're mad." She started to walk off back to the crew, shaking her head.

"Wait. I'll give you a hundred pounds for them. Please." Nina turned. She noticed his eyes as they occluded to a thunderous slate colour to match his hair. He was serious.

"Hey, forget the money." She held up her hands in defeat. "If they mean that much to you, jot down your address and I'll post them. They're old anyway." The wind tore at lips that couldn't help grinning. "No one's ever wanted me to take my trousers off for such an odd reason." The man grinned and daubed his name and address in paint on the remaining paper. He handed it over and Nina allowed it to flap in the wind to dry.

"And before you say it," he said as she glanced at the address, "yes, I'm trailer trash."

Nina tried to decipher the words. "Ingleston Park. I've never heard of it."

"Lucky you." He smiled again. "It's a shitty dump of a place on the outskirts of town. Only those down and out on their luck in this life and all their previous incarnations get to live there." He was laughing as he spoke. "No, really. It's OK. Just a cabin. In the woods."

"It sounds rather nice," Nina said, thinking of her own bedsit above the chip shop. "I bet you don't wake to the smell of fat and battered sausages."

"*Nina!*" the production assistant yelled.

"Looks like I'm needed," she said. "Expect my trousers," she called as she turned and ran back to the crew. The casual wave she flicked over her shoulder kept the artist standing on the dock until the crew van was out of sight.

"She's out like a light." Nina folded on to the sofa.

"They had a great time at the concert. I worry about her going out at night, though. Anything could happen to her." Mick sank on to the sofa next to his wife. "And if I'm honest, I don't think I'll be able to stand it when she brings a boy home. The thought of some grubby teenager laying a finger on my girl makes me . . ." Mick pulled a face and shook his head.

"Don't fret about that. She's sensible. She won't throw herself at the first boy who comes along." Nina laughed.

"That may be so, but you'll still have to tie me up when it happens."

They'd never thought that this time would ever come. Josie becoming a young adult, dating, going to parties, having relationships, had always seemed a million miles away. "I'm still not convinced that internet access in her bedroom is a wise idea, though. Did you update the parental settings?" This was Nina's main concern.

"Of course. I already told you that. She can't look at anything dangerous."

"It's not that. I trust Josie. It's other people that worry me. Chat rooms, all those social networking sites, photos and videos posted everywhere you look. She's ripe fruit for picking."

"It's all pretty harmless," Mick said. He stretched out on the sofa. "But it's under control. As you say, she's a sensible girl. I've already asked her about what she does on the internet. She plays some online game mostly. An alter world where you can pretend to be someone else. It's what they all do. She's just being normal."

Nina arced her head slowly. "That must be what she was logging off earlier. I got the feeling she didn't want me to see."

"Of course she didn't want you to see. She's fifteen. Now who's being paranoid?" Mick wiped his hands over a tired face. "I wouldn't worry about it, Nina. It's not even in the real world."

Nina nodded pensively. "But it's in her bedroom, inside her head." The most vulnerable part, she thought. "That doesn't mean she can't get hurt."

"Teenagers are programmed to be secretive. They don't tell us anything."

If Josie hadn't been home late after the concert, he and Nina would have already turned in by now. Mick yawned. "Worrying about a little bit of internet use is nothing compared to her having a real boyfriend." Mick pulled Nina's hand into his.

"You're right. I just need convincing sometimes. Bringing up a daughter is so scary. Every day you read about paedophiles and stabbings and —"

"Shh." Mick silenced Nina first with his finger, then with his mouth. He led her upstairs and they made love quietly and slowly — familiar bodies fuelled by trust and need.

Afterwards, with only a cotton sheet draped over her legs, Nina listened to the silence. In the room next door, she heard Josie mumbling through sleep, before she, too, slept restlessly, dreaming about things she'd long forgotten.

The rain swept across the garden at forty-five degrees. Purple-grey clouds hung heavy to the west over the estuary. It had been a washout summer so far. Nina knew weather like this and predicted a full day of rain.

"So much for the gardening," she muttered, climbing the stairs.

Mick had gone to his studio early. He was under pressure to deliver several new pieces by the end of the week. A respected gallery in London had recently commissioned him to paint for them regularly. Mick had been cagey about the details, bashful almost, as if he would jinx his good fortune if he bragged about the contract. If he didn't get them done, he said, there were plenty of starving artists waiting to take his place.

Nina knocked on Josie's bedroom door. "Honey, do you fancy a bit of retail therapy? You could do with some new jeans." When there was no reply, Nina went in.

The curtains were still closed and the room smelled of a mix of sweet perfume and dirty laundry. Josie swung round on her desk chair, startled by her mother's entrance. "Mum," she said, quickly shutting down the open window on the monitor. "I didn't hear you." Her face was red and, for a moment, Nina thought she'd been crying.

"You're not even dressed, Jo. I thought we could go shopping." Nina grabbed a handful of her daughter's messy hair and wound it into a knot. Josie swiped it down.

"Don't touch me, Mum." She shied away. "Do we have to go out?"

"You have anything better to do?" Nina pulled back the curtains and opened the window an inch. Rain settled on the inside sill.

"I just want to be alone."

"Given the chance, you'd stay on the computer all day." Nina scooped her daughter under the arms and heaved her up. Josie relaxed and made herself go heavy, standing reluctantly. She shrugged away from her mother, scowling.

"Get yourself into the shower, young lady, and then we're going out shopping." Nina bundled up the dirty clothes in her arms.

Josie hugged herself tightly, still feeling where her mother's arms had wrapped around her. "Why do I have to do what everyone tells me?"

Nina stopped in the doorway and turned. "Josie, don't force me to lay down the law. You have it pretty easy. An attitude lift wouldn't go amiss, OK?"

"I'm just sick of . . ." She stopped. Nina couldn't be sure, but she thought tears briefly swelled in Josie's eyes. Her daughter checked herself. "I'm sorry, Mum." She bowed her head.

"Just what is it that you spend so much time doing on that computer anyway?"

Josie sighed, anticipating what was coming next. "It's just a game, Mum. All my friends play it." She glanced at the floor, curling her toes into the carpet. "You worry too much."

"Then show me." Nina dropped the clothes into a pile by the door and sat down at Josie's desk. "Convince me it's harmless."

Josie shrugged and sullenly logged in to a website that was immediately dancing with crazy characters and 3D animations. "This is me, look. You can create little people that resemble you. They're kind of you but not you. Do you get it?"

Nina didn't reply. Pretending to be someone else on the internet didn't sound at all harmless to Nina. A frown pulled her eyes together and her lips parted. She watched as her daughter leaned over her shoulder and navigated her way around the site. "This is the house I made for myself. And look, I have a pet dog. My friends can come to visit me, or I can go over to their houses. I can get a job, earn credits, buy new clothes and stuff. You chat to people by typing in here then it appears in a box on their screen. It's cool." Josie suddenly buzzed with excitement, as if it really was better than real life.

Nina swallowed. "And you're sure you know everyone that you visit or talk to?"

"Of course," Josie said. "Only friends on my allowed list can come into my house and only when I say so. It's really safe, Mum." She planted a kiss on Nina's cheek. "I'm not stupid."

"Your character doesn't look anything like you. It has red hair, for heaven's sake." Nina laughed, trying to lighten things up. She didn't want to be a heavy-handed parent.

"That's why I love going there. It doesn't have to look like you. You can be whoever you want in Afterlife." Josie stared out of the window. "It's like a clean slate."

"In what?" Nina stared deep into her daughter's eyes, looking for signs of dishonesty.

"Afterlife. That's what the game's called." Josie happily logged off.

Later, when they had raided the shops, bought things they didn't really need, ordered milkshakes and doughnuts, tried on shoes, tested lipsticks and doused themselves in perfume, Nina found herself thinking about Afterlife and the chance to be whoever you wanted to be.

CHAPTER
SIX

I didn't encounter Adam again that first afternoon. I saw him through the window, striding across the courtyard, his long legs weaving a purposeful path back to school. The hems of his jeans were soaking. He'd obviously been walking through wet grass.

I pulled away from the window, my fingers trailing thoughtfully on the stone mullion.

It was just as well we didn't see each other. I wouldn't have been able to foil any friendly conversation, not without appearing rude, and I didn't want to answer any more questions.

Besides, after my duties were taken care of, I was left with little time to think, let alone sit and chat. From the minute term began, girls of all ages demanded my attention, and one teenager in particular latched on to me.

"It pisses me off that they don't care." Lexi, a blonde fourteen-year-old, hovered beside me. I checked off the inventory list in the linen storeroom. "They must hate me. Why else would they have dumped me here?"

I put down the clipboard on a pile of towels. "That's just not true," I said, although I hadn't a clue about the girl's situation. "Your parents love you. And please don't swear."

"Mum's dead," she continued. "And my dad's a big git." All this said with an accent that wouldn't be out of place in the royal household.

"But you said *they*." I continued counting towels.

"They as in the git and his sidekick. The bitch git."

I frowned, wondering how I could make her see her good fortune. But she'd told me her mother was dead. There was no good fortune in that.

"As soon as I'm at school, they go off on holiday without me. They lie on the bloody beach while I'm stuck in this dump." Lexi kicked a heap of sheets as hard as she could, but it didn't topple over. This made her even angrier.

"Look, Lexi. Have you ever considered that your dad might be finding things really hard since your mum died?" She was already shaking her head. "Or that all he wants is for you to love your new stepmum so that you can be a family again?"

"Then why ship me off to boarding school?" she retorted. There were tears building in her angry eyes, but she refused to allow them to escape.

"So you can get a good education, make new friends, become independent." I reached for Lexi's hand but she pulled away. "I'm sure your dad has his reasons for sending you here. Try to trust him."

Lexi finally broke down and fell against me. My shoulder drank up her tears. We sat on the floor amongst the clean linen, and for an hour she told me all about losing her mum, how she felt abandoned, an unwanted child. I stroked her head and just listened.

She was so upset, still drenched in snot and tears, that she didn't even notice when I said, "We have a lot in common then, Miss Lexi." And I wove my fingers tightly with hers.

Once a week there is a formal dinner at Roecliffe. Staff and pupils, stiff in their blazers, rack shoulder to shoulder at the polished oak refectory tables lined up like giant herring bones. A central path between the tables leads to the huge, empty, dining hall fireplace. At the end of the Advent term, Matron told me earlier, there would be a roaring blaze to accompany Christmas lunch.

"Silly health and safety rules won't allow it any other time," she'd complained, folding sheets, making beds, tidying the detritus that seemed to accumulate in the dorms as quickly as we could remove it. Gradually, through idle conversation as we worked, I was getting to know Sylvia, getting to know that she was a mother to just about every girl at Roecliffe. I remained sketchy when she asked me things, diverting direct questions with the snap of a sheet, or by diving under a bed to retrieve a sock. I reminded myself I'd not come to be friends with anyone.

My dinner sits untouched in front of me. "It's a shame," I say, staring into the empty grate. I imagine sparks jumping off knotty logs, purple-blue smoke escaping the draw and filling the hall with the scent of the forest, an orange rain showering up the wide black chimney, the bed of embers warming bare toes. Some comfort.

"What is?" Someone takes the space beside me and shakes out a napkin. I glance sideways and see that it's Adam with his wide upturned cuffs, showing a dash of sandy hair on his forearms. "What's a shame?" He sips his water.

I nervously laugh it off. "Do you want the pepper?"

"No pepper, thank you." Adam stares at me, frowning. He's holding his knife and fork poised above his plate. "When I sat down, you said *it's a shame*. I take it you weren't referring to me sitting beside you as a shame?"

"You want the truth?" I say. Meat falls off my fork. I can tell him this much. "The shame is that there's no fire in that empty grate." The flicker of admission makes my heart stumble over a beat.

"But it's warm. It's the end of summer." Adam turns away and eats his chicken, apparently disappointed with my confession. "We don't need a fire."

"I know, it's just that . . ." I take a mouthful of food. "It doesn't matter."

Adam shrugs, unaware what I'm thinking. He doesn't see what I see — a hearth on a winter's evening, ears cocked for footsteps, a churning belly, unsure if it's from fear or the excitement of sharing blackjacks and fruit salads that have been doled out.

"Do you think you'll be happy working here?" Adam places his cutlery on the edge of his plate and leans his elbows on the table. His shoulder brushes mine.

"Sylvia tells me that three of her assistants have left in the last year." I push a large forkful of food into my mouth, hoping he won't ask anything else.

"I said, do you think *you'll* be happy working here?" He laughs. "I know the others weren't."

"Oh?" I manage, forcing a reciprocal smile. I push in more food. My mouth is so full I can hardly breathe, let alone speak. I gesture apologetically.

Adam turns back to his food. "Don't choke," he says thoughtfully, satisfied with silence for the rest of the meal.

CHAPTER
SEVEN

Nina was in the kitchen, preparing food, occasionally glancing at Josie who was curled up on the sofa by the French windows. The teen's hair was wrapped in a pink towel and she was wearing a heart-covered dressing gown. Two hours ago, she'd asked to borrow Nina's laptop, saying the computer in her bedroom was running too slow. Nina tried not to show much interest, tried not to notice the rainbow of emotion that swept over Josie's face as she typed frantically. Nina guessed that she was on Afterlife. Josie sat hunched over the keyboard, her shoulders protectively winging the screen.

She wondered what it was that stirred her daughter. Her expression showed a mix-up of anxiety and desire. Nina kept quiet, but when Josie slid off the seat, shut the computer lid and went up to the bathroom, Nina took the opportunity to find out. It was her computer, after all.

Nina dried her hands, thinking that Josie had probably closed down the window she was using. But when she opened up the laptop, she was surprised to see that the page was still open and, as she suspected, Josie was logged in to Afterlife.

Nina read.

-*Have 2 go soon*, Josie had typed in a chat window. A symbol clearly showed a hug between Josie's character and another one. Nina caught her breath.

-*Don't go yet.* Then the characters had shared a virtual kiss.

-*5 more mins or i'll get it.* Nina imagined Josie's fingers shaking as she typed.

-*Wot u wearing?*

-*Duh. Wots it look like?*

She remembered Josie giggling out loud. Nina glanced at the door. She knew Josie was hanging out for the youth theatre's new production to begin rehearsals, but she hadn't expected her daughter to be passing the time quite like this.

-*Take them all off* the other character had typed. Nina saw that he was called Griff.

-*You know that's not allowed. Game rules.*

At least she has some sense, Nina thought. She recalled Josie clapping a hand over her mouth. Probably when she was typing this. She thought back to all the times Josie and Nat were hunched over the computer in Josie's room in fits of laughter. She shuddered.

-*Just ur knickers and bra then.*

-*No way!*

Nina remembered Josie mentioning this boy in the past. Griff was in the year above Josie at school. Apparently all the girls adored him. Josie had said that he'd never be interested in someone like her. Suddenly Nina felt a huge sadness for her, that her social life had been reduced to sleazy talk on the computer.

-I'm not taking my clothes off, Josie had then typed, much to Nina's relief. She knew her daughter was funny like that, even in front of her. She was very shy.

-*u going bowling tomoz?* Josie had continued. An attempt, Nina thought, to ask him out.

-*Nah*, Griff replied. She could almost sense Josie's disappointment, thinking that maybe if her character had just put on a bikini that would have pleased Griff. But Nina saw that the next thing to have happened was that Griff's character had faded to grey and vanished. He'd gone offline. Probably why Josie had left the room in a hurry.

Nina snapped the computer lid closed and rushed up to the bathroom.

"You OK in there, love? I've made a snack if you fancy something," she said through the door.

"K," Josie replied sullenly. "I'm going round to Nat's." Nina imagined she needed to confide in her friend about what had just happened.

"I can give you a lift if you like." Nina held her breath. Perhaps they could talk on the way.

"Nah," Josie said quietly. "I'll walk."

"Her moods are very up and down," Nina told Laura. "Never a dull moment with Josie." Her friend pulled a face, the same one Nina would have made in return if she hadn't had a mouthful of pasta. She swallowed. "If I'm honest, it started when she was about three. Sullen and moody way beyond her years from then on." The women laughed together, thankful that they had each other.

50

Once a month, they went out for a meal — just the two of them, to talk, to compare, to offer a little bit of support to each other in the world of bringing up teenagers. Laura had two kids — a sixteen-year-old boy, James, who had recently taken GCSEs, and Natalie, Josie's best friend.

"It's all so predictable in our house," Laura said. "I can virtually recite our morning breakfast conversation while James is shovelling up his cereal."

"Oh, don't." Nina tried not to laugh. "At least you have a morning conversation. Josie rarely even eats breakfast. She steps into her uniform in exactly the same spot that she stepped out of it the night before, refuses to brush her hair because she likes it messy, yet spends hours in front of the mirror perfecting her eyeliner. Most days, I only know she's gone to school because the house shakes when she slams the front door."

"You wait," Laura said. "When they've all gone off to university, we'll be bereft. We'll miss the surly silences."

"They'll be back often enough. When they run out of money, clean clothes, and get sick of eating beans on toast." Nina poured more wine, knowing they'd be sharing a taxi the short distance home. "Seriously, though, how are things with Tom?"

Last time the two women had met, Laura revealed that her marriage was running aground. Nina was shocked when Laura said it was like having marital cancer. "I reckon we'll only survive a short while longer," she'd confessed.

"We're still just hanging on," Laura said sadly. She downed several large mouthfuls of wine. "We had our first counselling session last week." She pulled another face. "My dear husband stormed out halfway through. He got particularly touchy when the counsellor suggested he should seek help for his anger problem. I'd already implied he'd been having an affair, so that was the last straw."

Laura's expression fell away from her usual taut, holding-it-together look. Her mouth drooped and her eyes lost their normal sparkle and turned downwards in a fan of lines. "I think the counsellor was right. The signs all point to another woman."

"Oh, Laura," Nina said. She offered her hand across the table but Laura didn't take it. Tears forced her to flee to the toilet. Nina followed her and found her sobbing over the basin. Gently, she turned her round and folded her into her arms. She plucked tissues from the box and wiped her eyes. Then she stood and hugged Laura, rocking her, not needing to say anything. In ten minutes they were back at the table, Laura as composed as if she were attending a job interview.

"So," she said brightly. "How's your work?"

Nina went along with it. "Well, I'm gearing up for the Charterhouse film that's about to go into production. Remember I told you I'd won the contract?" Laura nodded. "The first one's a horror movie called *Grave*. It's taking up most of my time at the moment, although I'm still doing some theatre work. I'll have to take on staff when shooting begins."

Nina sipped her wine. She felt guilty about being so excited when her best friend's life was shrivelling before her.

"That's wonderful," Laura said, hugging Nina across the table. They'd known each other since Natalie and Josie were in playgroup, had shared holidays together, helped each other out with childcare, and Nina had even lent out Mick when Tom had gone into hospital for knee surgery. Mick had spent several evenings at Laura's house using his engineering skills when her washing machine and car decided to pack up at the same time. The families were close; the women closer still.

"And what about Boss from Hell?" Nina laughed. She knew deep down Laura loved her banking job. "Admit it, you'd be bored stiff without him."

"He's not retired yet, put it that way." Laura shook her head. "He's still as cantankerous as ever. The department took on a new assistant last Monday. It meant I'd be able to eat lunch, perhaps have the odd holiday here and there." Laura shook her head. "The poor girl had resigned by Wednesday."

Nina laughed. "Guess he'll never change."

"Bit like Tom, then," Laura said, sighing. "You'd think with all the practice I get at work dealing with miserable buggers, I'd be able to figure out my husband."

"Not necessarily true," Nina said, knowing she wasn't really helping. She felt hideously guilty that despite the usual niggling disagreements, she and Mick were as content now as they were the day they'd married. Despite moaning about Josie's occasionally sullen behaviour, they had an easy ride compared to most parents. Having only one daughter meant their emotional focus was always on her. But they were equally careful not to overindulge her, although she'd had to chastise Mick occasionally for turning Josie into a daddy's girl.

They'd tried for another child over the years, but it hadn't worked out. They dealt with the strain that had brought, but it was nothing compared to what Laura was going through now. Once Mick and Nina had accepted that it would just be the three of them, life had got back on track.

She reached for Laura's hand, this time insisting it slipped into hers. She didn't know how to help. "Things will work out for the best." She thought for a moment. "Try focusing on what you've got, rather than what you haven't."

"I know. I know." Laura wiped her fingers down her face. "I'm lucky in so many respects. But I swear the counsellor was right, Nina. Tom's acting like a man distracted." She let out a sob. "The stupid thing is, I know deep down he doesn't want to hurt me."

Nina picked up the menu. "I prescribe two hot chocolate fudge cakes." She beckoned the waiter over. She understood Laura's reasoning. Knowing Tom for nearly as long as she'd known Laura, a part of her believed that, yes, he was capable of lying to his wife; that his slightly aloof character, his private side, could lead him into trouble. She could read Mick's every thought by the expression on his face, each little mannerism, but Tom seemed much more closed-off.

"I'll pass," Laura said, sending the waiter away. She quickly drank the remainder of her wine. "You'll have to let me in on your secret." Laura gave a warped grin and banged down her glass. For the first time ever, Nina detected bitterness. "Being so happy and all that. How do you do it? Is it something in the water down your street?"

"No, I think it's —"

"Nina, I wasn't being serious. But let's be realistic here. Your perfect marriage is probably as much a burden to you as my shit one is to me."

"What do you mean?" Nina stiffened. Her friend had had too much to drink.

"Well, think about it. When things turn sour, you've got further to fall than me, hon. That's all I'm saying." Laura stood and went to fetch her coat.

The waiter slipped the bill in front of Nina and hovered beside the table until she paid. Shaken, Nina joined her friend in the street. Laura was leaning against a lamp post, smoking a cigarette.

"I've never thought of it like that before," Nina said, removing the cigarette from between Laura's fingers, thinking about how far she had to fall.

CHAPTER
EIGHT

A few days into term and a stomach bug sweeps the school. Sick bay is full and first period after break I'm sent to fetch another fallen pupil. "Frankie, would you collect Lexi from the IT room? She's got the wretched cramps." Matron jots down a girl's temperature reading. "Another one down."

I pause a moment, soaking up Matron's strength and resilience. She is the type of woman to hold fast; to grow older yet stay the same. I imagine she's been a matron most of her life.

"No problem." I wash my hands. I've just changed yet another set of messed bedsheets. "Poor little lambs," I whisper as I wind along the corridors. I've not been to the IT room yet, although I've seen where it is.

A brilliant light shines out through the square of netted glass in the door, making me screw up my eyes. I enter and the glow and low-pitched hum and warm dry air of a dozen computer fans swallows me up.

"Another one," I whisper to myself. The pupils turn, shuffle and giggle. "Another one ill." A scraping chair switches my senses back on. "Matron told me that Lexi is unwell," I say to the teacher.

He points to a girl sitting in the corner with her head tilted over a metal waste bin. "Please, take her." He is annoyed that his class has been disrupted.

I weave between the desks. "Come on, Lexi." I scoop her up under the armpits. "Let's get you into bed." Lexi leans on me as I lead her from the class. We're bathed in an eerie light from the wide crescent of computers.

"Back to work," the teacher says loudly.

The girls quieten down and face their screens. It's as I'm guiding Lexi behind the bank of monitors that I catch sight of something that makes me freeze for a second; something that makes me study the two girls hunched and giggling over their computer so I can remember their faces for later — blue hairband, dental brace, long blond hair. I guide Lexi back to Matron with the image on the monitor emblazoned in my mind.

My arms are piled with laundry and my face is pressed into the scent of washing detergent. I am exhausted. With luck, he won't even see who is behind the stack of sheets; with luck he'll step out of the doorway and let me pass. But when I peer round the side of my load, I see that Adam is fixed firmly inside the doorway, deep in conversation with several of the older girls. He's clutching his laptop, gesturing with his free hand. He is completely blocking my way.

"Excuse me," I say. My elbows begin to sag under the weight of the sheets. "Can I get through?"

"Yes, sir," I hear one of the girls say. "Anything you say, sir." And then the peal of familiar teenage giggles. "*Anything* for you, sir."

"Could I just . . ." I feel like a character from a comedy movie. Any second my stack of washing will end up on the floor and a stampede of schoolgirls with muddy hockey boots will trample all over it.

"When, sir? When would you like us to do that for you?" More giggles. I approach the doorway, eyeing the long length of the corridor beyond. I grit my teeth.

"That's enough!" Adam's raised voice cuts through the laundry. Then I'm knocked for six, shoved against the wall as he storms off.

"Hey!" I cry, but Adam is gone, striding off through the school, clearly angered by whatever has just taken place.

As predicted, most of my laundry lies scattered on the floor, but no muddy stampede arrives, and nor does Adam turn back to apologise or help me gather the sheets. When I look up, the girls are gone. It's all I can do to stop myself curling up in the soft mess and falling into an exhausted sleep.

"Can't you just give me a tablet or something?"

I'm pairing socks while pretending not to listen. It's a thankless task. Tomorrow they'll all be back in my basket again. But it's a good way to learn the names of faceless girls, perhaps take a guess at their age by the size of their feet. I imagine their mothers stitching on the name labels.

"Sorry," Matron replies, shaking her head. "I'll need to examine you."

"It's just a sore throat. A bit of stomach ache."

My eyes flick from my task, across the five metal beds that writhe with ill, sweaty girls, to where Adam towers over Sylvia in the next room. Hours later, he's still clutching the laptop. And he still hasn't apologised.

"Mr Kingsley, there's a very nasty bug going around this school. The doctor is on his way to examine the sickest girls. If too many of our staff fall ill, then the school may face closure. Now, if you wish to have some medication then please allow me to run a few basic checks."

I glance up again. Nine odd socks so far. Adam is a tall, strong man. This afternoon his shoulders are angled forward, and his lean neck is struggling to keep his head from wilting. Some of his hair is stuck to his forehead in bronze strips. He doesn't look at all well as he grudgingly nods defeat to Matron. She leads him into a private room and I return my full attention to the basket of navy blue socks.

Ten minutes later, Sylvia emerges again. She stops at a couple of beds, checking on the patients, before walking by me and my growing pile of balled socks.

"It's never-ending," she says with a sigh and a smile. She's the sort of woman who thrives on a crisis.

"Do you need any help?"

Sylvia rummages in the storeroom. "Ah, found it," she calls out, not hearing me. She emerges holding a brown bottle. "Poor Adam. He won't like being laid up with this bug, especially not now."

"Oh?" I say.

"When he's not teaching, he's obsessed with his research." Sylvia vigorously shakes the bottle. Sludgy liquid turns frothy before separating again. "He's writing a book." She squints at the label. "I'm not sure how old this is," she says. "But he's told me to make him better no matter what." She grins. "That's how desperate he is not to fall ill." She pulls a face at the medicine, which looks as if it's from the nineteen seventies. "Tough types, these Australians." She walks off laughing, shaking the medicine as if it's a maraca.

Australian, I think. He said he was from the south, like me. Twelve thousand miles further south.

I take another handful of socks from the basket. I am doing my best to appear polite yet reserved with the other staff. No one has dug too deep into my life yet.

"He's not at all well." Matron glides past me again. This time she is shaking down a thermometer; pursing her lips. Then Adam emerges from the consulting room. He has mushroom-coloured circles under his eyes and his mouth stands out like a bruise on his pale face.

"Oh dear," I say, completely unable to prevent the comment.

"Oh dear indeed," he replies solemnly. "I need to call for a sub. I have three history classes this afternoon," he says to Sylvia. "Can you help?"

"Leave it to me. Just get back to your room and rest." Then there's a wail from one of the girls in bed and Matron rushes over with a bucket. "Help Adam back to his room, will you, Frankie?" she calls out. "I don't want him passing out alone." Matron strokes the girl's head. I glance at Adam and then at my pile of socks.

"Really, there's no need. Carry on with your . . . socks." With his accent, it almost sounds humorous, but when I see his face, I can tell it isn't. "Look, I'm sorry about earlier," he continues. "I would have stopped to help you pick up but —"

"It's fine, honestly. It was just a pile of sheets." I wish I hadn't interrupted him. I am curious to know what was said between him and the girls.

"I really didn't mean to be rude," he adds, shuffling out of sick bay. As instructed by Matron, I escort him back to his room. "You don't need to . . ." He stops and stares at me, too weak to argue. "This way then."

"So you're an Aussie. Which part are you from?" I wonder if I should take his arm to help support him.

"Who says I'm Australian?" A diluted version of the grin that I'm becoming familiar with appears on his ill-looking face.

"Sylvia did." I swear the corridors in this place tangle and change overnight to confuse me. One dark passage gives way to another. One knotted with the next. "Which way?" I ask when we are faced with a fork. Adam nods towards the left.

"I'm as English as you are," he says. His voice is flat, as if all his concentration is being used just to stand up. I feel sorry for him. He doesn't look well at all. We go up another staircase and he leans on the rail, sucking in breath as if it's his last.

"You don't sound English," I add.

He puffs syllables between gasps. "We don't all necessarily sound like what we really are," he replies. Sweat beads on his face. He takes a bunch of keys from his pocket. "This is my room."

"No," I say. "I guess we don't." I turn to go. "I hope you feel better soon." I walk off down the corridor.

"Murwillumbah, if you're that interested," he calls out after me. "I lived there long enough to get a twang."

"Mur-what?" I don't turn round. I force myself to consider the danger of making friends, the slip-ups, the gradual leakage of information, the jigsaw puzzle that is me. I can't allow myself to get drawn in.

"Some place in Australia that grows bananas," he says. Then I hear the click of his door and Adam is gone. I hurry away, once again lost in the maze of corridors.

CHAPTER
NINE

Nina had never been good with heights. The ladder wobbled. She grabbed the wooden rail and a splinter pierced her finger. "Ouch! I can't quite . . ." She sucked away the blood.". . . reach," she said, trying to slide the dusty box off the shelf.

"You haven't climbed high enough. Get down and let me have a go." The stagehand standing below, a pleasant girl not long out of college, reminded Nina of herself a couple of decades or so ago — reckless and determined to succeed.

Nina's legs shook as she slowly climbed down each of the rungs. She felt giddy as she stepped back on to the floor. "Sorry," she said, shrugging away her obvious fear. "I thought I'd overcome my phobia." Nina swallowed, and choked trying to laugh away her embarrassment. "But in actual fact, it's got worse . . ."

"Hey, stand aside." Petra grinned. Spritely and lithe, she shinned up the ladder like a teenage boy. Her hair was cropped short and her skin was clear and free from make-up. Nina had wanted to try out a new blusher between scene rehearsals and asked Petra to be a model. She'd flatly refused, claiming the only thing ever to go on her skin was water and organic olive oil.

"Be careful," Nina said, staring up at the girl's trainers balanced on the thin rung. "I can't afford for you to hurt yourself. I need you to help me with the chorus change. That soot's a nightmare to get off between scenes." Nina was trying to joke but couldn't help trembling as Petra leaned over to reach the box.

"Got it," Petra announced and was swiftly on the floor again beside Nina. Nina let out the breath she'd been unconsciously holding. "You really do have a problem, don't you?"

Nina shrugged, suddenly feeling rather old in the girl's company. "Not really," she said. "I've been up higher than that before." She pulled a silly face.

Petra smiled and tapped the lid of the box. Dust rose and swirled in the shaft of light that entered the small storeroom through the tiny window at the back. The Victorian theatre was familiar territory for Nina — she'd worked on many productions there over the years — hence everyone asking her where various props were stored. And in a couple of weeks' time, Josie would begin rehearsals there for the youth group's production of *Chicago*. She'd landed the lead role of Roxie Hart, beating dozens of other hopefuls in the auditions — a dream come true for Josie. Nina was so proud of her daughter. She came alive on stage, as if stepping into character relieved her of all her teenage troubles.

"Perfect," Petra said, after peering inside the box. "What do you think?"

"I think you deserve one for fetching them down from up there." Nina smiled and held up a couple of the tarnished medals. "They're just what our soldiers need. How's your sewing?"

"About as good as your fondness for heights." Petra patted Nina's shoulder playfully, and the two women left the storeroom.

"See you at lunchtime," Nina said. She headed off back to the dressing rooms, knowing they'd be empty. The cast had been called by the production team for a meeting on stage, giving Nina the ideal opportunity to experiment with a new type of quick-preparation wound for the war scene. During the play, she had exactly twelve minutes to massacre the faces and arms of three lead characters and wasn't sure exactly how she would pull it off. Live theatre was always a challenge, but she loved the buzz and the pressure.

Nina went back to the smaller dressing room, and, just as she was about to enter, she thought she saw someone disappear down the passage leading up to the stage. "Hello?" she called out, wondering if one of the cast needed her. She shrugged when there was no reply.

She went on into the room where she'd left her holdall and make-up cases. She always packed up and took them home at night, having learned the hard way over the years that absent-minded actors often helped themselves to her stock and usually forgot to return it. The products were too expensive to keep replacing.

"Odd," Nina said, feeling for the light switch along the wall. It was pitch black in the windowless room. "No one ever turns lights off around here." She assumed the production manager was having a clampdown on expenses. Running a company was a tough business these days and making a profit was hard. "Probably what the meeting's about," she said to herself.

Her fingers found the switch and she clicked it on. At first, Nina didn't notice the mess. Actors weren't known for their tidiness and with quick changes between scenes, they relied on the assistants to sort out the costumes. Clearly the meeting had been called in a rush because not much of the floor was visible. Hanging rails bore empty hangers and most surfaces were strewn with clothing. Nina sighed.

"Well, I'm not tidying —"

Then she saw her special effects case on the shelf below the spotlit mirror. She frowned. "What the hell . . ." Anger swept over her. "I just don't believe this." Foundation, pots of fake blood, packets of scabs and wound wax — everything had been tipped out of her bag.

This stuff is expensive, she thought. I can't have anyone just helping themselves. She froze again. Reflected behind her, Nina saw the contents of her other make-up cases tipped out all over the floor. Her usually neat and organised corner of the dressing room had been upturned into mayhem. "Oh *no*," she cried. "Who's done this?"

Nina crouched down amongst the tubes and tubs of theatrical make-up and brushes. She began to scoop them up but stopped. She wondered, fleetingly, if someone had broken in. She continued shovelling her belongings back into the bag. Thankfully, nothing seemed to be missing. Why would anyone make such a mess of her stuff? Did someone in the theatre have a grudge against her?

She thought hard, suddenly recalling the temper tantrum that Rosalind had let rip last week when the director insisted she wear the grey wig — a suggestion made by Nina earlier during rehearsal. Vain Rosalind, not known for her quiet temperament, had gone out of her way to make the entire day miserable for Nina.

Rosalind. Nina shook her head at the woman's childish behaviour. She would have a word with the producer later.

"I just wanted to ask you if you knew where . . . Good heavens, what a mess." Petra stood in the doorway.

"It must have happened while we were in the storeroom. What a nightmare." Nina's voice shook and her mind raced. She was angry. "Someone here clearly doesn't like me." She didn't name names.

"Are you sure the mess was deliberate?" Petra winked. "You know what these thespian types are like. Just plain messy buggers."

"No. No, I clearly remember it being tidy when I left." She bent down and picked up a nineteen-forties dress. "How can anyone be so thoughtless?" Nina stood, wondering what she would say to Rosalind next time she saw her.

Then, distracted by the predicted stampede off stage, Nina returned to her work. During the course of the day, she gradually tidied up. It was only as she was packing up for the night that vague thoughts began to stir.

★ ★ ★

"What would you do," Nina began, "if Tom found out that you . . ." She trailed off, unsure how to explain exactly what she meant. "Well, if Tom discovered that . . ." Again, words failed her. She sighed and sloshed boiling water on to coffee granules. After the day she'd had, what she really wanted was a stiff drink.

"For heaven's sake, Nina, spit it out." Laura opened the refrigerator and took out the milk. Something was up. Nina never usually called round on the way home from work. "So? If Tom found out what?" Laura snorted out a half laugh. "Tom wouldn't notice if I was nailed naked to the kitchen table with another man sprawled on top of me."

"Oh Laura, I'm sorry," Nina said, thankful for the diversion. What she really wanted to say just wouldn't come out right. Instead, she touched a hand on Laura's arm as she took the milk.

Laura pulled away. "You can't leave me hanging like that. Tell me what you were going to ask." Laura slurped her drink then emptied an entire bag of oven chips on to a baking tray. "Get this. Tom said he'd cook every other night to *share the domestic burden* after I asked him if he'd forgotten where he lived." She said it in a demented voice. "So far that's amounted to him bringing home two takeaways in the last week and suggesting we eat out for his other shift." Laura shoved the chips in the oven and cracked the ring pull on a can of baked beans.

Nina watched her friend blast angrily through the evening's domesticity. She found herself thinking back to last night and the prawn curry Mick had whipped up. He'd even made his own naan bread. "Men are lousy cooks anyway," Nina lied, hoping it would make Laura feel better. "They make too much mess and we're the ones left —"

"I just can't bloody take it any more, Nina." Laura slammed her mug on to the worktop and a circle of coffee pooled beneath it. "All I do is moan. It's soul-destroying. And all my moaning is about him. It never used to be like this. There's someone else. I'm sure of it." Laura's brittle voice was desperate. Nina had never witnessed her so close to breaking. "It's over, Neen. I give up. I want a new life." Laura briefly sank her face into her hands, let out three or four pitiful sobs before wiping her eyes and fixing a smile on her face. She was adept at burying her feelings. "Now, damn well tell me what you came here to get off your chest."

"Forget what I was going to say. It's not important." Nina burned her tongue as she gulped her coffee. "Talk to Tom. Talk to anyone. Just get help."

Nina helped by slapping sausages on a baking tray and snipping the twist of skin joining them. "Nothing like a bit of home cooking, eh?" She laughed.

"The kids like sausages," Laura said dismally. She took the greasy wrapper and chucked it in the bin. "It wasn't meant to be like this." She dropped her arms against her thighs. "You know, sausages, arguments, two kids who grunt to communicate, and a husband whose personality warrants a search and rescue team."

Nina threw her arms around her friend. "Oh Laura," she said. Their faces were close, a mass of tangled hair and tears. Laura let it all out on Nina's shoulder.

"You'll get through this," Nina whispered. She held Laura at arm's length and laughed when she saw the scribbles of mascara on her cheeks. "It takes me hours to achieve that look," she joked, but then she was reminded of what happened at the theatre.

"I'd better get going," she said. "Hungry hordes at mine too, you know." She pulled her car keys from her trouser pocket.

"Wait. Are you OK? Really?" Laura asked, noticing Nina's deep sigh.

"Yeah. It's nothing," she said, smiling brightly.

Laura shrugged. "Get out of my house and go back to yours. Hug Josie and Mick for me and send Natalie home when you see her. That girl would live at your house if she could." She gave Nina a tight squeeze.

"I will." Nina went outside and got in her car. Laura waved and closed the front door.

The street, similar to Nina's only a short distance away, was deserted apart from another vehicle about fifty yards along the road. The car was stationary so Nina continued rolling backwards out of Laura's sloping drive. She wondered what was in the refrigerator at home.

Suddenly, her head was jolted as her car was clipped from behind. Her foot instinctively jabbed the brake as she was knocked sideways.

"Christ! Watch out!" she cried, rubbing her sore neck. The impact rang in her ears and it took her a moment to regain her senses. She turned and stared down the road, watching the big dark car driving off at speed. She saw 5 and 7 and M in the number plate, but that was all.

"Stupid, stupid man," she wailed, pumping the horn way too late. "Damn him," she said, slumping forward, wondering if she could offer even a vehicle type to the police.

Shaking, Nina got out of the car to examine the damage. There was a dent along the rear quarter of her small red car, framed by a dark green streak of metallic paint. She ran her finger along it, as if it might give a clue to the car's owner. Was it a Rover? A Jaguar? she wondered. Definitely a male driver, she recalled, trying to re-create an image of the face she saw flash past, but it had been too fast.

Nina glanced at Laura's house but somehow couldn't face adding to her friend's troubles. She got back in the car and drove off, slowing at every dark car she saw in case it had a dented front and she could get a number plate.

At home, the kitchen was a mix of teenage giggles, something burning, and a laptop balanced precariously on the edge of Natalie's knee as she sat on the worktop, swinging her legs and kicking the cupboard doors with an annoying beat. The girl was hunched over the screen, her fingers jabbing at the keys with the skill of a speed typist.

"What's that smell?" Nina asked. She had dumped all her make-up kit in the hall. It could stay there until morning.

"Toast," Josie replied. A shower of black crumbs rained on to the floor as she scraped the blackened bread. "It burned."

"No way," Natalie cried. Without looking up from the screen, she pulled the toast from Josie's fingers and bit into it. "You'll never guess who Kat's going out with?"

Nina shook her head and went into the downstairs toilet. Her head was throbbing from the wretched day she'd had. The girls' voices faded to distant whoops and incredulous laughter as she locked the door.

Nina flicked on the light and leaned against the wall. She just needed a moment.

"You in there, Mum?" Josie said, hammering on the door. "Hurry up. I'm desperate."

Nina stood and flushed the toilet. She was being ridiculous. She was tired, stressed about her extra workload, even though it was exciting. And she'd not been sleeping all that well. Mick had been restless because of his new commitments. They were no different to many families she knew.

Nina splashed water around the basin and opened the door. "Sorry," she said, and she was squeezed against the wall as Josie rushed in.

Mick suddenly came through the front door.

"Oh God, I'm so glad you're back," she said, delivering a long kiss on his lips.

"Mmm, I should go out more often." Mick hugged her fondly with one arm, dangling a shopping bag with the other. "I've been hunting," he said, pausing,

72

frowning at Nina's worried expression. "Chicken OK?" he asked. "Come and help me prepare it."

Nina followed him, glad of the distraction.

"Christ, has there been a volcanic eruption?" Mick asked, wiping the worktop free of black crumbs. Then, "Nina?" He paused, hands spread wide on the laminate — clever, capable hands that Nina just wanted to have encase her and keep her safe forever. "Are you OK?"

"Sure. I'm fine." She snapped out of it and helped unpack the groceries.

Perfectly safe, she said over and over in her head as later, in bed, she tangled the sheet around her restless body. She was hot. She was sweating. She couldn't sleep. Instead she listened to Mick's gentle sleep-breaths as they bordered on a snore. She was, of course, perfectly safe.

CHAPTER
TEN

Still my dad didn't come to visit. "Been forgotten?" the horrid man asked, shoving me back on the cold window seat where he'd found me. I cowered as he raised a hand, but he thought better of it as one of the female carers walked past with a bunch of kids in tow.

I stared out of the window, willing my dad's car to appear. My eyes were still smarting from the glare of the light in that horrid room, and my heart pumped a rich mix of cold blood and fear. I gripped the stone window sill and stared down the drive, pressing my nose to the glass. I focused hard on the trees, the tarmac, the dingy grey sky, and prayed that my father would come to save me.

As dusk fell, so did my eyelids. Once or twice I dropped off — sweet oblivion where me, my dad and my mum were all back together. Vague memories of a slim woman with a ponytail, the scent of her skin — face cream and lipstick — teased me into believing she was still alive for several blissful moments even after I woke.

It was a smell that brought me round the third time I nodded off. It made me feel ill. Disinfectant overlaying the stench of fear — *my* fear — and that's when I realised I'd wet myself. Too scared to tell anyone, I crept off the dirty cushion and sloped off to the dormitory. As I peeled off my knickers, I realised that the ugly man had been right. I'd been forgotten. My dad wasn't coming today, and he probably wouldn't come tomorrow either. Or even the day after that.

So far I'd spent my time at Roecliffe Children's Home ducking and diving, smiling sweetly, innocently, getting by any way I could. I longed to be a shadow, a picture on one of the grimy walls, a rat scurrying about in the basement. The other kids were harsh, sometimes sad, sometimes bruised, and sometimes screaming with laughter. They were a rainbow of every emotion, from the tots gurgling in their prams to the teenagers who punched the walls as they idly walked past. Me, I was somewhere in the middle. Trying to hide, trying not to be noticed. If my father didn't come to fetch me soon, I vowed I would fly away. Ava, his skinny little bird.

The carers trudged through their duties each day. I mistook one or two of them for kids from the home, they were so young. Others were older, weary, grey, and most of them filled with resentment. None of them seemed to like us.

I tried to find my mother inside everyone I met, just in case, but none of the carers resembled her. I wanted to make friends with the grown-ups, but they couldn't be bought with a gum-lined grin or a cut knee — not like Dad — and it was impossible to play a sneaky prank to get more bread at tea. I soon learned that ferocious punishment followed even tiny steps out of line. Once, I went up the back stairs, forgetting they were strictly off limits. Each step hit my head as I was pushed back down by a shadowy figure at the top.

I wasn't stupid, far from it, and mostly kept quiet and watched the goings-on, learning how it all worked, especially when I first arrived. I didn't want to get taken to that room again, to see what was behind the bright light. No, I just kept my head down and waited for Dad to come back because he'd promised me he would.

It was on one of those waiting days, sitting, staring at the wall, swinging my legs, biting my nails, when I noticed that one of the carers, Miss Maddocks — who seemed about a hundred years old to me — wasn't quite as scary as the other grown-ups. She bustled about the home more like a mother; someone with a heart.

I thought back to my first night at the home, when I'd had no idea who anyone was. It was Miss Maddocks who had stroked my forehead until she thought I was asleep. I'd been sobbing for my dad, and eventually lay quiet but completely awake — too terrified to realise that she was being nice — as she ran her papery hand over my damp head. Through my tightly shut eyes, I stared at the backs of my eyelids, seeing the warped face of my father as I was prised from him, the grim expression of the children's home director as I was brought here, and the feral whoops of the other kids when they found out about me. The new girl.

"What did you do wrong?" a grimy boy of about twelve asked me on my first morning. He passed me a bread roll and allowed me to wipe up the scrapings of jam on his plate. There was nothing else left. I'd spent most of the night sobbing and, when I did finally sleep, it was as the other children were waking and rushing for breakfast.

"Do wrong?" I asked. I wasn't very hungry and didn't like the look of the bread. "I didn't do anything wrong. My mum died and my dad couldn't cope. I tried to help." The other children fell silent and listened to me, even the older ones. "But I can't have done it very well because they brought me here." I shrugged. It was the way things were, but that didn't mean I had to like it.

The grimy boy patted my shoulder. His hair was all messy and he smelled. "Never mind," he said. "You're with us now."

I looked around the group of children that had gathered. It felt as if I was in a circus and that made me want to howl and sob until my dad came for me. I didn't want to live here with Miss Maddocks or any of the other carers who skulked in and out of the shadows. I didn't want to eat dry bread for breakfast, or sleep in the lumpy cot next to a dozen other kids. I didn't want to do anything except go home. I wanted things how they were.

"How do you run away?" I whispered to the boy. It made me feel sick to think of it. I had never done anything bad before. I didn't want to appear ungrateful or hurt anyone's feelings, but I didn't think I could spend another hour in the horrid place.

There was a round of laughter followed by silence. "You don't," whispered the boy, his eyes as black as coal. "Because there's nowhere else to go."

Later, we were given different things to do. Two of the big girls had to clear and wash the dishes; another couple were instructed to strip the beds in B dorm and take them to the laundry. The boys were given brooms and had to sweep the hall then polish shoes, while the tall bony lady giving out instructions asked the rest of the group to shower and clean their teeth. These were things that I'd done at home every day for as long as I could remember. Why, then, did it seem so cold, so wrong, so cruel as the woman ushered everyone along with the back of her hand?

"I want my dad," I said when I was the last one sitting on the bench. I would tell him everything, I vowed. About how horrid the place was.

The bony woman crouched down beside me. "Hey, orphan Annie," she said with a smile. "Have you got any muscles?"

I shook my head. Was she nice too, like Miss Maddocks, perhaps?

"Well, you're going to have to get some, living here." The woman gently squeezed the tops of my arms and smiled. "Ah, you have the muscles of an ox. Now would you like to help me carry in a basket of logs so we can get the fire lit?"

I shrugged. I didn't want to do anything except go home.

"Come on. No use moping about. You want to be able to tell your dad about how you've been a helpful girl all week, don't you?" The woman lifted my chin with her finger.

"OK," I said, sliding off the bench and following her. "But can I strike the match to light the fire?"

"Of course you can," she replied and told me her name was Patricia. She seemed nice. "I work here when Miss Maddocks has gone home."

"You mean you're allowed to go home?" I stopped. It didn't seem fair.

Patricia laughed. "Of course. I have a son living at home. Miss Maddocks has to feed her cats."

I was worried. "But what if everyone goes home? Who will look after us?" I didn't fancy the thought of all the older kids bossing me about. Most had been friendly, but one or two looked like trouble. I kept my head down and didn't cause a fuss.

"That never happens," Patricia assured me. "There's always someone on duty and some of the carers live here."

My shoulders dropped. Without really noticing, we'd walked along several corridors, down a flight of stone steps, through the endless basement until we arrived at a small room that smelled of wet forests and moss. "The log and coal store," Patricia announced. "It's freezing today and I think we need a fire." She grinned as if everything might not be so bad after all. I wiped away a tear and took the small basket Patricia held out. "You pick out all the little bits of wood. You can carry the kindling upstairs and lay it in the grate."

I did as I was told and within the hour a group of children had gathered around the massive stone fireplace to soak up the warmth of the blaze. For some reason, I felt proud, maybe even a little warm inside myself. I had struck the match, held the tiny flame to the newspaper knots that Patricia had shown me how to tie, and these in turn had ignited the kindling. Soon, giant logs were crackling and popping in the grate, while plumes of black smoke rushed up the chimney. Lost in my make-believe world, I stared at the flames, fascinated as insects scurried from the logs in panic.

"Do you think they'll get a new home too?" I said to the boy sitting next to me. We'd been given biscuits, and I sucked on mine to make it last. The boy shrugged as if I were a mad child.

But I didn't feel mad at all. Neither did I feel like orphan Annie, or Cinderella, which one of the older girls had called me for helping with the fire. No, I was bursting with fresh hope, with purpose, with a lust for life that I'd long forgotten existed. For that one day, I had a feeling that everything was going to be all right. It was in my tummy; it was in my bones; I could even taste it. All I had to do was get through the next ten years to prove myself right.

CHAPTER
ELEVEN

Even in the rain, Mick spotted the dent. From the window, Nina saw him crouching next to the rear end of her car, running his fingers through the beads of water, wondering if he was seeing things as he walked out to the street to add another bag of rubbish to the already full dustbin. Squinting through the summer drizzle, Mick frowned and viewed the damage from several angles, just to make sure it was really there.

"Damn," Nina whispered. Her breath fogged the window of the utility room.

As she heard Mick stamping his feet on the front door mat, Nina bunched up the pile of ironing that was still warm from the tumble dryer.

"We need to recycle more," Mick said, washing his hands. Nina dumped the laundry on the kitchen table and put up the ironing board.

"Do we?" Perhaps he wouldn't mention the car. She wasn't entirely sure why she hadn't told him. Mick would understand. Accidents happen. She plugged in the iron. Flattening clothes, stacking them in neat, pressed piles.

"The bin's stuffed. Surely there are things we could take to the —"

"I do," Nina snapped. "Every week I go to the bottle bank, the paper recycling depot. Tins, cardboard, clothing, plastic. You name it, I recycle it."

Mick paced the kitchen, wondering what had got into his wife this morning. He watched her slamming the iron on to the garments, adding more angular creases than she was taking away.

"I'm not cross," he said finally. Nina looked up, the iron mid-swipe. "The car," he added, raising his eyebrows.

"Oh," she said glumly. "I . . . I . . ."

"Didn't know how to tell me?"

Nina nodded like a little girl. She screwed up her eyes as her hair thankfully fell forward to cover her lie. She'd decided not to tell Mick about the accident or the mess at the theatre.

"I'll drop in at the garage later when I'm out. We'll need several quotes for the insurance company." Mick filled the teapot.

"Insurance?" Nina pressed hard on the hot iron. "But won't they want a crime number from the police or something?"

Mick turned, the kettle steaming in his hand. "Police? Christ, Nina, what did you do? Run someone over?"

Nina shook her head so vigorously that her brain ached. "No, of course not. I smacked into a lamp post while . . . while I was trying to park, OK?" Suddenly, smelling something, she lifted the iron to reveal a

82

triangular scorch mark on Josie's new T-shirt. The printed words had smeared to plastic goo in the heat and stuck to the iron plate, ruining the garment and the iron. "Oh no," she cried. "Josie'll kill me."

Nina felt the iron being pulled from her hand. Mick held up the T-shirt like a flag, laughing. "What does it say now?" he asked.

Nina stared hard at the words. It had said *I'm an accident waiting to happen*. Both Josie and Nat had bought one a couple of days ago. "It looks like *I'm an ant waiting to happen* now," Nina replied, also laughing. "She loves it. She'll never forgive me." She stuffed the T-shirt into the waste bin. "I'll buy her another. She won't even know."

"And don't worry about the car," he said before going off to his studio to work. "I'll sort it." He winked before clicking the door shut behind him.

Nina's shoulders uncurled. She pulled the phone book out of the cupboard and looked up the number of the boutique where she knew Josie had bought the T-shirt. "Hello," she said. "I just wanted to check that you have an item in stock." She tapped her fingers on the worktop and chewed on the end of the pen. Her daughter would never know the difference.

"I just thought you ought to know," Laura said down the phone. It had rung only moments after Nina had finished talking to the boutique.

"Know what?"

"I wasn't spying on them exactly."

"Laura, for God's sake. Just tell me."

"And I'm not one for tittle-tattle either, but they're our daughters and I know how you, especially you, feel about these things."

"Laura, just spit it out."

"They were both in Nat's bedroom, Neen. On that bloody laptop Tom gave her from work. They were in total hysterics. I was just walking past, putting stuff away, so I stopped and listened. I peeked through the door crack too but couldn't see much. Just Nat on the bed, rolling about, hugging a pillow. Josie was curled next to her, the computer between them."

"Go on."

"Nat said to Josie, 'He wanted you to *undress?*' It sounded as if they were discussing something that had happened to Josie earlier."

"Yes," Nina said flatly.

"They hooted and giggled. I'd told them earlier that I was going out, and they thought they were alone. Anyway, Josie told Nat 'not to get too excited because she hadn't done what he'd wanted'. Apparently 'he got annoyed and logged off' were her words, whatever she meant by that." Laura paused. Nina heard her sip tea. "Then they decided to go back on to that stupid website. I have to admit, it was Nat's idea, little minx. Josie was quite envious of the laptop, though. Nat was telling her how easy it is to hide it under the covers at night."

"Oh God," Nina said, wondering how many times her own laptop had been taken and used by Josie in a similar situation.

"Turns out Nat's online a lot more than I realised. She was telling Josie. She must think we're stupid." Both women suddenly felt exactly that.

"Anyway," Laura said, sighing. "They were definitely on Afterlife and Nat was glamming up Josie's character and trying to make her look 'not frumpy' as Nat put it." Nina was grateful that Laura had always been honest about how pushy Nat could be. "Nat appeared to be controlling Josie in the game. She'd put her in provocative clothes and was parading her around the public space for teens in this area. She'd even given poor Josie a pair of big boobs. Wait till I see her later."

Nina couldn't imagine her daughter taking kindly to Nat doing those things. But then she thought of the chat she'd read on her laptop. "I guess they're just being kids, Laura." Nina couldn't believe she'd just said that, but she was trying to echo what Mick would say.

"Some boy turned up online. Clearly it was someone Josie fancied like crazy because she went absolutely scarlet. I think she quite liked it that her new look had done the trick and brought him to her online."

"Was his name Griff by any chance?"

"Yes, it was." Laura paused, wondering how Nina knew. "I have to say, Josie didn't seem to be comfortable with the whole online thing. She kind of froze."

"Really?" Nina wondered why. Surely all teenage girls were up for a bit of a giggle with boys. She was fifteen, after all.

"I knew what they were typing because they were reading it out to each other. This Griff character was definitely coming on to Josie. He even asked her to come round to his place."

"What?" Nina was shocked.

"Relax. He meant his online place in Afterlife."

Just as bad, Nina thought.

"When she went there . . . oh, I don't know how it works on that game, but it's as if you're suddenly in someone else's room with all their personal stuff there. Anyway, when she went, the girls hooted with laughter although I could tell they were quite shocked."

Nina swallowed.

"I heard Nat say that it was like some bondage den. Some kind of Goth or Emo black and red place. Josie seemed quite scared, but here's the thing — and you'll be proud of her for this — Josie didn't trust that it was someone they actually knew."

"Oh Laura, I don't know what to say. It would be so easy for a perv to get chatting to two girls." Nina sat down.

"They commented that he seemed like a different person entirely. Josie then went on to test him about stuff he should know if he really was Griff. She's taken heed of whatever you've been telling her."

"I don't get why you're telling me then, Laura, I'm not keen on Josie spending time on that website but it sounds as if she's being utterly sensible."

"That's not exactly what I'm calling about," Laura continued.

"Oh?"

"Nat got a bit fed up with Josie for not flirting with this boy. She stormed out of the room to get a Coke. I managed to duck into the spare room just in time. When Nat had gone, I checked back on Josie through the gap in the door. She didn't see me, but she was crying. Sobbing and choking on her words, talking to herself. She was saying, 'No one's ever going to want me now,' and that she hated herself."

Nina thanked Laura and hung up with tears welling in her eyes. She gripped the edge of the table with whitened knuckles, wondering what was going on inside her daughter's mind.

CHAPTER
TWELVE

Nothing about Geoffrey Palmer particularly surprises me. Nothing about the small flat he occupies in the west wing of Roecliffe Hall is out of the ordinary — the maroon patterned carpet, the porcelain ornaments on the mantelpiece, the magazine rack with a dozen issues of *Country Life* stuffed between the bamboo slats.

Geoffrey Palmer is the perfect person to captain Roecliffe Hall School for Girls through the next decade or two. He read history at Oxford. He is a governor of another boarding school. He chairs several charities, is a committed Christian, and takes a safari in Africa every year. He creates an excellent impression on the parents, manages his staff with a firm yet caring manner, and is popular with the girls — not least because he runs the film club on a Friday evening. Once a month he invites the sixth-form girls to his private quarters for a special horror movie night.

"Interesting," I say as he hands me tea. I gaze up at the wall again to indicate what I'm talking about. "Photographs," I add, and he nods a slow arc.

"The Gambia, two thousand and four," he says proudly. "And that's Kenya, Zimbabwe and Tanzania, plus Kruger National Park."

"Amazing," I say, thinking of the charities he supports. There's a picture of him standing with a dozen African children, thin as pencils. Palmer is grinning beneath a khaki cap, while the children's eyes are wide as owls'.

Mr Palmer moves on. "The reason I asked to see you, Miss Gerrard, is about your job description."

My heart stops, refusing to add another beat until I know what he means. "Oh? There's nothing wrong, I hope."

"Far from it, Miss Gerrard. Sylvia tells me that you're doing a fine job of looking after the girls and, in view of that, we've decided to enrich our programme of PSHE."

I stare at him.

Mr Palmer explains. "Personal, social and health education for our girls. Worries or concerns they may have. Things like that." He looks away, clearly embarrassed by the connotation of any personal problems that a teenage girl might suffer. "Anyway, we were thinking that you would be just the person to take these sessions. Currently we have a member of staff offering classes, but she's very busy with sports clubs. Would you be interested?"

"I'm not sure that . . ." I sip tea to wash away what I should really say. "I'm not sure that I'm the best person for this role, Mr Palmer, although I am very flattered that you considered me." What does he think I know about teenage girls? What good would I be to any of them?

"I'm not sure you quite understand, Miss Gerrard." Mr Palmer smiles, but it doesn't take much to read that it's not a smile of pleasure. "I'm not asking you if you'll do it." His icy blue eyes needle me, staring intently, waiting — *ordering* — me to accept. "We really need your help."

A sharp breath counters the hiccup that forces out. "I see." Staring back at Mr Palmer, in this room, the look he's giving me, sets off something in my chest. Tight bands of fear tug my ribs together, making it hard to breathe. I grasp the edge of the table. Words are hard but they finally come out, dry and unbelievable.

"Do I . . . do I know you?" It's his skin, the papery folds sliding over bent bones. That stoop; the stare, circling my face like the beam of a lighthouse.

I change the subject quickly before he answers. I don't want to know if I know him, because if I do, then it means that I can't stay here. Yet there's nowhere else to go. "What about training then?" I ask. "Do you really think I can do this job?" His eyes are so difficult to read.

Finally, he says, "You're just what the girls need, Miss Gerrard. Still young enough to relate to them, yet at an age where they can look up to you." Palmer smiles, satisfied it's all sorted. "You are the perfect mother substitute," he adds, standing up and wringing his hands. He clearly wants me to go, even though I haven't finished my tea.

"Good," he says when I just sit there.

"Fine," I reply, rising slowly because all the blood has left my head. "I accept."

"Don't be scared of them, Miss Gerrard. They're just teenage girls, after all."

"Yes," I say, leaving my tea, leaving the room. No reason to be scared at all.

I see the laptop before I see him. There's a sticker on the lid — a flag — and as I walk past, I see it's the Australian pennant. The computer is perched on the edge of the reception desk about five feet from where Adam is standing with his back turned to the rest of the hall. He's with that fifth-form girl again, and suddenly his hands explode off his hips and punch the air above his head as if he's conducting the final bars of a symphony.

"For God's sake, Katy, not again. Don't you know when to stop?" I slow down, listening, pretending to look at the pupils' work stapled to the pinboards. I hear the girl chime a bitter retort: *That's not the end of it, Mr Kingsley.* When I turn, they are gone, just the echo of their departing footsteps in the air. Adam has left his laptop behind.

I swear the route has changed; that this place morphs daily, twisting on its foundations, creaking through alterations as if ghostly builders are at work each night, changing walls, bypassing doorways, adding passageways to the already complicated network. Finding Adam's room takes me several attempts. I knock and, as if he's been standing behind the door waiting, he's suddenly there, directly in front of me, gripping the edge of the door with both hands so that his knuckles are white. His pale face is crested red on his cheeks and his eyes look bloodshot.

"Feeling any better?" Last time we spoke was when I escorted him back to his room as the sick bug swept the school. Most of the girls are recovered now.

"Yeah, thanks," he says. His lower jaw trembles.

"Anyway," I say, when I realise the silence has gone on too long. "I found this. It's yours isn't it?" I hold up the laptop and Adam's eyes widen to saucers. He glances back into his room to where I see a desk beneath the window.

"Yes. Yes, it is. Where did you find it?" He snatches it from my grasp.

"You left it in the reception hall about ten minutes ago."

Thoughts fly through his mind, perhaps wondering if I could have data-plundered in such a short time. "Thanks," he finally manages. "I'm grateful." He lifts the lid and snaps it shut again.

"I didn't look at anything, if that's what you're worried about. I thought I was doing you a favour by bringing it up. You had your hands full with that girl before."

Adam wings the door closed to all but a foot. "All under control," he says flatly. "And thanks for this."

I put a hand on the door, against the old latched planks. "I'm in charge of PSHE now," I say. "If she needs someone to talk to, if there's a problem, tell her she can come to me."

Adam nods and closes the door.

CHAPTER
THIRTEEN

The stories went like this. If you were naughty, you got taken in the night by the evil gremlin from the woods. There would be no warning. There would be no escape. The only thing to do was relent and be taken. One boy said he'd seen the gremlin come three nights in a row for a young girl that refused to eat or speak. At the end of the third night, she never returned to her bed. Another girl said she'd seen the gremlin wearing a green mask and a hood, spitting and hissing as it trod the boards through the dorms, deciding who'd been the naughtiest.

Another told of a wicked demon landing on the window sill and clicking its long nails on the glass. The first child to open their eyes, to set a gaze on the knotty body of the creature, would be the one taken, the one tortured, the one brought back by morning wishing they were dead.

Someone passed around a tale of a vampire, and another boy cried as he recounted his brother's pleas to save him from the imps that came for him. There were whisperings of evil old women, rumours of murderers, bogeymen and burglars, and late-night banter about the ghost of Roecliffe Hall.

It was me who told them not to be so stupid, that if they didn't shut up, I'd tell Miss Maddocks or Patricia about their silly tales. Didn't they realise the stories had been made up by the carers so that everyone would be good?

I'd had enough. I jumped up and stood on my bed, shouting at the top of my voice. A dozen children, all of us meant to be in the bathroom, stopped messing about and for the first time since my arrival at the home, they noticed my existence; they actually fell silent and listened to me. Before this, I had blended into the plaster, been so meek that once the flurry after my arrival had died down, I hadn't caused so much as a whisper.

"You're wrong," I said. The shock of seeing them all staring up at me closed my throat. "There aren't any monsters or gremlins." My cheeks burned scarlet. I wanted to fall through the bed, slip through the floorboards below, disappear through the bottom of the home, and drop into the centre of the earth.

"Who said?" asked a boy older than me. He was the one who'd given me his jam when I first arrived.

Hands on hips, chin jutting forward, I continued. "My dad said that there's no such thing as monsters." I sniffed. They seemed to be listening. One or two sat down. "I used to get scared in the night after my mum died. I thought the monsters would come and get me too."

"What happened?" asked Sally, a girl with plaits.

I shrugged. "No monsters ever came, even though I'd seen their shadows on the landing."

"That's what happens here," another girl said. She was younger than me, although dressed in clothes fit for someone twice her age. "They wait until we're asleep."

I crouched down beside her, suddenly feeling way more grown up than I really was. "If you don't believe in them, then they won't be real. They need our thoughts to survive. They feed on our fear."

"Really?" she asked. She had pretty eyes, soft and brown, and skin the colour of sand. I held her hand.

"It's true. The monsters are all made up by grown-ups." I whipped a look around the group. "Don't believe and they won't come." There was silence. Just a cough, a scuff of a shoe on the floor.

"Try telling that to Keith Bagwood," someone cried out. "The gremlin came and got him last week and he never came back."

"And if they do come back, they won't speak about it 'cos they're too scared." Voices of dissent rained around me. "I hope they come for you, Miss Know-it-all." One by one the other kids grumbled agreement with each other, calling me stupid, pulling my hair, pinching me.

"I'll tell on you," I wailed, but they weren't listening. A circle of the meaner kids had formed around me. They danced about, singing a vile little rhyme that made my bones turn cold. *Tell-tale tit. Your tongue will split. And all the dogs in our town will have a little bit!*

Tears welled in my eyes. They scoffed at me, filtering off to the bathroom when Patricia came in and shooed everyone away with two sharp claps of her hands.

Were they right all along? Had my father lied to me about the monsters not being real if I didn't believe in them? After all, he'd promised me he'd visit every weekend and he'd lied about that. My shoulders collapsed forward and my waist buckled. I lay down on my bed, breathing in years of other children's sobs as I buried my face in the thin pillow. I cried silently.

"Ava," Patricia said. Her warm hand cupped my heart through my back as she rubbed gently on my ribs. "What's upset you?"

Reluctantly I prised my face from the damp pillow. "They said there are monsters," I told her. "That they come in the night."

"Just listen to how silly you sound. Do you think I'd let monsters hurt any of you?" Patricia was one of the nice ones. She smelled of apricots and the skin was soft on her hands as my fingers crawled into her palm.

I shook my head. "No." She wasn't my mother but perhaps I could pretend.

"We lock all the doors and windows at night. No one can get in or out. You're quite safe here at Roecliffe, Ava. That's why your daddy asked us to look after you."

My voice wobbled. "My dad said that if I didn't believe, there wouldn't be any monsters. I tried to tell the others."

"Well your father was quite right," Patricia said, smiling. She leaned forward and kissed the top of my head. "You're a sweet girl, Ava. You just keep believing what your daddy told you and everything will be fine. If anything bad happens, you come and tell me."

I frowned. "It's wrong to tell tales," I said. "The others said the dogs would get my tongue."

Patricia shook her head and smiled, dismissing my silly fears. "You have to brush your teeth now. It's bedtime." She pulled me off the mattress by my hands and I trotted after her to the cold tiled bathroom where the other girls were drying their faces. They glared at me as I walked in with Patricia.

"Scoot," she said, and they disappeared like wisps of ghosts in their nylon nightdresses and bare feet. "Don't be long," she said to me before leaving the room.

I shook my head vigorously. The vibrations dropped down my body to my freezing feet. I couldn't stop shaking. *I don't believe . . . I don't believe . . . I don't believe . . .* I thought, flicking a brush over my chattering teeth.

As I pressed the towel against my mouth, as the shadow swept across the doorway, as the odd scent blew in on an unlikely breeze, it dawned on me that to not believe in something meant it must have been there in the first place.

CHAPTER
FOURTEEN

Nina walked between the vans and trailers, avoiding the mud and puddles, squinting through the summer drizzle that hadn't let up for days, looking for number nineteen. Part of her wanted to run away, yet part of her was still intrigued by what had happened back at the harbour with the enigmatic man and his painting.

Some vans were not much more than old metal boxes with curiously decorated exteriors — horseshoes, bright paintwork, indoor furniture sitting tiredly beside them in the wet. Did they belong to gypsies or travellers? Nina wondered. Some cabins were clearly derelict, or so she thought until a door opened and a man with a bare chest and filthy jeans staggered out. He sauntered over to a bush and urinated. Nina looked away, shocked.

Eventually she found number nineteen. She hesitated before knocking on the corrugated green door. Her heart thumped. What was she doing here, all alone in this remote place? Then that other part of her made her pull her mac over her head so she didn't look a complete washout when he greeted her. As she waited, she wondered who would live in such a depressing place, and she wasn't sure she wanted to meet someone who did. But then she thought of her own situation — as a junior make-up artist, she scraped together the rent for a poky studio flat above a chip shop in a rundown suburb of the city — and suddenly it didn't seem much better.

When the door remained closed, Nina shrugged and turned to go, deciding any further meeting with the man from the harbour wasn't meant to be. Half of her was relieved. But two breezeblock steps back down into the mud, and she walked directly into him as if he'd been standing there all along, watching her get drenched, watching the air leave her lungs with disappointment when she thought he wasn't home.

"Oh," she said, smiling. "You're here."

"Here I am," he confirmed. His voice resonated through the rain. He was wearing a black shirt and jeans and was even more soaked than Nina. The curling hair she'd been thinking about since they'd met at the harbour was heavy and dripping, trickling in straight dark chunks down his forehead. His irises were blue-black ink syringed on to a brilliant white canvas. Even in a mess like this, he caused tremors deep inside Nina's chest.

"My trousers," she said proudly, holding up a plastic bag. She felt ridiculous.

"Really?" He was delighted. "I will have them framed." The smile alone was invitation enough as he unlocked the door to his trailer. "It's not much," he warned as they stepped inside.

Nina breathed in the scent of darkness, masculinity and paint. As her eyes adjusted to the dim light in the small rectangular space, she saw that every surface was covered with paint tubes, brushes, half-finished canvases or sketches. Jars of murky liquid adorned sills and ledges, and what could be a bed was blanketed in magazine cuttings and dramatic photographs of skies, seascapes, and close-up portraits. He made quick work of gathering up a particular stack of photographs — Nina thought she saw a nude — and stuffed them into a folder. He patted the clear space for her to sit, but she stood, staring around her.

"Gosh," Nina said, virtually speechless. "It's . . . it's . . ." She didn't know how to describe it. "I'm Nina, by the way."

If his surroundings indicated what was going on in his mind, then Nina was already fascinated by him. She guessed him to be dark yet creative, moody but not inaccessible. She wondered if days would go by when he never spoke to anyone, when he just immersed himself in his work, producing genius quality sketches, oil paintings and watercolours.

"Mick," he said, holding out his hand.

"I know." Nina offered her fingers in return. Mick drew them into his palm. He held on to them as if he were gauging her life story. "You wrote it down, remember?"

Inside, Nina sighed. This was the point where things got tricky — post-introductions, the place where she usually exited faster than she'd entered. Making friends wasn't easy, had never been easy.

"I thought you were going to mail me the trousers." Mick's face was deadpan. Did he want her to confess to being curious, admit to wanting to see him again?

"I was just passing and —"

"No one passes here. Ingleston Park isn't even on the map." Mick again indicated that Nina should sit.

"OK. I admit. I thought I'd come to see you in person. I like art. I wanted to see what else you painted besides my leg." Nina wasn't lying exactly. Neither was she telling the entire truth. But after she'd left the wind-lashed harbour the week before, she'd taken away a seed of intrigue about the man and his paints. He could obviously see things that other men couldn't. She liked that. If she was honest with herself, she couldn't believe that she was actually here, that she'd allowed that seed to germinate.

"Anyway, here you go." She handed over the bag. Mick immediately took out the garment.

"Just as I remember," he said. "Although not quite so striking now that they've dried." It was true. The vibrant sea-greens and moody greys that had bled and blended so stunningly on the black cloth had faded to a powdery ghost-like stain. "Thank you."

Nina shrugged. Away from the wind, out of the torrential rain, Mick appeared older than she recalled — eight, maybe ten years older than her. In fact, she didn't recall noting his age at all when they'd first met, just that he was an unusual man with wild hair, who had been desperate for her trousers.

"Coffee?" He asked, his mouth curling through the fine grazes of lines on his weathered face. His eyes

101

sparkled yet hung heavy with something — perhaps sadness — as she admitted to herself that she found him incredibly attractive.

"Thanks, but I'd better be going. I'm on the news set at five tomorrow morning." Nina was unable to take the first step towards the door.

"So, what, do you go to bed at two in the afternoon?" Mick glanced at his watch and laughed.

"I have things to take care of." She couldn't help but be wary of strangers. Even offering her hand for a shake and giving up a first name made her spine stiffen. It was what she'd been taught and the way things were.

But she was becoming tired of living her life as if she were see-through; fed up of being on the periphery of commitment. Would it be such a disaster, she wondered, to move a little closer to someone?

"You know what? Perhaps I will have that coffee." She perched on the edge of the messy seat, her hands clasped expectantly in her lap, and watched as Mick swilled out a couple of mugs. I wish, she thought as she glanced at each of his paintings — ghostly nudes, washed-out landscapes, unidentifiable slashes of colour — that I could apply a layer of paint to myself; colour in the paint-by-numbers that has become my life.

Tess, Nina's assistant, phoned almost hourly to check details for the Charterhouse job. She fussed over tiny things when there were more pressing problems to deal with, such as the contract itself. Nina was already late for a meeting with her solicitor to discuss the terms of the new commitment.

"Did you contact the staff agency, Tess?" Nina glanced at her watch. "Can you call them, please, unless you fancy learning how to make zombie children and fake wounds yourself?" She was unnecessarily snappy. "It's more important than anything right now. I need to hire someone reliable, someone who's got experience in the industry." She hung up.

Grabbing her bag, she glanced in the hall mirror before leaving the house. She looked awful. Lack of sleep had engraved dark circles beneath her eyes, and too much coffee made her hands shake as she tried to touch up the damage. She bowed her head and gripped the hall table. "Stop overreacting," she told herself.

Nina drove quickly to the solicitor's office. "There's nothing to worry about in the contract. All seems straightforward to me." He was charging her several hundred pounds to tell her the fifteen-page document was watertight.

She nodded, grateful that Charterhouse Productions was offering fair terms. It was one less thing to worry about. "So there's nothing that could get me into hot water later?" Nina wanted her money's worth. Sitting in the dark office for six minutes hardly justified his fee. He'd not even offered tea.

"Not unless you go and die," he said flippantly. "There's no provision for your company's release from duties if . . . if anything untoward should happen to you. Not a bad driver, are you? No terminal illness, I assume?" The small man chuckled and leaned back in his squeaky office chair. "Because you pretty much *are* Chameleon FX. Quality of work depends largely on your skill. I understand that you're not the only company Charterhouse has contracted for their productions, but if you were unable to fulfil your obligations for any reason . . . well, I assume you have insurance for those circumstances anyway."

"Yes, yes of course." Nina was thinking. *If anything untoward should happen to you.* "What would it take to add in a clause to cover me? You know, in case that bus did come from nowhere?" She tried to laugh but only a warped sigh left her lips.

"Nothing too tricky. I can draft a clause and put it to your client, if you wish."

"Yes, please do that. Make it state that if anything happens to me, then Chameleon FX is released from any liability whatsoever to Charterhouse. Something like that." Mick was a director of her company. If the worst happened, she didn't want to bequeath business liabilities as well as a legacy of lies.

"I'm not so sure they wouldn't want some kind of indemnity —"

"Mr Wenlock, I assume you'll be charging me for this short clause?" Nina stood. The floor dropped away from her and her head spun.

"Of course I will have to make a small fee but —"

"Then please, just do as I say and insert the clause. If Charterhouse takes issue with it, then I'll have to rethink the entire contract with them." Nina thanked her solicitor and asked him to be quick with the revision.

She walked out into the bright sunshine, her head now fizzing with the start of a migraine, and headed back to the car park. She approached her car, about to unlock it, but froze. The door was already open.

What the hell . . . I know I locked it. She thought back to when she arrived at the car park. She'd definitely beeped the car locked. Hadn't she? She peered inside the car. Nothing was taken. Her jacket still lay on the back seat. CDs were still strewn on the passenger seat. Even her satnav was on the dashboard. Surely a thief would have taken that.

She tried to solidify her melting thoughts. Am I going crazy?

Nina pulled her phone from her bag. She would call home to make sure Josie was OK, ask her what she wanted for dinner, ground herself. Her hands trembled and she hit the wrong buttons. Perhaps she had disturbed someone trying to steal her car. She dialled again, stalking around the car park for a better signal, glancing around, wondering if anyone was watching her. The phone rang, eventually answered by the machine. "Josie, are you there? Pick up if you can hear me. Josie? Call me as soon as you get this."

Then she dialled Josie's mobile number. Voicemail.

Feeling stupid for even worrying about Josie, she dashed back to the car, jammed the seat belt into its slot and drove out of the car park. Should she notify the police? But what would she tell them? My car door was open but nothing was taken. Maybe she'd just forgotten to lock the door.

The drive across town was slow. She called home a few more times, but there was still no reply. She didn't care if she got caught using a phone while driving. Oh

Josie, *Josie*. Just answer. Irrational thoughts started flashing through Nina's mind, even though she knew her daughter would, in all probability, be absolutely fine. It wasn't the first time she hadn't bothered to pick up the phone.

Jabbing the brake, she stopped the car abruptly on the drive. She ran up to the house. She forced the key into the lock and burst inside. "Josie, are you home?"

The living room and kitchen were empty. As she went through the hall, she could see that no one was in the dining room. "Josie, where are you?" Each step was a mountain as Nina ran up the stairs. She smelled shower gel, body lotion, hairspray as she passed the bathroom door. Steam hung in the air, indicating Josie had recently showered. She probably hadn't heard the phone.

"Josie?" Nina burst into her daughter's bedroom without knocking. The curtains were still closed and the blue glow of her computer lit one corner of the room. As Nina's eyes adjusted to the darkness, all she could make out was the usual disarray of a teenage girl's bedroom. Josie wasn't there.

Nina dashed out. It was when she was in the kitchen, redialling Josie's mobile number that she saw something that made her heartbeat race then stall. "Oh, thank heavens," she cried, and ran out through the back door, on to the deck, down the steps, and straight into Josie's arms.

"Whoa, Mum. What's wrong?" Josie was suddenly the adult as Nina trembled against her daughter's shoulder. She buried her face in the soft fabric of her dressing gown. Josie hadn't even dressed yet.

"Don't mind me. I'm just being a stupid paranoid mother." She laughed and hiccupped and sniffed. Josie was safe. Josie was at home where she was meant to be. No harm had come to her. And nothing, Nina tried to convince herself, was going to happen. "I just had this stupid feeling, that's all. I'm OK now I know you're safe. Why didn't you answer the phone?"

"Sorry. I didn't hear it. Dad wanted me down in his studio." She scowled, thinking she was going to get told off.

Nina laughed and fought to contain the hysteria. "Who's the chosen one, then, being allowed in there while he's working?" An inappropriately large smile spread across Nina's relieved face. She had been completely irrational and stupid. In her tired, absent-minded state, she'd obviously left the car door unlocked. She was lucky all her stuff hadn't gone missing. Nina draped her arm around Josie's shoulders and led her back to the house.

"Dad said he needed help with something." Josie faltered. "Besides, my clothes disappeared and I wanted to find out if he knew where they were." Josie sounded grumpy.

Nina froze. "What do you mean, your clothes disappeared?"

"It was really odd. I went into the shower cubicle and left the clean clothes I was going to wear draped over the towel rail. I showered and it got all steamy, but when I got out and was drying, they were gone. I can't find them anywhere. I thought you might have taken them for the wash before you went out, thinking they were dirty."

Nina's throat closed around her words. "No," she managed. "I didn't." She glanced around the garden. Her skin prickled and the hair on her arms stood up. She hugged herself, suddenly feeling chilled to the bone.

"Josie, listen to me. When you were in the shower, did you hear anything at all? I was out at the solicitor's office and your dad's been in the studio all morning."

"No, not at all. That's the strange thing. I guessed you'd come back early, but when I couldn't find you, I assumed Dad had moved my clothes for some reason." Josie bowed her head.

Nina's thoughts raced. Mick simply wouldn't do that. He would never dream of interrupting Josie in the bathroom. And he wasn't really one for practical jokes, either. "You know, I bet Dad took them as a joke," she said, not believing a word of it. "He's probably hidden them under the sofa." Nina forced a smile. "Come on. Let's go inside and get a drink." She swallowed, but her throat was dry and rasping.

"Nope. I already asked him. I'm so annoyed. They were my new jeans."

"I'll buy you some more," Nina said quietly. She poured juice for Josie and then she couldn't help it but she went round the house shutting and locking the windows. She double-locked the front porch and secured the door leading on to the deck.

"Mum, we'll swelter. It's so humid today. What's got into you?"

Nina tried to hide her shaking hands from her daughter. She smiled as much as she could manage. "Well, as it happens, I'm cold. Probably a bit stressed or going down with something. The new contract's a huge responsibility. But I'll be OK. Don't you worry about me." Nina's words were flicked with brightness.

Josie frowned. "Whatever, Mum. Just let me know if my stuff turns up." She took her drink and went to her room.

"It's OK. She's always losing things," Nina muttered, pacing. Tennis racquets, books, sweaters, homework, even footwear — Nina recalled the day Josie had walked home from school barefoot because she'd misplaced her new shoes. A few missing clothes weren't out of the ordinary.

"Stay home the rest of the day, yeah?" Nina called up the stairs. Keeping Josie in the house would be unsustainable long term, she knew, but the thought of letting her out right now wasn't appealing.

Nina hadn't thought she'd ever have to do this. A remarkably happy family life, she'd believed, had eroded the need to worry. She sighed and spent ten minutes collecting her thoughts before deciding what to do.

Finally, she fetched her handbag and sat down at the kitchen table. She rummaged through the bag — a gift from Mick last birthday — and dug out the battered notebook. It was concealed in a zip-up compartment and went everywhere with her. In the past, the fabric-covered book had been used for notes and lists and reminders. It was full now and never got used. But at the back was written the most important telephone number she had ever been given.

Nina stared at the number and her heart sank. It was so outdated, it was unrecognisable. But, peeling out the original number and adding a modern code, Nina dialled and held her breath. She recalled his last words. "If there's trouble, you know where I am."

All she wanted was reassurance, just to be certain.

After four rings, a woman answered. "Claire's Bakery, can I help you?"

Nina's head dropped to the table in despair as she hung up.

CHAPTER
FIFTEEN

A dozen pair of eyes focus on me. The common-room walls are painted with swirls of red, making me feel as if I've been swallowed up by my worst nightmare. I'm being digested alive.

"So." I clear my throat. "I'm Miss Gerrard and I'll be taking you through the PSHE syllabus this year." I'm shaky, nervous, unqualified. "There's a lot to cover, but I want to make it fun and get to know you all at the same time." Silence fills the room with its vaulted ceiling and huge windows overlooking the school grounds. But despite this, it's a friendly space with bean bags, a couple of squashy sofas, a television and a rack of DVDs. There's a fridge, a small sink, and a worktop with a kettle and sandwich toaster in one corner, while on the opposite side of the room there is a desk with a lone PC. The monitor rotates with a screensaver featuring photographs of the school's various sports teams.

"I thought I'd start our sessions off with a subject that's sometimes hard to talk about." A couple of girls glance up. "Bullying is a serious issue." Someone groans and a couple of girls giggle. One yawns and snaps open her mobile phone.

"We did that last term," a pretty girl with dark hair says. The girl I saw talking to Adam.

"Then I expect you to be an expert on the matter." I already sound like a teacher. "I'm sorry, I don't think I know your name."

She stares at me for longer than necessary, squinting her devious eyes up and down me, sizing up my worth, deciding whether or not I'm fit to take the class. "Katy," she tells me. "And I don't know yours either."

"Miss Gerrard. I already told you." More giggles as Katy mumbles something to the cluster of heads that have drawn around her. "If you like, you can call me Frankie. It's short for Francesca." The name crunches off my tongue.

It takes a while, but the group finally settles to listen to what I have to say. I show them a short film to discuss afterwards, but it seems rather basic for a bunch of worldly fifteen-year-olds.

"Miss, Katy shouldn't have watched that." A girl's arm shoots up into the air as she speaks.

"Katy?" I ask. More giggles as I wait for her response. I look back and forth between both girls, raising my eyebrows.

"Her parents don't allow her to watch television. They've signed a form." A spray of laughter ensues.

"Can Katy speak for herself?" I imagine myself hauled in front of a red-faced Mr Palmer, Katy's angry parents making a complaint against me. "Is this true?" The girl nods, clearly stifling a grin. "Will they mind that you watched this little film?" Katy nods again, and my session in the headmaster's study becomes all the more real. "Why didn't you tell me this before I switched the film on then? You could have waited outside."

"Because I wanted to see if what's happening really *is* bullying," she says. Katy's eyes darken and her mouth pouts, pulling her cheekbones inward so that she suddenly looks more vulnerable than a lamb without its mother.

"And is it?" I ask. At last, we are getting somewhere.

"Oh *yes*," Katy replies, wide-eyed and smug, suddenly animated again, suddenly very much fifteen and cocksure. The rest of the class explodes into fits of raucous laughter.

Lying underwater, I am encased, warm, safe, and everything is silent except for the dull sound of me tapping my fingernail on the side of the cast-iron bath. I blow out bubbles. In one swift move, I am sitting upright again, dripping, gasping, completely exhausted of oxygen.

The underwater tapping has been replaced by a similar sound. Someone is knocking on the bathroom door. "I'm nearly done," I call out, sighing. It's late. I thought I'd be guaranteed peace in the bathroom once the school had settled for the night.

"It's me," a female voice whispers through the old wood. "Katy," she adds.

"Katy?" I reach for a towel. "Do you need to speak to me?"

"Yes," she sends back urgently.

"Just a moment then." I am up and out of the bath, wrapping my dripping hair in a towel. I pull on my robe, tie the belt, and open the door. "What's up, Katy? It's nearly midnight."

She slips into the steamy bathroom and slumps down on the closed toilet. She is wearing her pyjamas — white ones with pink bows dotted all over. Her feet are bare, her toenails painted. I crouch in front of her, touched that after one rather chaotic session with her class, she feels she can talk to me.

"There's this problem," she says. Her face puckers like a baby's. "It's really hard."

"Take your time," I say.

"There's someone that's after me." She sighs. "Really after me," she adds. "And it's scaring me."

"Is this to do with the bullying you mentioned in class?"

Katy nods. "He tried to . . ." she trails off. The bud of her chin tightens and her lips curl. She's trying not to cry. "He made a move on me and . . ."

"And you didn't want him to?"

She nods again and covers her face. I hear a sob, which, if I couldn't plainly see the pain she is suffering, I would have taken to be a snicker, based on her behaviour in class.

"This isn't something you could talk about in our session, is it?"

Katy pulls off some toilet paper and blows her nose. "No way," she admits. "I'm sorry if I mocked what you were telling us." She looks up at me as I pull back the curtain of her hair. Pain radiates through me at the simple act. She smiles as a strand gets stuck on her wet cheek.

"Is it someone you know through school?" I ask. "Or a boy back home?"

"It happens while I'm at school," she says. Suddenly she looks like a very naive child, rather than the fifteen-year-old that she is. Her age, depending on how far this has progressed, presents an array of extra problems. Whoever's doing this is messing with a minor.

"Can you tell me who it is?"

Without a thought, Katy shakes her head.

"That's OK," I say, not expecting a name just yet. Courage is a seed; Katy has sown hers. "How far . . . how far has this all gone, Katy?" I'm asking if he's had sex with her . . . forced her to have sex.

Katy just stares straight ahead. With every breath, her body shudders. Her mouth gapes open; something trying to escape. I rub her back. "No need to speak," I say. I look round at the ceiling, the walls, the cracked windowpanes, wondering about all the things this building has seen. I reach over to the bath and plunge my hand underwater. I pull the plug. "All in your own time." I shake my arm. We sit and listen to the water draining, each hoping that what we are thinking will be washed clean away.

The term forges on in an unstoppable schedule of lessons, sports events, musical preparation and, for Sylvia and me, an endless stream of motherly duties ranging from laundry to sprained ankles to homesickness.

"Adam was looking for you earlier." Sylvia snaps out a sheet and deftly folds it on to the ironing board. With two quick shots of steam, she has it pressed, crisp, and folded on the stack of others.

"He was?" My heart skids and I don't know why. So far I've done a reasonable job of keeping my colleagues at arm's length. Angie Ray, English teacher and netball coach, asks me almost daily to join her and some others on their Friday night drink at the village pub.

"You'll meet people," she always says.

But I don't want to, I think, while smiling politely. "Perhaps," I tell her. "Maybe." Then the headache comes, or the extra duties for Matron, or the made-up excuse about a family get-together an hour's drive away.

"It seemed quite important." Sylvia moves on to pressing school skirts. Then her pager bleeps and she flicks off the iron. "Someone's been hit in the face by a hockey ball," she says, rolling her eyes.

"Did he say he'd come back?" I ask before she shoots off with the first-aid bag.

"Adam?" Her gaze flicks behind me. "Speak of the devil." She grins and slips between the door frame and Adam, who's standing there, looking awkward, hands on hips so that his elbows zigzag the space.

"Hi," he says, when Sylvia is long gone down the corridor. If he's been sent by Angie, then the answer will be the same. I don't want to join their happy little

116

pub nights. I don't want to meet people. All I want is to keep my head down.

"Hello," I reply. "Haven't lost anything else, have you?" I switch the iron back on. I will tackle the skirts for Sylvia.

"Maybe," he says. Adam's tone is gravelly and serious. He sits in the saggy old armchair by the gas fire. "I came to ask you about the PSHE classes you take with the girls."

"Yes?" I glance up from the board.

"Have you met a girl called Katy Fenwick yet?"

"Katy?" I say. It gives me a moment to think. Last night she was in a terrible state; now Adam is asking me about her. "No, I don't think so. I've probably seen her around but —"

"Will you let me know if she says anything to you?" Adam shifts in the squat chair. He looks uncomfortable, both body and mind.

"Like what?" I can't betray her confidence. "Is she OK?"

"Just let me know if she says anything." Adam stares down the long room, past the banks of washing machines and dryers, over the stacks of clothes, and beyond the tall window that looks out over the sports field. Distant spots of green and yellow, the school colours, flash through the early autumn mist as the girls dart about the hockey pitch.

"They're gunning for me," he says, suddenly standing and striding away, the remnants of his voice leaving me wondering if someone really is out to get him, or if he is perhaps not the man I thought he was.

CHAPTER
SIXTEEN

Sometimes I got asked to help with supper. The other kids stared as I was singled out and led off by the arm to the kitchen. I didn't want to be special, I thought, the first time Patricia took me. I just wanted to go home. The kitchen was huge and filled with car-sized machines that were covered in a greasy yellow film that stayed on my fingers even after I washed them. The smell put me off my food.

Patricia stayed in the kitchen with me, but she didn't exactly cook. She watched as Chef tramped about, sweating from the hot, food-heavy air. She said I could help him. She thought it might cheer me up and help me to settle in, make me feel at home. I scowled when she nudged me towards Chef because, honestly, how could chopping celery into little horseshoes make me feel as if I was back with my dad, with all my toys, with my pet cat? Anyway, I didn't even know you could boil the silly stuff, so when Chef scooped it all into a huge saucepan bubbling with water, I wondered what we were making. He ran his fingers down my arm, making my skin tingle as if it was boiling too.

"Is it soup?" My voice rang tiny through the steam and smells.

Patricia laughed fondly. She was leaning on the wall, watching Chef in his chessboard trousers and funny hat. "You'll have pie and vegetables," she called out, not taking her eyes off Chef. Patricia was leaning in an "S" shape against the wall. Her hips stuck forward and her legs bent back, ending in pencil points. In the kitchen, Patricia acted differently to anywhere else. It was as if she forgot herself, became someone else entirely.

"Pie?" I asked. "I don't see any."

Chef laughed and when he did, his face reddened. He glanced at Patricia. He had a moustache that sparkled as if it was wet. "Pie's in the oven, girl." His voice was too high for his chunky body — a voice that should sound like beef and dumplings, not lemon meringue.

"Can I see it?" I asked. I'd never seen a pie cooking before. Chef beckoned me over to the oven. I heard Patricia's soft laugh as I was scooped under the armpits and swept up to peer through the glass door. My own face was reflected over the browning crust as the pastry and gravy smells sent me wild with hunger. Breakfast was ages ago and the pie smelled so good.

"That looks yummy," I said. I was slipping from Chef's hands. At nearly nine years old, I was a bit too big to be held up. My arms began to hurt and I wriggled, so Chef pushed his arm between my legs like a bicycle saddle.

"Now you can watch the pie cook, little one. And afterwards, I will give you some ice cream as a treat. Strawberry or vanilla?" He couldn't say vanilla properly.

"Why is there a blackbird poking out?" I thought it looked cruel. I fidgeted. I wouldn't like to be that blackbird in there, all hot and trapped.

"It's not real. It's made of china. It lets the steam out of the pie. It's like the nursery rhyme."

Then, as Chef moved me about on his arm to keep hold of me, I heard the rhyme being sung. I was uncomfortable now and just wished he'd put me down. When he finally did allow me to slide off him, I realised that it had been Patricia's soft voice humming the tune all along. She leaned against the wall smiling, looking happy, looking quite pretty, watching me and Chef. It gave me a funny feeling I didn't like.

"My daddy says my name means little bird," I told him, pulling down my skirt. "You won't put me in a pie, will you?"

Chef laughed. "No, silly. But now you can be my little bird. My secret helper in the kitchen." He took my hand and led me to a big silver door and pulled it open. Clouds of fog fell down on me. "Time for ice cream," he said in such a sweet voice it made me grip his hand tighter.

"If you ever feel sad, Ava bird, just come into the kitchen for a treat." I can't remember if it was Chef or Patricia who said it, because their voices were nearly the same. But it made me feel oddly happy, as if I shouldn't have this secret with Chef, but I was special because I did. He made me promise not to tell.

CHAPTER
SEVENTEEN

Nina left Ingleston Park without noticing the sodden litter spilling from the dumpsters. She didn't notice the tied-up German shepherd baring its teeth at her as she walked between trailers. The echoes of a slap and a woman's screams didn't make it into her consciousness either, and neither did the wail of a baby or the thud-thud of loud music.

"Mick. Mick Kennedy," she said to herself over and over. She was soon soaked by the rain as she walked back to the main road. Half of her was still back in the messy trailer.

It was a long walk to the bus stop, but she didn't care. Mick had done strange things to her mind in the hour that she had spent in his company. He exuded the kind of inner strength she'd not seen in a man before. Through the detritus of his trailer, through his extraordinary paintings, shone a mind that she felt she would like to know better.

Thursday seemed a lifetime away. It was only a drink in a pub, but he had asked her, which meant he liked her, which meant that perhaps things weren't so bad in her life after all. That getting up at 6 a.m. every morning, padding across the sloping landing to the shared bathroom in the hope she would reach it before the other tenants occupied it for hours, wasn't such a hardship. That chasing coffee and bagels for the news team when she'd been trained to do their make-up didn't really mean that she was just a lackey. That her bank balance wasn't as desperate as it had seemed yesterday.

Rising at the edges of Nina's life was a halo of hope. She didn't feel quite so alone, quite so abandoned, quite so unwanted — even though, if she was honest, getting to know someone new was about as terrifying as crossing the road blindfolded.

They didn't go to the pub in the end. Mick was pacing up and down the pavement when she arrived. In fact, she was a little early. But there he was, head down, hands shoved in his jeans pockets, a cigarette dangling from his lips. He's keen, she thought.

"Hey," she sang out. Nina had decided on a casual look, slightly bohemian. She thought Mick would like the flowing skirt and flower-print top. It didn't suggest anything other than femininity. In fact, Nina wondered if she looked too childlike. Before she left, she wrapped a woollen shawl around her shoulders.

"Nina." Mick stamped out his cigarette. "You look pretty." He dotted a kiss on each of her cheeks. She inhaled the lingering smell of smoke. She liked it. "Let's not go in there." He tipped his head to the door. "I hate pubs."

Nina laughed. "Then what shall we do?"

Mick chewed his bottom lip. She didn't think he'd shaved, but that was OK. Beneath his wild curly hair his face looked as if he had been concentrating all night long. He was both exhausted and vibrant, and exuded an energy that tingled Nina's skin.

"I know a place," he said. "But first we need supplies." A wicked grin led Nina to follow him across the road to a small supermarket. He took a basket and piled it with bread and cheese and olives and wine. At the counter he asked for more cigarettes and tipped the whole lot into a canvas bag he wore across his back. "Let's go," he said, taking Nina's hand and leading her to a bus stop. "I don't have a car," he said, and the grin flashed across his face again.

They headed out of Bristol and Mick announced they were going to the Downs. "It's a favourite place of mine," Mick said. "The view across the gorge is to die for."

"I've never been," Nina replied. "I'm quite new to the city."

"You're a northern lass," Mick said with a silly accent.

Nina reddened and hesitated.

"I . . . I went to school in the north," she said.

"But you're not from there originally?" Mick leaned his head back and suddenly Nina was dazzled by the setting sun. She didn't know what to say.

"Yes. I am. Sort of."

Mick laughed. "Well, you either are or you aren't. Where were you born?"

"I don't know," Nina answered. She'd used that before. It generally generated a laugh, from which she was able to change the subject. But Mick didn't laugh. He frowned instead.

"Were you adopted?" His voice was low.

Hesitantly, Nina nodded. "My mother died in childbirth and I never knew my father," she said. She left it at that, leaving Mick nodding slowly, thinking about what kind of childhood she would have had.

"Here's our stop." Mick picked up the bag and led Nina off the bus. It pulled away in a cloud of diesel fumes and they stood staring at acres of parkland.

"It's so beautiful," Nina said. "I had no idea this was all here."

"Follow me and I'll show you a view you won't forget." Mick walked off briskly and Nina followed, wishing she'd worn something more substantial on her feet than sandals. But the grass was warm between her toes, and the late sun grazed her shoulders like an extra shawl. Up ahead, Mick turned and waited for a panting Nina to catch up. She was laughing, holding up the hem of her skirt as she forced her weary legs up the slope. They'd climbed a long way. "Take a look behind you," he said.

Nina turned, feeling giddy after the exertion. The view was both unexpected and breathtaking. She squinted out over the gorge, the sides of which were laced together by a bridge that seemed to defy all physical laws. "It's amazing. It's crazy." She laughed.

"It's the Clifton suspension bridge," he said as if he were leading a field trip. "Designed by Isambard Kingdom Brunel, it was completed in eighteen sixty-four, five years after he died."

"I can't believe I didn't know this place existed." Nina shook her head, laughing at herself.

"It's amazing what can be right in front of your eyes. All you need to do is open them." Mick stood directly behind her, a warm breath away. Nina shuddered, not really understanding what he meant. But that was the thing with him. He said things that shocked her; took her by surprise with a glimpse into a future she'd never thought existed until she met him. How could such a short time of knowing someone feel like a lifetime?

They were silent for several minutes, taking in the view. Nina thought this place was way better than going to the pub. The river below them wound through the gorge in muddy arcs, and she thought she could almost see the glaciers damming and jamming and eating away at the ancient limestone.

"Hundreds of millions of years," she said pensively. "I read a book about it once."

"Oh?" Mick moved closer still. His chin hovered above Nina's right shoulder.

"And we take it for granted. Building a bridge like that is nothing compared to the feat that nature pulled off by producing this gorge."

"Try telling that to Isambard and his gang." Mick briefly squeezed Nina's arms and dropped down on to the scrubby grass. "Several men died during its construction. Time for some food, I think."

"You know a lot about the bridge." Nina joined him on the grass.

"I didn't bring glasses. You go first," he said, opening the wine with his penknife before handing the bottle to

Nina. "I trained as an engineer. They teach you all this stuff. Plus I like trivia. Apparently a Victorian woman survived when she jumped off the bridge. It was her long skirt that saved her, would you believe."

Nina tentatively sipped the wine. "That's incredible. I just assumed you trained as an artist."

Mick was shaking his head. Nina handed him back the bottle. "My father wanted me to follow in his footsteps and be a civil engineer. He refused to support me otherwise." Mick took a long draw from the bottle and wiped his mouth. "To be honest, I was always a bit of a no-hoper, so the prospect of my parents paying my way for a few more years was a good one, even if it did mean studying something I hated."

Mick's honesty and detail about his past stirred something within Nina. It was a cross between shame and envy, and a burgeoning desire to confide in someone. "Have you always painted?" she asked.

"Much to my father's disgust. He said it was a career for dropouts." Mick slugged again. "And guess what? He was right." Laughing at himself, he peeled the wrapper off the cheese and broke the bread into pieces. "*Bon appetit*," he said and sank his teeth into a large crust, eyeing Nina as he pulled and stretched the bread from his mouth.

"But your pictures are stunning. Do you sell many?"

"Hardly ever. The term starving artist isn't without reason. I do odd jobs on the side. Chopping wood, delivering newspapers. Working in bars. Anything to pay my way."

126

"I bet your father loves that, having supported you through your degree." Nina bit into her bread. She licked flakes of crust from her lips.

"I wouldn't know," Mick replied. "He's dead."

As quickly as that, the bond between the pair hardened. Mick didn't know it, but Nina felt an empathy towards him that would carry them onward towards love, marriage, a family, a future. They sat on the patchy grass, necking wine from the bottle, breaking off hunks of bread and cheese, their knees touching accidentally, their fingers brushing as they passed the wine, their thoughts entwining as they learned more and more about each other — Mick freely recounting stories of his past, and Nina carefully arranging her history like eggs in a basket.

"You look as if you've seen a ghost." Mick smelled of paint and turpentine. He wiped his hands on an oily cloth. "Are you OK?" He was back in from the studio.

Nina's hand bandaged the phone until her knuckles were painful white hillocks.

Claire's Bakery. It was meant to be a direct line, the eject button, a safety net. "I'm fine." Her voice was taut piano wire.

The grim truth was that it had been twenty years. People relocate, die, change jobs, and the telephone numbering system had altered many times since she'd been given this contact all those years ago. Like a fool, she'd been carrying it around as if it were a safety harness, something she could always fall back on. If she changed handbags, then the notebook was moved into the new one. The outdated number itself had become irrelevant. She realised it was what it represented that gave comfort.

"Who were you phoning?" Mick filled the kettle. "I need coffee," he said. "It's just not happening for me today. And I'm out of white paint. I have to go to the art supplies shop."

"No," Nina said. She didn't want to be left alone.

"But I've completely run out."

"Can't you order it online?" She noticed her hands tremble as she tucked her phone back in her bag.

"It won't arrive for a couple of days if I do that, and I need it to complete the piece I'm working on." Mick smiled and heaped coffee granules into mugs. "The work's finally coming in, Nina. I can't blow it." He was clearly pleased about the contract, but Nina could see it was taking its toll.

"Please . . . please don't go out. Or let's all go. Josie can come and we can go out for lunch." She spread her fingers round Mick's wrist. "Please."

"Nina, what's got into you? I thought you had mountains of paperwork to get through today." Mick allowed his wife to steady herself on him. "Josie'll want to see her friends later, not hang around with us."

"You don't understand." The colour drained from Nina's face. She thought she might faint. "I just don't want to be alone today."

Suddenly, Nina was back there, sitting on the grass with the evening sun blanketing their shoulders. The bridge cast a diagram-like shadow over the sludge of low tide in the crook of the gorge, and the warm cheese melted in their mouths. Josie wasn't even a glimmer of a thought between them, and the most pressing issue in Nina's mind was whether Mick would kiss her when they parted.

It was all so simple, all so unexplored, and over the following weeks, Nina and Mick grew closer than she could ever have hoped. He was an intelligent, enigmatic, sometimes moody, brilliant artist, and she was a young, naive and slightly nervous make-up artist living above a fish and chip shop. It seemed a lifetime ago now.

"I'll be back before you know it. A couple more hours' work and then how about we have a late lunch outside together. Bread, cheese, wine . . ." Mick enveloped Nina and pulled her face to his chest. They both knew what he meant; how symbolic that simple feast was. "You make your phone call, while I duck out." Forgetting to make the coffee, he reached for his car keys. "I'll be back in twenty minutes."

Nina grew worried. Mick often spent hours in the art supply shop without realising the time, chatting to the owner, browsing the brushes, running his finger over canvases, different paper grades, and trying out the various charcoal sticks that would end up snapped and stubby around his studio.

"OK," Nina reluctantly agreed. She couldn't press it further. She knew she was being ridiculous. "But please don't be long." Nothing would happen while he was gone. She would lock the doors and figure out a way to make contact with the only man in the world who could offer advice. "I'll see you soon."

She watched Mick drive off. Within seconds, the door was locked and the windows double-checked. No one would be breaking in again today.

CHAPTER
EIGHTEEN

The girl is naked. Moonlight swims over her young skin, giving the appearance of modesty yet not leaving an inch of her unseen. Flat stretches of muscle, gentle mounds, long youthful limbs, hair spidering down her back, I watch it all. She's performing a dance, or so it seems, right there under the tree, shrouded by the branches. She looks as if she'll never stop, as if she'll just keep on dancing for him.

I followed them. A sound woke me. It was late and as soon as I stirred — sitting bolt upright in bed — I sensed it was her coming to see me again, tiptoeing down the corridor, about to tap on my door, about to fall on to my quilt, about to cry, about to confess what was on her mind. Katy Fenwick had been to see me several more times since she'd interrupted my bath. As yet she'd not mentioned any names. She was a troubled girl, that was for sure, and it gave me something else to think about, something other than my own misery.

"*Stop*." The hushed command from outside my door stopped Katy's rap.

"Who's there?" Katy's voice rasped down the corridor. Someone had followed her.

I got out of bed and pressed my ear to the door. Two voices, one male, one Katy's. I froze. A breath the size of the one I wanted to release would reveal my presence the other side of the wood.

"Leave me alone," she said. Sobs welled in her throat.

"You're being ridiculous, Katy," he said. "We need to talk about this."

A sob finally erupted — the pathetic choke of an animal caught in a trap, its captor leering above. Then more talk that I couldn't hear, crying, muffled sounds, shuffling feet on the creaky boards, more whispers. It all grew distant as the pair retreated.

I grabbed my robe, pushed my feet into slippers, and unlocked my door. It was three twenty-five in the morning. *I'm thirsty; I couldn't sleep; I heard voices . . .* Excuses filled my mind in case I was caught.

Was it the scent of passion that led me on? Was it footprints of lust or a trail of forbidden love that directed me to the basement? Open doors, lingering words, an illicit scent . . . I smelled the fresh night air, cleaned and ready for the onset of morning, as I slipped out of the cellar. The door leading outside had been carelessly left open, showing me where they'd gone. I pulled my gown further round my shoulders and ducked under the low gothic arch. I climbed the steps to ground level and caught a silver trail of the pair as they ducked into a nearby thicket.

By the time I reached the edge of the evergreen spinney, by the time I'd drawn breath and steadied myself against a tree, by the time my eyes had widened enough to take in what was happening, I'd already seen Katy's nakedness; had already spotted that the man with her — his dark eyes swollen and transfixed — was Adam Kingsley.

Now, still watching, frozen, hoping someone will tell me the right thing to do, I stand here, paralysed. Katy winds herself through the undergrowth. Tears stream down her face as she performs her dance. "Is this what you want from me?"

My mouth falls open and my heart bounds in a million crazy beats. *This can't be happening.* I clap my hand over my mouth. Vomit or a yell, something is about to come out. I bend and duck away. *It's dark*, the voice in my head tells me. *It's dark and a girl is naked and crying in the woods.*

"No, Katy. You don't understand." Adam's voice is unfamiliar, altered by the situation — that he is watching one of his young students perform an erotic dance for him in the moonlight. Slowly, Adam removes his arms from his jacket. I watch, breathless, my heart thumping its own rhythm behind my ribs, as he begins his strip.

Katy holds out her hands to Adam; uses her youth to draw him towards her. It's unclear who is seducing who. I lay my hands on the scabby bark of the bush. Crouching in the thicket, I watch through the network of thorns and twigs.

"Oh, Adam," she sighs, and her tears subside. Everything about Katy is alluring and soft and the perfect feast for Adam, who doesn't know what to do with himself. Katy's legs are coyly crossed, her angular shoulders pressed back, and the moonlight is like brushstrokes of white across her skin.

Adam is free of his jacket. I wait for him to unbutton his shirt, but he doesn't. Instead, he approaches Katy with his jacket held before him as a bullfighter would spread his cape to the bull. "Katy," he murmurs. Adam is a hunter and Katy the fawn. Thorns scratch my ankles.

"But Adam . . ." she says. "Mr Kingsley. Mr *Kingsley*." She lets his name — the name of him as her teacher — roll off her tongue. She sidesteps the outstretched garment. She shakes her head and draws up to him from behind.

Adam spins round. "I want you to put —"

If there was a way to escape, I would. One movement from me and there will be three players in this game. Katy brings her face close to her teacher's. She presses her lips against his and delivers a kiss he will never forget.

I bow my head into the leaves. I can't watch. Following them was a mistake, but I wanted to make sure that Katy was safe. I had no idea it was Adam stalking her; no idea what his intentions were. No idea what I will do now, even though I should have learned that lesson long ago.

"No!" I look up just as Adam pulls away. "Katy, for heaven's sake, will you put this around you and get back inside." He recovers from the momentary paralysis Katy inflicted on him. His body is his own again; he has escaped from the teenage web she spun around them.

134

In an instant, he has the black jacket across Katy's shoulders. Once covered, Adam hunts around for her garments. He retrieves a flimsy nightie from the floor of the spinney and holds it out to her.

"It's what you wanted, Mr Kingsley." Katy is a child again. Adam grips her shoulders, tiny in the width of his jacket. He shakes her gently.

"No, Katy, it's most certainly not what I wanted. All this nonsense has got to stop." Adam's chest rises and falls. He's sweating.

"I thought you loved me," Katy says. Tributaries of mascara cut up her face. Her mouth hangs open. "Kiss me." She lunges at Adam. Her calf muscles stretch as she stands on tiptoe, desperately trying to deliver affection to her history teacher.

Adam intercepts her. His palms flat against the hollow beneath her collarbones, he eases her gently away. "No, Katy," he says firmly. "No more. I am your teacher and I do not want to have a relationship with you." His voice slams off Katy and ricochets between the trees.

"No!" she cries hysterically. She's laughing now, ripping the jacket from her shoulders.

"Katy, you've been drinking. You need to calm down and come back inside." Adam picks up his jacket and attempts to harness the girl within it again.

She's having none of it.

"You want me . . . you came to my room looking for me . . . you're always flirting with me in lessons . . . you grab me whenever we meet . . . you can't wait to get your hands on me . . ." Katy continues to mumble, staggering, ranting on and on until Adam silences her with a hand cupped over her mouth.

"You're imagining all this, Katy. It's a crush and it's got way out of hand. When you came looking for me tonight, I thought we could sort this out once and for all. But when you ran off, looking for Miss Gerrard, saying you were going to tell her everything . . ." Adam twists his head away. "It's just not fair on me, Katy." He drops his hand from the girl's face. "I haven't done anything wrong."

For a few seconds she is stunned into silence. Then, "I hate you!" she screams. "I'm going to report you." Katy's hand draws up and lashes across Adam's face. Her fingers are spread like claws, carving two scratches on his cheek. Adam recoils and watches Katy run back to school. It's over.

I don't move. I see the sadness, the despair as Adam takes one step after another in the trail of devastation that Katy has left behind. When he is completely out of sight, when I have counted to a hundred for good measure, I crawl out of the thicket and follow the shadows back to my room. I lie awake for hours, wondering who I should tell.

CHAPTER
NINETEEN

"Mick? Is that you back?" Nina called out. No one replied. "Josie?" She was sure she'd heard someone rattle the front door.

Nina went to the hallway and stopped. She listened, her breath rasping in her chest, waiting for proof that someone was there. It had been loud and clear — the firm pull and tug, the rattle of the handle. She knew the sounds of her own house.

"Mick?" she tried again. There was no familiar click of the lock, no jangle as he dropped the bunch of keys on the hall table and called out that he was home. "Josie," she half whispered, half cried up the stairs. "Can you hear me?" From where she was, she couldn't see the small glass panel in the front door; couldn't see if perhaps Laura had popped round, or if it was someone else peering in. Surely, she thought, if it was Laura, then she'd ring the bell or try the back door. Besides, she'd be at work now.

"What is it, Mum?" Josie stood at the top of the stairs, impatient, wondering why her mother was acting weird and looking frightened.

"Stay there," Nina whispered fiercely. "Go back to your room."

"Why did you call me then?"

Nina felt the vibrations as Josie slammed back into her room. Then the rattle at the front door again. Why didn't they just ring the bell? She dared to take a look into the porch, but no one was there. She thought she spotted a shadow flick round the side of the house. Her mouth went dry and her hands shook as she reached for her mobile phone. She clenched her teeth and dialled. Josie's safety was more important than anything.

Her stomach lurched as she was connected. She'd prayed she'd never have to do this. "Police, please."

Nina solemnly gave details, keen to stay calm yet desperate to get it over with. She begged them to hurry, wanting it all to be over before Mick returned. Explaining to him would take the rest of her life and that, she knew, she didn't have. She silently begged for the sirens to come, to frighten off whoever was prowling round her house. Perhaps that's all it would take. What might happen after that, Nina hadn't a clue.

They left the Downs in a fit of urgency and passion. Nina felt giddy from the last of the sun's strength, the wine they'd shared, but mostly from Mick's company. He was a heady concoction of masculinity and creativity. During their picnic, she'd discovered feelings within herself that she hadn't known were possible. Where she'd come from, honest desire, passion driven by love, simply hadn't existed.

Nina admitted to herself, as they tumbled down the hill towards the road, that she wanted Mick more than anything else she'd ever desired in her life. Her lust was both capacious and neglected — a balloon that had been expanding within for years, yet had never had the chance to bloom. Mick would be the fixer of all her problems; he would fill the gap, bring purpose, fulfilment and reason. They would be best friends, lovers, one day marry. She was working it all out.

"My place?" he said as they got on the first bus that came along. Neither of them knew if it was the correct one, or would be taking a direct route to the city. Neither of them particularly cared. For it wasn't a necessity to go side by side into Mick's messy trailer, or to strip without closing the blinds, or to drop with weakened knees on to the mattress. It wasn't essential that they locked bodies, forgetting whose skin was whose, or where lips had and hadn't been. Neither was that moment of silence, that rigid teetering place where two strangers felt like one, an essential part of the plan. For Nina and Mick, each of their minds greedily sucking up the possibilities, just sitting on the bus with all that potential at their fingertips was in many ways more desirable than having each other for real.

Nina nodded solemnly as the countryside transformed into suburbs and then the city streets. "Yours." They hardly spoke. Her veins hummed as they left the bus at some unknown stop. In a daze, as if they had both been waiting for this moment all their lives, they took another bus to the opposite side of the city. The walk to Ingleston Park was quick and silent, every footfall a step closer to their fantasies. Mick unlocked his trailer and they were greeted by the fallout of artistic smells

139

and unkempt van. Neither of them noticed nor cared. Each had the same idea about what would happen next.

It was three days before Nina left. She phoned work claiming to be sick, and apart from that call, little else was said during their time together. The windows wept condensation and the sheets twisted around their bodies. Surfaces were cleared of paints and dirty crockery by thrashing limbs; bodies desperate for a new place, a new way. They ate from cans and drank gin, water, tea and wine. They slept and they lay in each other's arms. When she finally left, Nina wasn't sure if she would see Mick again. He had delivered a lifetime's worth of need.

"Goodbye," Mick said solemnly. He stood in the trailer doorway with a towel slung around his hips. The lust in his eyes told her it wasn't goodbye at all.

"Bye," Nina said, head bowed, without looking back. Her hair hung loose in spent strands. Words seemed futile compared to what they had discovered about each other. It was as if they'd known each other forever, as if they'd been lovers in another time, and yet each time they'd come together it had been a novelty, stuffed with naivety, brimming with experience.

Nina slung her bag over her shoulder, scuffing through the dust all the way back to the bus stop. Once out of sight, the smile didn't leave her face. Happiness ran through her veins like warm honey. For the first time in her life, Nina felt as if she wasn't running away, rather running towards.

★　★　★

The approaching siren kicked up her pulse. Nina felt both sick and relieved. She swore she'd heard someone try the back door. What if Mick returned just as she was explaining to the police? What if they came back later to take statements? What if they arrested someone on the doorstep — someone she *knew* — and Mick saw everything? All this went through Nina's mind as she squatted uncomfortably behind the door, waiting until it was safe to come out.

The siren drew close then stopped abruptly. Then banging, the repeated ringing of the doorbell. This wasn't an intruder, this was the police.

"Mum, who is it? What on earth's going on?" Josie scurried downstairs as Nina slid back the bolts on the door. Glancing through the small pane of rippled glass, she drew back the safety chain. "Are you OK, Mum?" She saw her mother's pallor, the way her lips sat anonymously on a whitened face.

"I'll handle it, Josie. Just go back to your room." Nina's words were shallow yet commanding. Something in them told her daughter not to talk back. Nina pulled open the door and breathed out a hurricane, not even realising she'd been holding it in.

"Mrs Kennedy," the officer said. Nina nodded. "You made an emergency call. Is anyone in your property in immediate danger?" He was formal, programmed, and instantly made Nina feel both safe and under threat.

"I don't think so," she whispered. "I'm not sure. Please, come in." Nina bowed her head. The adrenalin that had set her mind and body alight waned as the two officers, one male and one female, stepped into her hallway. She suddenly felt like a time-waster.

"I'm Sergeant Naylor and this is WPC Shelley. I understand there was an intruder." The pair eased past Nina and went straight into the living room uninvited, looking around.

Nina bolted the front door again, but not before glancing each way up and down the street. There was no sign of anyone. Just a woman pushing a pram, a dog trotting beside her.

"I think someone was trying to break in." She joined the officers. "I'm worried that someone is trying to . . ." However she said it, she would sound crazy. "That someone's been bothering me. Perhaps wants to hurt me." Nina sat down. She felt faint.

The female police officer sat beside her. "Sergeant Naylor will take a look around and check out the property." She glanced at her partner and he nodded. He was clearly trying to combat a weary expression. He turned away and called back to the station on his radio. Nina heard him say possible false alarm.

"No, no, you don't understand." She stood but sat straight back down again when the room spun. "There's a situation that . . ." Nina sighed and collected her words. "It's a long story." She couldn't possibly say any more.

"How about a cup of tea?" Shelley smiled and waited for a reply. Nina's face was blank, pale, one step removed from reality. She shook her head, incredulous. She didn't want tea. "If you're anxious, sweet tea could really help —"

"I am not anxious." Nina did her best to stay calm. "Please, just look round the house and check everything." She cupped her face in her hands, but quickly dived out of self-pity. "There was someone in the house this morning. They stole my daughter's clothes."

Finally the officers exchanged looks which suggested they believed her. "Where is your daughter now?"

"Right here," Josie said. "I don't see how anyone could have taken my stuff, Mum." Josie's calmness made Nina seem almost hysterical. "I was here all the time. Perhaps you just put them in the wash and forgot."

"Did you actually see or hear anyone in the house?" Shelley asked.

Josie was shaking her head vigorously. "Nope. Just my dad, but he was down in his studio."

"Was anything else missing?" The sergeant replaced his radio.

Josie shrugged and looked at her mother. "No."

Nina closed her eyes, then blurted out, "Someone ran into my car the other day. I think it was on purpose." She hesitated. "I wasn't going to report it, but now this has happened." She dropped her head into her hands. She hadn't wanted Josie to know.

"Could any of your friends have played a prank with your clothes, love?" Shelley asked Josie.

Josie shrugged. She stared at her mother. "Maybe. I dunno. Mum, why are you lying about the car? Dad said that you reversed into a lamp post when you were parking."

The officers exchanged glances. "Is there damage to the vehicle, Mrs Kennedy?" Sergeant Naylor peered out of the rear window, across the garden to the studio. He rattled the French door handle but it didn't give.

"Yes, a dent and some paint left behind. Do you want to see?" She led the officers out on to the drive, having to steady herself on the door frame.

"Mum, are you all right?" Josie was concerned. "What's going on?"

WPC Shelley took hold of Nina. "Take it steady, Mrs Kennedy. You look rather pale."

"There," she said, pointing to the rear quarter panel of her car. "I was pulling out of my friend's drive and there was a parked car further up the street and it just drove at me."

"Did you get a number plate? A description of the car?"

"Yes. It was dark green. Metallic paint. You can tell by what's left on my car." The sergeant was running his finger along the dent, looking underwhelmed. "There was a five and maybe a seven and an M in the number plate. It might have been one of those big Rovers or a Jag."

"Hardly a write-off, is it, Mrs Kennedy?" the sergeant said. "Have you contacted your insurance company? Why didn't you call the police when it happened?"

Nina shrugged. "I guess I didn't . . ." She bit her lip. "I didn't want to . . ."

"Why don't you come back inside the house, love?" Shelley was kind, calm, considerate. She'd dealt with

144

women like this before. In fact, it was light relief being called out to a non-threatening incident. The morning had been arduous so far, and she hoped they might even have time for a quick break before heading back to the station.

Nina was close to tears. "Look, someone was trying to get into my house this morning." She swallowed. "And someone took my daughter's clothes." She found herself being guided back inside.

"Now listen, I insist you have that cup of tea." The constable somehow coaxed Nina back to the living room and persuaded Josie to make her mum a drink. She spent a few minutes writing details. Finally, she said, "Do you have any idea who it is that might be bothering you?"

"Perhaps." Nina didn't hesitate as she'd thought she would.

WPC Shelley sighed with relief. At last they were getting somewhere. She wrote some more notes and then waited for Nina to give a name.

"But I can't tell you," she finished. Josie stopped in her tracks as she carried a mug of tea to her mother.

"Mum, if you know who it is, you have to tell the police." Josie veered away from her mother and dumped the tea on the table. "What the hell's got into you? You're acting so weird."

Shelley glanced between mother and daughter. She didn't know what to make of it all, but guessed the whole thing was possibly fuelled by an uncomfortable domestic situation. A divorce or separation, perhaps from a violent partner. Maybe there was a new man on the scene. It could be that the mother's ex was the guilty party, or there was tension between a new man and the daughter. The policewoman had seen it all before. Nothing surprised her these days. "That's not very helpful, Mrs Kennedy. If you say you know who's bothering you but you won't reveal a name, there's little we can do." She watched Nina's reaction closely.

"You don't understand, you *can't* understand. But please, trust me. I need your help. Can't you take fingerprints from the front door?"

"Mrs Kennedy, no crime appears to have been committed. There's no evidence of a break-in, and quite honestly the damage to your car looks consistent with you backing into something. Arranging for a forensic team to visit your house to take fingerprints is hardly an appropriate use of police resources." Sergeant Naylor put his notebook away.

Nina pressed her teeth together. "Josie, give me a moment alone with the officers, will you?"

"Mrs Kennedy —"

"Please." Nina knew she sounded pathetic. She steadied herself on the back of the sofa. "You have to take me seriously."

"If you would just tell us why anyone would want to break into your house or threaten you, then I can establish if there's a need for further action. As things stand, there is nothing we can do." Sergeant Naylor folded his arms and shifted the balance of his weight on to one leg. He was a hefty man, the sort, Nina thought, who would show sympathy to a wife-beating husband because he thought the woman was being awkward.

146

"I can't." Nina hung her head. She remembered his words. *Trust nobody.* "I'm sorry." It was final.

"In that case, Mrs Kennedy, seeing as your property and everyone in it is safe and secure and . . ." Naylor glanced around to justify his statement. "And not apparently in any danger, we'll be going."

Nina felt a sense of panic inside. They were leaving. She and Josie would be alone. In desperation, she fished some paper and a pen from the detritus on the floor, and wrote down her number. She handed it to WPC Shelley rather than the sergeant. "If you change your mind about helping me," she whispered, "then please call." Nina's hands dropped to her sides. "Please?" She eyed the female officer in the hope of establishing a sympathetic bond. The officer nodded slowly — a brief flash of female understanding? — before she followed her sergeant.

"Any trouble, you know where we are." They were standing in the porch. The sergeant slid back the door bolts. "But make sure there's actually some trouble first, eh?" He laughed and walked out, Shelley following. The constable glanced back at Nina once more before pushing the paper into her pocket.

Nina bolted the door. The house was silent. She leaned against the wall, head pressed back, palms flat against the cold plaster. She had never felt so alone.

CHAPTER
TWENTY

One particular Sunday, I sat on the stone window seat and waited for my father's car to break the drab winter landscape. I almost turned to stone myself, the way the cold seeped from the ancient building into my bones. Everyone else — nameless carers and kids I didn't really know — ran around doing their morning things, while I just sat there, transfixed on the ribbon of drive that disappeared into the woods surrounding us. To pass the time, I trailed my finger down the glass, following the snaking beads of water that collected from the drizzle.

"Not got nothing to do?" asked a woman who made my neck prickle. She seemed to fold herself out of the furniture or the walls, appearing everywhere at once. The other kids said she was the eyes for all the others; that she was watching and waiting for us to do something wrong. Some said it was her who came in the night. Her tight black hair scared me. It made her face look white and dead.

I blinked up at her, suddenly believing all the stories I'd heard. "I'm waiting for my dad," I told her. Her laugh hung in the air long after she disappeared.

He came eventually. I knew he would. My entire body lit up, just like the flames racing through the newspaper and kindling when we lit the fire. At ten past three, after I'd been waiting for nearly five hours, his car cruised down the drive and parked outside the front door. He got out with a big grin on his face, most likely in a good mood from the drive. My dad doted on his car — a nineteen seventy-three Ford Granada, he told everyone, solid as a tank — and he always took one glance back at it after he'd parked. I reckoned he was imagining that he'd pulled up at a fancy hotel or a stately home where a lord and lady lived. That was my dad. Always pretending he was someone else; always believing he was better than who he really was. I ran to the big door to greet him.

"Hello, doll," he growled as I launched myself at his waist. He ruffled my hair, perhaps wishing I was a boy so that he could take me to see the football on a Saturday, or have me help him polish the Granada. He once told me that I reminded him of my mum and then he got angry at me because she'd died. "You have her pale skin and almond eyes," he told me. Then he didn't speak to me for a week. He drank until he passed out, and when the lady next door found me playing alone in the street, I was taken away to be looked after by someone else. All I remember are the cakes. A nice lady fed me sponge cakes until I felt sick. She said it would help, until my dad got better.

"I've been waiting for ages. Where have you been?" I didn't want him to see I was sad, but I couldn't help it.

My dad glanced at his watch. "Only an hour or so late."

"Three *weeks* late," I reminded him. But there was no getting through to Dad. He did his own thing in his own time.

"So, where do you want to go, princess?" He smelled funny. Of someone else.

"How about the zoo?" I asked, wide-eyed. Then Patricia was in the hall, her heels clicking on the tiled floor and her slim body curving towards my dad. She eyed him up and glanced out of the window at his shiny red Granada. He saw her admiring it. He stuck out his chest.

"Not the zoo," he said quietly. He walked up to Patricia. "Any ideas where I can take a little girl for a spot of fun?" Dad pulled open his sheepskin coat. His stomach curved above his belt and pushed out against his shirt. His arms winged from his pockets.

"You could go anywhere you like in that car." Her face stretched to a smile. She tucked a loose coil of hair behind her ear.

"She's a beauty, ain't she?" My dad fingered his moustache. Sometimes there was food in it. "So what's a bloke to do around here?"

The woman laughed and bent herself even closer to my dad. I didn't like it. "I finish work soon. I could show you some sights." Her black top clung to her concave waist. Hips like ledges shifted from side to side. My dad looked at it all.

150

"What's wrong with the zoo?" I said. Dad wafted a hand at me. It did the trick. I shut up, knowing what would happen if I went on.

In the end, we just walked around the grounds of the children's home. He pulled a can of Pepsi from his huge pocket. I sucked on it while I showed him a couple of dens that the other kids had let me make with them. Dad kept looking at his watch. He brushed leaves off his coat. "She'll be getting off work soon," he said.

He scrunched me in his arms as we headed back to the building. It stood looming through the trees like a big old prison. "Worked out all right then, didn't it?" he growled into my ear. I stiffened until he put me down again. "You being here worked out right dandy. Are you happy, princess?" Dad wove his big rough fingers into mine. I didn't reply.

Back inside, I unfurled my arms from his waist and watched as Patricia appeared in my place. He hooked one hand under her elbow and cranked the big front door open with the other. He said goodbye to me over his shoulder. I heard him ask her name.

"Patricia," she said. "Patricia Eldridge." Her voice was a whisper in the distance.

I climbed back on to the stone window seat and watched the Granada sail off down the drive. Dad's arm snaked across the back of the passenger seat. I sat and stared at the exhaust trail until day was lost to night. Now I would have to wait all over again.

CHAPTER
TWENTY-ONE

Mr Palmer walks into the room with a stack of papers clutched to his chest. He ignores us even though we've been waiting ten minutes already. His secretary sent for us, said we were wanted by the headmaster, said we should be in his study in half an hour. Adam and I stand side by side like a pair of naughty children. I have no idea what it's all about. Before anyone speaks, I cast a glance around the room. A sick feeling rises in my throat as I take in my surroundings.

The headmaster sits down, rearranges things on his desk, sips from a cup before pulling a face at the cold dregs. His stern demeanour commands the respect needed to captain the school. It's the controlled silence, in spite of the bursting redness on his nose, and the veins on the back of his hands, the way they hang like a roadmap to nowhere. He still doesn't acknowledge us.

I take a breath. "Mr Palmer," I say. "You wanted to see us?" I will not be afraid of him, even though for some reason I am.

He looks up. A grave expression sweeps his face. "Yes. I was hoping you could help me, Miss Gerrard. It's a delicate matter." He stares hard at Adam. There's sudden tension between the pair. "Mr Kingsley, perhaps you'd like to enlighten your colleague." As the seconds pass, the sick feeling grows. I have a good idea what this is about.

The smile lines around Adam's eyes and the crescents that frame his mouth, the tightness of his jaw and the stiff posture of his shoulders dissolve as he forces out his breath. "There's been a complaint," he says flatly. His face is emotionless. He stares straight ahead. "The complaint's against me. A pupil is claiming that I've had . . . relations with her." A swallow too big for his throat works down his neck before he continues. "It's not true, of course. Because of your role with the girls, because they talk to you, we were wondering if you have any reason to believe that —"

"That she's lying," Mr Palmer interrupts, getting to the point. "It's a serious business. The parents have already got their lawyers on the case." He glares at Adam, clearly not believing that his employee is entirely free from guilt.

Adam continues, staring from me to the headmaster and back. "The girl — Katy Fenwick — states that I've been . . . that over a long period of time we've . . ."

I hold up my hand to prevent him having to give details. "Really, you don't need to say any more." I'm back there, hiding in the thicket, hardly daring to breathe, watching them, watching her naked. "I understand the situation." My breathing quickens. Pinpricks of sweat break out on my top lip. I have to get out. I remember the wet earth, the smell of it on pale flesh. The mist as it crept through the woods, dulling the sound of fleeing footsteps.

"I'm speaking to a number of staff in the hope that we can sort out this mess," Mr Palmer continues. "The school's legal team has requested this process as part of the investigation we're duty bound to undertake. Then I'll have to compile a report for the board of governors." He sighs heavily. "Even though you've only been at the school a few weeks, Miss Gerrard, I'd appreciate it if you could give some thought to what you know about the girl. If anything relevant comes to mind, any comments she may have made about Mr Kingsley, then please let me know. It may just help." Mr Palmer's neck flushes and his fingers flick around a silver pen.

"Of course." I nod solemnly. I don't look at Adam, even though I know he's staring at me, willing me to say something that will save him. I remain silent, biting my lip. Then I turn to go.

"Anything at all," I hear Adam say as I click the door closed.

The car engine turns over then cuts out. I try four more times and on the fifth attempt, the engine sends out a death wheeze. I'm no good at fixing things, but I pull the bonnet release and get out to take a look anyway. I prop open the rusty lid and stare at the twisted assortment of oily metal that I paid five hundred pounds in cash for. I'm amazed it survived — no, amazed *I* survived — the journey here. The battery terminals are loose and caked in scum. Black gritty seepage drips from every joint and anything rubber is

154

perished and cracked. There is half a dead bird clogging the air vent intake.

"Oh hell," I say. "Now what do I do?" I kick the front tyre.

"Going anywhere nice?"

I peer over the top of my sunglasses. A male teacher is walking a dog. I've seen him in the staffroom but we haven't spoken yet.

"No." I laugh. He might help if I'm friendly, however painful it is to smile, to pretend to be jolly. "I think the dealer warranty's probably expired." I'm giving him my nicest grin, under the circumstances. I remove my glasses and fork them on to my head.

"This is Alfie," he says, marching up and thrusting out his dog's lead for me to hold. "And I'm Doug." He pushes up the sleeves of his old sweater and bites his lip. "Head of physics. Let me take a look."

"Thank you. That's kind." The dog runs round and round me, wrapping my legs in the lead. Finally, he slumps on my feet, unable to move any more, and chews the toe of my shoe.

"Not good news." Doug emerges from beneath the bonnet and scratches his nose, leaving a black streak. "There's a serious oil leak. Head gasket, I think. Plus that battery's seen better years. All the hoses are shot, and see down there? That's the manifold. Doesn't look good to me. I could go on."

"Please don't."

"Where were you off to?" Doug bends down and takes hold of Alfie's collar. The dog yaps. They walk anti-clockwise round me, unwinding, making me giddy.

155

I'm unsure what to say. With two days off work, I was going to take a trip, one mile at a time, to see how close I could get. It seems stupid now, reckless and dangerous. I lay a hand on the rusty wing of the car, silently thanking it for preventing me setting out. I doubt if I would have even made it further than the end of the drive in this old heap. I'm not thinking straight. "Just into town," I lie.

Doug glances at his watch. "There are only two buses a day from Roecliffe. If you walk briskly to the village, you'll make the second one." The dog stands up against my legs, reaching my knees. Doug pulls gently on the lead and walks off. "Hurry now," he says without glancing back.

I head down the long drive, each footfall tentative. I stop and turn, looking back at the building's façade, seeing a pale face at the window, just to the right of the huge front door — a pupil perhaps, watching me leave. I break into a run until I reach the iron gates. The hairs on my neck stand on end as the metal gates creak open and I step out.

The church spire rises above the deciduous woodland flanking the south side of the gates. A flicker of pale gold whips through the leaves as a breeze heralds my walk. The start of autumn already. It feels odd to be outside school grounds. I am conscious of the risk, aware that I have to keep my head down even though I have changed considerably.

I walk down the single-track lane in the direction of the village church. I jump as a crow flaps out of an oak tree to my left. I watch it fly away towards a building sitting squat in a clearing through the trees. It's the old chapel, part of the Roecliffe Hall estate. It's dark and derelict, crawling with ivy, the windows are boarded-up, and the graveyard is completely overgrown so that none of the headstones are visible. A wire fence surrounds the building. Clumps of sheep's wool hang on the barbs like forgotten laundry.

I walk quickly on. The journey to the village seems interminable.

I arrive in Roecliffe just in time to see the bus leaving in the opposite direction. A blue-grey trail of diesel exhaust dissipates slowly. "Damn," I say, although somewhat relieved. Taking a trip to Skipton would have been pointless. It was only so I didn't have to explain my intentions to Doug. Following my original plans would have ended in disaster one way or another.

There's a car coming towards me, remarkable only because there aren't any others visible in the quiet village. I turn my back to the road, not wanting to be seen, but it slows and draws up alongside me. The driver toots the horn and when I reluctantly turn round, I see Adam in the driver's seat. He leans across and winds down the window.

"Hello," he says awkwardly. He's peering up at me, his brow crumpled. We haven't spoken since we stood in Mr Palmer's office.

I nod a greeting. Nervously, I cast a glance around the street. I suddenly feel very vulnerable. What was I thinking by leaving the school? A woman and two young children step out of the post office.

"Out for a walk?"

"Not exactly." I bend down to the window so I don't have to speak too loudly. "I missed the bus into town."

"Skipton? I've just been there." He pats a pile of library books on the passenger seat. "I'd have given you a lift if I'd known."

"Spur of the moment thing," I lie, shrugging.

"Do you want a lift back to school?" Adam shifts the stack of books, tossing them one by one on to the already cluttered rear seat, avoiding his laptop. His car will be safer than being exposed like this. He holds a copy of a non-fiction book that has "murder" in its title.

"Thanks," I say, nodding. I don't want to be rude. I open the stiff door and get in.

"Hey, you got your car from the same dealer as me." I buckle the seat belt.

He laughs. The book he's holding lands on my knee. "*The Ritual of Murder*," I say. It looks quite dated, perhaps from the eighties. "Bit of light reading?" I comment. When he doesn't reply, I shove one hand under my legs and cross my fingers, praying that he doesn't bring up the business between him and Katy Fenwick.

Adam nods briefly and drives off. He quickly works through the gears. But before we make it back to the school entrance, he slows down to second gear again and turns his face to me several times in quick succession. He wants to say something but doesn't know how to start. A rabbit darts from the hedge, stopping and starting, crazed with fear, making Adam

158

halt completely while the creature makes up its mind. It gives him the chance he needed.

"Did you think about the . . . incident?" he asks.

"Yes, yes," I say immediately. I don't want to be drawn into this — police, lawyers, perhaps court — but how can I not tell anyone about what I saw?

"And?" Adam's fingers drum on the wheel. I'm not sure if he's impatient because the rabbit just sits in the road, its nose twitching at the stench of exhaust fumes, or because I'm hesitating. Adam doesn't want to lose his job.

"And . . ." I trail off. The rabbit scampers off into the hedge. Adam moves the car forward again. We pass the school gates and I'm about to tell him we've missed the turn, but he pulls into a gateway a little further down the lane. He turns off the engine and suddenly all I can hear are crows. They sound as if they're inside my head, not the fields around us.

"I can wait," he says solemnly. He pulls a small tin from a crammed glove compartment. Sweet wrappers, scrunched papers, old tissues flutter out. Inside the tin are a pouch of tobacco and some Rizla papers. He rests his right elbow on the open window and begins to roll a cigarette. It takes him an age just to get the strands of tobacco in a line. Then a breeze blows them out of place, some falling on to his jeans. Patiently, he picks them up and lays them on the paper again, waiting for me to speak.

"I don't really know Katy very well," I say. "I think she's a bit troubled." That's an understatement, I think.

"At the first PSHE session I did with that year group, she claimed she was being bullied."

Adam snorts. A shower of tobacco rains on his jeans again. Piece by piece, he collects it up. I watch as finally he rolls the cigarette, holding it deftly between slim fingers. He licks the paper and sticks it in place. Finally, he holds it close to his mouth, between bent knuckles. "Bullied," he says. He breathes in the scent of the tobacco. Then he shakes his head slowly, an incredulous gesture that needs no explaining.

"She's not allowed to watch television," I say, as if it's some kind of excuse for her behaviour. "Strict parents, probably." How can I tell him I was spying on them that night?

Suddenly, Adam turns to me. "I can't lose my job." There are flecks of panic in his eyes. Adam's reasons for not wanting to leave are different to mine.

"I don't suppose you will," I say, sounding more sympathetic than I intended. Oddly, I have an urge to touch his shoulder, to offer some comfort, to just get close. "Aren't you going to light that?" I rein in my need.

He glances at the cigarette. "I don't smoke," he replies and tosses the roll-up into the back of the car. When I look round, I see a dozen others abandoned on the floor. Adam puts his hand on the keys. "Is that really all you know about her? That she's not allowed to watch TV and she thinks she's being bullied?"

"Pretty much." Not a lie exactly. A pheasant walks across the gateway, speeding up when it sees us. "Sorry."

Adam nods stoically. He starts the engine, does an easy three-point turn, and pulls into the entrance of the school. Punching in the security code, he says, "I've never laid a finger on her. Just so you know." He stares straight ahead.

"I believe you, Adam," I say as we cruise down the drive, wondering what it will take to make everyone else think the same.

CHAPTER
TWENTY-TWO

Nina lay in Mick's arms. The scent of his body enveloped her as she remembered last night. He'd swept away her anxiety, sensing it from the minute he returned from the art shop. In spite of a pressing deadline, he'd forgone an afternoon's work and stayed in the house with his wife. He made her feel better. They'd talked about everything, from the times before Josie was born, to what they would do with the extra money the new work would bring in. Mick had suggested a new bathroom, perhaps even an extension.

Later, he'd cooked supper for the three of them, and rented a movie for Josie and her friends when they called by. All of Josie's friends adored him, which, of course, embarrassed Josie no end.

Nina had seen to it that Josie clearly understood she mustn't concern her father with tales of the police and false alarms. That he had enough on his plate, that worrying about such things would only stress him out and kill his creativity. "Your dad's got deadlines," she'd said, convinced Josie understood. "I guess I was mistaken about what happened, although it really is a mystery." They'd even laughed about it.

That night, to escape the teenage whoops and laughter coming from the living room, Mick had taken Nina upstairs, away from the noise. He'd run a bath for her, and given her a massage on the bed. But Nina had halted him when he was halfway down her back, pulling him on top of her, removing his clothes, pressing his flesh against hers.

Next thing she knew, the light was breaking through the gap in the curtains. She waited for the rush of adrenalin she'd suffered the last few days to wrench her heart. But it didn't. Any fears that she was under threat had dissolved with the dawn; out of her system like the end of a bout of flu. She stretched out her toes, trying not to wake Mick. She needed to get up, but instead lay still, watching the clock flash from one minute to the next.

It was bound to happen sometime, she thought. Like a delayed reaction; post-traumatic stress, she supposed. Explaining her behaviour, from an outsider's point of view — which she was trying to take — was simple. The mess in the dressing room, the car accident, Josie's clothing, someone rattling the door, could all easily be explained away as coincidental happenings that actually meant far less than the sum of their parts suggested. "No one," she whispered through the tiniest breath, "is trying to hurt me."

Mick wheezed gently through early-morning dreams. Nina shifted her head and saw his eyelids flickering. Today, she resolved, she would get up, not think about anything that frightened her, and simply focus on gearing up for the Charterhouse job that was looming. There was work to be done.

Nina prised herself out of the warm nest of Mick's shoulder. She stepped on to the carpet and padded naked to the bathroom. In the mirror, she saw Mick open his eyes. He smiled as he watched her leave.

In the shower, her mind was back on work. She felt bad for having left Tess to sort out most of the logistics so far. She would invite her round later, make her some lunch, and they could prioritise remaining jobs. After all, there was not much more than a week to go before Chameleon FX made its debut appearance on the movie set at Pinewood. This was a big deal for Nina. Rinsing her hair, she made a mental note to check how the bulk orders she'd placed were progressing. She didn't want anything going wrong at the last minute.

"Morning." Nina raised her eyebrows as her daughter silently retrieved the breakfast she had made for her an hour ago. It was nearly eleven o'clock and Nina had already ploughed through last month's accounts, made a dozen phone calls, emailed the director of a future production at the Old Vic theatre, made a salmon and asparagus quiche for Tess's arrival later, and placed another online order for some prosthetic gel for the fake burns she was going to create.

Josie didn't say anything to her mother. She swiped the limp toast from the plate, gulped down the orange juice and headed straight for the door.

"Nice to see you, too, sweetheart. Are you still walking round to Nat's house today?" Nina thought she saw a vague nod of her daughter's head. "What time are you back? Would you like me to fetch you?" Nina thought it would be a good chance to see Laura. They could talk about the girls' internet use.

Josie held up five fingers over her shoulder before disappearing from the kitchen.

"I'll fetch you at five then," Nina said, bemused. "Teenagers," she muttered after Josie had banged the front door closed. Ten minutes later, she resisted the temptation to text her daughter to see if she'd arrived safely at Nat's.

It's only a few streets away, she reminded herself. Nothing is going to happen.

Nina settled back at the kitchen table and replied to several emails. One was from Tess, saying that she would be a little late for their meeting. Her youngest child had a dental appointment. Nina didn't mind. It would give her a chance to really get ahead; catch up with the backlog of the last few days. Her head hadn't been in the right place for work, and she couldn't afford for things to slip further. A couple of years from now, Nina saw herself with twenty or so employees, premises, and multiple film contracts. "We might even be able to afford a holiday," she muttered while checking an invoice.

The doorbell stopped her. "Now what's she forgotten?" Nina said to herself, pushing out the kitchen chair.

She strode to the front door. The band in her loose ponytail slid from her hair so she pulled it out completely. Her bare feet trod softly on the carpet. She opened the door but no one was outside. She leaned out and glanced around the front garden. Her car was on the drive, the cardboard boxes still in a pile ready to take to the recycling depot, and the dustbin sat on the street waiting to be brought in. There was no sign of Josie. Had she imagined the doorbell?

"Just kids messing," she said out loud. "Long summer holidays make for silly pranks."

She frowned and turned to go back inside, but she stopped suddenly, having trodden on something. When she looked down, she saw an envelope. She picked it up. It was obviously just junk advertising — blank on both sides to entice you to open it. She took it into the kitchen, ready to toss it into the recycling bin. The postman had already delivered the mail, so she knew this was nothing important. She despaired of the rubbish that came through the door.

Nina filled the kettle, still holding the envelope. She wondered whether Mick would be hungry yet. He'd been out in the studio for hours already, determined to get the current painting finished. She was just about to throw the paper into the bin when she felt something hard inside; something lumpy. She frowned, particularly disliking free gifts in promotions.

"Another cheap pen that won't work properly." Whatever it was would have to come out before the paper could be recycled. But when she tore open the envelope, there was no paper inside; no sales pitch for insulation or fake brick cladding.

Nina pulled out the object and let the envelope flutter to the floor. Her hands shook as she examined the contents. Her lips parted and her eyebrows tugged together in a frown. Her heart began to race as she remembered, as the memories dragged through her mind on barbed wire.

Oh God, no.

She couldn't believe what she was seeing; that it was real. A child's hairclip, old-fashioned, slightly bent, with one side rusty and missing its paint. The ceramic strawberry was still there, fat and shiny with black painted dots and a once bright green stalk, now dulled with age.

"Oh Mick," she whispered, shaking. "Josie . . ." Frantically, she punched in a text to Josie asking if she was at Nat's. Within seconds, a reply came back. *Yep xx.* She breathed a sigh of relief.

Nina leaned against the kitchen counter. She tipped back her head to contain the sobs, to help herself think.

Looking out of the window, she saw her husband's studio, the bright light spilling from the small windows as he worked. She saw Josie's lacy cardigan draped haphazardly over a chair, a hairbrush fallen on to the floor, and a pair of flat shoes squashed down at the heel. Her face reddened at the normality of it all. And now, suddenly, it wasn't. Then she saw herself reflected in the glass cupboard door — a woman lost, a woman scared. She saw the long road ahead.

Nina took a deep breath, swiping away the tear that wet her cheek. She turned the hairclip over and over in her fingers, before stuffing it into her jeans pocket. She made tea for Mick and tossed a salad for her lunch with Tess. She fixed her make-up and changed her top, and she put on a load of washing. She ran the dishwasher and wrote a shopping list, and then she slid down the wall, each knob of her spine aching with the pressure, and said, quite matter-of-factly, "It's over."

CHAPTER
TWENTY-THREE

Katy's chin juts forward. She chews on the inside of her lip. She stands with her ankles crossed, her arms folded, and her eyes stare at the floor.

"Katy?" She hasn't said a word since I called her into sick bay. Matron has a day off so I'm on duty alone. "What have you got to say for yourself?"

"You can't prove it," she says.

"No, I can't, but I can at least ask you to explain why you did such a horrible thing to Mr Kingsley."

Katy shrugs. "Just for fun. It was a dare at first."

"Fun?" I half scream.

"It's not like he has a wife or anything. He didn't *have* to look at me naked." Katy sighs heavily, as if I'm making a fuss about nothing. "It wasn't just about the sex, or some silly crush." She flicks back her hair. "I . . . I didn't like it when he said no."

"So you thought you'd trap him into it?"

Katy shrugs. "It was just a dare." She looks up at me. We are getting close to the truth. She snorts and blushes, a far cry from the naked young woman in the woods. "All the girls really fancy Mr Kingsley. It's not our fault there aren't any boys here." I nod slowly, not wanting to put her off. "Someone said that Mr Kingsley

169

had been looking at me in history, and that I should go for it."

"Go for what?" I ask.

"You know." She turns crimson. "He's just so hot," she continues when I don't say anything.

"What did your parents say when you told them a teacher had been . . .?" I can't finish.

"My father went ballistic. He's got his company lawyers to sue the school. And the police are involved because I'm under sixteen." I notice a little shake in her shoulders.

"Is it because your parents are so strict? Do you feel you have to rebel?" I'd never anticipated saying these words to a teenage girl I didn't even know.

Katy sneers. "No. I can do whatever I like." We both know that's not true.

I nod, not wanting to anger her. "I think that your parents and everyone else would be very relieved now if you just told the truth."

I've already told Katy that I saw everything — that I'd woken up when she came down the corridor to my room, that I'd heard Adam trying to stop her, that I'd followed them into the woods. She listened and breathed in gulps as the realisation struck her that I couldn't be making it up. She didn't react when I said I'd seen her naked, tempting Mr Kingsley any way she could. She had been found out. It was over.

Suddenly, the breath Katy has been saving up leaves her body in a rush. She breaks down in tears. I step in and fold my arms tentatively around her — not nervous of how she might react or of the physical contact; no, I am nervous of this simple act of comfort because strangely, overwhelmingly, it is pure comfort for me too.

"So, are you going to tell me what happened?" Adam points to my face. The sun streams in through the floor-to-ceiling window behind us. The light touches my shoulder, sewing a warm passage through the fibres of my skin. We fork up our breakfast, aware that the assembly bell will ring any moment.

"I used to be a lion tamer at a circus." I'm deadpan as I touch the wound — a diagonal slice from the corner of my left eye to the summit of my cheekbone.

"Do you fly trapeze, too?" He scans my face again.

"I was in an accident. A car accident," I tell him. "I'm pleased it worked out OK for you, Adam."

He's already thanked me profusely, when I told him about my conversation with Katy and how I had seen them in the woods together, about how I had persuaded her to own up.

"Being at Roecliffe is so very important to me," he says, leaving me silently agreeing. "And what happened was every male teacher's nightmare. I just never thought it would happen to me."

"Katy's being offered professional counselling. It's more than we can cope with in school."

He nods and chews. "She gave a written statement to the police yesterday, confirming she was fabricating the allegations. It's all thanks to you, Frankie. I owe you." In his own way, this is Adam being emotional. It's the equivalent of throwing his arms round my neck and

171

sighing his relief into my shoulder. We've only known each other a short time, and it's been a vague acquaintance at best. Through this drama I have learned that, for some reason, he's holding back, just like me.

"I wasn't spying," I say again, just to make sure he knows. "I've told you the story. I had to get Katy to confess. I couldn't see your job go down the pan. She's grown up a lot these last few days."

I'd decided not to let anyone else know that I'd witnessed the scene in the wood. Mr Palmer need never know that I was instrumental in bringing about the girl's admission. I would rather he looked upon her as a brave young woman coming to terms with her mistakes, having the courage to confess. The ethos of the school, I imagined Mr Palmer telling Katy, while thankful the whole sordid business could be put behind them, is a lesson well learned. *Non scholae sed vitae discimus*, he would say to her. We do not learn for school, but for life.

"So would you like to?" Adam is talking to me and I've not been listening. The bell resounds through my head. "Come on a walk with me later?" he repeats, standing up from the bench.

"Yes. Yes, that would be nice." A few words, but some of the hardest I've had to say since I arrived. And as I watch Adam deposit his plate at the serving hatch, I realise that walking with someone, talking with someone, spending time with someone other than in a rushed work capacity, goes quite against everything I

172

ever vowed; goes some way, I realise, to making me feel normal again.

"You've just saved me," I say. "So we're even." I've put on a jacket. There's an autumn chill at each end of the day now that October is midway through. Half-term break sits like a gaping void next week. The prospect reminds me of plans, of holidays in Scotland, of log cabins and long walks, of the casual kisses that were never counted, of the hugs and bickers that went unregistered. "My evening would have been spent with the weepies. Sylvia stepped in to cover."

"They do get very homesick at this time of year. I don't think it's so much that they're looking forward to going home next week, rather it's the coming back to school afterwards that some find hard. Especially the first-years."

I nod. Roecliffe Hall reaches out its silent fingers around unsuspecting hearts.

"I went to a kind of boarding institution," Adam continues. "And I hated every bloody minute of it. Ironic that I've ended up teaching at one." He scuffs the dirt on the track as we walk away from the school. There's a public footpath stretching to the west of the building. Miles of flattened track, thousands of anonymous footsteps placed before ours. I think about what Adam has revealed — a speck of colour in the black and white of his life.

"Where was it?" I want to know more. It's unexpectedly sweet, this communication. A safe haven in all the chaos. It wouldn't have happened if it weren't for Katy's behaviour. I pull my jacket round me, matching one of Adam's strides with two of mine. "Banana land?"

He shakes his head. "No. It was a grim place in Birmingham. An odd situation, really."

"How come?" We are in a field of sheep — white smudges on a canvas of olive green now that the light is fading. The animals stop eating and stare at us as we walk past.

"Look," he suddenly says in a hushed voice. He stops and tenses, pointing to the corner of the field. "It's a hare." Adam crouches, as if making ourselves smaller will somehow disguise our scent. "Meant to be lucky," he whispers. "A sign of fertility, according to the pagans." The hare sniffs the air and tenses.

"He's on to us, look." A second later and the creature has darted fifty feet towards the cover of the hedge. Then he stops rigid, his black eyes and long ears twitching as Adam stands up and speaks normally again. "There are stories about witches shapeshifting into hares." He looks at me and grins. "Seriously," he says.

"Shapeshifting?" I say, not so much a question as an audible thought.

"Country folklore's full of it," he continues. "Where one living thing is able to transform into another at will."

"I see," I say thoughtfully, kicking off our walk again. From the corner of my eye, I see the hare speed off into the hedge.

"Do you think you'll stay at Roecliffe forever?" We're in the staff lounge sipping hot tea. We walked several miles and, by the time we arrived back at school, my cheeks had turned a shade of red to match my jacket. Adam laughed at my breathlessness, saying I should get out more. I smiled, suddenly finding myself wanting to explain why I can't.

"Forever's a long time. I want to get my book finished first."

"Book?" I say, pretending I've not already heard about it. Adam reveals another layer. It saves me from doing the same.

He nods, almost shyly. "I'm writing a . . . a kind of history of the school."

There's an awkward silence.

"Well," he continues when I don't reply. "It's a history of the actual building really, rather than just the school. I'm covering the village of Roecliffe, too. The things that went on." His accent stretches through the words, a twang that makes him as out of place as I feel. "It's had a pretty colourful past, by all accounts."

"How . . . come?" There's ringing in my ears.

Adam shrugs. "How long have you got?"

My entire life, I silently reply.

He slides over an antique chess table and pulls out the drawer. Black and white carved pieces lie stranded on their sides. "Fancy a game?" he asks.

I'm already playing, I think, while nodding that I would.

CHAPTER
TWENTY-FOUR

All that waiting, all that childhood, somehow turned into years. Strange how one glance at a clock, one look out of the window, one dash to the mail board to see if there's a letter pinned up with your name on it can turn into half your lifetime.

I grew used to my dad's absence. He came perhaps once or twice more after he drove off with his arm and his life wrapped around Patricia. I don't really remember. To begin with, I used to ask her about him. She seemed to know more than I did; wore a dopey expression when she mentioned his name. *William Fergus*, she liked calling him, as if he were posh. *William Fergus took me out in his car*, she'd say. *William Fergus bought me a hat. William Fergus and I went to the pictures. William Fergus held my hand.*

William Fergus, I thought bitterly. Couldn't even be bothered with his own daughter.

Besides, when she told me they'd held hands, I knew exactly what that meant. We had a television in the home. We saw what grown-ups did after they'd held hands. I ran off when I found out. My tight shoes bit my toes, stopping me from crying, as good as a punishment. But what I didn't understand was if my dad and Patricia were friends, if they were together, then why did I have to live here? Why couldn't Patricia be my new mum? Why couldn't I go home?

Simple, I deduced eventually. My dad hated me.

And so the days went on, turning into weeks, into months, into years. All of us waiting, biding our time for something to happen, something or someone to save us. A few of us went to school. I was one of the lucky ones and was allowed to leave Roecliffe for six hours a day. Until the age of eleven, I walked to the village primary school with a cluster of other trusted boys and girls. We scuffed our way to the playground, where we suffered the taunts of the other kids. We were the ones without parents. The kids no one loved. The dirty kids. The troublemakers. The children who stank and who no one wanted to sit next to or hold hands with. As we got older, some of us went on the bus to the secondary school in town. Sometimes we got beaten, kicked, bullied, but sometimes we just kept quiet and got on with learning.

When we weren't at school, we drifted around the children's home. The boys scrapped and fought, broke things, ran away and screamed when they were dragged back. The girls turned inwards, became sullen and quiet, and spent their time making things. Always making stuff from nothing. Rubbish from the bin. Old clothes fit for scrap. Rags were woven, cardboard was glued, and string was crocheted. We made crude dolls. We made bracelets and charms. We made pictures and presents, some of us saying they were for our parents. By then, we didn't remember what parents were.

All the while we were waiting for something to happen.

Then she came. The girl that would change my life. There had been a quiet patch at the home. "No new customers," Miss Maddocks joked, when nothing had happened for weeks.

I found her by accident, standing in a puddle of pee. She was crying and her bare bottom had the sting of a handprint — the adult fingers reaching right across its width. She was naked apart from a stained vest.

I was nearly thirteen but my body looked two years older. Everything I owned was too small for me. I was virtually the size of an adult woman yet wore the clothes of a ten-year-old. When I stumbled upon her, the look on her face told me that she thought I was a carer — *one of them*. To her, I must have seemed a hundred years old.

There she was, standing in the dark corridor with a thousand confusing doors leading off, stretching out her arms to me as I walked past. She wanted me to pick her up. She was making a brave, last-ditch attempt to be loved by someone.

"Hello," I said. I crouched down. She couldn't have been more than three years old. Tentatively, she wrapped her arms round my neck. Her cherry-red face buckled with anticipation. She wanted to feel the warmth of another human; convince herself that she wasn't alone. This little girl was acting on pure instinct. She needed someone to love her in order to survive.

"What's your name?" Her face drew close to my neck. Every indrawn breath was a hiccup or sob.

She leaned close and whispered, "Betsy," in my ear. The stench of urine closed around me.

"I'm Ava," I told her. "You're new, aren't you?" I'd not heard that anyone had arrived, and I'd been here long enough to know how the system worked. Someone would spot the social worker's car at the end of the drive. The news would quickly spread around the home that another one was being brought in, one grubby mouth whispering to the nearest ear. A writhing cluster of kids would congregate at the big old front door, straining at the window, waiting for the latest catch to be brought in. Then the whooping would begin, followed by ugly catcalls, dancing, play-fighting, poking at the new kid, until they were shooed away by the carers' impatient arms. I would stand back, palms pressed together in prayer, sizing up the newcomer, before rushing to my bed to defend my belongings.

The little girl began to lick my neck. I prised her away and held her at arm's length. "Where did you come from?" I angled her into the light from the small window high above us. She wouldn't speak. "Can you talk?"

She stared at me blankly, huge blue eyes set beneath red-gold curls that were matted with dirt and most probably full of lice. Then she pulled up her vest and started sucking on it. She was starving. "Come with me," I said, wanting to help her. Hot sticky fingers wove their way into my fist as I led her to my dormitory. Two other girls were sitting cross-legged on a bed. One was cutting the other's hair with plastic play scissors.

I rummaged in my bedside cupboard and pulled out a crumpled paper bag. Sugar showered from a hole and the girl dived to the floor, pressing the grains against her fingers before sucking them clean. "You really are starving, aren't you?"

I tipped the contents out on to my bed. We were given sweets once a week. Usually jellied sugary things bought in huge drums. I'd been saving up, just one or two a week, and now I had a fine stash that I was planning to eat alone, under the bedcovers when I was sad. Survival when those waiting moments turned into years.

The child greedily scoffed the coloured mess on my bedspread. Then she scooped up the fallen sugar until there was nothing but a damp patch left.

"What's her name?" Alison asked. She tugged at her friend's hair with the blunt blades. "Does she want a cut?"

I pushed my fingers through the girl's hair, opening the knots down to the scalp. As I'd guessed, she was teeming with head lice. I pulled a face and nodded. "She's called Betsy," I told them. "And cut it all off," I instructed Alison. Last time there were lice, Patricia went mad and we had a night awake gagging from the treatment she doused us in.

"She's sweet, isn't she?" I opened my chest of drawers and pulled out the smallest skirt I could find. "She's mine," I warned the others. "Finders keepers." I handed the skirt to Betsy, but she just stared at it. I opened the waist and the child stepped in, as if it was something she was used to doing, as if she once had a mother.

Patricia was in the doorway, glaring at me. "There's the wretched creature." Then she smiled. "There's a bed come free, child. You can have that." I'd never quite got the measure of Patricia. She was an unreadable force in the home. Her moods ranged from motherly, to fun, to downright sinister. I always knew if she'd been with my dad. Her mood was as light as meringue.

"Whose bed will she have?" I asked. The child launched herself at me. I felt as if I'd finally been given a purpose inside all this waiting. Something hot spread within me, burning my heart, racing through my veins, expanding them, thawing them, taking away the void. "She wants to stay with me," I told Patricia.

"She can have Dawn's bed. Dawn's gone now." The words fell from Patricia's mouth as if she were spitting out gravel. Her cheeks reddened.

I didn't say anything. I knew better than that. Sometimes kids left without a trace. Sometimes they went away, then came back days later. Some of them never spoke again. Sometimes we asked what happened to them, and sometimes we got a clout.

"Can she sleep beside me?" The little girl had pushed on to my lap and balled up like a kitten. I pressed her safe against me, still feeling the heat driving through me.

"Did you find out her name?" Patricia's thin arms winged out from her hips. Her face shot into an arrowed expression, as if it was a test. Tell me her name and she can sleep next to you.

I stared down at the child, desperate to protect her. Close up, I saw the creatures on her scalp, the matting of her hair, the sheen of grime on her skin. I wanted to bathe her, to make her warm, brush her hair and feed her. Someone for me to care about when no one cared about me. My living doll.

"She's called Betsy," I told Patricia. "She said that her name is Betsy and she wants to be my friend. I will look after her. You won't need to bother with her if you let her sleep next to me."

At that, Patricia visibly relaxed. She always moaned how busy she was, that they were understaffed, that the council should give the home more money. Carers came and went. Patricia and Miss Maddocks said they'd been working at the home forever, knew everything there was to know about it.

"All right," she said. "I'll have the spare bed shifted next to yours. We don't know much about where she came from, just that the last children's home kicked her out because they couldn't cope with her." Patricia shook her head and walked off, stopping after a couple of paces. "And don't let her piss everywhere, Ava, or you'll be on your hands and knees scrubbing it up." She left, satisfied that there was one less thing to worry about.

"Alison," I said grinning, excited by my mission. "Set to work." I sat Betsy on my bed and let Alison hack off the knots. Within an hour, Betsy had a new style. It was ragged and chopped close to her scalp and made her look like a boy, but when I washed it, my fingers slipped easily between the strands. I picked out the lice one by one and drowned them in the bath.

"Nasty creatures," I told her, showing her one. She smacked it into the water and let out a noise that I hoped was a laugh. Then I rubbed soap all over her, stripping the layers of dirt and revealing pink skin. I scrubbed at her neck and cleaned in between her toes. Then I wrapped her in my towel and sang nursery rhymes to her.

"You know, Betsy," I said as we padded the corridors back to my dormitory. "I've always wanted a little sister or a brother."

Betsy suddenly stopped and sat down on the cold floor. She huddled within the towel and began to rock. "Bruvver, bruvver, bruvver . . ." she whined over and over. I scooped her up in my arms and held her tight. It was the first time she'd spoken. A clue to her past.

"Do you have a brother, Betsy? Where's your brother?" She grabbed my hair as I set her on the bed.

She nodded and stared right inside my head. "Bruvver gone," she said in a voice that reached around my heart. And then she repeated this a dozen more times before stripping off the towel and pulling my bedspread over her head.

Later, I dressed Betsy in some clothes that I'd found in Dawn's chest. The girl was eight and small for her age when she disappeared. I didn't really think it odd that Dawn had left all her belongings behind; didn't really think it strange that my little Betsy stepped right into her shoes as if the other girl had never existed at all.

CHAPTER
TWENTY-FIVE

It's like the tide going out. A reversal of the influx of pupils I'd watched only a few weeks ago. So much has happened in that time, yet nothing has really changed. From my bedroom window, up in the eaves, the girls look like angry ants, impatient for their parents to take them home.

Katy told me that she's off to Italy with her parents for the half-term break. A fine punishment for her display of irresponsible adolescent behaviour. Since I saw her with Adam in the woods, I've dreamed about her several times. In the morning, I wrote down the details in the hope it might stop them coming. If anything, it's made them worse. In the last one, the police were exhuming Katy's naked body from a shallow grave of wet earth in the exact same spot I saw her with Adam. A faceless man was hiding in the shadows. I woke up drenched in sweat, frozen with fear.

I huff breath on to the windowpane and wipe an X in the mist; a farewell kiss for each of the girls as they leave Roecliffe for half-term. There's a gentle tap-tap on my door. I ease it open from its old frame.

"Lexi," I say. "Are you OK?" She has mascara streaking down her cheeks and the thick eyeliner she keeps getting told off for wearing makes the seam of black look as if she's been thumped.

"He's going to be late," she says. "Bloody late at half-term. I'll be the only one left." She's talking about her father.

"You won't be alone. I'm not going anywhere." The words sit thick as concrete on my tongue.

"You'd think that he'd want to see me." She storms into my room and hurls herself on my bed. She picks up my scarf and winds it through her fingers. "You're lucky," she continues. She reaches to my dressing table for a tissue. "You can just up and leave whenever you like."

I am about to tell her that I can't, that I will be staying at Roecliffe instead of taking a break by the sea, or staying with family, or going on a walking holiday. I will be trying my best to avoid the handful of diehard staff who choose to remain at school, who, like me, have nowhere else to go, but I stop. I know Lexi well enough to know that she would ask why.

"How late is your dad going to be?"

Lexi doesn't answer. She picks her way through my scant belongings on the dressing table as if they were her own.

"You don't have much make-up," she says. "And is this what you put on your hair?" She pulls a face and opens a bottle of supermarket brand shampoo. "Yuk. It smells like toilet cleaner."

I doubt that Lexi has ever cleaned a toilet in her life, let alone knows what the cleaning products smell like, but I humour her. "It does fine for me." Truth is, money has been tight. My pay has so far been two hundred pounds cash in advance from the bursar who told me, rather impatiently, that until I submit my bank account details, I won't be getting my salary.

"If you ask your hairdresser, they will recommend something. Daddy sends me to London every holiday and buys me a day in a salon. They do whatever I ask and it's all paid for —"

"Take it." I hold out the pale blue bottle. "Try it. You might be surprised."

Lexi's hand rises slowly and she takes the shampoo. She holds back the scowl that's forming, and actually finds it in herself to thank me.

"If it turns your hair to frizz, just pour it into your dad's girlfriend's shampoo bottle." We both laugh. "Now, will you be staying here overnight?" Sylvia and I have already stripped the beds.

Lexi shrugs. "I could be here for the whole week," she says glumly. "It wouldn't be the first time that's happened. And what did you mean when you said a while back that we have lots in common? Did you get dumped at boarding school while your parents went off having fun?"

"Not exactly," I reply. I think of different answers — some are lies, some skirt around fact, and some crush me with the truth. She wouldn't believe any of it. "I was headstrong like you when I was younger. I got angry when other people let me down, just like you're angry at your father now."

"What did you do?" Lexi sits cross-legged on my bed, hugging the scarf and shampoo as if they are her only worldly possessions.

"I guess I just changed over time," I tell her.

The kitchen staff don't work during half-term. For those who choose to stay on at school during the break — and those who have no choice — a supply of food is left in the giant refrigerator. I'm staring at it all, wondering if I should offer to cook for the others. But that would mean conversation, a gathering, a meal shared, stories told, questions asked. I pull out a block of cheese and set it on a chopping board.

"There you are."

I swing round, knife in hand, mouth gaping open. Adam holds up his palms in mock self-defence.

"Whoa," he says. "I was only going to ask if you wanted to join us all. We're going down to the village pub for a bite to eat. Kind of a celebration."

"Celebration?" A shard of light reflects off the knife, dancing around the kitchen walls.

"It's half-term," he says. "A bit of peace."

"Peace?" I say, chopping the cheese.

"Are you going to repeat the end of every sentence I say?" Adam glances at his watch. "Meet us in the hall in ten minutes?"

I stare at Adam, not seeing him, rather someone else entirely. Someone I'd rather be with, someone not quite so tall, someone who would wrap their arms round me and, if I didn't want to go to the pub, someone who would lead me up to my bedroom and fetch a tray of food for me, lie beside me, comfort me, laugh with me. "Sorry," I say. "I'm a bit tired."

I concentrate on the cheese but it's gone all blurry, as if it's melting. I wipe my eyes on the back of my wrist.

"Have you been chopping onions?" Adam asks. I shake my head. The sniff draws him closer, leaning the other side of the stainless steel counter. He peers at me. "Are you OK, Frankie?" I know that he'd rather be fetching his coat, stamping his feet impatiently in the hall, waiting for his friends to gather, to walk down to the village pub for some cheer.

"Yeah, I'm fine." *Please go away*, I think, even though I don't really want him to.

"See you tomorrow then."

"See you tomorrow." And I wait for the sound of his footsteps to disappear completely before I hack up the entire block of cheese.

The fire is quick to start. It was the matches sitting on a shelf in the kitchen that set me thinking. I turned the box over and over in my fingers, wondering where I might find wood. The library waste bins provided enough old newspapers to set the entire building alight, so I carried a few bundles back to the dining hall and dumped them on the hearth.

"Logs," I pondered, wondering if anyone would notice a couple of missing school benches. I headed off to the basement, feeling my way along the rough damp walls until I found a light switch. A network of rooms and low-ceilinged passages finally led me to a stash of broken furniture that had been crudely hacked up, perhaps for the single winter fire that was allowed.

I grabbed an armful of wood and took it back upstairs. Then I went down and fetched more. I did this until I had enough wood to last the evening. I shook out the newspapers and rolled them into knotted twists. I put a dozen into the fireplace and stacked the smallest bits of wood on top in a wigwam shape. My heart was in my throat.

Then I lit a single match and held it against the paper. I watched as the tiny flame spread, taking only seconds to rise between the splintered wood. In ten minutes, the fire had taken hold and the stack settled and dropped to a steady blaze. I went back to the kitchen and fetched the tray of food I had prepared.

So here I sit, a lone chair dragged next to the chimney, the tray set between my feet, my left cheek pricking scarlet from the blaze. I'm chewing slowly on cheese and crackers. I helped myself to the supply of wine left for staff and find that, after several glasses, it helps wash everything away.

I chuck more wood on the fire and watch it ignite. A fresh wave of heat makes me take off my cardigan. Time drags slowly, silently, as I think of the others in the pub. It's quarter to nine. I saw four of them leave — a woman who I think teaches Latin, Mr McBain the IT teacher, plus a new teacher recently over from Paris who works in the languages department, and, of course, Adam.

I pull my feet up on to the chair, hugging my knees. "I suppose he doesn't have a home to go to either," I mutter to myself, sipping the wine. Something about the heat, the alcohol, being alone, sends me to a place I don't want to be. Setting the drink on a small table nearby, I pull a photograph from my back pocket. It's in a sealed plastic bag, slightly crumpled, and the faces in it appear ghostly and silvered because of the shiny bag. I push my fingernail through the seal and open it up.

Then I scream.

"Oh my God, you scared me half to death." Relief turns into a hysterical laugh.

"That was exactly what I was trying *not* to do." Adam bends down, laughing, and picks up the photograph I dropped. "Here." He hands it back to me after giving it a quick glance. "I'm sorry."

He drags another chair and places it opposite me. My cosy dinner for one is over, but deep down I'm grateful for the company.

"What's all this?" he asks, pointing at the remains of my food, the blazing fire. "And who doesn't have a home to go to either?"

My entire face reddens, not just the side that is closest to the fire. "I thought you were at the pub," I say, sidestepping the question.

"Would you rather be alone?"

No, please stay with me, I beg in my head.

I shrug. "Up to you," I say, sliding the photograph under my leg.

"Nice-looking kid. Family picture?" he asks.

"No. Just a photo a friend sent me. Do you get many letters from banana land?"

Adam snorts a laugh. "Sadly not," he says. "I don't have any family in Australia. In fact, I don't have any family anywhere apart from an ex-wife who, if she did have my address, would probably send me rotten bananas."

My turn to laugh. "Don't tell me. She liked hers with ice cream and you liked yours spread on bread with jam."

"Something like that." Adam touches the bottle of wine. "Mind if I join you?" In a moment, he's back from the kitchen with more wine and another glass.

I try to convince myself that the company is harmless, that it doesn't mean I'm betraying anyone or putting myself at risk. He's just another teacher, not even from this area. The risk is low.

"No family anywhere, then?" I ask. If we're going to do it, if we're going to spend the evening together, then I only want to talk about him. "And you didn't tell me why you came back from the pub."

"No, not anywhere, and because I was worried about you. Satisfied?" Wide-eyed, almost mischievous, Adam fills our glasses. He shifts closer to the fire, to me. "There's a real chill in the air tonight."

"You didn't have to worry about me," I say, angry at myself for liking it that he did. "I'm absolutely fine. It's been a busy few weeks."

"You'll become institutionalised in no time," he says. His lean body bends towards the heat like a plant seeking the light. "Outside of Roecliffe Hall, I'm officially homeless." He pushes the iron poker into the fire and the wood drops down into the bed of embers.

He chucks more wood on, sending a rain of sparks up the chimney.

"How does that make you feel?" I put my cardigan back on and stretch it around my legs.

"Free," he admits, nodding. "For the first time in my life, I feel free."

"Did you feel trapped in your marriage, then?"

Adam sighs and waits, wondering if he should tell me. "Claudia is a beautiful woman. She's every man's dream. But when we met, we were only nineteen. She was just starting out in her modelling career and I'd not long been in Australia." He shakes his head, smiling at the memory. "Then she got whisked off to London, New York, Paris. She became quite famous and ended up with more money than sense. A few years later, she was back in Australia. By then, I was living and working in Sydney. She looked me up and things kicked off seriously from there. We were married within six months." Adam takes a breather, inhaling the heady fumes of the wine.

"Our relationship, if I'm honest, was based around nothing more than lust. Look any deeper and it was clear that we were completely incompatible." His accent wins over, perhaps to conceal embarrassment.

"In what way?" I clasp my fingers around my legs.

"I was teaching history in a city state school. She was an international model. You work it out." He grins and pushes up the sleeves of his striped shirt. "I think it was a novelty for her to take an academic to her glamorous parties."

192

"Worlds apart then," I say, hoping that's the right answer. "Literally now," I add.

"Claudia was always at some social event, always obsessing about her looks. She went from studio to nightclub, to health club, to studio. In the end, we never saw each other." Adam waits for a response but I sit silently, hoping he will continue. "I loved her. And she loved me. But if I mentioned kids, she broke out in a sweat." He laughs. "And as for the house, the car, the dog, the camping holiday in the hinterland every year — the whole happy family thing — forget it. Claudia was a penthouse apartment girl. It was me that left her in the end, in case you're wondering. I did it to be kind. No one should change themselves that much."

"Sometimes it's necessary," I find myself saying. Then, "So is that what you want? The whole happy family thing?" I chew on a nail, watching Adam intently.

He shrugs. "I guess it is, eventually. Isn't that what we all strive for ultimately?"

"Everyone except Claudia." I laugh in an effort to disguise my sadness.

"And you?"

"Maybe one day," I say quickly. "Although I'll have to hurry up, huh?" The humour clearly doesn't hide anything. "So is it very different teaching in England to Australia?"

"It's more roundheads and cavaliers than aboriginals, but I cope. I did my training in Australia, but studied European history as well. Have you ever been

193

married?" It seems that Adam is as skilled as I am at shifting gears.

"I guess half the battle is how you teach the kids, rather than what it's about. After all, anyone can read a few books —"

"I'm not entirely sure that's true." Adam stands and leans against the heavy oak mantelpiece. His long legs are stiff, outspread, soaking up the heat. He has his back to me and I see the rise and fall of his chest.

"I didn't mean that in a bad way. Just that I'm sure *how* you teach is as important as *what* you teach."

Adam turns round again. "The girls here enjoy my classes."

"A little too much, it would seem." I grin.

He covers his face. "Oh, don't remind me," he says. "Listen, thanks again for doing what you did. To say I'm grateful isn't enough."

"You don't have to keep thanking me." I mean it. "Tell me about the boarding school you said you went to. Was it anything like Roecliffe?" Strangely, it's helping, learning about Adam, learning about things outside my own sealed-off bubble.

"It was about as far removed from this school as any place could be. It was in the worst part of Birmingham. It was awful. Horrendous." Adam sits down again. His mouth folds into an attractive smile beneath a mass of hair that doesn't know which way to fall. He has strong features, yet somehow carries himself with gentleness.

"But I thought boarding schools were for the privileged, that they cost an arm and a leg. Surely your parents must have complained about it if it was that bad."

"It wasn't a boarding school, Frankie. It was a children's home. I was in and out of it from the minute I was born. My parents didn't have any money." His face falls flat. He's trying to wear a mask, but it keeps slipping. "I spent some time with my family, but mostly I was in care. I was fostered for a while."

"What about your parents? Where are they now?"

He shakes his head. "They couldn't look after me. It was the usual. Drugs, crime, violence. I had a younger sister. I was fourteen when she was born. She was taken into care too, but we got split up. Eventually I was told that my parents were dead and I lost touch with my sister."

"That's a tragic story." I pour more wine and offer up some of the cut cheese. Adam takes a piece. I stuff two lumps into my mouth. It stops me saying something I know I'll regret.

"So you can see why I made a new life in Australia. As soon as I got out of the home in Birmingham, I worked hard and saved enough for a ticket. I was one of the lucky ones. I'd studied at school and eventually got some qualifications. That got me a place in teacher training college."

I nod, curious why he came back to England. But I don't get to ask. Suddenly we hear a piercing scream.

"What was that?" Adam rushes to the double doors and throws them open. Then there's another scream followed by the vision of a pale, shaking figure in a nightdress.

"*Lexi*," I say.

CHAPTER
TWENTY-SIX

Nina peered through the studio window before entering. She balanced a tray on one hand as she opened the door. She prayed she didn't look as if she'd been crying.

"Hey," she said softly. Mick didn't like being startled or interrupted when he was working, but she'd needed to see him, just for a few moments. Her excuse was to take him lunch before she got embroiled with Tess.

She saw the concentration in Mick's muscles, the tight strapping across his shoulders as he leaned in to the canvas, applying a tiny amount of white paint to a huge picture. "The sparkle in the eyes," Nina whispered. "You've just brought her to life."

Mick turned and removed a brush from between his teeth. He drew a deep breath as if he'd been holding it all morning. "She's beautiful, isn't she?" He made a satisfied noise from the core of his artistic soul. A strand of dark hair curled across one eye. Nina unconsciously noticed the threads of grey. She adored the way her husband looked when he worked. Absorbed, lost, content. As she'd hoped, seeing him went some way to soothing her mind.

"I brought you lunch." She slid the tray on to a side table, pushing dozens of curled and squeezed paint tubes aside. The air was scented with linseed, turpentine, and imagination. "Did you hear back from that other new gallery that emailed you? Are they still interested in your work?" Nina was doing her best to appear normal. The prospect of even more work for Mick was exciting, yet she worried about how he would cope.

Mick tossed the brushes into a jar of blue cloudy liquid. "They want to meet me. I tried to call but had to leave a message."

"I'm so pleased you're finally getting the recognition you deserve." Nina looked at the painting. It was slightly different to his usual style. There were more colours, for a start. Mick's trademark palette was soft, natural, fleshy hues with one key accent colour to focus the eye. But real-life subjects and realistic backgrounds had given way to an impressionistic feel with a surreal theme. The young woman, a nude, was looking out of a balcony window. There was a hint of a street scene below, but only a hint, while the eye was instantly drawn to the scarlet pumps she wore. "I love it," Nina said, kissing Mick's neck. She closed her eyes and breathed in his scent. Again, she felt a rush of relief, security, need. But after only a moment of closeness, Mick pulled away. He was keen to get back to work.

"Enjoy your lunch," she said, wishing she could stay in the studio for the rest of her life. "I'll see you later."

As she was walking back to the house, Nina's heart stuttered again. Her fingers twitched inside her jeans pocket. Only when she was back in the kitchen did she remove the hairclip for another look. She stood in front of the mirror and held the strawberry slide against the blond hair at her temple. Nina's mouth opened in a little gasp. Blurring at the edges, her vision played tricks and she saw someone completely different staring back.

Nina swung away from the mirror. She reached for the phone and dialled Tess's number. She was probably already on her way, so she left a message on the voicemail. *Sorry, Tess. Something's come up. I can't meet today. Can we reschedule?*

Nina tore the clip from her hair and jammed it back into her pocket.

"Probably just a mail order error," she said, not believing a word of her self-styled rationale. "Or maybe parole for good behaviour." She paced the kitchen impatiently, pulling back her hair. She bit one of her nails down so short it bled, and rhythmically kicked her toe against the table leg until it throbbed from the pain.

Nina lifted the lid of her laptop and opened up the internet. "Surely," she whispered, "he can't have disappeared off the face of the earth."

She typed in a search and drummed her fingers as she scanned down the list of Google results. There were thousands to trawl through. Mark McCormack, she muttered over and over. Nothing caught her eye; none of those mentioned seemed to be *her* Mark McCormack. She typed again, adding the outdated phone number from her notebook to the mix. Nothing came up. Then she typed *Mark McCormack CID*. Results showered down the page, but at first glance none of them seemed relevant to her needs. She clicked on a couple of links but the site content was irrelevant.

Finally, Nina typed the man's name again before adding two further words that made her stop dead and consider the danger she was in. They glared back at her from the white box before she hit the enter key.

Eagerly, she scanned the results. Among the listings were blogs by people with either the name Mark or the surname McCormack. There were a couple of articles that caught her eye but turned out to be nothing, plus a website listing movies on the theme of her search. And so the list went on. Nina wasn't able to find anything specific to her situation or the elusive Mark McCormack. She supposed, given the nature of his work, he wouldn't be advertising his whereabouts.

"This is useless," Nina said, getting up and walking away from the computer. She was angry. What was it he'd said? *I'll be here for you. I'm only a phone call away.* And what else had she been told? Self-sufficiency in the community was key, as was reduced contact with the programme support team.

"Not this reduced," Nina said bitterly. She turned back to the laptop and brought up the contact details of Avon and Somerset Police headquarters. She dialled the number and waited for a response. She had absolutely no idea what she would say. All she knew was that she needed to make that first contact, to perhaps get a message forwarded to Mark, wherever he was. At the very least, she needed to know that someone was still on her side.

"I want you to connect me to the CID, please," Nina stated clearly.

"Which department, please?"

"I . . . I don't know."

"Do you have a contact name?"

"No, not exactly," she said. "Can't you just put me through?"

The receptionist sighed and the line went quiet for a few seconds. Then it rang again and a male voice answered. "Public Protection."

"I was wondering if . . ." Nina stopped. "Do you think you'd be able to . . ." The words just weren't there. "I'm trying to contact someone in the force that . . . that I knew a long time ago. The number he gave me doesn't —" Nina stopped when she heard the chuckle.

"Aren't we all, love," he said. "Give me a name and I'll give the department lists a quick scan for you."

"He wasn't actually based in Avon," Nina confessed. "I don't know which force he came from. Can't you just run a search on his name?"

"It's not quite that simple. Who am I speaking to exactly? Let me enter your details into the system and see what we come up with. I may be able to help if —"

Nina quickly pressed the phone back on to its base. She lifted it up and jabbed it back in its socket several times, to make sure she was really cut off. She let out a desperate whimper. She couldn't remember feeling such despair or panic since the day the ultrasound technician had had trouble finding her baby's heartbeat.

200

"Nothing will happen," McCormack had said to her. "You'll be fine now." How could he have been so sure? Looking back, she had believed him, she *trusted* him. Nina recalled his wise features, the mature way he allayed her fears. Mark McCormack, from the first time she'd met him, had taken control of her life, managing everything from enrolling her in college to arranging for funding. He'd even helped her choose a new wardrobe when she wouldn't go to the shops alone.

"You've let me down," she whispered. She took the hairclip from her pocket and tossed it on the table. She felt like a caged animal with the door wide open — except there was nowhere for her to run.

There was a hopelessness to the way she pressed the laptop lid shut — limp wrists, curled fingers, arms hanging heavy from her shoulders. She dropped her head on to the table and allowed her thoughts to spin. Perhaps Mark McCormack had never really been there for her at all.

"Yes. Yes, I think so," Nina said, without knowing if that was an appropriate answer. She was distracted and couldn't even repeat what Laura had just said to her. She glanced out of her friend's kitchen window and adjusted the net curtains so there weren't any gaps. She'd driven round to Laura's to be close to someone. Her mobile phone rang in her pocket.

"Is your mum OK, Josie?" Laura whispered while Nina was on the phone. She'd made the girls lunch, and a mug of sweet tea for Nina. Her friend was clearly upset about something.

Josie shrugged and pulled a face. It was true her mum had been acting a bit weird these last few days, but then mums were weird, weren't they? Nat had said that hers was always crying in her room, always arguing with her dad. Hormones, they'd agreed, were the cause, happy to throw that one back at their parents.

"Yes, see to that as well, will you?" Nina's shoulders uncurled and her mouth relaxed from the pursed button it had been since she'd arrived. "We're going to need loads of them. And get me some more fake tears. Thank you, Tess. You're a huge help." Nina hung up. "Tess," she said, holding up her phone. "She's virtually running things at the moment."

"Oh?" Laura asked. She quietly busied about the kitchen, knowing that asking Nina directly what was wrong wouldn't provide answers.

"If we get this film right, the work will come pouring in." Distracted, Nina thought ahead — she saw herself taking on more make-up artists, renting premises, hiring Tess full-time. But then the sick feeling returned as she remembered.

"Shall we go on Afterlife?" Nat said as they thumped up the stairs with their food. Their plans grew more distant until finally the slam of the door marked Laura and Nina alone.

"Right, kiddo. Tell me what's going on." Laura dragged out a chair and sat down. She spread her palms face down on the table. "Your turn to dump on me. And before you ask, before you change the subject off yourself as you always do, my marriage is still a disaster zone. Tom didn't come home two nights ago . . ." She trailed off when she saw the tear crest Nina's cheek. "Oh, Neen. What's wrong?"

"Does . . . does Natalie ever say to you that it's wrong to tell tales at school? That dobbing someone in, snitching, is bad?" Nina blew her nose.

Laura thought for a moment then said, "I know that Nat would never rat on a friend willingly. Kids who snitch have a pretty hard time at school."

Nina let out a crazed laugh. "And what do you think about that?"

"I think it's bad news. Kids should be encouraged to tell if something's happened. From an early age, there's this pressure to keep quiet and —"

"Well, you're wrong, Laura. Just so you know." Nina forced a smile, one that told Laura not to argue the matter. "If they want to survive in the playground, then they have to keep quiet."

Laura shrugged, wondering where this was leading, hoping Josie didn't have problems at school or, worse, that it was something to do with that Afterlife website again. "Fair enough," she said. "If that's what you think."

"No," Nina replied. "I don't think it. I *know* it."

"What does this have to do with you looking as if the sky's fallen in?" She plucked a tissue from a box and swished it at Nina. "I'm not budging until you tell me."

Nina blew again and attempted a laugh. "Nothing. Really. Wrong time of the month. Pressure at work. Maybe I have a virus."

Laura was shaking her head. "I don't buy a word of it."

"Just leave it, will you?" Nina snapped. "I can handle it." And her head dropped to the table with thoughts of quite the opposite spinning inside.

CHAPTER
TWENTY-SEVEN

"What on earth's wrong, Lexi?"

The girl is shaking and her lips are tinged blue. I coil my arm round her shoulders and guide her towards the fire. "Come and sit down. You're freezing."

Lexi lowers herself on to the chair. Her bones are thin under my hands, her skin papery and cool to touch. Adam takes off his jacket and drapes it around her shoulders. "She shouldn't even be at school," I tell him. "Her dad got delayed."

"There was a face," Lexi whispers, terrified. "Staring in at my window."

"It was probably just a dream," Adam says matter-of-factly. "Who would be looking in through an upstairs window?"

I recognise the fear in Lexi's voice, see it sweep across her in waves. Each time she breathes out, her body quivers.

"There was a man's face," she says. "And I wasn't dreaming. I hadn't even gone to sleep."

"Not an upstairs window, Adam. Lexi was the last one here so I said she could sleep in a sixth-form room. They get the suites on the ground floor, directly beneath the night matron's room." My voice has thinned and I'm praying the worst isn't true. "Sylvia and I had stripped all the beds upstairs. As a treat, I let Lexi have a room with its own television and en-suite bathroom. It didn't seem fair she was stuck at school on her own." I'm breaking out in a sweat.

"I was lying on my bed," Lexi says, "just reading *Cosmo Girl* and half watching the telly. The curtains were still open. When I looked up, I saw his face. He ducked down as soon as he saw me." Lexi cups her face in her hands. "Then I screamed all the way up here, miss." Another shudder. "It was horrible."

"Should we call the police?" Adam asks.

"No," I reply immediately. They both stare at me. "It's probably just an old tramp looking for shelter. Maybe he knows it's the holidays and he thought the building would be empty." I smile, trying to make light of it all.

"Or maybe it's an intruder looking to nick a few computers. I think I should call the police to be on the safe side."

I stand up. "Really, you'll be wasting your time. They're so busy these days, it'll be ages before anyone —"

"Frankie, I don't think that's what Lexi wants to hear." Adam crouches down in front of the girl. I glance out of the big dining room and sweep a glance around the great hall, half convinced I'll see someone scuttle past. "Can you describe the person you saw, Lexi?"

She shrugs. "He was ugly. Kind of old, I think."

"What about hair?" Adam asks.

Lexi shrugs again. "Maybe," she answers vaguely.

"I'm going to make you some hot chocolate," I tell her. "Then you can spend the night with me. I bet all you saw was a reflection of someone on the television, right?" My words are jagged and clipped, virtually giving Lexi no choice but to agree with me.

"Probably," she says, following me into the kitchen.

"No more of this nonsense," I tell her, as the milk begins to simmer in the pan. "There was no intruder." After a second or two, after she has seen how serious I am by the lock of our eyes, Lexi nods in agreement.

When the milk has come to the boil, when I have sloshed it on to the chocolate, when I have stirred it so hard it spins over the top of the mug, I march Lexi back through the dining room. We say goodnight to Adam, who says he'll make sure the fire's out, and I escort Lexi up to my room. There's a camp bed beneath my bed and, between us, we haul it out and sheet it up. She sits cross-legged on it and sips her hot chocolate.

Fifteen silent minutes later, punctuated only by her snuffling into her drink, Lexi is hiding from what she saw at the window, curled up like a cat beneath the blankets, locked safe in sleep away from the man's staring face. When I know there's no chance she'll wake, I creep downstairs and go into the sixth-formers' bedroom.

The television is still on — some talent show with a tuneless singer strutting about the stage. I flick it off. Lexi's magazine lies on the bed, along with her robe and a wet towel. I cast a glance around. Nothing is out of the ordinary — the curtains are open, as Lexi said.

207

The bed has been lain on, but not slept in. A chocolate bar wrapper brushes my foot and a hairbrush slides off the sag of the mattress when I sit down.

Only then, when the angle of light is changed, do I notice the distinct handprints on the windowpane. Squinting at the spread-out shapes, I step over to the window, knees bent to keep the view, and hold my own hands up to the print. I know the greasy shapes are on the outside of the window because when I try to rub one of them away, nothing happens. They are a mirror image of my own sweating hands, only larger, more masculine and . . . and . . . I stare hard at what I'm seeing.

The left hand is clearly missing a thumb.

"An hour?" It doesn't make sense.

Adam is leaning over me, dabbing at my head with a ball of wet cotton wool. I swat his hand away. "I drank the rest of the wine, made myself some soup, checked the fire had died down enough to leave it safely. I even watched the first part of the news on the staffroom television."

"A whole hour?" I say again. I'm spinning in circles, mind and body.

"I saw the lights on down the sixth-form corridor. Based on what happened earlier, I thought I ought to check things out. That's when I found you on the floor. I carried you up to sick bay." He does the cotton wool again.

"Ow!" I yelp. "That hurts."

208

"You should have seen the chest of drawers," he says. Then he lightly touches a finger down the maroon scar on my cheek.

"Don't," I say, flinching.

Adam shrugs and gets back to bathing my new wound. "You might be concussed. I should take you to accident and emergency."

"I'm fine," I tell him.

"Do you feel sick, dizzy, have a headache?"

"Nope," I lie.

Adam sighs impatiently. "If you're sure," he says, already knowing better than to argue with me. "Can you remember what happened before you passed out?"

"Yes," I say. "I saw handprints on the windowpane. One was missing a thumb. They were probably the prints of the man who frightened —"

"Do you think you can walk?" he asks. I nod that I can. "Then let's go and take a look."

Back in Lexi's bedroom, I see that the pale blue curtains are now drawn. The bed, the magazine, the television, everything else looks just the same. I pull away from Adam's guiding arm and snap open the curtains. "Right here," I say. "But you have to crouch to see them." I bend my knees. My head throbs. I frown. I don't understand. "They were here before," I tell him. "Can you see them?" I glance up at Adam, who is not crouching.

"Frankie," he says soothingly. "You had a nasty bump on the head. You had wine."

"But the handprints were here before I fainted. A pair of them on the outside of the glass. The left hand was definitely missing a thumb." I sway from side to side, angling the light differently in case the prints magically reappear.

"Maybe when you hit your head you —"

"No!" I say. "I'm not dreaming this up. Someone must have wiped them off." I shiver. "Does that mean that whoever stared in at the window came back?"

"I doubt it." Adam's strong arm is round my shoulder, forcefully pulling me back from the window. "You're tired," he says. "Let me take you up to your room. See how you feel in the morning."

I stare up at him. He's a good six inches taller than me. He's not going to take no for an answer. His strong hands grip my wrists.

"I don't want you falling again," he says, guiding me to the door. I don't argue when he leads me up to my top-floor room. Neither do I argue when he turns his back so that I can change and slip between the sheets. Lexi huffs through irregular snores, and Adam casts a glance at us both before flicking out the light.

"I'll leave the door open," he says, staring at me, frowning, offering a forced smile that I catch in the half-light.

"Thank you," I say, unsure if I'm grateful for the care he's shown me or that he could actually be right — that I probably just imagined it all.

CHAPTER
TWENTY-EIGHT

Michael was very ill, Miss Maddocks said. Contagious, she told us. Needs to rest, she insisted. Leave him alone, she grumbled, shaking her head as we gathered outside the room where Michael had been sealed off. Every so often, we heard a crash or bang coming from inside.

"I heard him crying in the night," one boy said.

"Did he puke?" asked another.

"Scoot, the lot of you," Miss Maddocks said. "Before the gremlins come for you, too."

"Was it the gremlins that made him sick, Miss Maddocks?" I held back as the others scattered, knowing I wouldn't get told off. Betsy clung to my hand, coughing up the nagging tickle that had plagued her for the last couple of days.

Miss Maddocks stared at me, perhaps thinking that at nearly thirteen, I was too old and too smart to be fobbed off with gremlin stories. I was hoping she was going to let me in on an adult secret, be party to the workings of their grown-up minds, finally discover what the night-time goings-on really meant. But she just stared at me, settling her hands on my shoulders. Betsy whimpered at my side.

"There are some things," Miss Maddocks said, "that you or I don't need to know about." Close up, she reminded me of a witch. Her breath smelled musty and her wrinkles sagged from her bones. I half expected her to reach for her broomstick and fly away. "Best keep your nose out if you don't want to find out for yourself."

I pulled Betsy close. Miss Maddocks was scaring me. "Find what out?" I asked.

It was in my nature to discover. I'd been doing it ever since I gave up waiting for my dad to come back. If something was going on, I wanted to know about it. Occasionally I would tell the carers if one of the other kids was being bad — hurting or stealing or breaking. They gave me sweets in return, told me to keep watch for them. They patted my head with a fond palm, nodding approval, giving me the attention I craved.

Other times I would spy on the cooks, see them pick up food from the floor, slap it back on the baking tray. Or I'd sneak around the grounds, watching when the council men came to chop down trees or ride the great big mower around. They didn't know I'd seen Letitia, the cleaner girl, sneak into a hedge with one of the men, come out all rosy-faced and with a skip in her step when she later circuited the floors with her bucket.

Once, I ventured down the corridor that was most strictly out of bounds — the same place that I'd been taken to years ago and been dazzled by that light. The carers were playing cards, the telly was on loud, most of the other kids were watching a movie. I was bored; it was the holidays. No school. Nothing to do. I wasn't naughty — far from it. Just eager to please. Keen to spin a tale or two; keen to be loved. So I went exploring.

Down that corridor, there were many doors. Some were ajar so I peeked inside. The desks, filing cabinets, dying pot plants, old cabinets were dull as ditchwater. Nothing to discover there. I ventured further down the corridor, and jumped out of my skin when a floorboard creaked, froze against the wall when I heard voices, held my breath until they faded away.

I tiptoed deeper into the forbidden zone, reaching out my hand to the knob of a door that appeared locked. But when I wrapped my small fingers round it, twisted it as carefully as I could in case there was someone the other side waiting to pounce, it turned and gave, allowing me to swing it inwards. I held my breath in case it made a noise. When it was six inches clear of the frame, just enough for me to get my face through, I peered inside.

I wished I hadn't.

It must be where the gremlins live, I thought, terrified. It reminded me of the dungeons in those books about princesses and beasts and castles and giants.

Several metal chairs were chained to the floor right in the middle of the ugly room. Bare bricks with flaky stuff growing on them lined the walls. It was dark, but the corridor light allowed me to see that the floor was dirty and littered with horrible tools like saws and iron poles and racks. There was blood. Several cameras sat on tripods around the room like long-legged insect monsters. A wretched smell wafted in my face, making me slam the door shut again. Vomit rose in my throat as I ran back down the corridor. I wouldn't be going in there ever again.

When I got back to the living room, panting, I nestled amongst the other children, pushing up close to them so that I could feel safe again. Later that night, sitting on Alison's bed while she brushed my hair, I told her what I'd seen, told her all about the room — where it was and what was in it. In the mirror opposite, I saw her mouth fall open. I saw her cheeks turn scarlet.

"It's true," I stuttered back. Talking about it sent my heart skipping. "This horrid place where all the devils live." My voice was filled with childish awe, as if I'd discovered a new and dangerous world.

"Liar," she said suddenly. "You're a dirty liar." Her face was burning up.

I thought Alison was my friend. She dug the brush into my scalp, pressing my head down into my neck. "*Liar, liar, liar,*" she screamed, hitting me with the bristles.

"Ow, stop it, Alison!" I ducked away from her flailing arm. Then she fell on to the bed, sobbing into the sheets, hammering the mattress with her fists. "What's got into you?" I asked, peeling back the hair from her face.

Alison stared up at me, calm for a moment. Her head shook in the socket of her neck. "Years ago," she whispered through hysteria, "they took me there."

"Who did?" I ask.

"Them," she replied. "Them in those dark hoods."

214

I didn't say anything else; just stared at her, frowning, wondering. Alison cried some more and I stroked her back until she fell asleep. She was still in the same position in the morning — curled with her knees drawn up to her chin, thumb in her mouth, even though she was a year older than me.

"But I want to *know*," I whined to Miss Maddocks.

"Like I said," she told me as we stood outside the room where Michael was banging about. Screams pushed out from under the door. Betsy clung to my side. We heard Michael throw up. "There are things that a young girl like you doesn't need to know about."

I frowned. "But *you* know."

"I'm not young," she said, walking off.

"Just tell me, tell me. Is it the evil spirits or the ghost or the imps and gremlins? Did they come for Michael? Did they give him his disease?" I grabbed hold of Miss Maddocks' arm, surprised at how cool it felt, as if she wasn't really alive.

She gave me a kind look. "Yes," she said, nodding seriously. "The bad gremlins came for Michael." She turned to go but stopped, offering a few more words. "But I shouldn't have told you that much," she whispered before shooting off down the corridor.

CHAPTER
TWENTY-NINE

By the end of the movie, Josie had tears cascading down her cheeks. "Oh Mum," she said. "It was so sad. I didn't think it would end like that. That poor girl."

Nina turned to her daughter. She pulled her close and wrapped her arms round her shoulders. Josie's hair smelled of the expensive shampoo she'd pestered for. "No, neither did I," Nina replied in a measured voice.

They'd come back from Laura's house together after lunch, Josie protesting that she'd been invited to stay the night, that she and Nat had plans, that there was talk of a party, and shopping the next day. Nina's eyes had darted nervously to her rear-view mirror all the way home.

"Well, your plans have just changed, young lady," Nina had snapped when Josie pulled a face in Laura's kitchen. "We're spending the rest of the day together," she'd informed her daughter, thinking that if she had to stick to her like glue the rest of her life, then she would.

"Things rarely turn out the way you expect." Nina's eyes were completely dry after watching the movie that she'd bribed Josie with. She hadn't been paying attention to it, preferring to stare anywhere but the screen. Above all else, she'd simply wanted to spend a

216

couple of hours in Josie's magnetic field, to help forget. "I love you," she said spontaneously.

Josie recoiled with embarrassment. "Er, you too, Mum," she chirped, suddenly bright — *too* bright. She leapt off the sofa. "Think I'll go to my room. I just want to be alone."

"Not on that computer again. Why don't you help me in the garden?" It wasn't a very tempting offer, Nina knew, but she needed something as mindless and mundane as weeding to keep her overactive mind occupied until she figured out a plan. Josie's company would help, and at least they'd be near to Mick in the studio.

"I'm going to read. I'm into a really good book." Josie passed through the hall and went upstairs, leaving Nina alone with memories that she thought had long gone.

She fingered the rusty metal of the hairclip in her pocket, thankful that at least Josie was oblivious to everything. Nina would strive to keep it that way, and keep it from Mick, too. Once again, she checked that the front door was securely locked. She went round rattling every downstairs window, deciding not to bother with the weeding. She would just sit, stay inside near to Josie, and think. She would make best case and worst case scenario plans.

Nina made herself a cup of tea and curled up on the sofa with a blanket. Work issues would have to wait. She stared at the wall ahead, the one she and Mick had painted together late one night when Josie was young. They'd fallen into bed, their hands tacky with emulsion, stamping prints on each other's bodies. *Marking my territory*, Mick had said, before they'd made love.

Nina kicked the knitted throw off her legs. She was sweating. She was shaking from the realisation that, when it came down to it, there was very little distance between the best and worst case scenarios; that if things were to turn out well, she would first have to pass through the worst.

"Are you sure you don't mind if he comes for dinner?"

Nina snapped out of her reverie. She didn't know how long it had been since she curled in on herself — ten minutes, ten hours? "What did you say?" She smiled up at her husband. One moment she shook, another she poured sweat. Shock, she thought.

"I'm really sorry it's such short notice. I finally got an email back from the new gallery owner's secretary, telling me that the boss was in the area and wanted to meet up immediately. I emailed back and suggested he come for dinner. I'm afraid I don't know anything about him."

Nina sensed Mick's excitement, but it did nothing to lift her mood. She felt happy for him, of course, but when she understood what he was asking of her, when she realised that in a few hours they would be entertaining a man who could help change their finances forever, she wasn't sure if she was up to it. Even applying mascara seemed an insurmountable task, let alone cooking a dinner that was fit to serve to an important guest.

Nina's eyes were heavy. Mick noticed immediately, countering the imposition by wrapping his arms round her as he sat beside her. He felt her respond, relax, push back against him. "Interest from yet another gallery is such a great opportunity for us all."

Nina suddenly turned and kissed her husband, pressing her mouth fiercely against his. She gripped the sides of his head between her hands, wanting to become a part of him, to crawl inside him, to hide forever.

She pulled back, took a deep breath. Mick's eyes were swimming. "We're taking on the world, you and me," she said. Her voice was deep, convincing, and it turned Mick on. "A West End gallery."

"West End indeed," Mick agreed. He lowered his lips on to the soft skin at the nape of her neck. He wanted more of what she'd just offered him, but if they were to be ready before their guest arrived, there was no time.

As Mick nuzzled her, Nina remembered the one and only time she'd not welcomed his affections. She was back there in the hospital, staring at her face in the small mirror in the patients' toilet.

"Dead," she said to herself. She saw a face, some lips, and heard the words, but they didn't seem to be hers. "How can my baby be dead?"

It was a routine scan at twenty weeks' gestation. Mick had promised to meet her at the clinic, but he'd had a puncture on the way. There was no way of contacting him — he didn't have a mobile phone; in fact, they could barely afford the old Fiat he drove around in. So Nina had gone into the dark room on her own, changed behind the screen, and lay down on the couch. There was a lone chair set out on the opposite side of the great humming ultrasound machine. A chair for partners, she thought.

"That's unusual," the sonographer said after a short while, then she didn't say anything else until, "There's baby's face, see?"

Nina gasped. "Oh," she said, quite unable to speak at the sight of the little snub-nosed profile.

"But I'm having trouble finding a heartbeat, I'm afraid." Whatever else the technician said after that, Nina couldn't remember. The world became skimmed with a protective film that prevented the truth drilling into her.

A consultant was called, further scans performed, a pregnancy test run at record speed. The baby had died; four weeks ago, they thought. Nina wondered what she'd been doing when her baby decided to give up.

Then Mick arrived, red-faced, apologetic, covered in oil from the car. "Have I missed it?" he asked, grinning. Nina was lying on her back, her face as white as the gown she was wearing.

"It's dead," she said flatly. No one had told Mick before he came into the scan room. The clinic receptionist had sent him straight in — just another late father who was going to get it in the neck.

Mick stood still. He asked if it was still inside her. He asked if the baby had come out yet.

Nina didn't know what to say. With her eyes, she implored the female consultant, who was preoccupied with writing notes, to suggest what might happen. But she didn't look up, didn't see the look of horror on Nina's face, didn't notice when, gown flapping at the rear, she heaved herself off the couch and ran into the bathroom. Mick followed his wife, wrapped his arms round her lifeless yet still swollen belly.

"Don't touch me," Nina spat out. Mick ignored her. He pressed his face into her hair, stricken with grief that their baby was gone.

"Dead," Nina said, staring at herself in the mirror. "How can my baby be dead?" She felt as if she was dying herself, from the inside out.

"Or we could go to a restaurant if you prefer," Mick suggested. There was a squeeze on her shoulder, bringing her back to the present. "Nina, I said we could go out for dinner if you prefer. Save you cooking."

Nina snapped out of the memory. Her mouth had gone dry. She occasionally thought about Josie's older sister, even though they hadn't named the baby. That would have made her too real and therefore harder to lose. There was no grave, just ashes scattered in the river close to where she was conceived one late-night picnic with wine, with stars, with bats skimming between the trees around them. The child was just a breath on the wind, as if she'd never been real.

"I have some fresh fish," Nina said. Her words were wispy and fragile, stretching through time. The present-day dilemma hit home again, hammering her head. Her stomach lurched; a feeling of having nowhere to run — and if she did run, what about her family? Were they only allowed a certain number of years together? Should she just be grateful for the twenty she'd already shared with Mick, the fifteen she'd cared for Josie? She'd envisaged growing old with Mick; always imagined a Cornish cottage, a dog perhaps, Josie coming to visit with their grandchildren.

"I'll cook," she said, striding into the kitchen and lifting the wrapped fish from the refrigerator. It would take her mind off things, if only for a few hours. Mick followed, mumbling how grateful he was, that he would help any way he could.

Nina stared at him for a second, swallowed, and then slapped the fish on to a chopping board. Without knowing how it would help, she stabbed it over and over with the sharpest knife she could find.

CHAPTER
THIRTY

Dozens of crows flap out of the trees as I skirt the perimeter of Roecliffe Hall. They caw indignantly, flying through the early-morning mist that hangs in the trees as if someone has draped giant net curtains over the school grounds. I stick close to the building, following the buttress of stone flanking the earth. I look up. Five storeys of Victorian red brick reach up to the brilliant blue sky that's just visible beyond the haze. It's a beautiful morning, although nothing about my mood matches the day.

"Not this one. Not this one," I say, marching past window after window. Most of these rooms are sixth-form accommodation, with some of this wing also being used by staff. It's school policy to mix up the female staff rooms amongst those of the girls. Supervision is natural rather than enforced, Sylvia told me. All the male staff accommodation is in the same wing as Adam, apart from the headmaster and his wife. They have their own flat. My room is one of only two staff rooms in the attic. I asked Sylvia if I could use the spare room up there for sorting out games kits, but she told me it was locked. "Headmaster has the key," she said. "Waste of good space, if you ask me."

I recognise the pale blue curtains. All the others are lilac. The ground slopes away beneath this window, making the sill head height to me. I look back along the row and see that looking in at the other end would be easy because the ground is higher. I stub my toe on something. There's a rock — a large one that looks as if it was once part of a rockery — directly beneath the window. It's grey-green from lichen, but my heart skips when I see the muddy footprint on the flat surface. There are grooves in the grass where it's been dragged to the window.

"Someone *was* here," I say. The sunlight breaks through the mist and light darts off the panes of glass. I see a smeary patch in the lower section, as if it's been wiped. Grimy streaks pattern the glass.

Then I see something caught on a splinter of wood on the window frame. I pluck off a piece of snagged tissue — all the proof I need that someone wiped away the handprints.

In the cold light of day, I don't think Adam will believe me when I tell him what I've seen. I can hardly believe it myself, that someone was spying, looking for something — someone — in the virtually deserted school. As I walk back to the front entrance, the piece of tissue rolling between my fingers, I wonder where it is that a person hides when there's simply nowhere left to go.

I've barely walked inside the hall, barely wiped the dew from my boots, when Adam is upon me, bright and cheery, asking me things that I can't take in.

"I was wondering if you'd like to join me. If you're feeling up to it, that is. It's a beautiful morning." Adam is wearing a bright blue jacket, like someone walking up a mountain would wear, and I see he's put on walking boots. He's fresh-faced and smells of coffee. His hair is slightly damp from the shower. It settles around his face in darker, tighter waves than usual. I can't help staring at it.

"Sorry?"

Adam pulls a half-grin and sighs. "I said, would you like to visit the old chapel with me? I've arranged access. It's in the school grounds so you won't have to walk very far." He stamps his feet on the old tiled floor as if he'll have a mini tantrum if I refuse. His interest in me has grown since the ordeal with Katy Fenwick. By doing the right thing, I've strung a thread of trust between us whether I intended to or not.

My mouth drops open.

"A chap in the village has the keys," he says. "With a bit of string-pulling, I managed to wangle half an hour in there to do some research for my book. It'll be interesting. The building's sat derelict for twenty years. I could use the company."

Adam's broad shoulders fill the weatherproof jacket, and one of his strong arms leans against the wall as if he's holding up the entire building. His face travels through a range of expressions, from eagerness to hopefulness to impatience. I want to push my head on to his chest, to seal myself off from everything. I want to cry on him, howl on the nearest, strongest, most

225

trustworthy person I can find. It doesn't sound like my voice at all when, shaking, I say, "Yes. I'll come."

"Tell me more about your book. Is it going to be published?" There's a lacy splattering of light on the mossy grass as the sun filters through the tree canopy. The lane is dappled and the mist has all but burnt off. Together, we walk towards Roecliffe village. With Adam beside me, I feel oddly safe setting foot outside the school grounds. Together, I am part of a credible couple — not what anyone would be looking for; not likely to be recognised. Although after last night's scare, there isn't much reason to feel safe within the school property either. I know I'm yearning for the familiar closeness that can never be mine again — the joke that doesn't even need to be told to be understood, the shared laughter, the knowing look. But if Adam did take my hand, I'd probably snap away — ashamed, guilty.

He grumbles and makes an indignant noise about the difficulty of getting local history books published. "I'm going to get it printed myself if I have to. It's not about the money."

"What is it about then?" I ask quickly.

He thinks for a moment. "It's about the truth," he says carefully. "Researching local history is a lot like archaeology. Miss a piece and you risk misinterpreting the whole event. Damage something and you'll never know exactly what happened." We walk in silence until he says, "It's about putting things right."

"So why Roecliffe Hall?" I ask. "I'm sure there are more interesting places to write about." I'm hoping that Adam is simply passionate about architecture — after all, Roecliffe is a fine example of Victorian gothic folly. As we approach the chapel, my feet fall heavily on the road. I swear there is lead in my boots. "Is there something special about it?" I need to know what he knows.

Adam stops abruptly and pulls on my arm to bring me to a halt. His face is serious while his electric-blue eyes flash excitement. "Don't you know?" he asks incredulously. "I thought everyone here knew." He shrugs and walks on a couple of paces, before stopping again.

"It's the murders," he says, lowering his voice. His eyes flash around the lane as if he thinks we're being watched. "Roecliffe Hall used to be a children's home until the late eighties. Terrible, ghastly things happened and it was closed down. Those poor little mites." Adam shakes his head. I think I see his eyes fill with tears. "Bodies were found all over the place."

"That's shocking."

Adam's face soaks up the dappled light. It masks his expression, making him appear sad and determined all at once. "When the body of a little girl was found buried in . . ." His lungs deflate with sadness. "The police found many others. It was terrible." He swallows back a grief that suggests he knows a lot more than he is letting on.

I look up at Adam, shielding my eyes from the sun; from the past, and from the future, too. "You seem to know a lot already," I say, unsure if I should continue. "You sound as if you were there," I add, my gaze unwavering, looking for even the tiniest reaction.

Frazer Barnard dangles a pair of keys on a chain. His other hand is shoved deep inside the pocket of his dirty tweed jacket. "No one's wanted to go in there in years," he says in a gruff voice. "Not after everything was all stirred up."

His front door had opened before we reached the end of his weed-strewn path.

Adam reaches for the keys. "Thank you very much, Mr Barnard," he says loudly. "I appreciate this."

I stare at the keys.

"Not so quick," he replies, whipping them back. "And no need to shout. Rules state that no one can go into the chapel without an approved person accompanying them."

"Approved person?" I say. "Rules?" Frazer Barnard glares at me, as if he's not noticed me yet. His face is spidered with drinker's veins, the little remaining hair he has is grey and glued down to his skull. His clothes are filthy and, even standing six feet away, I can smell a bitter odour seeping from him.

"Not a problem," Adam says. "Who's the approved person?"

"Me," Barnard growls.

In my mind, I hear the single bell tolling through the woods. I see a procession of adults walking slowly down the path with a clutch of children following in their wake. Bluebells drench the lush grass with brushstrokes of azure and indigo. Sun sparkles off the small stream beyond. I hear the excited chatter of children anticipating the Sunday picnic after the service. I see the arched door of the little chapel being unlocked. Then it all goes black as the children are led inside.

My legs falter and my breathing becomes shallow. Frazer Barnard beats his walking stick from side to side, smashing down the nettles and brambles that have spread over what was once the path. Vaguely, I hear the sound of gravel crunching, of laughter; I smell the scent of flowers mixed with the tang of the man I am following — the stench of fear, survival; of everything that was normal.

Finally, we arrive at the arched door. My heart thumps madly. A heavy iron padlock hangs from a chain around the old latch. I think of those that passed through the doors. I think of those that never came out.

Barnard glances at his watch. "Half an hour is all. Don't touch anything." He unlocks the padlock and removes the chain. He pushes open the door and a rotten smell escapes into the autumn air. Despite the vague warmth of the sun, goose bumps chill my skin. "Dead rat," he says, laughing when I crumple my face.

"I can't go in," I blurt out to Adam. I find myself gripping his arm. It goes some way towards providing the safe haven of contact I crave — the touch of someone who might understand. "I'll wait outside." I'm standing on the top step, teetering on the edge of the darkness beyond. Nothing could make me go in. Sweat erupts on my forehead, fear leaks into my veins. I stand steadfastly, arms crossed, face turned up to the sun.

Adam glances at me. "You're scared of a dead rat?"

"Yes," I say quietly. "I really don't like them." I accidentally catch a glimpse of the chapel's interior over Adam's shoulder. Light falls in coloured stripes from the stained glass above the altar, highlighting a fallen cross, stone steps, a table. I can't make out anything else because it's too dark — that, or my eyes won't let me see.

"Come in when the smell's cleared." He's disappointed to be going in alone. Adam clutches a clipboard and a Dictaphone. He gives me one last imploring look — perhaps because he's scared himself — and turns, disappearing through the arched door. The cold, dank atmosphere inside wraps its arms around him, pulling him in until he is completely out of sight.

I step away from the entrance and feel my heart going crazy in my chest.

"What is it you're really scared of?" Frazer asks, hacking as he speaks. He turns away, fumbling with a packet of Superkings. Eventually he gets one lit.

"Nothing," I say, shrugging. "I'd just rather wait in the sunshine."

"Think all them ghosts are going to come and get you, do you?" His wrinkled face puckers meanly.

My head whips up. "I don't know what you're talking about." I walk down a couple of stone steps. The edges are crumbling and lichen crawls over them. "*You're* not

230

going in. I'm sure Adam could use some local knowledge for his book."

"He'll figure it out. Eventually." Frazer Barnard laughs and coughs at the same time, still finding enough breath to draw on his cigarette. "Unless he dies of old age first."

Suddenly, there's a loud noise from inside the chapel followed by a yell. "Adam?" I call out, running back up the steps. I feel dizzy.

"I'm OK. Everything's OK." Adam's voice echoes from deep within the chapel. Someone calling out through the years. A lost voice.

Frazer shakes his head. "Touch nothing, I said."

"It's dark in there. He probably bumped something by accident."

"P'raps it's that young gal's body, eh? Come to get him." Frazer Barnard has a gruff Yorkshire accent, broad and loud, bitter and hard. I wonder if it's living in Roecliffe that has made him this way, or being keeper of the chapel that sets his cruel tone. He laughs. "As if a waif of a little girl could do any harm."

My mouth is dry. I don't feel very well at all. I sit on the step and drop my head between my knees. *Waif of a little girl*, I think. I bite my tongue until I taste blood.

"You all right, lass?" His compassion surprises me.

"I feel a bit faint." I drop my head and run my fingers through my short hair. "I'll be OK." I squint up at him, wondering how I could be so stupid as to allow myself to be seen by someone from the village. Barnard is silhouetted against the sky, steeped in as much history as the chapel. He rummages in his grimy tweed jacket pocket for something. God, I wish I'd not come on this stupid walk.

"Here," he says, pulling out a single pill and handing it to me. "Take it. I've got dozens."

"What is it?" But before Frazer replies, Adam comes striding out of the chapel. His face is contorted and his chest heaves inside his jacket.

"Frankie." That's all he says, breathless. Just my name. We stare at each other as if an entire story passes between us. I frown, ignoring Barnard's outstretched hand. Adam is telling me something. What has he discovered?

"You should come inside with me." His voice is suddenly flat. "There are some interesting . . . features." He stares at me for ages. No one speaks, not even Barnard, who is watching us. I hear the birds sing, the rustle of a breeze through the woods. Adam mumbles into his Dictaphone. I shake my head.

"She don't feel so good," Frazer finally says. I take the pill he's holding out and roll it between my fingers. Whatever it is, I have no intention of taking it. "Best be hurrying along, before she keels over." But Adam doesn't hear. He is already back inside the chapel. "Eat up, then," Frazer says, turning back to me, slumped on the stone steps. "I've got lots. It'll help your head. Help you forget everything," he whispers, grinding his cigarette butt into the lichen, not taking his eyes off me.

CHAPTER
THIRTY-ONE

Betsy never sat still in chapel. The only bit of going to say our prayers that she actually liked was the skip through the woods on the way there, and of course the skipping again on the way back. We weren't allowed to run.

She'd clutch my hand and strain at my arm, pulling to get ahead. I made her little gloves for winter, knitting them out of scraps of wool, unravelled old sweaters left behind by other kids. Sometimes they fell off, so I picked them out of the mud before the line of kids trampled them into the mush. I pushed them back on to her freezing hands. "Tanks," she'd say, skipping off until it happened again.

Summer would see Betsy in one of two flowery dresses. I sewed one of them — a patchwork creation cobbled together from whatever I could find in the drawers. The other dress came from a pile of clothes left by the gone children; the ones who didn't come back. If they were missing for a day or two, we helped ourselves to their stuff. Any sooner, and it wouldn't have seemed right.

Betsy looked a pretty sight, all strawberry-blond curls, eyes the colour of forget-me-nots, cheeks hand-painted. She giggled through those summer months, as if her little spirit was warmed by the long days, the hot sun, the times we played outdoors chasing each other through the woods and thickets.

But Betsy didn't like it when I went off to school. She cried when I left and, according to Patricia and Miss Maddocks, she curled up on her bed and whimpered until she knew it was time for the school bus to drop us at the end of the drive. Then she'd sit on the stone window seat and watch for me, just like I'd watched out for my father.

Betsy liked the school holidays best and, of course, Sundays, except for when we had to sit quietly in chapel for a whole hour and thank the Lord for our blessings. "Wassa blessin'?" Betsy whispered to me. She scratched her head fiercely.

"It's all the good things God gave you," I replied as quietly as I could. Mr Leaby preached above us, his arms flying about in the pulpit. One of the male carers turned round and told me to shut up. I didn't like him; didn't even know his name.

"But why do I have to count them?"

Betsy was nearly five. She knew some numbers and that B was for Betsy. She was slow to learn. "You just do," I told her. But she'd made me think. Why *did* we have to count our blessings? And what if we didn't have any to count in the first place?

Then I saw Betsy peeling her fingers away from her palm, mouthing the numbers that she could remember. She stared up at the chapel ceiling, gazing at the dusty oak beams as she totted up her blessings.

234

"How many?" I whispered as the first hymn started.

She thought for a second and stared straight at me. "One," she told me. "I counted it over and over to make sure." She grinned.

"One?" I said into her ear. Her hair got between my lips. "What is it?"

"You," she said.

The carers used the picnic as a week-long bribe to make us behave. After the service, if we'd been good and the weather was fine, we walked to the end of the bluebell wood where it opened into a patch of scrubby grass. Enough space for the girls to set out the rugs while the boys marked out a cricket pitch with their sweaters. If we were bad — and it only took one of us to step out of line — there were no tartan rugs, no packed-up food, no rustling packets of greaseproof paper to tear off the soft sandwiches, no plastic cups of squash that refused to stand up on the uneven ground, and no lazing around in the sun after we'd eaten. It would be at least another week until the prospect of fun loomed.

The picnics took place, I'd worked out, only about once a month. Lots of the boys were naughty, causing everyone to forfeit their fun. But when a picnic was planned, all the carers came along, even the ones that didn't do much looking after. They were the ones who lurked in the rooms down the forbidden corridor, wearing dark suits, talking in deep voices, using words I didn't understand.

"What's a conundrum?" I asked Patricia.

"It's a mystery," she replied.

"And what's a predica . . . predictament?"

"Predicament. That means a situation. Something you got yourself into. A pickle."

"And what's assaulted mean?"

Patricia stared at me. She snapped closed the book she was reading as if I were the biggest nuisance out. She shook her head and went to sit under the oak tree along with some of the men carers I didn't like. She whispered to them, glancing back at me.

Betsy crawled on to my lap and rested her head on my knee. She often slept after the picnic. Her belly was full of crisps and cake and all kinds of stuff that we didn't usually get. They were happy days, those Sundays after chapel. As long as someone hadn't been bad that week, as long as the weather was fine, as long as I could hear Betsy snuffling through the night, as long as no one was taken.

I'd never felt like this before. Was I ill? My head fuzzed up like cotton wool and my eyes wouldn't stay open. It was sweets day. I'd only been able to eat a couple, and so stashed the rest in my cupboard. Soon afterwards I felt groggy, strange, as if I wasn't me at all. I went to lie down on my bed.

When I woke, it was the middle of the night. It was the music that stirred me. My belly ached and folded in from hunger. I'd missed supper. I'd missed the fuss and noise of bedtime, and I was still wearing my clothes. I sat upright. Had I heard someone in the room? In the half-light, I saw Betsy lying in the bed beside me.

236

Breath puffed from between her lips. Her eyelids flickered.

"Who's there?" A chink of light fell across the floor from the landing outside. The curtains were drawn, rippling slightly from the open window behind. I couldn't see anyone.

There was music downstairs. A dull thud-thud. They were having one of their parties. Shrieks and whoops, overlaying the repetitive beat of the bass, pierced through the noise that we'd all learned to sleep through when the staff let their hair down. We liked it the next day, when they were all too tired and grumpy to be bothered with what we got up to.

The door suddenly opened and two figures were standing there, silhouetted by the light outside. I could see clearly that they were men. One had a bald head, one had shoulders the width of a house. I froze and my eyes stretched wide in the darkness, trying to see who they were.

"Who's there?" I whispered.

A flashlight shone in my eyes, blinding me. Then a hand was over my mouth, forcing my scream back down my throat. His fingers smelled of cigarettes and his breath stank of beer. I was tangled in arms and strange smells as the other man helped hoist me from my bed. I kicked and pushed and would have bitten too, had my mouth not been smothered.

This is it, I thought. *I am being taken by the night creatures. This is what it's like.*

I reached out for Betsy as I was half dragged and half carried past her bed. I cycled my legs, trying to break

237

free. They strapped my arms round my body and manhandled me from the bedroom.

"Thought you said she was dosed-up," one said. The other man grunted. His face was red and pockmarked from acne. He was young, maybe only nineteen or twenty. The bald one reminded me of my dad, and wheezed as he dragged me. His fat belly rolled over my legs as they carried me down the stairs and along the corridors. When we reached the forbidden passageway, the music got really loud. Some song I'd heard on the radio pounded my head.

"No!" I managed to scream as the hand on my mouth came away.

Then a sting as the hand skimmed my cheek. "Shut it, stupid," the older one said. "You want to get us all into trouble?" They stopped walking and my legs dropped to the floor. I tried to run for it, but they still had hold of my arms. I ducked my head to bite one of them but I got knocked back against the wall. For a moment, I saw nothing; just heard a tingling in my ears, saw a bright light in my eyes.

"Do as you're bloody well told." He hit me again. I nodded frantically, praying he would stop if I did what they said. When the grip loosened, when they muttered between themselves, I legged it down the corridor, back towards the light at the end, back towards my bed.

Then I was on my face, tasting the dust on the floor. They dragged me back by my ankles. My clothes rode up and my belly burned as my skin rasped along the wood. I bumped over a door frame and was hurled into the room where the music was. I saw legs all around me, smelled the beer, heard the calls as I was rolled over, my top up around my shoulders. When I tried to pull it down, I was kicked in the ribs. I froze, breathing in quick bursts. My eyes were unblinking, my mouth dry as chalk. I stared up and saw half a dozen faces peering down at me. Someone spat in my eye.

Then it all got muddled, out of order. I was suddenly naked, but don't know what happened to my clothes. I stood shaking until my legs ached, worried that everyone was looking. I pressed my hands against my chest. I don't know what came first — the laughing or the snap of the cane as my arms were hit down.

The chair was cold on my back and my wrists ached from the straps. I know I peed myself because I felt the warm pool settle under my bottom. The chair was tipped over, with me strapped in it. The wet ran up my back, soaked into my hair. Another few hits — some on my head, some on my shoulder, some from a boot. Some from a cane.

Then they ignored me. I was just left on the floor, bent through ninety degrees, the wood of the chair digging into my back. I shivered until my muscles ached. My eyes shot round the room, trying to take it all in, trying to figure out an escape. I saw Chef chatting with some other men. He wasn't wearing his uniform. Why was he letting them do this to me? I thought Chef liked me. And there was the man from the village shop, where we sometimes bought sweets. The others blurred into anonymous faces.

Was this where everyone got taken when the night monsters came? I was sobbing; more scared than I'd ever been in my life. The straps cut into my ankles. The pain wasn't pain any more. I wanted my dad.

They got on with their party. A *party*? I screwed up my eyes when I saw one of the men who had carried me from my bed kissing a woman. Patricia and Miss Maddocks weren't there. I called out their names but got belted in the head.

Eventually, I gave up screaming, even when one of the men hauled me upright again; even when he removed the straps and forced me to stand. I couldn't run. I was exhausted, groggy and fuzzy-headed. My legs wouldn't work and I didn't even care that I was naked; didn't care about anything as the room spun around me. It was as if I didn't have a body any more; it was just me in my mind, floating high above the room, wondering what was happening to that poor skinny girl down below as one of the men took off his trousers.

I saw her pain, watched the agony on her face. When she crumpled to the floor, he stretched her out again. The circle of onlookers clapped and cried out. There was blood. Her fingers and toes had turned blue, as if her veins had closed down. Her head flopped on a neck with no strength, and her heart struggled to beat slowly in her chest.

"Don't bring this one again," he said, zipping up. "She's a menace."

When I woke, I was back in my bed. Slowly, I turned my head to the side and saw Betsy's profile — her little snub nose, the pout of her young mouth. I reached out and brushed my fingers through her soft hair. There

240

they stayed, entwined in the locks, as I stared at the ceiling through bruised eyes, counting my blessings as tears flowed silently on to the pillow.

I came back, I said over and over in my head. *I'm one of the lucky ones.*

CHAPTER
THIRTY-TWO

The doorbell rang just as Nina finished tossing the salad. She would be cheerful, go some way to acting like a good hostess, for Mick's sake. She would pretend she was busy in the kitchen, visit the toilet, hide in the bedroom for as long as she could get away with. The thought of socialising made her feel sick, even if it was going to help secure a better financial future. Mick had suffered the classic starving artist jibe for enough years now. He was good at what he did and deserved to be recognised. This was his chance. However wretched she felt, Nina refused to ruin it.

"Right," she said, wiping her hands on a tea towel. She wouldn't put the fish under the grill until they were nearly ready to eat. It would only take a moment to cook the thin fillets. "Set the table," she reminded herself.

She heard Mick let their visitor into the hallway. The man sounded brash as he greeted Mick — almost a shout. She heard the usual exchange of introductions, envisaged the handshake. But then it fell completely silent. Nina wondered if they'd gone to the living room, but when she peeked in from the kitchen, it was empty. Mick would be hanging up his guest's jacket probably.

She closed the door again, not wanting to be watched while she was cooking.

Nina decided she would allow them to talk a bit more before she introduced herself. There was still enough to keep her occupied in the kitchen for another ten minutes or so. Then she heard voices coming from the living room, confirming they'd moved on. She hoped the dealer was looking at Mick's paintings. There were several pieces hanging on the walls. Nina grew excited at the prospect of Mick selling work at prices he'd never imagined. They'd talked again of an extension, perhaps a new bathroom; even with everything that had happened, Nina held on to the dream. It was all she had left.

She pressed her ear to the closed door, straining to hear what was being said. They were talking so quietly — discussing time, passing years, she thought — but she couldn't make out much. Mick was probably nervous, she guessed. He wasn't the best at promoting his work.

"Drinks right about now," Nina said, returning to the stove. She imagined Mick pouring from the decanter. She heard the chink of glasses and muttered toasts. "To Mick's good fortune." She raised her own glass of wine. Something positive in all this mess, she thought.

Nina washed her hands just as Josie came into the room. "Will you set the table, love?" She tossed some napkins at her daughter and opened the kitchen drawer. She rummaged through the bills, pens, and assorted oddments before finding her lipstick. In the mirror, she applied a coat of pale pink. It was Mick's favourite. She wanted to bring him luck, even if she wasn't having any of her own.

"Do I have to?" Josie grumbled, gathering the cutlery. She did it in spite of her protests, muttering that she'd only come down for some crisps, that she was talking to friends on Afterlife.

Nina stared at herself in the mirror and sighed. In the reflection behind her, through the door to the dining room, she saw Josie slowly arranging knives and forks on the table. A feeling grew in the pit of her stomach, a cross between rage, love and fear, and she had to clench her fists to stop herself lashing out. She wanted to smash everything up, destroy her life and everything in it before anyone else could. She shoved a hand into her pocket and pulled out the hairclip. She stared at it closely and then stuck the sharp end against the mirror. She dragged it hard against the glass.

"Ow," Josie squealed as a knife dropped to the floor, jabbing her foot. "That hurt."

Nina stuffed the clip back into her pocket, shaking, fearful, as if she had just caused her daughter's pain. She glared at herself, trying to get a grip. "This is Mick's night. Don't ruin it."

Mick paused in the kitchen doorway. Nina knew he was staring at her. When she turned, she thought he looked anxious, slightly pale. He was sweating.

"Not going so well in there?" Nina asked. She wondered if Mick was out of his depth, dealing with these London galleries.

244

"It's fine," he said unconvincingly. "I . . . I think we can work things out." Mick reached for a glass and filled it with cold water. He gulped as if he hadn't drunk for a week. When he'd finished, he said, "You look beautiful." He stamped a kiss on her cheek. "Thank you for going to so much trouble." He gripped her shoulders for a moment — the exact same gesture she had wanted to make to him — and went back into the living room without asking her to join them.

"*Let me introduce you, darling . . .*" Nina mocked, pulling a face. "Unless you're ashamed of me," she said stupidly, knowing that wasn't the case. Mick was just nervous. This was a very big deal for him.

Nina heard the men's voices again and decided it was time to make an appearance. She quickly fingered her hair as she walked past the mirror, noticing a thin scratch on its surface from the hairclip. A fracture in my perfect life, she thought bitterly.

She went into the living room.

The adrenalin hammered her heart long before she knew why. Nina felt as if she was striding across the room, but she'd actually stopped dead with her false smile dropping away. She stared at the guest, unable to move.

He slowly stood up and extended a hand to Nina. His face was blank. He was average height, she noticed, a little shorter than Mick, and everything about him was pointed and sharp, from his hands and feet to his spiky hair and chiselled nose; even each individual tooth appeared to be honed jagged. And he sent her into paroxysms of fear.

Nina forced her hand out in return. She had to stay in control.

She looked at him.

Was it?

Then he gave her a tight smile.

She tried to withdraw her hand, but it was too late. They were touching. He was already gripping her fingers between the points of his.

Surely not him. Her mind was playing tricks again.

The hairs on her neck prickled. She tried to focus on his face through the dizzy waves that were threatening to swamp her brain. She blinked, worried she might pass out. But her body was fighting back instinctively, driven by self-preservation, by survival.

It must be a mistake, she pleaded desperately in her head. *It can't be.*

"Welcome . . . to our home," Nina said, speaking as carefully as her trembling jaw would allow. Did he recognise her? It had been so long, after all.

"A real pleasure to meet you, Mrs Kennedy," he replied. Each word was precise, weaselled out of his thin lips like staccato bullets. Nina flinched.

She swallowed, trying to think, but her mind was a whirlpool of emotion. "Call me Nina," she said, glancing at Mick, who had completely forgotten to do the formalities.

"I'm Karl," he said. His eyes drooled and his chin angled forward. "Karl Burnett," he said.

The name sent her reeling.

He was here, in her home. How had he found her?

"Delighted," he continued, pausing for effect, "to meet you."

Nina pressed her other hand against the outside of her pocket. She felt the hairclip nestled inside. He'd sent it to her as a warning and now he was here, in her house, silently threatening her. Avoiding recognition wasn't an option. He knew exactly who she was. Worst of all, she thought, by being here, he was threatening her family. He could end it all with one private sentence whispered in Mick's ear.

For Mick and Josie's sake, she had to hold it together — at least until she'd had a chance to think what to do. Nina prayed for the evening to pass quickly, for the three of them to stay safe. She could hardly speak, her mouth was so dry.

Mick finally found his voice. "Darling, Karl owns a gallery on New Bond Street."

No he doesn't, she screamed in her head.

"Really?" she managed weakly, shooting a look at her husband. Mick seemed bowled over by the man, judging by his wide-eyed expression. She willed him to unconsciously pick up on the danger signals she was sending out. How could she tell him that Karl wasn't really interested in his paintings; that it was *her* he'd come to hang, not a landscape or delicate nude. She hated it that he was using Mick to get to her.

Nina breathed fast, clinging to the hope that if she acted normally, the evening might pass without trouble.

"I'm so pleased that there's been such interest in Mick's work recently." The gossamer-thin words barely made it across the room. Nina saw both men had drinks. She leaned against the dresser and poured herself a large gin and tonic.

Karl paced around the living room. His manner was confident and slick, his expression giving nothing away. A blank face sat atop bony shoulders that were capable of moving the world — Nina's world. He was dressed entirely in black. He touched a couple of ornaments, picking up a china bird that Josie had given to Nina last birthday. "Mick tells me you have a daughter." Then the smile again, drilling into Nina's heart.

The mention of Josie, the very fact he knew of her existence, made Nina erupt in a cold sweat. "Yes," she said, mustering all her resolve. "Would you like another drink?" She had to steer him away from talking about Josie.

Then it happened so quickly, yet seemingly in slow motion, that if asked to describe it later, Nina would only be able to tell of the deep ache in her heart, the fear rising as bitter as bile in her throat.

Josie sauntered into the room, lighting it up in her carefree, captivating way — a knack she'd had since she was able to walk. She paused briefly in the doorway, eyeing up who was there, until her father stepped towards her and wrapped his arm adoringly, protectively, around her shoulders. Mick, Nina thought, was glad of the reprieve Josie provided.

"This is Mr Burnett from London," Mick said, when Josie looked up at her father. Nina prayed that he'd sensed the tension between her and Burnett, picking up on the silent messages she'd been sending him. She just wanted this evening to end.

Josie, oblivious to everything, grinned. Her straight white teeth sat perfectly within full young lips. Nina held her breath. Her daughter had changed into a pretty summer outfit with a low-cut top. It was as if she hadn't even noticed her womanly curves before now. The white broderie anglaise bodice fitted snugly, sitting prettily over a colourful skirt that hung just above her knees. Wedge shoes gave Josie three extra inches and the light make-up she wore — the colours suggested by Nina only a week ago — made her look at least eighteen. Despite this, she still exuded innocence. Childishness on a woman's body. Nina clenched her teeth; felt the pressure growing in her head.

"Hello," she said sweetly. "It's very nice to meet you." As she had been taught, Josie politely held out her hand. Karl, however, ignored it and moved towards her with his arms wide open. He left a lingering double imprint on her face, one each side of her shimmering lips.

"Mick, Nina." He glanced at them both. "You have an absolutely stunning daughter. I'm jealous as hell." Karl's hands slid down Josie's bare arms and locked with her fingers. He leaned back, examining her, his devious eyes sweeping up and down her length.

Nina let out a little gasp. *Mick, do something!* Beads of sweat erupted on her face as Burnett leered at her daughter. *Take your filthy eyes off her*, she yelled but nothing came out. If she made a scene now, it would put them all in danger. No, she had to remain calm; get through the evening and give herself time to think, to get help, to protect Mick and Josie. It could all still, *somehow*, be an innocent mistake, a coincidence, couldn't it?

She excused herself and went into the kitchen.

"We could go away," she whispered through the steam of the vegetables as her trembling hand spooned them into a serving dish. "All of us. We could just disappear. He'd never find us." Nina played over how it could work, how she would explain everything to Mick. Then suddenly there was a big void in her mind.

Where were the others? Her hands shook as she removed the stack of plates from the warming oven. Frantically, she tried to recall the sentences passed by the judge. If they were all out, then this was just the start of the nightmare.

"Who are you talking to?" Mick was suddenly next to her. He seemed calmer now, although his knuckles were white as he gripped the worktop; the muscles on his forearms tight beneath rolled-up sleeves. Nina longed to fall into those arms, wishing she could take time back.

"Oh, no one," she sang rather too brightly. "Here, take these through to the dining room, will you?" She handed Mick a pair of serving dishes then froze. They stared at each other.

"Are you sure you're OK, Nina?" Mick frowned and swallowed. He walked away then stopped, turning back. "Nina?"

He sounded serious. Nina wasn't sure she could handle anything else.

"We're in this together, aren't we? Just the three of us, through thick and thin?"

Nina laughed, nervously, uncontrollably, filled with relief. "Yes," she said, touching his arm. "Of course we are."

"I couldn't lose you, you know."

Nina swallowed. Whatever happened, she must keep her cool. She needed to think. "Where's Josie?" she said. It suddenly struck her that Karl would be alone with their daughter.

Without waiting to hear Mick's reply, she grabbed the wine bottle and sped through to the dining room. Burnett glanced up as she entered. Was she imagining his slow blink, his leering smile, each suggesting a thousand threats?

Conversation bounced awkwardly between Mick and Karl. Nina dissected her food, spreading the fish to the edge of her plate. In all, she had consumed two tasteless mouthfuls. The whole evening was a nightmare, with Josie the only one apparently enjoying herself.

"So, Josie," Karl asked. His fingers toyed with the cutlery, and his legs jittered beneath the table. "What are your favourite subjects at school?"

"I love drama," Josie announced. Immediately, she fell into role. Her keen face spread wide as she thought of her passion. She'd loved acting, dancing and singing since she'd been able to walk. She leaned in across the table, pulling nearer to Burnett as if she were his leading lady. "I want to be an actress when I'm older."

"Do you now?" Karl flicked a glance to Nina, who quickly looked away.

"I auditioned recently and got the part of Roxie Hart in the youth theatre's production of *Chicago*. It's going to be on in the autumn."

"Drama queen, more like," Mick said, relieved not to be discussing art. Nina noticed how her husband sympathised with her mood. Her unease was clearly making him nervous too. They would lie in bed later, discussing the evening. Hopefully Mick would fall asleep, not so convinced he wanted to work with Burnett after all. Nina would lie awake, staring at the ceiling, remembering, watching the light seep around the curtain edges, too scared to close her eyes, planning what to do, fearful for them all.

"Thanks, Dad," Josie said. Her eyebrows drew together and her lips plunged into a pout. "Mum takes me backstage as often as she can with her work in make-up and special effects. She's just got an amazing contract with a big production company. I'm going to go to Pinewood with her. I might meet a director who —"

"Really?" Karl interrupted, turning to Nina. "You are successful in business as well as having a beautiful family. Perfect." Karl set down his knife and fork and raised his wine glass. "To the Kennedy family," he said precisely. "May they get everything they deserve."

CHAPTER
THIRTY-THREE

Sylvia hands me two paracetamol. She's been visiting her aunt, but now she's come back to school. She likes to use the last few days of half-term to catch up with things while it's quiet, she told me. Truth is, like the rest of us here, I don't think Sylvia has anywhere else to go.

"Get to bed," she orders. Her hands are propped on tilted hips and she's wearing lipstick that matches her scarlet nails. She sees me looking at her. "I was going out, but with you like this, I'm not so sure."

"Please don't cancel. I'll be fine." I glance at my watch. "Going anywhere nice?"

Her cheeks redden for a second. "There's this chap from the village. He wants to take me to the pictures." She glances in the mirror above the sickroom basin and puckers her lips. "Are you sure you'll be OK?" Without the girls here, Sylvia is a different person.

I nod that I'm sure.

It'll give me a chance to speak to Adam. Since we visited the chapel, since he let on that his book isn't just about the architecture of Roecliffe Hall, or local walks or wildlife, I haven't been able to get out of my head just what it is that he knows. He's aware of the murders, discovered that there were bodies, I know that much. But why is he so interested? Besides, I don't want to be alone up here in case that prowler comes back.

When Sylvia has gone, I leave sick bay, head down the main staircase, along several corridors, across the hallway, and down on to the lower level of the school. My spine prickles in the half-light. I feel along the wall for the light switch. I go up the rear staircase and along another corridor until I reach Adam's room. I knock and the door swings open.

"Adam?" I say. "It's me." *Me.* I wonder how we got so familiar.

I step inside but he's not there. It's bigger than my attic room and every available surface is covered in books. Textbooks, hardback books, old books, new books, paperback books, foreign books, modern glossy books, and ancient dusty books. I run my finger along a pile. Under the window there is an antique desk. His laptop computer glows pale blue. "Not one for tidying up," I whisper, intrigued by this glimpse into Adam's private life.

The bed is unmade and several days' worth of clothes lie crumpled up on the end. In the middle of the bed, beside his discarded jacket, lies Adam's Dictaphone. I reach down and pick it up. I look back at the door and turn the volume down to low. Heart thumping, I press play.

"*. . . Several altar cloths, stained, a broken crucifix, and on the tiles below the altar are a pair of . . . of old trainers. Nikes size ten. Near to where it apparently* *happened. Cigarette butts. Bottles. About thirty oak benches, rather ornately carved for a private chapel. The north window is . . ."* Then a familiar bang and cry reminds me of dashing up the chapel step to check if Adam was OK. I press fast forward for a second or two and then press play again. *". . . You should come inside with me. There are some interesting . . . features,"* he says loudly. It was when he was speaking to me outside the chapel. There's a pause, some breathing, then whispering. Adam talking privately into the machine. *". . . She's stunning . . . Her legs, her fingers, the pattern of her skirt. I do wonder about her, though."*

I press stop and toss the Dictaphone back on to the bed. When I turn, Adam is standing in the doorway.

"Oh! I came to see if you'd like to have a coffee with me in the girls' lounge?" My heart flips into my mouth and my cheeks burn like embers. Adam doesn't say a word.

He sits cross-legged on the floor of the boarders' living room. His shoulders slump forward as if he's totally relaxed about this. He spots a stuffed rabbit under an armchair and pulls it out. "Yours?" he asks.

"Hardly," I reply. "It belongs to one of the girls. They sit in that chair and pour out all their problems." Most of the pupils bring a cuddly toy to school with them, even the sixth-formers. "It's quite sweet that they need something to love." For some reason my eyes prickle with tears.

Adam hears my sniff, sees my lower lids brimming. He passes me a tissue from the box. "Do you want to sit in the chair and talk?"

I laugh, shaking my head, wishing I had the courage to say yes.

"Are you having second thoughts about the job?"

"Not at all," I reply, lying. "First thoughts are hard enough."

"Cryptic," he says, passing my coffee from the tray. He believed me when I told him I wasn't prying in his room, that I'd just come to see if he fancied some company. I half wonder if he wanted me to hear that recording.

"So," I say, trying to sound bright. "Tell me about the chapel. Why does it intrigue you so much?"

Adam sighs and draws a long sip of coffee. He stares at me over the rim. This game we are playing — you say first — hangs silently between us. We both sense that the other has an interest in the place, and, for different reasons, an interest in the other.

"The chapel's a very important part of the story I'm researching." He hesitates for some reason. "It's where the murders took place. One in particular." Hearing him say it makes it sound like folklore, as if none of it happened. "But it's real people I need to speak to now. I want to find locals who remember what happened."

My head whips up. Has he found anyone with a story to tell? Suddenly, I am overwhelmed with curiosity.

"Today, I wanted to get a sense of place," he continues. "To . . ." He pauses, clears his throat. "To really feel where it all happened. It was awful, Frankie.

I could virtually smell the fear in there." Adam bows his head. "*Her fear*," he whispers.

"You could?" It's not surprising the villagers called for it to be boarded up and never used again.

"It was what made me spin round and knock over that huge candlestick." Adam's face betrays more than merely an interest in writing a local history book. Anguish overlaid with sorrow.

"Why Roecliffe?" I ask, trying to figure him out. I have to be careful.

He thinks for a moment, draws a deep breath. "Have you ever felt that a place has such a pull on you, that there's something so huge you need to discover, you'd travel from one end of the earth to the other to find out?"

My heart kicks up a gear; my lips part, but I can't find the right answer.

"Roecliffe Hall has dragged me kicking and screaming all the way from Australia, Frankie. What began as a quest on the internet, a desire for knowledge, an unravelling of my past, has ended up as an obsessive mission to dig down to the tiniest detail. There are things I need to find out, for my own peace of mind."

I stare at him, imploring him with my eyes to continue.

"I'm looking for my sister," he confesses, once again unemotional, as if he's lost a book or a tie. Adam reins himself back, whereas I can't even let go. "She lived here a long time ago, when it was a children's home."

He drains his coffee, as if the answer might be found at the bottom of the mug.

I finally manage to speak. My voice is thin and vapid. I don't feel real. "Your sister?" I say, standing up, shaking, making my way to the door by holding on to the wall. I have to get out. "I doubt you'll find her here."

The last Sunday of half-term and school explodes with noise, chatter, clutter, weeping mothers and excited girls. The first-years are thankfully happy to be back, used to school life, refreshed from their break. The older girls get on with settling back into the school routine, sharing stories, waving a casual goodbye to their parents.

Lexi's father doesn't come inside with his daughter. He doesn't even wait to watch as she drags her bag up the steps of the front entrance. "Hey," I say. "Did you have a good time?" She was finally picked up the day after her fright. Since then, there haven't been any more strange faces appearing at windows.

"It was OK, I suppose," she says. I help her heave her bag over the threshold. "I was on my own for most of it." I escort her to her dorm and help her unpack the things she's brought back to school. At the top of the pile is a gift box of expensive-looking shampoo and conditioner. "For you," she says, handing me the silver box. "The stuff you gave me was horrid." She grins. "I did what you said and put it in my dad's girlfriend's shampoo bottle."

"And?" I take the cap off and inhale. It reminds me of the beauty products I used to buy. I give her a grateful hug.

"My dad told her that her hair smelled gorgeous and they disappeared for hours. I just can't win. He wishes I didn't exist."

"Nonsense," I tell her, wondering exactly when it is that someone becomes invisible, even if they haven't actually gone anywhere at all.

It's the blue hairband and braces that remind me, and the long blond hair — a mental note to ask questions when I next saw them. It's been a while since I noticed the girls in the IT room — when Lexi was sick — but the image from their monitor is still emblazoned on my mind. I even tried to get on to the website myself from the computer in the girls' lounge, but the site was denied access. Some over-zealous IT technician, I supposed, or fate telling me to leave well alone.

"Will you tell Mr McBain?" The girls' eyes widen and droop apologetically, simultaneously — a teen device that won't wash with me. I know how most of them work.

"That depends," I say. I don't like doing this but I have a burning need, a desire so deep that it may, just may, help me fill in a tiny portion of the desperate hole that has become my everyday life.

"On what?" the second girl asks. They both stand in front of me, hands clasped at their waists.

"On me having a go," I say as if it's quite normal for a woman of my age to be asking such things. They look at each other and I catch the first quiver of smiles on their faces. Relief.

"You're not serious?" the taller one asks.

"Why not?" I try to sound indignant. "You don't want Mr McBain to know that you were messing about in his class, do you?" It's a horrible thing to do, but I can't help myself.

"Of course not, but if you tell him we were on that site, we'll just deny it."

"And you think he'll believe you over me, do you?"

"Yes, because technically, you can't get on it through the school firewall. All sites like that are banned." The girls pull faces, half from the thought of inappropriate websites and half because of nervousness. They don't like being blackmailed any more than I like doing it.

"Then how come I saw it on your computer?"

"Because we're experts."

"Geeks," the blonder one says. "Nerds, you know, tech-heads. That's what we do."

"So you have a way to log on even though it's not allowed in school?" I'm incredulous and, unlike these two, not very technically-minded. I always thought if something was blocked it was blocked.

"Sure. We've set up our own proxy server. As long as the IT admin doesn't find out the address, we're safe. The only reason we got sprung was because Lexi got sick and you saw our screens. Mr McBain always stays at the front of the class." The girl leans against the wall. "So are you going to rat on us?"

"Rat?" I ask.

"You know, tell tales. Dob us in."

"Tell tales," I repeat slowly. "No, girls, I won't do that."

I weigh them up. They are pretty enough, pleasant enough, dressed smartly enough despite the usual customisation that goes with school uniform — shortened tie, turned-up collar, pushed-up sleeves. Like every single teenage girl in this school, they make my heart bleed. I sigh. "Your secret's safe with me. But I do want to go on that website and I need your help."

They look at each other and nod. "Deal," the taller one says. "I'm Fliss and this is Jenny. Welcome to Afterlife." Fliss holds out her hand and I tentatively shake it. It won't be long now, I tell myself.

CHAPTER
THIRTY-FOUR

Nina dropped a plate. It fell from the top of the stack that she was holding and tumbled in slow motion on to the floor tiles. Shards of china exploded across the kitchen. She saw every piece skid and slide and disappear under the table, the sideboard, the fridge.

"I'll get that," Mick said, seemingly appearing from nowhere again. "How do you think it's going?" He pulled Nina against his chest and squeezed her tightly as if he wouldn't see her again for weeks. He kissed her mouth. She didn't respond. "Are you OK?" He removed a single shard of china from her fingers.

"I'm fine." Nina reanimated and bent to collect the rest of the broken plate. She cut her finger and blood seeped immediately, thick and dark, dripping on to the tiles. She sucked the wound.

"Here," Mick said, producing a sticking plaster from the cupboard. "You're exhausted, honey. I'll bring coffee through in a few minutes. Josie's already said good night." Mick seemed in need of a break too.

Nina let out a jagged sigh of relief that at least their daughter was out of the way. But she wished Mick wasn't implying she go back and talk to Burnett. He was right, though. She was so tired she could fall asleep standing up, but that didn't mean she would trade the kitchen for sitting down in the same room as that man. She made a feeble protest that really, she would rather make the coffee.

"I won't be long," Mick said. Nina knew there was no point protesting. She had to help Mick out here. He didn't know it, but they were both in danger. Reluctantly, Nina went back into the living room. Burnett had left the table and was staring at a group of Mick's earlier works hanging over the fireplace.

"They're very different to what I would have expected," he commented, glancing at Nina as she hovered nervously near the door. "Not as . . . sensual as some of your husband's works have been, I believe."

Nina shrugged. "He has many others."

It was a poor defence, Nina thought, but she didn't care what Burnett thought of Mick's art. She just wanted him to go.

"Then I insist on seeing them." Burnett approached her. "I already told your husband that I want you to show me his paintings alone. Artists are so hopeless at promoting themselves." Karl turned and scanned the artwork above the fireplace again. "He agreed completely."

"Just take him to the studio," Mick suddenly whispered from behind. He must have heard. "Once he's seen them, he'll probably just go."

Nina shook from the inside out. *No, please,* she begged silently. *Don't make me.* She was grateful, at least, that Mick seemed to have also taken a dislike to him. Her feet dug into the carpet as Mick pushed gently in the small of her back, urging her towards Burnett. The other man's arm extended and folded easily around Nina's shoulders. Her skin crawled.

"Lead on," Burnett said. His pale hair fell over one eye, obscuring half of his delighted expression. He grinned, pushing back the wayward hair. "Tonight is turning into a real treat indeed."

Mick opened the French doors that led on to the decked area outside. Warm estuary smells washed inside as Nina and Karl stepped out into the humid evening. The sun had already dropped behind the spinney of trees beyond their garden, so Mick flicked on the outside lights to illuminate the path to his studio. As soon as they came on, they went out again.

Mick groaned. "A fuse has blown. Or could be a faulty bulb," he said, turning to go to the understairs cupboard to check. But he stopped, reaching into his pocket. "You'll need this," he said to Nina, holding out his studio key. A three-way glance shot between them as Karl led Nina out into the darkness.

Nina swallowed and watched as her shaking hand reached for the key. It didn't seem like her hand. How she longed to make a grab for her husband's fingers. Didn't he know what he was doing by sending her out into the night with this man?

"Thank you," she said quietly and, for a brief moment, she thought she saw Mick hesitate; thought she saw doubt in his eyes as he glanced at Burnett and then back to her. But no, Mick just walked off to the fuse box in the hall.

The grass brushed a cool fringe around Nina's ankles. Silently, she led the way to the studio, knowing exactly where all the rocks were that marked the edge of the flower borders. She and Mick had set every one of them last summer.

I could make a grab for one, she thought, and smash it on his head. It would all be over before it began. Mick would understand. I'd tell him everything. We could all go away —

"You have a very pleasant garden," Burnett commented beside her. Nina didn't know how he knew — it was quite dark with the lights off. "In fact, I'd go so far as to say your whole life is very pleasant." His voice was deeper now, thicker, and weighted with something sinister. She didn't reply.

They reached the wooden studio and Nina felt for the padlock. She fumbled and twisted it round, but she couldn't get the key into the lock.

"Allow me." Now Burnett was talking as if he were her gentle lover, offering to unfasten a stubborn zip or tight buckle. His nimble hands were suddenly wrapped over hers, skilfully removing the key from her fingers and inserting it into the padlock. "There," he said into her ear. "Easy."

When they were inside the studio, Nina felt for the light switch. She frantically flicked it on and off but nothing happened. "It must be on the same circuit as the garden lights. We may as well go back up because you won't see the paintings." Nina made for the door.

"I can see everything I need to," Burnett replied. His voice had hardened again.

Nina stopped and faced him. The light from the kitchen window drizzled a pale streak across Burnett's face, highlighting his sharp nose and angular jaw. She saw his pupils flick over her, no doubt seeing the same eerie outline on her as she could see on him.

Without a word she turned to leave, but an unexpected band of pain around the top of her arm stopped her.

"I said, I can see everything I need." Burnett levered Nina against him. "This is all the art, all the beauty, all the convincing and proof I need. Your husband's skill doesn't lie in his paintings." Burnett laughed. His breath smelled sour, like the mudflats at low tide. "It lies in his choice of wife."

Nina whipped her face away. She screwed up her eyes — unable to cry, unable to scream. What did he mean — Mick's choice of wife? It wasn't coincidence that he had come to their house, and neither was it coincidence that he was using her husband as a way to get at her. He had no real interest in Mick's art. For twenty years she had tried to deny that this moment would ever happen. A comfortable existence, a loving family, her own home and business had left her with no reaction, no instinct, no grand plan. Even McCormack had failed her when it came down to it.

"I . . . I don't know what you mean."

Burnett laughed deeply. He pulled her closer still and prised her face round with his fingers clipped beneath her chin. "Haven't you even thought about me once over the years?"

Nina shook her head. Words were out of reach.

"Well, I've thought about you," he continued. "I've had your little-girl charms in my head every day for the last two decades." He was so close that Nina could smell — almost *taste* — the sweat on his face. "Thought about what I would do to you when I found you."

He pulled Mick's work chair towards him and sat down. It creaked under his weight. He yanked Nina down towards him, but she suddenly whipped her arms away and kicked him in the shin.

"No!" she screamed, lunging for the door. Before her hand was even on the handle, Burnett grabbed hold of her again, this time pulling her roughly down on to him as he sat in the chair. She hated the feel of his muscles against her legs.

"I thought of nothing but you during those lonely nights," he crooned, stroking her hair, tucking it behind her ears. "And life's been good to you, Mrs Nina Kennedy." He snapped out the syllables of her name. "You've hardly changed a bit." Burnett dragged a finger up her cheek, through her hair, pinning it back at the temple as if a clip were in place. "And I hope you liked the gift I sent you. Pretty, isn't it?"

Nina swallowed, nearly choking on her own spit. She thought she was going to pass out.

"Do you know what it's like to have two decades of your life taken from you because of . . ." Burnett panted stale breath in her face. "Because of a *little girl*?"

Nina shook her head. She couldn't look at him. Her body was stiff with fear.

"I spent nineteen years, four months and seventeen days in that shithole because of you." He suddenly stood, and Nina was pushed back against the wooden wall of the studio. Something crashed from a shelf beside her.

In the dim light, Burnett tracked his finger over a canvas propped on an easel. "I don't care much for your husband's paintings," he said quite normally, as if he were choosing something for his living room. "And I don't care about your airhead daughter, either." He picked up the large canvas and carried it across the studio to Nina. "But I do care about *you*. Life won't be so good any more."

Nina let out a little whimper. It didn't sound like her voice. Her fingernails dug into the rough-sawn wood of the studio wall.

"You are going to die." He said it quietly, although it expanded to fill the entire studio, bursting through the thin walls and out into the night. "Tell anyone, and your daughter dies first." Burnett drew a line with his finger across his veined neck. "She looks like you," he said pensively.

"Keep your filthy hands off her." Nina could hardly speak.

"Oh, she's too old for me now. You should know that, Nina." He reached out and caressed her face. "Once you're dead, I'll be on my way."

Burnett slammed his foot through the large canvas just as the lights came back on. Nina stared at the painting as her eyes adjusted to the brightness. It was the beautiful picture that Mick had done of her.

Burnett's greedy eyes drank up every inch of naked flesh that hadn't been destroyed by his boot. There was a gash right through Nina's heart.

"You'll just have to tell Mick you had an accident, won't you?" Burnett pushed the canvas and watched as it toppled flat on its face.

"You're evil," Nina sobbed. "Pure evil." Fighting hard against the terror binding her muscles, she turned and ran out of the studio, through the floodlit garden, and up towards the house. She batted away the tears as they poured from her eyes — tears of fear and anger because her perfect life was being destroyed. She held back the wail that filled her chest, and tripped as she ran through the grass.

How did he find me?

As she came up to the back door, she saw Mick through the kitchen window. Nina was sure of only one thing — that by the time she got inside, she must appear composed and calm, as if nothing at all had happened, as if she had had a perfectly pleasant time in the studio with Burnett. Nina knew that when she faced her husband, she must be a different woman entirely.

CHAPTER
THIRTY-FIVE

I tried to tell them. It took two days before I could get the words out. They thought I had laryngitis. Patricia gave me some medicine.

"And Chef was there," I told her. She looked at me for a moment, shook her head, then decided she didn't have time to listen to the rest. When Miss Maddocks came on duty, she told me off for messing up my clothes.

"What are these doing crumpled and bloody under your bed?" She whipped out the stiff, sticky garments that I'd been wearing when they took me. She screwed up her nose at the smell.

"Those men hurt me," I whispered. "And Chef was there."

Miss Maddocks stared at me, stretched her mouth in thought. Then she went around the dormitory harvesting dirty clothes, picking up toys off the floor. "When will you girls learn," she mumbled. "Mess, mess, mess."

"Miss Maddocks," I begged. "Please listen. They did bad things to me." I started to cry. "Things they shouldn't do." They were tears of frustration. Why wouldn't she listen? Why hadn't any of the other children told?

"Ava Atwood, you are the biggest tittle-tattle I know. One day those dogs are going to have a feast of your tongue."

Men from the council came. An inspection, Patricia told us. We had to scrub the place from top to bottom, even the horrid old dusty rooms that never got used. The building was huge and we weren't usually allowed in half of it. Betsy trotted after me, too young to be of any real help.

"What's a spekshun?" she asked.

"I don't know," I admitted. "But I don't like it much if it means we have to do all this cleaning." I slopped a wet mop on the old floorboards. A warm musty smell rose from the wood. Betsy jumped in the wet bits and made footprints in the dry areas.

There were half a dozen of them, five men and one woman, all wearing dark suits. We were made to line up in the dining room and sing a song while they drank coffee. I recognised one of the men, remembered his red nose, the brown flecks on his forehead. I screwed up my eyes.

"Very commendable," one of them said to the home director, Mr Leaby. We only ever saw Mr Leaby when there was an emergency or someone from the council came. "You're running a tight ship."

There was a clatter of crockery as they finished, a clap of hands as one of the older male carers sent us away, and then the people from the council spread like an infestation of beetles throughout our home. They spent three days observing what went on, watching how the staff dealt with us, poring over files and accounts in the office, and making a note of what we were fed. It was the best few days of my life at Roecliffe. We ate better food, all the staff were nice to us, not just Patricia and Miss Maddocks, and they even played games and allowed us to watch what we wanted on television.

And then my father came.

"My little Ava bird," he said, standing in the doorway to the living room. They'd lit a fire. It was warm and cosy and Chef had made us cakes. I was sitting on the floor with Betsy. We'd been given a jigsaw puzzle to do. It was new because of the inspection. I had my hand over half a face and a bit of sky. I was forcing a piece in.

"Dad?" I said quietly. Was I seeing things?

There were two men from the council sitting at the other end of the room. I stood up, not taking my eyes off him in case he disappeared again. My legs fizzed from pins and needles. "Dad, is it really you?" I walked over to him. He was still wearing that old sheepskin coat.

"Ava bird, how you've grown!" He held out his arms and blanketed me in a hug that I'd dreamt about for years.

"I've been waiting for you," I told him. On my fingers, pushed deep into the shaggy lining of his coat, I counted the years. "I've waited for five years, Dad." I wanted to hit him, but my arms went limp at the sight of him. "Have you come to take me home now?"

272

"I've come to see Patricia," he said. His eyes darted around the room. My heart slopped from my chest, into my belly, and down into my feet. I couldn't even cry.

"She's not here," I said. "It's her day off." I knew all the staff schedules; knew when to keep out of the way when the nasty ones came on duty.

"Damn," my dad said. "When's she back?" He pulled a packet of cigarettes from his inside pocket and put one between his lips. It wiggled as he spoke. "I need to see her." His eyes darted everywhere, as if doing that would make Patricia appear.

Grudgingly, when he realised that he'd had a wasted journey, Dad drove me to McDonald's. On the way, he told me that he and Patricia had got married two years ago.

"But she left me soon after," he said, adding a third sachet of sugar to his coffee. I had a Coke and a cheeseburger. We were sitting in the smoking area and it made me cough.

I didn't say anything about him getting married, about him not telling me, about him not even asking me to the wedding. He showed me a photograph of it, all crumpled in his wallet. "Doesn't she look beautiful?" he said.

That would explain that hairdo, I thought, remembering, noticing the way it was pinned up, ringlets at her cheeks. Ages ago she had come into work looking like that, but a bit less neat, and with rosy cheeks. There was a boy in the photo, wearing a smart suit.

What's worse? I wondered after I told Dad that the photograph was nice, that Patricia looked pretty, that I was happy for him even though she had left him; what's worse, I thought, swallowing away the lump in my throat, your dad getting secretly married, or being raped by a stranger?

I wasn't sure. And to be honest, I wasn't sure if I'd even been raped. I'd seen some things on the news, and at school I'd overheard the bigger girls gossiping. What I didn't understand was that, in all the cases I'd heard about, the victims had wanted to die. I'd felt a lot of things, but not that.

The first time Betsy went missing, it was for a whole day. They found her up a tree, stuck like a kitten. She clung on to the knotty branch of the apple tree, her arms and legs wrapped round it. Her face was pressed into the bark.

"I wanted an apple," she wailed. Patricia called for the gardener to fetch a ladder. "And I was going to get you one," she told me. Instead, what she got was a whipping by one of the nameless nasty carers, and an early bedtime with no supper. I saved her some sausage and some bread.

I sat on the edge of her bed and took them from my pocket. The sausage had gone cold and was covered in fluff. Betsy didn't care. She nibbled at it and cried, telling me she wanted to go home, wherever that was. I couldn't help her, and that made me angry. When I got angry, I bound it all up and stashed it deep inside. If I couldn't help myself, how was I supposed to help her?

274

Like everyone else, we just waited for one day to turn into the next.

That sausage was pretty much the last thing, apart from sweets, that Betsy ate for a year. The next time she went missing was one winter evening. She was back in her bed by morning, seemed fine, stared at her cereal, so I didn't ask questions, didn't think to probe into the secrets that lay behind her silent eyes as she drizzled milk off her spoon. I knew better than that by now, and besides, there was nothing to say. Simply nothing to tell about the ones who got taken. They went, they came back, they got on with life. What else were we to do? And if they didn't come back, there was certainly nothing else to be said — just a race for their clothes, their toys, and, if we were lucky, a bag of sweets left behind in their cupboard.

When I told Miss Maddocks that Betsy wasn't eating, that she was getting thinner, she stared at me. She carried on filling out the forms. Some tales, I'd learned over the years, weren't even worth telling.

CHAPTER
THIRTY-SIX

I'm risking my job as well as expulsion for Fliss and Jenny. But they're up for it, especially when I tell them I'll give them twenty pounds each to keep their mouths shut. "Even if Mr Palmer strings you up by your necks and whips your bare backs with a willow branch?"

"We're not stupid." Jenny's voice is crisp and sieved of all lazy accents. Fliss wears an expensive perfume and carries the latest iPod.

The girls look at each other as if I'm their mother; as if I'm so old they can't contemplate ever being my age. *Yeah, right, Mum,* they would say before skulking off to their rooms to text or instant message their mates.

"It's probably best if we go to the IT room now," Jenny says. "It's nearly study time and won't look too odd if we're in there. If anyone asks why you're there with us, just say one of us came to get you because the other was feeling ill."

"I'm excellent at fake fainting," Fliss adds with a smile that is no doubt costing her parents thousands in orthodontic treatment.

"You'll only have to do this the once," I tell them. "I won't bother you again." I flicker a smile back, not wanting them to think I'm weird or stalking someone online. They don't need to know reasons and, with twenty pounds pressed into their palms, I doubt if they'll ask why.

The IT room is hot and humming and, thankfully, empty. Jenny boots up a terminal and Fliss drags over a couple of extra chairs so we can all see the monitor. Fliss looks at me sympathetically. "There are websites that adults go on, you know, to meet people their own age. Do you want me to find one of those for you?"

I shake my head. "No. You know the site I want." I glance at the door. "Can you hurry?" Several teachers pass by, glancing in through the square of glass. If Mr McBain comes in, there'll be questions that no amount of fainting will disguise.

"OK," Fliss says, nudging Jenny. When the terminal is ready, Jenny brings up an internet window and types with lightning speed. Her fingers dance their way to an unknown website, where she enters usernames and passwords and then, suddenly, a log-in screen resolves in front of us.

"You're going to need an account," Jenny says, sighing. "That means you have to think of a nickname for yourself and enter lots of details. It'll take time." The girls are already fidgety.

"Can you log in to yours, so I can have a look around?" I assume they have an account because I saw them on it before. If this works, then I know I'll want to make one of my own, somehow find a way to come back to the site often. I rein in my anticipation, trying to keep my breathing quiet as I lean close to the monitor.

"Sure," Jenny says and again her fingers slide swiftly across the keys as she enters her username and password.

"Oh my God," Fliss shrieks, and suddenly it's as if I'm not there. "Look, he left you flowers."

"I adore him *so* much," Jenny replies, blushing the same colour as the bunch of roses that are on her virtual doorstep.

"They cost a whole load of credits. He must really like you."

I watch the pair immersed in their oh-so-real world that doesn't exist outside of their minds. To Jenny, the flowers mean as much, if not more, than if the boy in question had hand-delivered the bouquet. I watch as she clicks to accept the gift. A messenger boy character asks if she would like to send a gift in return.

"Oh, make him wait," Fliss advises. "Play hard to get."

I clear my throat and they turn to me. "Is it possible to find someone specific?"

"Sure. There are lots of search options." Jenny wiggles the mouse pointer over the flowers. In another two clicks, they are in a vase in her pink virtual bedroom.

"But you can't be that person's friend unless they accept you. It's a safety thing."

I nod, smiling, willing away the tears. "That's good."

Fliss looks at me oddly then pulls a packet of tissues from her blazer. "Take these, miss." The girls eye each other warily, feeling sorry for me. Jenny brings up an advanced search form.

"Do you have a username to search for?" she asks.

I think hard, blowing my nose. "No, I don't." Is that it then? I wonder. A brief glimpse into another world; a world with a lure so strong, I can feel the tug in every cell of my heart.

"You can still search using a real name. But if you're looking for a Jane Smith, then expect to trawl through hundreds of results."

The girls are being kind, yet I sense their impatience. Jenny's fingers are poised above the keys, the cursor blinking in the box. I look at each of them, wondering if their mothers are thinking about them at this particular moment, hoping they are enjoying school, that they are eating properly, that they have friends, that they are doing their homework, that, most of all, they are happy.

"Why don't you phone your parents later?" I suggest. "Tell your mums that you love them." Jenny and Fliss don't actually laugh although I can tell they want to spray out a giggle. But deep within them, I see a glimmer of thought, as if maybe it's not such a stupid suggestion.

"Mine's on holiday in Florida. She won't be up for hours."

"And my mum's always in meetings. She'll get really mad if I interrupt her." Fliss picks at her nails. The varnish is coming off.

"I bet they love you so much," I say wistfully.

"Miss, we don't want to be rude but if a teacher comes in . . ." Jenny pulls a face. "Do you have a real name I can search for?"

"Yes. Yes I do," I say, standing up and leaning over Jenny to get a better view of the screen. This is it, I think. This is the moment when the past catches up with the present, when everything I've been holding back becomes real. I hold my breath, close my eyes. Then, with my lips close to her ear, my voice not much more than a warm whisper, I say, "I want you to search for a Josephine Kennedy."

CHAPTER
THIRTY-SEVEN

Nina did the washing-up twice. She scrubbed the table and swept the floor. She rummaged in the cleaning cupboard until she found polish that made the dining table shine and the windows gleam. She took the rubbish to the dustbin, emptied the dishwasher for the second time, vacuumed the living room carpet and the upholstery, as well as swiping away fine threads of cobwebs from the ceiling with a feather duster. She took to the door handles with brass cleaner, and bleached and cleaned the downstairs toilet. She put the tablecloth and linen napkins they had used at dinner into the machine and put them on a boil wash.

At 2a.m., Nina sat on the edge of a cane chair overlooking the garden. The garden lights leading down to the studio were still on.

"Hey, what are you doing up?"

She turned. Mick was beside her, wearing only his check pyjama shorts. His face was puffy with sleep. She welcomed his closeness yet wanted to shove him away. Nina's thoughts spun as fast as the washing machine. It had been the worst evening of her life — *nearly* the worst — and she hadn't a clue what she should do. Her priority was to keep her family safe.

"I've been clearing up." Nina didn't recognise her own voice. Cleaning like a whirlwind was her way of blocking out what was happening. What had always been going to happen, if only she'd stopped to think about it. She'd been wearing a blindfold, conning herself, her husband, her daughter.

"But we already did the washing-up. I heard noise." Mick glanced around the spotless room and frowned. "You've been cleaning at this hour?"

"I wanted to get rid . . ." Nina turned and stared back out of the window. "I wanted to get it done."

Mick caught her chin with his finger and turned her to face him. He squatted beside her chair. "Are you upset about something?" His breathing was on a similar precipice to hers — jerky, shallow, tight.

Nina shook her head. She couldn't look into those eyes, the same ones that had watched her transform from young woman to mature businesswoman and mother. "I'm fine," she said, forcing a smile. "Just tired."

"It was too much for you tonight." Mick sighed. "I wish I'd never agreed to the stupid meeting in the first place." He stared down the garden, following Nina's gaze. Then he turned and left a kiss on her cheek. It was slow, vaguely sorrowful, loaded with regret. "If it's any consolation, I have to do some paintings for him."

"Oh!" Nina's cheeks flushed. "Well . . . that's great," she added, feeling guilty that Mick was trying to play down his success. This was terrible news.

"He says he has clients lining up to buy artwork that's, well, a little different." Mick shifted and folded

282

his arms. "He's asked me to do some paintings that will fill a gap in the market."

"That's great," Nina said flatly. She didn't want to sound too downbeat, but this was the worst possible outcome. Explaining to Mick was not an option. Normally, she'd sleep on problems, but this time there would be no restful separation of night and day, no recharging, no bright-eyed decision-making while consulting the rest of the family. How dare Burnett use Mick to get to her. He was gutless as well as deranged.

Mick hugged her — a tight, close embrace that to Nina symbolised both the end and the beginning. Tears made her vision blur, obliterating the very centre of the life she adored. "Oh Mick," she said, hiccupping back a sob.

"What is it, love?" He held her at arm's length. Nina saw a window of opportunity, a moment in their lives when she could be totally honest with her husband. Did he sense her despair?

But Nina remained silent, unable to utter a single word to describe how she felt. She was flotsam on the tide, heading inexorably to a whirlpool that would suck her down into the darkness. She knew she was about to drown. She knew she would have to go alone.

"Come to bed. I won't sleep properly knowing that you're downstairs. I'm sorry tonight was stressful." Mick stood, pulling Nina up with him. His hands trembled as he guided her towards him.

"Mick, there's something I have to tell you." Nina was cold in his arms. Her back was rigid, and her eyes glassy and staring.

"Go on."

Nina sighed. "You're going to kill me but . . ." She pressed her hands over her face. It had to be done. There was no room for emotional leakage. "It was an accident and . . ." She let out a sob, not entirely forced. "When I was showing Karl your work down in the studio, it was dark and I stumbled and knocked over . . ." Nina prised apart her fingers a little, so her voice wouldn't be muffled. She didn't want to have to say it twice. "I knocked over the beautiful painting you did of me and when I tried to save it, my foot went straight through the canvas." Further sobs joined into one cry. From the heart. "Oh Mick, I am so sorry. I didn't want to ruin the evening by telling you earlier."

"Nina, Nina, Nina." Mick pulled his wife to him and held her as tightly as he could. He felt her ribs strain against his arms as she breathed. "That explains why you came back from my studio looking as if you'd seen a ghost. For a moment, I thought that Karl had said something to upset you or even made a move on you." Mick was almost laughing with relief. "And for heaven's sake, don't worry about the canvas. I can repair it so you'll hardly know it happened." He kissed her neck and told her not to be silly, not to worry, that everything was going to be all right.

"Thanks, Mick," she whispered into his shoulder, knowing that it wouldn't.

She must have slept because she didn't remember it getting completely light. She'd seen the first streaks of dawn push through the sides of the curtains, heard the

284

milkman hum and clink down the street, and felt the bed rock a little as Mick prised himself from under the duvet. When he didn't return, Nina assumed he'd got up early to work.

Then she remembered.

The grace that a couple of hours' sleep had provided slid from her as quickly as the down quilt. She got up and went into the bathroom. She turned on the shower and stared into the mirror while she waited for the water to heat up. Gradually, her face disappeared as steam filled the bathroom.

"Gone," she whispered, opening the glass door and stepping into the hot flow.

Nina allowed the water to flood over her, soaking her hair, flattening it on her shoulders. She dragged her hands down her face — an attempt to wash away the grainy tiredness. It didn't work.

Last night's food — not that she'd eaten much — sat heavily in her stomach. She thought she might be sick. Nina pressed her hands against the tiles and leaned forward. She stared down at her feet, just letting the water flow over her.

Afterwards, she stood wrapped in a towel, dripping, staring into the steamed-up mirror. Gradually, the surface cleared. Gradually, Nina saw her face reappear. Gradually, as if she were being reborn, Nina forced herself to imagine it was a different person staring back.

CHAPTER
THIRTY-EIGHT

In the library there are paintings, and in the paintings there are faces. The cold eyes stare down at me as I walk along the length of the wall, studying them, whispering to them, wondering if they've seen as much as I have.

"Some of them are meant to be valuable."

I don't turn round, even though my instinct is to be startled, to spin round wide-eyed, to gasp, make an excuse, tell him I'm busy, apologise for my sudden exit.

"Mr Palmer is an avid art collector." Adam stands behind me, a breath away from my back. My neck prickles from his closeness. I don't move.

"It takes a good while, you know, to appreciate a painting properly." It wasn't what I'd meant to say. I was going to scuttle off with my pile of laundry.

"Go on," Adam says as if he's teasing an answer from a student. He doesn't realise how hard it is for me to talk to him now. I am learning that the past runs faster than the present — way faster than me. Eventually, it becomes the future.

"I just meant that they take a long time to paint. Therefore, looking at them should be a slow process too. To really appreciate what the artist did." Slowly, not knowing exactly how close Adam is, I turn round. I find myself pressed against the wall, face to face with him.

I burst into fits of laughter, even though it feels so wrong. "What on earth do you look like?"

He pulls a dejected face; the face of a sad clown with a daubed-on smile. "You don't like my outfit?"

"It's not that I don't like it. I'm just curious to know why you're wearing yellow tights, a pink stripy tunic, and a blue fuzzy wig." My hand half hides my face. "And silly shoes."

"These are my normal shoes," he replies, joking. "Don't you know anything, Miss Gerrard? It's the school fun run today. Didn't you get the email that was sent out?"

"No. Why would I? I don't have an email address or a computer."

"How long?"

"What?" Adam keeps me confused.

"How long do you think it took for the artist to paint these portraits?" His mind switches between past and present like mine.

"For a start, there's more than one artist here." I scan the line of ten or twelve portraits. "There are four different styles. That last painting is unique. I love it. It's very Matisse. You can tell by the colours, the composition, the lighting. If I ever invested, it would be in something like this."

"Your knowledge is impressive, but there are five artists." Adam's square features speak earnestly from beneath the face paint and wig.

"I don't think you're —"

"And you do have an email address. Everyone who works at the school has one. It will be your initials followed by your surname at the school's domain dot net."

"It will?" Bright colours spill from Adam, dazzling me. His slightly crooked nose looks even more prominent under the dark eyeliner he has whizzed around his eyes. His broad jaw sets a wide expression on the clown's painted mouth.

"Checking your email regularly is important at Roecliffe. Just think, if you had read your emails, you could be dressed like this too, and preparing to run, walk or crawl five miles around the village for charity." He adjusts his wig. "Then I wouldn't have to beg you to come with me, would I?"

My bemused smile drops away, wondering if it will ever not hurt — from the cut on my cheek that's taking an age to heal, to the internal bruising that makes me live life blank-faced. "What a shame I didn't see it then," I say. I make a mental note to find out more about staff emails and the internet.

"So, you like Henri Matisse," he states. "I score one point for finding something else out about you."

"You're keeping score?" I ask incredulously.

"Would you like to go to a gallery at the weekend? There's an exhibition in Leeds that I think you'd love."

"I'm no art critic. I have uniforms to put away and sports kits to fold and . . ." I shake my head, walking away. But I stop when I see the empty road ahead, the vast blank landscape of my life stretching before me. I turn back. "Maybe we *could* go to a gallery one day." I close my eyes. "I think I'd like that." It's hard to tell him how much.

"You can wear my wig if you join in the fun run," he calls out, making me smile, shake my head, quite unable to take another step away from him.

Fliss and Jenny promised not to tell. Although after I broke down and sobbed on to the keyboard, they were wary of me. "Miss? Miss, are you going to be all right?"

I heaved up my head. They hovered by the door, keen to get out before they were caught. They had essays to write.

"Go," I told them. I nodded a thank you and they left, leaving me crying on to the desk. What I'd just seen had loosened every tendon, every muscle, every cell of resolve in my body. I was limp from sadness.

After Jenny had finished swooning from the flowers that some boy had sent her on Afterlife, she ran my requested search. Eight Josephine Kennedys appeared on the screen — a more common name than I imagined. The one I was tracking down was third on the list.

"There," I said, breathless, shaking. I stared at the tiny photograph, intrigued by the unfamiliarity of her face. I swallowed but my mouth was dry. Beneath her name, I read *Location: Portishead*. My heart galloped through a run of palpitations at the prospect of getting a glimpse of her remote world.

Jenny clicked on the name. "She hasn't been online for about two weeks."

"How do you know?" I gripped the edge of the desk. It was information. Already more than I expected.

"It says here, look." Jenny wiggled the mouse pointer over an information bar. "Last login was the tenth of October."

Now I know what Josephine Kennedy did on the tenth day of October. I marvelled at that simple fact.

"What do those mean?" I asked. I wanted more. There was a row of little icons next to her name.

Fliss and Jenny glanced at each other and sighed. "Game stuff. It's a summary of information about how she plays, what she does, what she has." The girls enjoyed knowing more than I did.

"This heart means she's looking for love." Fliss smiled.

"She is?" My heart raced. "And what's that?"

"It means she has her profile set to private. Unless you're on her list of friends, you won't be able to see her details."

"And to get on her friends' list, I have to make a character, right?"

Jenny glanced at her watch and then at the door. "Right."

I was about to give up, about to thank the girls for the glimpse into this other life, when suddenly Josephine Kennedy's profile lit up from its dim offline status. "Online Now" blinked in neon green beneath her name.

"What's happening?" I asked. I leaned in to the screen. My eyes gaped wide to drink it all up, while my fingers spread rigid across the desk. I didn't think I'd have the wherewithal to operate the mouse.

"You're in luck," Fliss said. "She's just logged in. There's always someone you know hanging out on Afterlife. That's why it's so cool."

"She's at her computer *now*?" My breathing was quick and shallow.

"Yeah, of course." Jenny sounded incredulous at my ignorance. "Do you want to say hi? I can send a hug or a smile. It's a kind of no strings attached 'hello'."

"No! No, don't." I sat staring at the screen until it flickered once again.

Jenny refreshed the browser. "Look. She's just changed her mood and tag line."

"What do you mean?" My eyes were cloudy. Focusing on the tiny words was nearly impossible.

"She's set her current mood to *unstable*," Fliss said.

"And her tag line just states: *Why?*" Jenny added, sounding puzzled. "Usually people put a favourite quote or saying in there."

My hand came up to the screen, my fingers spreading a distant safety net around Josephine Kennedy's virtual life. Everything in the IT room became insignificant and blurred. All I could see was the glowing screen, a halo of light around her words.

"Because I had no choice," I told her as my throat clamped shut.

My head dropped on to the desk as the first proper tears began to flow. When I looked up, I saw that Josephine Kennedy was offline again as if she'd never really existed.

★ ★ ★

The villagers of Roecliffe spill from their houses to watch the annual spectacle. Some have made banners and some have stuck bunting to their front windows. They cheer as the girls run past, throwing coins into their buckets.

"I didn't . . . realise that I was . . . so . . . unfit." I also didn't realise that looking ridiculous would help take my mind off things, but it does. I am wearing a pink tutu and fairy wings dug up from the bottom of the drama group costume box. A sixth-former lent me some knee-high stripy socks. Lexi painted bright circles of turquoise around my eyes and daubed on scarlet lipstick. Hardly a professional make-up job, but it makes me the perfect partner for Adam as we jog through the village. "What's this in . . . aid of? It'd better be worthwhile." I attempt a smile.

"A local children's home," he replies, hardly sounding out of breath at all. "We do this every year. The kids get to go to Scarborough for a day. It pays for the coach, meals, gifts, that kind of thing."

It stops me in my tracks. "Children's home?"

"Yes. It's in Harrogate. It's council-run and funds are low." Adam stops beside me, forgetting he looks ridiculous. "It's a cause very close to my heart."

I'm panting, trying to collect my thoughts, prevent my insides from pouring out.

"After the children's home in Roecliffe was closed down, the locals wanted to raise money for a similar charity. From what I've heard, everyone was very badly shaken by the horrendous events going on right on

292

their doorsteps. It was their way of making good from bad. It's a tradition now."

"I don't see how throwing a few coins into buckets is going to help . . ."

Adam isn't listening to me. He steps on to the pavement, pulling me with him as half a dozen men jog past dressed as nurses. Bystanders whoop and clap.

"To begin with, it was just the villagers who raised money, but when the hall was sold off and the school opened, the pupils were invited to help each year."

"I see," I say, my heart rate returning to somewhere near normal. "So the children's home in Harrogate has nothing to do with . . ." I make a gesture back towards the school.

Adam is already shaking his head. "None of the pupils or staff associate what happened in the nineteen eighties with life at school here today. It's not something the headmaster broadcasts to prospective parents."

"So Mr Palmer knows about what went on . . . the murders?" It's hard to say the word.

"Of course," Adam says, surprised. "Back then, he was a teacher at the village primary school. He's a local man through and through."

The cries and calls of the crowd shatter my thoughts. Mr Palmer was a teacher at the primary school. Like a photograph album flipping in the wind, I see images of children, of schools, of worn-out shoes, of blackjack sweets, of toothless grins, of whips and bloody backs. I smell the wood smoke, taste the foul food, feel the desolation — once again, I see the faceless man.

Mr Palmer, I repeat over and over in my mind. The name means nothing to me.

"Why the sudden interest? Has my book whetted your appetite for a bit of mystery?"

"I'm just careful about charity donations. I like to know where my money's going." Adam's crazy colours glow neon. I can see he doesn't believe me.

"And here's me thinking you wanted to help me interview one of the locals." Adam's eyebrows rise hopefully.

"Come on," I say. "We're being left behind."

It's true. The carnival-like group from the school has jogged down Roecliffe's main street and is nothing but a wash of banners, whoops, and brilliant colours in the distance. Adam kicks off running again, a slight tinge of dismay creeping across his clown face. His pace is nothing compared to how we started out. By the time we draw level with Frazer Barnard's cottage, he has stopped and stands with his arms folded in the middle of the street.

"What's wrong? Giving up already?" I turn and jog on the spot. I just want to get this over with and return to the monotony of folding sheets and sewing on name tapes.

"Would you like a drink in the pub?" Adam asks.

"I thought you wanted to support the charity run? A drink in the pub is hardly the idea, is it?"

"What if I promised to make a fifty-pound donation on our behalf? Would you come then?"

Up the street, the group of runners is nearly out of sight. I can just hear the sound of coins being chucked into buckets. "You promise to make a donation?" I imagine the kids singing on the coach to Scarborough, see them licking ice creams, hear the pinball machines ringing as they pump in the loose change from our buckets. It makes me want to empty my pockets.

"I'll drive the kids to Scarborough myself if I have to." Adam pulls off his wig. "To be honest, I hate running." His hair sticks up from static, until he sees me looking, until he flattens it down. He seems oddly at home in the Yorkshire village, even though his accent, sandy hair and tanned skin place him on an Australian surf beach. He ruffles his hair again, suddenly self-conscious.

"I'll have to be quick then." My hand rises to my mouth. I just agreed to go to a pub with Adam. It feels good, even though I'm filled with guilt. "It'll be mayhem in the dorms once the girls get back from the run."

Adam says he wants to smoke so we sit outside. It's mild for the end of October and there are several tables on the pavement in front of the Duck and Partridge. I straddle a bench, sipping on the half-pint of ale Adam bought me. He rolls a cigarette. The dappled light, the young couple sitting at the next table, the bag of cheese and onion crisps that gets tossed my way, even the silly costume make me feel just one per cent normal.

"I'm having trouble," Adam says. The unlit cigarette hangs from between his lips. A flurry of ideas swims behind his intense blue eyes. He thinks I know what he's talking about.

"With what?" I bite a crisp in half.

"My book, of course. It's always the book. I can't concentrate on anything else."

"Do you think writing it will help you find your sister?" He glares at me as if only he is allowed to mention her.

He ignores my question. "So will you come to that exhibition in Leeds with me? I saw a leaflet for it. It's only on for another few days. 'Beyond Expressionism'. Sounds good, eh?"

"Answer my question, Adam." My voice is soft, resigned, nearly a whisper. It makes his pupils dilate, even in the sunshine. I don't know what's come over me.

He shrugs. "By writing the book, I'm hoping to find out *about* her, not where she is." In return, his tone is soft, accommodating, as though he understands that we are tracking a delicate dance around each other. "Now you tell me about your interest in art."

"Did I say I had one?" It's in Adam's nature to dig and delve. He wouldn't be a historian otherwise.

"It was just the way you were looking at the portraits in the library. Stacked up with laundry, one eye on the subject, the other on the artist. And what you said, about the pictures taking a long time to appreciate, it's true. Most people only give a painting a quick glance. Considering how many hours' work go into —"

"Will you help me get on the internet at school?" I interrupt him on purpose. This has to stop.

"Of course," he says with the unlit cigarette still bobbing between his lips.

296

"I'm looking for someone too," I blurt out. "Only this person's not lost."

Adam withdraws the cigarette from his mouth and holds it between his thumb and forefinger. He exhales, as if there's been something to inhale. He squints at me through non-existent smoke, taking an accompanying sip of his pint. "You're like the leaves of a book, Miss Gerrard." And before I can pull away, Adam is drawing a line underneath the cut on my cheek saying, "There are more than two sides to every tale."

CHAPTER
THIRTY-NINE

In nineteen eighty-four, Roecliffe Children's Home was given a special award by the council. It was cause for celebration. Many homes across the area had been closed down or failed inspections, according to Patricia, but Roecliffe was the council's flagship institution. It was a shining light in the land of lost children.

That summer, there was a presentation. The mayor came, all draped in gold chains, and a shield was presented to Mr Leaby. He told us, through gritted teeth and a smile I'd never seen before, not to touch the trophy as he posed for the local papers. He didn't want our grubby mitts on it, he said.

"Get a couple of the kids around you, sir," one of the photographers called out. Mr Leaby stood stiffly next to the mayor. I was pulled by the arm and pressed between them. "Smile, love," the man behind the camera said. Mr Leaby's hand slid down my back and settled on my bottom just as I was blinded by a hundred flashes from the camera.

"Oh, Ava, look, you've got your eyes shut," Miss Maddocks said, chuckling, as we all pored over the half-page spread when the *Skipton Mail* came out three days later.

Eyes screwed up, more like, I thought. I was fifteen. I knew what it all meant. After nearly eight years at the home, I'd figured it all out. It was arranged in layers, a bit like the trifle we had only at Christmas. Us kids were the fruit at the bottom — the overripe bananas and peaches with brown dents on our skin. We were the stuff nobody wanted but didn't have the heart to throw away.

I almost got used to Betsy going missing. She was six. She chatted away, mostly about nonsense. She lived in a different world to the rest of us — a make-believe paradise that she'd been born into long before she came to Roecliffe.

She didn't go to school. They enrolled her and she lasted two days. I was at secondary school by this time so, even though I walked her down to the village on my way to the bus, even though I kissed her goodbye at the school gate, even though I put an extra sweet in her pocket for break time, she still peed herself, still rocked in her chair, still pulled out her hair and bit the other kids.

Betsy, they said, was anti-social. She was marched back from school and got a beating by one of the nameless male carers. I found her, curled up on her bed, looking like a bruised apple — little rosy cheeks with soft smudges of battered flesh beneath. Her legs were spotted blue and looked like the skin of a dead fish. When I bathed her, I asked her why she wet herself.

Betsy shrugged, her bony shoulders bumping her ears. "Because I can," she said. I knew exactly what she meant.

After her bath, we went for a walk. It was warm. I wanted it to be just us, to pick daisies and chain them together. Something normal.

"My mum died," I told her. There were cows in the field opposite the paddock that we meandered through. When she was with me, Betsy was just like any other kid. Quiet, but she behaved well and affectionately. I needed her as much as she needed me — the contact of someone who knew. "It was ages ago though. I don't really remember her."

Betsy ran up to the post and rail fence that separated us from a hundred beasts. She mooed and spiked her fingers out from her forehead, pretending to butt the fence. We were the same. Parentless, lost, waiting for childhood to pass. Banging our heads relentlessly against nothing. The only difference was that I *knew* this now. I'd lost the benefit of childish ignorance.

"She got cancer," I said. Betsy found a long stick and poked it through the fence. She pushed it into a cow pat; squealed when all the flies buzzed off and swarmed around us. "I've not seen my dad for ages. He got married to Patricia. Did you know that, Betsy?" She wasn't listening, but it was good to talk all the same. "But then they split up." I'd always wondered why Patricia didn't talk about her marriage to my dad. I think she was embarrassed that she was my stepmother, that she'd got a kid of her own who was free, living a normal life. Such a waste of family, I thought, when here's me with none.

It was on the walk back that we found James hanging from a tree in the orchard, his neck all purple from the rope, his head bursting with blood.

Betsy spotted him. She stared ahead, her lips stiff and thin, her eyes big as the cows'. We shook at the sight of James's elongated body slowly turning beneath the biggest branch of the apple tree. His feet weren't far off the ground. The sun shone through the leaves, making his face blotchy. I screamed and dropped the daisies.

"No, no, oh no!"

Betsy's eyes transformed from disbelieving moons into slivers of wonderment as she stared at the body. It was as though she'd spied a fairy up in that tree, that James was beautiful now, untouchable, and came from the same place as her.

We stood for a while, each of us just a tiny bit envious that he'd gone, that he'd escaped his demons. He'd suffered from terrible nightmares, but now, at sixteen, he was old enough to realise it wasn't dreams he'd been having all these years.

When we were brave enough to draw closer — our feet dragged on by curiosity — we could make out the deep groove carved into his neck by the rope. It was a twine necklace, layers of thin parcel string plaited together to make a long thick strap. We couldn't take our eyes off him.

"He planned this," I said. I reached out and touched his shoe. The black leather shone in the sun. He was wearing grey socks and navy shorts. His shins were mottled with bruises like Betsy's. I stared up at his face. It looked nothing like James. James was pale and shy and quiet as a mouse. Everyone thought he was about eleven even though he was nearly a man. His voice was as high as a girl's, and his top lip smooth. James barely had the muscle to haul himself up the tree, but ultimately he proved he had guts.

"Goodbye, James," I said.

"Bye, James," Betsy mimicked. She threw the stick at him, but missed. "What's James doing?" she asked.

"He's dead," I told her.

"Like your mum?"

"Yes."

We stared at James for a while. A fly landed on his knee and I brushed it off. Red spit oozed from the corner of his mouth, and he wouldn't stop staring at a cluster of apples growing level with his face.

"Come on," I said to Betsy. "Let's go back." I didn't tell anyone what we'd seen. After all these years, James deserved some peace.

"Will we get dead?" Betsy asked. She picked up a handful of gravel from the drive.

"Maybe one day," I said, wondering why I'd not thought of it before.

CHAPTER
FORTY

In return for his help on the computer, I reluctantly agree to go with Adam to interview a woman from the village. I silence the inner voice that tells me not to be reckless. Adam wants to find out more about his sister, and if I'm honest, so do I. Besides, I like him and I want to help him.

He hunches over his laptop, finally resorting to thumping it when it locks up for the third time. "I need a new one," he mutters. Then he grins and stares at me, as if he finds my presence amusing. I'm perched awkwardly on the edge of his bed while he sits at the desk. There are books and papers piled everywhere. Even in the dim light, I can see the skin of dust on everything.

"Fourth time lucky." He stands, walks across the room with its sloping floor and knotty beams, and shocks me by clamping his hands on my shoulders. "I'll drag you into the twenty-first century if it kills me." He recoils when he realises what he's done.

"I'm not from another planet," I say. "I have used the internet before." I grin. He's just trying to help. He's becoming my friend and, even though I'm quite unprepared to cope with the feelings that brings, I like it.

"Finally," he says, sliding his finger over the touch pad to bring up the internet. He beckons me over.

"You sit here." He directs me to his chair. "This, Miss Gerrard, is called the internet. It's an amazing other-worldly place where you can connect with people from China, from Australia, even, I imagine, from space." He pours the tea, carrying on as if I'm a complete technophobe. "We do make tea in banana land," he says when I stare at the pot rather than the screen. "Now, let's get you registered on the school *intranet*."

Adam leans across me with one hand resting on the back of the chair. "Then you can read all your missed emails. A bulletin goes out every day with school news." He smells of sandalwood, of the forest, of fresh rain. I don't want to notice these things. "Only staff and pupils can log on to the intranet. And staff get a higher grade internet access. So if you want to catch up with friends on Facebook or have an eBay addiction, there's no problem. No barred websites. School policy keeps the girls on educational sites only."

"Sorry?" Suddenly I'm listening. Having the internet explained to me is not something I either need or asked for. "No barred websites?"

"Not for staff." Adam towers above me. He's wearing jeans rather than his usual dark grey work trousers. Instead of a smart shirt, he's put on a faded T-shirt with the name of a rock band I don't recognise splashed across the front. His chin is grazed with a day's worth of stubble, darker than his hair. Above all, Adam looks tired, weary, fed up. Of what? I wonder.

I watch and listen as he registers my school email address and shows me how it all works, how to log on, how to get on to the internet with unlimited access. "Easy, see?" he says. I ask to do it myself, repeat what he's shown me. For a second, our hands fumble over the keys.

"You can use my laptop any time. The staff terminals aren't always free."

"Thanks," I reply, wondering if I should take a peek now, just to see if it really works. Hacking through the firewall with Jenny and Fliss, having them peer over my shoulder, wondering why a grown woman is hanging out with teenagers, was never going to work. "Could I use it now?" I ask, hoping my shaky voice doesn't betray the enormity of what I'm about to do.

"Of course," Adam replies and opens up a new window. "It's all yours."

The whole world is suddenly at my fingertips. Another life is only a couple of clicks away. Adam sits on the bed with his mug of tea. He flicks through a couple of books, but soon he is lolling back on his elbows. I hear him put down his tea; hear him sigh, plump his pillow, ease himself further on to the creaky mattress.

I swallow. I glance back at Adam. He's reading a book, not watching what I'm doing. From Google, I head to the Afterlife log in page. I stop, as if I've reached a locked door, as if I wasn't invited to the party.

"Adam," I say. I find myself wanting a virtual squeeze of his hand before I step inside; to know that there's another person nearby — especially one that has such a curious interest in Roecliffe. "Have you ever done something so irreparable, so damaging and life-changing, something you can never undo or take back — not without hurting those you love most in the world — that you can hardly stand to wake up each morning?" My shoulders drop. "That you wish you'd died instead?"

I hold my breath, waiting for his reply. When it doesn't come, I turn to find him asleep, snoring gently, the book spread open on his chest, his lips puffing apart every few seconds.

The sigh bursts from my lungs.

It takes ten minutes to create a basic account. It's free unless I want to upgrade to an account with extra benefits, or buy more than the standard-issue belongings for my virtual apartment. I choose a name for myself, enter some personal details — all made up, of course — and finally confirm my identity through a school registered email address.

I feel like a different person as I create a little icon to represent me in this strange new world. I choose a body type, hair colour, facial features — having already confirmed myself as female and fifteen years old. Suddenly, my icon changes to a pretty teen with scarlet hair and painted nails. Once clothes are added — jeans, T-shirt, sandals — I know I will fit right in, look like

306

any other fifteen-year-old girl wasting away her time by chatting, flirting, gossiping, redeeming.

Chimera–girl28 is born.

"OK," I whisper, careful not to wake Adam with my clumsy keystrokes or laboured breathing as Afterlife creates my new living environment. I find myself in a room that's simply furnished. Several icons and banners flash at me from the top and bottom of the screen. There's an advertisement suggesting I upgrade for only £2.99 a month.

After a while spent clicking various links, experimenting, I find myself in a public area. Then I discover how to search for a specific character. I repeat what Jenny did the other day, and up comes the list of all the members called Josephine Kennedy. I click on the correct one, the one from Portishead, and notice that she has changed her character's look. The little cartoon picture looks sad, unkempt, as if its owner doesn't care any more. As if Josephine Kennedy has given up.

"Send a hug?" or "Say hi?" it asks me. Other alternatives include blocking this person from my friends' list, adding them as a friend, rating this friend, or inviting this friend to an event. I'm baffled but focused. I don't want to just say hi to Josephine Kennedy, I want to crush her in my arms. I don't want to block her out because, I think, tears fuzzing the screen, I've already done that.

"Add as a friend," I whisper, clicking, biting my lip in frustration when it asks me how I know this person. There are a couple of standard options — at school together, friend of a friend, related — but none really fulfil my reasons for contacting Josephine. There is a space for typing a message to confirm to the other person how you know each other.

Hello Josephine, I type. *Can't believe I've found you after all this time. Would love to be your friend again.*

I stare at it for ages, mouse pointer poised above the "Confirm" button. I go back and add, "*We were friends at primary school*," hoping that she'll take the bait. I click and wait, as if her arms are going to burst from the screen and embrace me, pull me against her in a tearful yet ecstatic hug, as if she will forgive me with just the click of a button.

After twenty minutes, when Josephine Kennedy's icon remains offline, I log out and close the window. I shut the lid of Adam's laptop. I will not be going home today.

I leave Adam sleeping. He doesn't even wake when the bell for supper sounds. I don't eat much. Sylvia is glowing and tells me about her night out. She snaps at a couple of girls who want off-games notes for no good reason. "Don't be so lazy," she tells them. "Go and run it off on the hockey pitch."

The sixth-formers swagger away with pouting lips and torrents of hair spilling down their backs. I grip my knife and fork and mash the broccoli on my plate. I force a smile when Sylvia frowns.

"Do you need me tonight?" I ask.

I am exhausted and empty. Since I've been at Roecliffe, I've been everything from cleaner to counsellor, laundry maid to sports assistant. I've iced hundreds of pulled muscles, found girls who'd skipped lessons, spoken with concerned parents, and combed out matted hair. I've sat up all night and watched over ill pupils, and slept beside the homesick ones when they refused to be left alone. I've kept food diaries of our poor eaters, and ironed countless uniforms. I've dealt with Katy's crush and Lexi's tantrums, but worst of all I've lived in constant fear of being found out.

Sylvia rests her hand on mine. "No. I don't need you. Why don't you get away for a few hours and forget this place exists."

That will never happen, I think, nodding appreciatively.

Later, when the girls are immersed in their evening activities, Adam catches me in the library looking at the paintings again. I wanted to see the one hanging on its own at the end of the long room. Vigorous brush strokes cross-hatch the large canvas in a style quite different to the nineteenth-century portraits hanging nearby.

"Who are they all?" I ask.

Adam shrugs. "The chap in this portrait built Roecliffe Hall. The Earl of somewhere." He drags his fingers through his stubble, thinking. "He died young and his widow couldn't stand to live here without him so she killed herself."

"That's horrible."

"But rumour has it that she isn't really dead. That she faked her own death and the ghost that's meant to be her isn't really a ghost at all, but rather her still living secretly in the corridors of Roecliffe Hall."

My mouth opens but nothing comes out.

"Of course she'd be dead now anyway but —"

"And the others?" I blurt out. I wish I'd not come to see the wretched paintings. Huge faces glower down at us.

"Haven't a clue. Mostly nineteenth century. All except this one."

Adam points to the picture I'd been staring at. The pale face of a young girl is half turned away. I can't tell if she's smiling or crying. She is wearing a nightdress and standing at the end of a long corridor. "It's modern, of course. You can tell by the colours, for a start."

"I like it," I say. It resonates with me; makes me want to take the hand of the little girl and lead her out of the darkness that spills around her. I shrug and gather up several hockey shirts that have been left on a chair. "But what do I know? I must get these put away before my evening off. Bliss," I say, forcing a laugh to hide everything else.

Adam halts me with a hand on my shoulder. "Shall we meet at half past seven then?"

"Half past seven?" I'd forgotten he wanted me to go with him to the village. I'd been planning a quiet night alone, but I don't want to disappoint him. Adam is the only ally I have.

"To talk to the woman from the village, remember? The one who worked here when it was a children's home. She gave evidence at the court case."

"Evidence?" I'm paralysed. He didn't say that she worked at the home.

310

"That's what I'm going to find out about. She must know something about my sister. Perhaps she even knew her."

Suddenly I'm dizzy and it feels as if I'm falling. The wind pushes up my nostrils and balloons my lungs. My skin draws up my body and my arms and legs burn from the effort of control. Impact never comes.

"I . . . I don't think I can make it."

Adam scowls and frowns. "Oh, for God's sake, Frankie, make your mind up." He turns away briefly, hands balled, shoulders hunched. "Why do you have to be such a bloody mystery?" He's angry. I've not heard him speak like this before. "I like you, OK?" He falters, wondering if he should justify the admission. "You seem to . . . to understand about my research." Then he surprises me by drawing me close by the shoulders. "Please come with me tonight?" His tone has changed back again, winning me over. "You promised you would."

I nod reluctantly. This goes against everything I know is right. I am agreeing only because I know how much it means to him.

"Thanks," he says. "See you later then." He gives me a little shake on the shoulders and strides off, laptop tucked under his arm.

It's half past seven exactly — I know this from the staff computer terminal I've just shut down. I am still shaking from what happened online, but somehow this meeting now seems right.

I wait by the big oak door with my coat slung over my arm. I trace a finger around the heavy iron latch ring, remembering.

"Bang on time." Adam comes up beside me. "Thanks for coming." He brandishes a clipboard and the Dictaphone. "It should be interesting."

"Indeed," I reply, pulling on a knitted beret. I've applied heavy eye make-up and altered my cheekbones with some blusher. I found some weak glasses in lost property. Adam does a double take as I shrug into my coat, but says nothing about my eyewear. I pull up the collar, thankful that the cold wind allows me to shrink beneath my clothes.

"Let's go then," I say before I change my mind. I wrap my fingers round the latch and Adam's hand is suddenly over mine, freezing time for just a moment.

There's no hiding our journey to the village in his ancient car. We leave behind a trail of black smoke as the engine struggles. "I don't take her on long journeys," he yells and cranks down his window to let out the fumes that have seeped inside. It jams halfway.

"Good job," I shout above the noise. The short drive is illuminated by crooked and dim headlights. The left verge and the trees high up to our right are visible, while the road ahead is virtually unlit, as if it's not even there. It makes me think of the rest of my life.

A few minutes later, we chug into Roecliffe. In the street light, I see several couples walking towards the pub, wrapped up against the autumn chill. Adam slows down as we pass the pond and small patch of village green. He pushes his foot to the rust-lined footwell and

312

the old Fiat halts abruptly. The engine immediately stalls.

"I want to show you something," he says. He leans across me and opens the glove compartment, rummaging through the mess. He pulls out his cigarette tin and a packet of mints. "Want one?"

I take a mint, peeling off the silver wrapper. I hold the sweet between my lips, hoping it will prevent me saying something I might regret. We get out of the car and Adam leads me on to the little village green. A couple of street lights illuminate our way. The grass is damp and doesn't look as if it's been cut since summer — a straggly reminder of better days. There are rows of dead snapdragons and geraniums lining the perimeter of the triangular-shaped communal space. Everything appears the wrong colour in the orange light.

Several paths lead to the centre of the green where there's some kind of memorial. A couple of benches face the pond beyond. Last time I was in the village there were ducks sculling across the water. "What is it?" I look around. There's nothing unusual here.

"This way," Adam replies. I hear him crunching his mint. He follows the path and stands beside the memorial, rolling a cigarette while I take a look around. "Go on." He urges me up to the stone structure.

On each side of the obelisk's broad base, there are plaques with lists of names engraved in the metal. "Locals who died in the two world wars," I say, squinting at the inscriptions in the dim light. I remove my glasses, imagining the poppy wreaths laid out in November. With their surnames first, inhabitants of the parish who were killed in action are listed alphabetically. The year of death is inscribed above each batch of names. "So many lives lost from this village."

"Sadly, yes," Adam says. "But look over here." He steps over the low chain-link fence to the rear-facing side of the stone quadrant. "There was a massive wrangle with the parish council about getting these extra names added to the memorial." Adam's cheeks flush as he waits for me to cross the fence. "It makes me so angry." His jaw clenches. "That there was so much fuss to remember them properly."

When I scan the list of names, I feel dizzy, unreal. I am standing beside Adam, trying to focus on the few names chipped into an added-on plaque as if it was an afterthought. I am sinking in the soft earth, dead summer flowers brushing my ankles, the musty scent of the pond and the remains of car exhaust threading through the cold air.

"Why are you showing me this?" I swallow. I blink. I swallow again.

"They are the dead children," he says softly.

I hardly hear him. My eyes soak up the names again, just to make sure. As each one weaves a dance through my mind, I hear their tears and laughter, feel their pain, watch the thinness of their lives evaporate while everyone else's continues as if nothing bad ever happened, as if they never even existed.

Tilly Broady, Abigail Nicholls, Oliver and Ken, Owen Fisher, Jane Dockerill, Samuel Seabright, Megan Seabright, Jonathan, James McVey, Alaister Peters,

Dawn Coates, Andy J.R., Michael Price, Craig Knott . . . The list goes on but I can't read any more.

"How . . . how did they . . .?" My mouth's so dry that my tongue sticks to my lips. "Who . . . What happened?" I'm stopping because I know the answer to each of my questions.

"They were all murdered, Frankie." Adam is solemn. "They were abused and killed at Roecliffe Hall when it was a children's home." He steps off the flower bed and walks over to the pond. I follow him.

We sit on the lichen-covered bench, imagining ducks, imagining children playing, imagining the past, the future. An unlit cigarette droops from Adam's mouth. "It's all going to be in my book."

I'm not listening — *can't listen*. I see myself running away, fleeing to another town, another country, another continent, looking over my shoulder for the rest of my life.

"Police uncovered a paedophile ring at Roecliffe Children's Home during the nineteen eighties," Adam continues. "All the children named on the memorial were systematically abused and murdered over many years. For ages, no one knew what was going on. After the home was closed down, children's remains were found in the grounds of the hall. Some were never recovered. Apparently the police worked for years to locate the missing children, unsure if they'd been murdered or had somehow escaped. Record-keeping at the home was poor. Some of the kids didn't even have last names or dates of birth registered."

Adam takes the cigarette from his mouth and rolls it between his fingers. "I don't believe the list of dead is complete by a long way. Since I've been in England, I've spoken to the local force, even interviewed retired officers who were involved in the investigation. But doors have slammed in my face. It makes me wonder who I can trust."

No one.

He pauses, frowns, maybe wondering if he can even trust me. "I came here to find out about my sister, Frankie. We were split up when she was a baby. I hardly knew her, but I've got her birth certificate, mapped some of the homes she was dumped in. She was in and out of care, like me, from the minute she was born." He draws breath. "Some people shouldn't be allowed to have kids."

Suddenly my hand is on Adam's arm, preventing his nervous movements. "Don't upset yourself," I tell him. "When you try to change the past, you can't help but alter the present. That makes a very different future to the one you expected. Are you sure you want that?"

He stares at me. "What is it about you, Francesca Gerrard, that makes me think you're a lot wiser than you make out?" Tears collect in his eyes. I fight the urge to draw him close, to hold on to someone who cares about the very same past as I do. That single link spans the entire universe, not just the few inches between us.

"Maybe it's that I understand what it's like to lose someone," I reply. My cryptic side kicks in automatically. "If you keep looking, you'll find your sister," I tell him. "If not in real life, then you'll find her in your heart." It's the only comfort I have these days. Passing it on to Adam isn't too revealing, I decide.

"But I know exactly where she is," he says, reaching into his pocket for a lighter. The flame bends as he sucks. "She's dead."

My mouth opens ready to say the usual things, but nothing comes out. I lean forward and pluck the dried head of a weed between my fingers. It gives me another moment to think before I have to fill the gap between us. "I thought you didn't smoke."

"I don't," he says sourly. He blows out smoke and pulls a face. "Want to know something?"

I nod.

"You're the only person I've ever told about my sister. No one else even knows I had one. Not even Claudia." He sucks deeply on the cigarette. Ash falls from the end.

"What was her name?" I feel so desperately sad for Adam.

"Elizabeth," he replies. He presses the unfinished cigarette into the wet grass. "But I always called her Betsy."

No one was using the computer terminal. The staffroom was quiet except for the cleaner collecting dirty cups, emptying the bins, running the vacuum over the floor. She was old, moved slowly, and had thin white wires coming out of each ear. "Like my ear pods?" she said too loudly, winking at me. I could hear the *tss-tss* of the music even from across the room. "Granddaughter gave them to me." She smiled proudly.

I turned back to the computer, wondering about the passage of time, about technology, communication, how easy it's all become, yet how the human race probably spends less time in actual conversation than ever — so close, yet light years apart. I thought about all the texts I used to receive and send, missing them desperately. *Where are you? Can you get bread? What do you want for dinner? Love you x.*

Just as Adam had instructed me, I signed in to the staff network. In a few more moments, I'd opened a web browser and was connected to the internet. Logging in to Afterlife was easy now, and as soon as I'd set foot inside the other world I saw that I had two alerts.

Josephine Kennedy has accepted your invite. You have one new message.

My heart slowed then accelerated. It meant she'd read my words, wondered who this primary school friend called *chimera–girl28* was. Two more clicks and I was reading a message from *dramaqueen-jojo*.

"Drama queen," I whispered, waiting for the page to appear. I heard her voice, imagined her soft lips curling around the words.

Hi chimera girl. Thx for adding me but do i know u? I cant see ur real name. jojo.

"Jo-Jo," I said, then repeated it over and over. The cleaner pushed the vacuum head towards my feet. I shifted them to one side. When she'd moved away, mouthing the words to a song, I rolled the mouse pointer over various icons and buttons, trying to get my bearings in what was a complicated game. I didn't care about playing it. I just wanted to be near Josephine Kennedy.

"Friends list," I said, simultaneously clicking on the words. A list of one name appeared, with a small picture of *dramaqueen-jojo's* character beside a few basic details. There. She had chosen to reveal her real name alongside her nickname, whereas I, on checking, had selected to remain anonymous.

I thought back, thought of suitable names, of primary school children, of packed lunches and grazed knees, of long white socks and reading books. I reeled through the homework, the friendships and break-ups, the SATs tests and music lessons, the ballet shoes and the dressing-up clothes. I counted every one of the cuddly toys arranged on the window sill, and named each picture book on the shelf.

Amanda Wandsworth, I told myself, recalling a little girl with sleek brown hair. She was everyone's friend, but eventually moved away. I checked there was no one else already registered under this name, then I went to the profile section of my character. I entered my new details. Then I clicked "Show real name", hoping this would fool Josephine when she read it.

Suddenly, I received another notification. Flashing in the bottom right corner of my screen was a green icon that looked something like a person. When I held the mouse over it, a tag read, "You have one friend online."

My fingers clutched the mouse as I imagined *dramaqueen-jojo* sitting at her desk at that precise moment. Her shoulders would be a little hunched and she wouldn't have bothered with make-up. Her clothes would be creased and her hair perhaps hadn't been washed in a while. She probably wouldn't have eaten a decent meal in ages. I froze, not knowing what to do when a bright blue box popped up on screen and the words "*Mand is that reli u?*" appeared inside. Beside them was a tiny picture of *dramaqueen-jojo* and a space for me to type my reply.

I was shaking, sweating, not wanting to blow my one chance.

-*Yes, it's me. How are you?* My words looked incongruous next to Josephine's abbreviations. Somehow clumsy set against her quick dance of words. A few minutes passed before another message appeared. Perhaps my rather formal reply had scared her off.

-*had bad time. trying 2 survive. u?*

-*wot happened? im ok ta.* I held my breath waiting for the reply, hoping my language now fitted in. I imagined Josephine's fingers poised over the keys, perhaps typing something then deleting it when she thought better of it.

-*my mum died.*

I sat, stunned, gripping the edge of the desk, gasping for air as I read the words. Shaking, my fingers replied while the rest of me reeled.

-*i am so sorry for you. was she ill?*

There was a long pause.

"'Night then, duck," the cleaner said. She'd coiled up the vacuum cable and had four mugs looped through the fingers of one hand. One of her earphones hung down her shoulder. "Don't work too hard." She smiled and dragged her vacuum out of the staffroom.

-not ill. wish she had been.

I didn't type anything. She had to tell me in her own time. Eventually, another few words appeared on my screen.

-she killed herself.

The air left my chest as if someone was standing on me.

-its been the worst time of my life.

-i am so sorry 4 u. That is really tragic. How is yr dad coping? I couldn't imagine what losing a parent must be like for a fifteen-year-old. Would she remember the laughter, the hugs? Would she pick through her mother's wardrobe, pressing her face into a favourite sweater? Would she pluck make-up from her dressing table, hoping to look like her mother? Or would she just lie on her bed and stare at the ceiling, always wondering *why?*

-dad not good. we get by. where do u live now?

-London. With my dad. I lost my mum as well. Three years ago. Cancer. The lie came easily. I was not Francesca Gerrard any more as I sat at the computer, logged in to another world.

-oh mand im so sorry for u 2. lifes not fair.

There was a pause as we both soaked up this information, became virtual sisters.

-Does the hurt ever get less? Will i wake up one morning and not have it fill my head?

All the typing in the world wouldn't ease her grief.

-what helped me was knowing that my mum wouldn't want me to be sad. I knew that she loved me.

I knew she didn't want to go. The reply came quick as lightning and I realised my mistake just as fast.

-*yeah well mine did. she obviously didn't love me.*

-*No!* I replied. *Your mum loved you. Don't ever think it's your fault.*

-*nothing makes sense anymore. Everything on its head. Thought mum happy. Thought she loved us. Dad gone crazy.*

A long wait, me staring at the doleful character Josephine Kennedy has chosen for herself, wondering if she was gazing at the image I had chosen to represent Amanda. Then she asked, -*Don't you wanna know how she did it?*

-No, I type. I couldn't stand to hear.

-*Everyone else does. Do they ask about ur mum?*

-yeah, I lied. *I just tell the truth. It shuts them up.*

-*my friends didn't know what to say to me. Still don't. I'm the odd one out.*

-*does ur dad talk to you?*

-*no. he's always working. It's as if he's in prison camp. He's really changed. Not the dad I knew.*

-*that's terrible. You need to get help. Can u see ur doctor?* I wanted to help her but we were lifetimes apart. I wanted to wrap my arms around her, never let her go, make everything better.

-*nah. no point.*

-*u need to talk to someone. There's help out there for you if only you'd ask. You could join a group or talk to a therapist. It sounds as if your dad would benefit from counselling too. People move on. People recover. You'll never forget your mum. Just know that she loved* you. *But you have the rest of your life ahead of you, everything to live for. She would want you to do that.*

Only when my message appeared on screen did I realise just how much I had typed, how little like a teenager I sounded.

-*dont lecture me! Ur not my mum.*

Suddenly the lit-up icon of *dramaqueen-jojo* faded to grey and she was offline.

Tears fell in torrents down my cheeks. My head dropped to the keys as I cried out my reply to her, praying that across all the miles, she would hear.

CHAPTER
FORTY-ONE

On the face of it, it was a normal day. Late summer sun warmed the garden. Mick had work coming in faster than he could paint and was already down in the studio. Josie would surface in another couple of hours, bleary-eyed, seeking Cheerios, tea and television. Nina's current work was piled on the counter in the kitchen — a stack of papers filled with opportunity, potential, everything she had ever wanted. Life, theoretically, was perfect.

Why then, when the phone rang, did Nina stare at it, shaking, feeling that if she answered it the world might end?

"Hello?" She held the handset between finger and thumb, slightly away from her head as if it might separate her from anyone undesirable.

"Mrs Kennedy? It's Jane Shelley. I hope I'm not disturbing you."

It took a moment for Nina to place the policewoman who had visited her home in response to her emergency call. "That's OK." Nina's mind raced, wondering if the WPC had found anything out. Perhaps they believed her after all, although now she would have to backtrack swiftly and tell them she had been mistaken, that there was no intruder. She couldn't risk police involvement now.

"It's just a courtesy call really. To make sure that nothing else has happened to upset you."

There was something about the constable's manner that made Nina think this was not an official call. Plus, a mobile number had shown up on the caller ID on her handset. Nina doubted police numbers would be so easily identifiable. WPC Shelley was making a personal call to Nina.

"That's kind of you," Nina said obliquely. "But everything's fine." Revealing anything about Burnett was tantamount to writing her own death certificate.

"I believed you," Jane Shelley said. The line was bad. Nina wasn't sure she had heard correctly. "About the intruder and the car. I believe you weren't making it up."

"It was probably nothing," Nina said. "My imagination."

There was a sigh on the other end of the line. "I've seen cases like this before. It's tragic. I can't let another one slip through my fingers."

Nina didn't think Jane Shelley had been in the force very long, but clearly something had affected her during her short career. What, how or why, Nina didn't care. She wanted her off the line; she needed to think what she was going to do.

"There was a woman, bit younger than you," the constable continued. Nina could hear background noise, as if Shelley was with a group of children. Screams and giggles all but drowned out her voice.

"She'd got a kid. A little boy. Only four. Her partner beat her senseless most nights. The son saw everything."

Nina frowned. She didn't want to hear this. Through the window, she saw Mick emerge from his studio and gasp lungfuls of fresh air. He stretched and rocked his head back, supporting it in his arms. Then he dropped forward and leaned on his knees. If Nina hadn't known better, if she hadn't guessed he was taking a breather from the mountains of work he had building up, she'd think he was lost in despair.

"That's very sad," Nina replied. "But it hasn't got anything to do with me."

"I was the one who found her body," Shelley said. Her voice was loud and clear now, no kids in the background. Nina thought she heard the vague hum of a car engine. "Well, actually, her four-year-old son found the body. He was poking her, begging for his mummy to wake up when I found them. Her partner had beaten her to death."

Nina paced around the kitchen. If it was a trick to get her to admit the truth, then it wasn't working. She had no intention of divulging anything to do with Burnett to the police. Nina knew that if she was to have any chance of survival, she would either need to find Mark McCormack and beg for his help or deal with things herself.

"She'd called the police out several times, claiming there'd been an intruder, a break-in, a burglary, when really her husband had been battering her. When we asked her to make a formal statement, she denied everything. Said she'd made a mistake. That she'd fallen over."

"My husband is *not* beating me up," Nina said indignantly.

Another sigh. "I have a little boy," Shelley said. "I've just picked him up from nursery."

"That's very nice for you."

"I'm a single mum," she continued. "I left his father last year. He used to knock me about."

Nina almost felt like laughing. "But you're the *police*," she replied.

"In this game, everyone's equal. You've got my number. If you want to talk, just call me." And then the line went dead.

Nina had worked on a production years ago as part of her theatre make-up course at college. It was a short piece that the film students were working on for their final exams. Several professionals had been brought in from the industry to offer advice to the students, as well as scout for potential talent once they had qualified. Everyone on the theatrical courses was involved.

Nina had been particularly intrigued by Ethan Reacher, stunt and effects coordinator to the stars, who had agreed to give a oneday workshop to the students. Nina was enthralled for the entire day, taking copious notes, puffing with admiration for the man whose name she had seen roll by on countless film credits. His knowledge of the industry was endless, his dedication to detail flawless.

"Take *Silent Dreams*," he roared. Normal volume was apparently too ordinary for the great man. "Not once did the director call upon a special effects team for the death scene, but he still managed to create a film so believable, so raw, so terrifying, that several of the actors couldn't even stand to watch the premiere."

There were hushed whispers as Ethan delivered the facts. Nina sat mesmerised, learning that with just the tiniest detail, the biggest effects could be achieved. That, she thought, is how my whole life has been.

"The arm was largely prosthetic," Reacher continued. "But we made sure the fingers were real. The close-up shots were stunning. No need for clumsy cuts." He gulped from a pint glass of water. "Minuscule muscle movements are key to scenes such as the cliff-falling take. When the actor was finally forced to let go of the rock, the viewer was inside his head. Those close-ups weren't close-ups. They were *mind*-ups."

There was snickering. About half the students were on the course to pass the time. Of the rest, some were vaguely interested. One or two, including Nina, were riveted. Since beginning her course in theatrical make-up, Nina felt she had finally found a purpose in life. Everything that had gone before suddenly added up and didn't make a number less than zero. She knew that changing people's appearances, characters, was what she wanted to do.

"So did you have to shoot the cliff scene last?" some cocksure student asked. "Surely the actor would have been killed after a fall like that."

Ethan Reacher had shown the scene several times before his talk. A classic example of simple effects pushed to the extreme, he'd said. A ripple of laughter followed the question.

"Stand up, young man." Reacher strode to the front of the platform in the lecture theatre. He glanced around at the few who were still laughing. "That's not such a stupid question." Reacher clutched at his chin with stubby fingers. He didn't look as though he'd be able to undertake any of the stunt work himself any more, Nina thought. In his mid-sixties, Ethan Reacher's body betrayed a stiffness, perhaps one accident too many in the past, to allow him to body-double for anyone now.

"The actor in question broke both legs on impact," Reacher announced. A wave of disbelief as the students listened. "He flatly refused a stunt double. This kind of fall, from such a great height, even though it was into water, takes great experience. You should have seen the reams of paperwork he had to sign before the producer would let him undertake this one." Reacher let out a bellow of a laugh, silencing any noise from his now captive audience. "The director put the deleted scenes back in. Got the aftermath. Close-up face shots, the blood, the agony, everything."

Nina winced at the thought. She'd never liked heights. Wondered why anyone would want to tackle such dangerous work. She preferred to stay behind the scenes.

"So how do you survive a fall like that?" another student asked.

"Mostly you don't," Reacher explained. "Best trick of the trade that I know . . ." he paused, "is either do a different stunt, or pray to God."

Several students gathered round Ethan Reacher after the workshop. They'd been given a glimpse into the world of special effects and been allowed to demonstrate their own skills to one of the best in the business. Now they wanted to thank him personally. Nina queued up to shake the man's hand.

"I noticed your work earlier," Ethan said to her. He downed more water and at close range, Nina could see why. He was pouring sweat. "You stood out. You plan to make a career in theatre or movies?"

"Oh yes," she replied. At twenty, Nina had never been so overawed by anyone. Most people she had met in her life so far had only ever let her down. "It's everything to me."

"You're good," he said, nodding, looking her up and down. "Take my card. Give me a call when you're qualified. How long have you got to go?"

"Another year," Nina said. Her heart beat frantically. She could hardly believe that Ethan Reacher had singled her out. Suddenly the year loomed ahead like a decade. Why can't I be finished with college right now? she thought.

"What's your name?"

"Nina Brookes." Her voice was thin and breathy. "Thank you, sir," she continued. "For a wonderful day. I've learned a lot."

Ethan Reacher bellowed a laugh after jotting down her name. "If nothing else, you learned how *not* to fall off a cliff," he roared, before walking off with a group of students following in his wake.

It wasn't as if she hadn't tried. Josie was still sleeping and Mick wouldn't be back inside for a while. Nina phoned every police department she could think of, and looked up numbers on the internet. She made sure she dialled "141" each time, withholding her number. She didn't want anyone calling her back. Unless she found Mark McCormack, or at least someone who could confirm that they had stepped into his shoes, then Nina wasn't giving any details away.

"I'm sorry, there's no access to that area of CID without a special referral and contact name. Your liaison officer will put you in touch with —" Nina hung up.

"Mark who? Can you spell the surname?"

"That department has moved on, it's all centralised in London now."

When Nina rang Scotland Yard, she went through six departments, finally getting close to someone who could possibly help with witness protection. Just saying those words sent her into a flat spin. "Name and reference number please," she asked.

"Miranda Bailey," Nina said, plucking a name from nowhere. "I don't have a reference number."

There was silence for a while. "I'm sorry. There's no access on the system for a Miranda Bailey."

Nina hung up again. "No access," she whispered as her face pressed against the cold table. How can I tell them who I am? she thought in despair. Mark told me it was more than my life was worth to trust anyone that he'd not personally sanctioned. How can I tell just anyone in the police who I am, when several of the men arrested were in the force themselves?

"Nina?" Mick's voice was behind her. "What's up?"

Nina's head shot up off the table. She snapped shut the lid of her laptop. She attempted a smile. "You look like I feel," she commented. "What time were you up this morning?"

"I didn't go to bed," he admitted. "I need coffee." Mick banged about with the machine and cups, dropping the box of filter papers on to the floor.

"Don't you think you should tell one of these galleries that you need more time?" Nina hated to see Mick like this. She needed him fresh, on the ball, ready for action at any minute. As it was, he could hardly spoon the coffee into the machine without spilling it. "You're exhausted. You can't keep churning out work at this rate."

Mick turned and threw the teaspoon across the room, narrowly missing Nina's cheek. "Churning out work?" he yelled. "Is that what you think I bloody do all day?" He slammed the lid on the glass coffee jug and rammed it home. "We haven't all got the luxury to pick and choose when we work or not, Nina. You find it quite easy to take an afternoon off here and there, I've noticed, without a care about our next mortgage payment." Mick spat out an incredulous noise and paced the kitchen. He smacked the top of the coffee machine, wanting it to hurry up so he could escape back to the studio.

"I know you're under a lot of stress at —"

"You don't know what stress is," he retorted. "Not this kind of stress."

Nina didn't know what to say to make him feel better. She'd never seen him like this before.

"What about telling that man . . ." she couldn't bring herself to say his name. "What about telling that man from the new gallery that you can't do the paintings? Just concentrate on the Marley Gallery. They asked you first, after all."

Mick stopped dead still. His muscles tightened and pulled his face into an expression that Nina didn't recognise. "Tell him I can't do the paintings?" Mick was suddenly calm. Nina thought he was seeing reason; that if he agreed not to 'work for Burnett there was maybe a chance of getting him out of their lives for good, without Mick or Josie knowing anything. We could move, Nina thought. Maybe change our last name. Mick would understand if I made up an excuse, but he wouldn't understand that I'd lied to him about who I am for the last eighteen years.

"Tell him I can't do the paintings?" Mick yelled.

Nina jumped. "I just thought —"

He came up close to her. "You really don't have a clue, do you? Not a bloody clue about my work at all."

"I understand how precious this is to you. I know how many years you've struggled to get the recognition you deserve. Christ, I've lived with you for most of them." Nina backed off but Mick stuck to her. A thread of fear wound its way from her head to her heart, but

333

her heart rejected the emotion. This is your *husband*, she told herself, and it caused her to reach out to him.

"Don't," he said, recoiling. Mick yanked the coffee jug from the machine before it was finished. He sloshed some into a mug. "Just don't," he said again, before going back out to the studio.

Nina watched him walk down the garden, his coffee spilling over the sides of the mug. When he neared the studio, he hurled the cup into the air. It came down against the side of a tree, shattering in slow motion over the shrubs.

"What's going on, Mum?" Josie stood sleepily in the doorway. "I heard shouting."

"Nothing, nothing at all," she said, pulling back the tears. "What time do you call this to get up?"

"It's still the summer holidays. I wanted a lie-in." Josie reached for a cereal box and frowned when she felt the weight of the milk carton. "No milk?"

"You know where the shop is," Nina snapped but instantly regretted it. She didn't want Josie going out anywhere alone. Not until she'd resolved this mess.

"Fine. I'll go to Nat's for breakfast. Her mum does eggs and pancakes."

Nina thought of Laura beating hell out of the batter before splatting it into a frying pan and roughly dropping it on to a plate when it was blackened at the edges. Laura was no cook. She took out her frustrations in the kitchen.

"Oh, Josie." Nina reached out for her daughter, but she backed away with her eyebrows raised as if her mother was a stranger. "I'll make you eggs."

334

Josie walked off, shaking her head, slamming the door.

That's both of them, Nina thought. My husband and my daughter have each pushed me away in the last five minutes. She slid down the wall to become a puddle on the floor. Perhaps they are trying to tell me something.

CHAPTER
FORTY-TWO

Twenty-four hours after I died, I went dizzy and my vision blurred. I'd had a serious blow to the head and, even though I'd taken advice, researched the subject as much as time would allow, I can't say exactly what went wrong, what I'd misjudged. But the plain fact was, against all the odds, I was lucky to be alive. At least that part had gone to plan. The rest was out of my control.

A trip to the hospital was impossible. That first evening, I sat in the motel room watching a quiz show, shivering, wondering why I didn't know the answers to any of the general knowledge questions, or even have the concentration to count the vile flowers on the grubby curtains. I could hardly breathe in and out at the thought of everything; could hardly believe I was dead.

Had anyone read my letter yet? I wondered.

I bit into an apple. Earlier, the woman I hadn't yet fully become had plucked it off the supermarket display and taken it to the checkout in a basket also containing hair dye, scissors, biscuits, fruit, chocolate, water. I had handed over cash and then stashed my shopping in the boot of my new car — a twenty-year-old Ford Escort also paid for in cash from a dealer on the edge of town.

He didn't ask questions. If it got me where I was going, I'd be thankful. Soon enough it would be in a lay-by, keys in the ignition, ripe for stripping.

There was a knock on my door. I froze. My ribs contracted with pain.

"Hello? You in there?" Whoever it was banged harder. I jabbed the remote at the television to turn down the volume. I flicked off the bedside lamp but it was too late. "Open the door, love." It was a woman's voice.

I got off the bed and, leaving the security chain on, I opened the door a crack, just enough to smell the cigarettes on her. It was the woman from the motel front desk. "Yes?"

"I wanted to make sure that you were OK."

I frowned. I put up a hand to tuck my hair behind my ear, but my hair wasn't there any more. "Yes, I'm fine." I felt giddy and sick. I didn't want to know why she thought I might not be. I closed the door but she stuck in her foot. She was a big woman.

"It's just that you looked a bit upset when you checked in. You seemed agitated. As if something was wrong."

"No, everything's fine. Really." I smiled and pushed on the door but her foot was still there.

"Did you see a doctor about your face?" She raised a hand to her own cheek.

"Oh, that's nothing," I said. "I'll be right as rain in a couple of days."

"OK, love. If you're sure." She turned to go but then changed her mind. "It's just that we sometimes have women come to stay with us who've been, well, hurt by their men and —"

"It's nothing like that. I fell off my bike. Good night." This time she nodded and allowed the door to close.

I went to bed but didn't sleep. I listened to cars coming and going, to people chattering along the passageway outside my door. I listened to the pub fallout late in the evening, and I listened to the radio to hide the sound of my own sobbing.

In the morning, I put on a brave face, a new face, and I made a phone call. I had the rest of my life to take care of.

The woman is in her mid-sixties. When she opens the front door, she looks us up and down, taking note of everything, right down to the tape recorder that Adam is holding and the handbag I have slung over my shoulder.

There is a moment's hesitation as her eyes flick between us both, but she doesn't give anything away as her gaze lingers on my face a beat too long, making me wonder about her just as much as she is no doubt wondering about me. She looks familiar but I can't quite place her face.

"Thank you for agreeing to this," Adam says. He shakes her hand. Her grey hair is scraped back into a painful bun as if it hasn't been released for decades, and her powdered face is stretched clean of wrinkles by her startled expression. Despite all this hardness, the angular bones, the tight hairstyle, tiny mouth carved

338

into a man-sized chin, there's a softness about her. It's that, I'm assuming, that makes her stand aside and let us in.

"This way, please." She leads us into a small living room. There is a coal fire burning in the grate. There's no air and I feel dizzy. She indicates we should take a seat on the small tapestry-covered settee. Adam and I sit down beside each other, our legs brushing, while she occupies the single chair by the fire.

"I appreciate your time." He holds up his tape recorder. "Do you mind?"

The woman nods once and sends a glance my way. I detect a nip of her brow, a quiver of her jaw. She folds her hands in her lap and presses her ankles together. "I don't have long," she tells us.

Adam is edgy, tense, but excited too. He speaks fast, as if this woman is the key to finishing his book. I could tell him that she isn't; that he's going to have to dig deeper than he ever imagined if he wants a resolution. But I don't. Instead, I give him an encouraging look, which prompts him to switch on the Dictaphone.

"Can you tell me when you started working at Roecliffe Children's Home and what your position was?"

The woman clears her throat. "I started on the fifth of June nineteen seventy-one. I left when the children's home was shut down in nineteen eighty-seven. I looked after those children as if I were their mother."

I stare hard at her. My forearms chill and my feet go numb as it dawns on me. I bow my head.

Why did I come here?

"Can you take a look at this list of names and tell me if you recognise any of them?"

The woman holds the piece of paper at arm's length, squinting as if she usually wears reading glasses. After a moment, she nods. "Yes. I remember most of these names. They were at the children's home. Some of them were brought in as babies."

"And can you confirm what happened to them?" Adam is visibly shaking. His neck is flushed from the open collar of his white shirt right up to his hairline.

"Poor little sods all died, didn't they?" That's when I hear the woman from the past — a rough-hewn voice stained with weariness, with contempt, and fatigue. Gone is the forced accent, a veil of pretentiousness, and in its place is wedged someone else. "That's what the police said, anyway. I told them everything I knew back then."

"You'll know then that when the paedophile ring was first discovered, three men were convicted of abusing and murdering the children, before more of the network was broken up."

No one says anything. The fire hisses and belts out a heat so fierce my left cheek turns scarlet. The woman is suddenly tight-fisted with her words. Adam's Dictaphone wheezes in his hand. "Yes."

"But weren't there actually four men involved with the final murder at Roecliffe? One of them escaped and was never identified. He didn't go to prison like the others, am I right?" Adam's chest rises as he sucks in breath, holding it firm until the woman speaks. I find myself doing the same, focusing on picking the skin from my fingers instead of recalling the hooded, faceless monster covered in blood, bending over the altar like a surgeon at work.

The woman nods again. "If the police say so," she replies. The toes of her shoes rub together relentlessly. "Then it must be true."

"Do you know who that fourth person was?" Adam says. His voice is as tight as piano wire.

"If I'd have known that, don't you think I'd have told the police back then?" The woman sits upright in her chair. "I told them everything I knew in court." A veil of impatience drops over her face. Through it, she eyes me, squinting, perhaps remembering. Her fingers are restless on her lap, mirroring mine.

"Sometimes," Adam says, hesitating, "people are afraid to tell everything they know."

The woman's head jolts round to the fire. The embers glow within her dark irises. "People came and went all the time," she confessed. "There were gatherings. Men from the village came up to the children's home regularly. They had some kind of club going. That other man could have been anyone."

Adam and I daren't move — him because he fears that taking notes or holding the tape recorder any closer will stop her talking, and me because I can't stand to hear what I already know.

"I kept out of it. My concern was looking after them kids. Right pathetic, some of them." She leans forward and jabs at the fire with a poker. I see her brandishing it, yelling, then I see her quiet as a lamb with kids nestled around her as they listened to a story. "Dirty business went on down those corridors. Best not to know. I just kept my head down, did my job, got paid. Wasn't any other work around here."

"Do you remember a little girl called Betsy?" Adam clears his throat and coughs. It doesn't hide his sadness.

"She was the last one to die, weren't she?" The woman finishes what Adam couldn't bring himself to say. There's a look in her eyes — glazed, regretful, fearful.

"Yes."

"Poor wretch. It was because of her that all them perverts were locked up. Dirty, dirty business," she says again.

"What was she like?" Adam leans forward eagerly, his elbows resting on his knees and the Dictaphone stretched forward as much as he dare without putting her off.

And suddenly I see it all revealed in his eyes. He doesn't care about Roecliffe Hall or the people in it. Adam wants to prove that his little sister's existence wasn't a waste. His book isn't about Roecliffe's past, it's about salving his conscience. He wasn't there to save his sister when she needed him, so he's trying to do it now. He wants the fourth person — the one who killed Betsy — found and convicted. He wants to put things right.

The woman thinks, trying to find the correct words. "All them kids were well looked after," she says. "Some of them had their problems, of course. Most had been dumped by parents who didn't want them, or they were orphans."

I screw up my eyes.

"But what about Betsy?" Adam asks impatiently.

"She was a funny little thing. All eyes and curls and not much to say for herself."

"Go on."

I stare at her, making sure she knows I'm listening intently. Then it's as if a switch has been flicked inside her, turning off her memory. Her lips draw together as if someone has pulled a string. "I don't remember anything else."

"Did she have any friends?" Adam asks. Perhaps he is hoping to track them down, find out more. But the woman is already standing, indicating she has had enough of us.

"She had one friend," she says, looking over at me. The news relaxes Adam's shoulders. "No one knows what happened to her though."

"But what about the fourth man? The one that was never identified." Adam is filled with panic. He doesn't want the meeting to end. I can see his mind whizzing with all the things he was going to ask. There may not be another opportunity. "They say that he was the one that —"

"The hooded one?" she asks, suddenly interested again. "None of the others arrested would tell. They offered more lenient sentences if they gave a name, but they all clammed up. That's what them lot do, protect each other. Don't suppose they'll ever get him now."

I stand up, feeling sick and dizzy. I need to get out. I can't believe I was stupid enough to set foot outside the school grounds again. I don't feel safe.

"Goodbye, Patricia," I say, head down, indicating that we are done, that we will be going, that she will never see us again. Adam follows my lead, reluctant, deflated, yet somehow relieved. There is a triangle of silence on the doorstep as a three-way nod marks our departure.

Adam slams the car door shut; drives off.

My fingernails dig into my palms. I turn to the side window; press my forehead against the glass. I don't say a word. Suddenly Adam slews the car into a gateway and roughly pulls me round by the shoulders, staring into my eyes with such intensity that I'm not sure if he's going to kiss me or hit me. He does neither.

"How did you know her first name?"

"Didn't you say it when we arrived?"

"No." I flinch as his words strike back. "I didn't even know her first name was Patricia. How did you know? Have you met her before? Tell me, Frankie. For God's sake tell me what you know."

I stare at Adam, fully believing that he's going to keep me holed up until I divulge everything. Only when I start weeping does he silently drive back to school, fingers drumming impatiently on the wheel; on my heart.

CHAPTER
FORTY-THREE

Sometimes Betsy and I tracked huge circles round the lawn while I told her stories about when my mother was alive. How she'd plait my hair while I sat on the edge of her bed; how she'd let me lick the batter from the whisk after she'd baked; how she let me feel the lump growing in her neck.

Betsy had some stories to tell too, but they were disjointed snaps of pain barked from a mouth that didn't know any better. We trod a careful path through the bluebell woods as obscenities flowed out, similar, I thought now I was old enough to understand, to her constant wetting and soiling.

"See those buds?" I said, bending down. "Those are going to be the bluebell flowers. They're beautiful. They make the woods look underwater when they come out."

Betsy worked as hard as she could to snap and destroy as many plants as she could until I caught and restrained her.

"Get off!"

"Betsy, why do you do things like that?" Her behaviour, even aged eight, was no better than a naughty toddler's. I'd tried to show her right from wrong, good from bad, but every time I thought I was making progress, every time she showed me a glimmer of understanding, they went and knocked it out of her again. There was nothing I could do to stop her being taken; to stop them cutting up and reshaping the essence of her soul. I worried that she would never be normal.

"Hate them," she said, yanking from my grip. "And I hate you!" She spat a foamy globule at my sweater and her eyes fizzed with mischief. Being bad was her way of taking control. Her way of showing the world that however terrible things got, she could do something worse.

"No, Betsy," I said, pulling her pants back up. "Wait until we get home." Reluctantly, she did as she was told and we continued with our walk through the woods. We joined the path that we were all herded along on a Sunday when we went to chapel.

"I want a picnic," Betsy cried. She stopped and lay down on the twig- and leaf-covered ground and mimicked eating a sandwich. It was the exact place we'd had our last picnic and it seemed a lifetime ago. The carers didn't bother to do anything nice for us these days. Since the home won the award and escaped closure like all the others, it was as if everyone had breathed a huge sigh of relief and didn't need to bother.

I was counting the days until I could leave. At seventeen, I'd soon be able to get out, get a job, live on the street if I had to. Life after Roecliffe had always seemed impossible, light years away, as if disappearing or something worse was the only choice. I'd already decided that I would be taking Betsy with me.

346

As fast as they came into the home, kids vanished like whispers — nothing left of them other than their belongings in the drawers. It eventually struck me that the ones who went were the ones who had no one to bother about them. At weekends, some kids would get trips out with their mums or grandparents. Others would spend a week with a foster family. A few would even be allowed back to their real homes for good.

These kids rarely got taken in the night, didn't suffer at the hands of men in hoods, didn't know what it was like to have their backs lashed or their bodies bent open. Maybe I'd noticed this, unconsciously, sooner than I realised. Maybe that's why I'd spent so many years of my life waiting for Dad's car to cruise down the drive — to prove that there was someone out there who would miss me if I mysteriously disappeared; that I wasn't a good choice, that someone cared.

Only a part of me truly believed I waited for my dad because I loved him and he loved me right back. I only saw him a handful of times during my teen years. He was usually drunk. Once, he fell off his chair in a café and was taken off in an ambulance. I walked five miles back to Roecliffe when I could have walked five miles in the opposite direction.

Betsy screamed. She stared at the chapel and peed herself. I scooped her up in my arms, puffing under her weight. She was tall for her age. A damp patch formed on my waist. "We're not going in," I told her. Everyone hated going to the chapel, sitting through the mighty sermon that Mr Leaby took it upon himself to deliver once we had finished singing hymns. There was no vicar or chaplain. Just Mr Leaby and another man from the village.

"Unclean thoughts don't remain thoughts for long," he told us once. "Just remember that your bodies were born dirty and only with God's forgiveness will they be cleansed. Pure thoughts lead to a pure body."

Another time he told us a story about a little boy who told fibs. "Crying wolf," they call it. "It's a sin to tell tales," Mr Leaby said, red-faced and looking like my dad did when he was about to pass out. "No one will believe you anyway," he instructed, ramming home to every one of us that telling tales was wrong, that our tongues would be ripped out by the stalks if we dared breathe a word of our sinful thoughts.

They told me that my dad was dead. Mr Leaby, with Patricia standing beside him as if she'd switched allegiances, broke the news one morning. Apparently it had happened three weeks ago and they'd only just remembered to tell me. They said, as I waited for the tears to come, that there wasn't any money, that his things had been taken away, sorted out, bank accounts dealt with, that the house was being sold. His divorce from Patricia hadn't quite gone through, I was told. She'd been kind enough to take care of affairs, so I shouldn't worry.

The tears didn't come and I walked slowly back to my dormitory. Betsy was sitting on my bed cutting her hair. Strands of gold feathered from her head. She giggled at the sight of it. Her forehead was bleeding where she'd caught herself with the scissors.

348

"Are you sad?" she asked.

"My dad's dead."

"You're like me now," she said.

I nodded and bowed my head towards her so that she could hack off my hair. Betsy dropped the scissors and hugged me close. "I'll look after you," she told me, and I fell on the bed, sobbing until my lungs collapsed. My cries weren't because I wanted my dad. I was crying because now there was no one to miss me; no one to stop *them* coming in the night.

CHAPTER
FORTY-FOUR

"Spill," he says. His breath smells of cigarettes and Polos. Since we've been back he's smoked virtually an entire pouch of Golden Virginia and crunched his way through two packets of mints as if that will counter the reek he's making in his room.

I'm pacing like an animal, treading the old boards like a lioness in a cage. Adam hasn't moved from the door, reaching across to a small table to flick his ash into an old coffee cup. "You're not leaving until you tell me."

"I'll scream," I warn him. It's hot in his room. Central heating pipes clank and gurgle beneath the bowed floor. "Sylvia will hear."

"I'm not letting you out until you tell me how you knew Miss Eldridge's first name." Adam is quite calm about my kidnapping, but still angry nonetheless. He pushes up his white shirt sleeves, feeling the heat too, and leans sideways on the door. "I'm quite happy to stand here for the rest of term if need be."

I curse in my head. I refuse to show him I'm bothered. I can't allow Adam to think he can unravel my past to patch up his own.

"OK," I say finally. I've whipped up a vague story that will no doubt knit itself into believable form once the words leave my lips. Over the last two decades, I've become adept at fabricating just enough truth from too many lies. Tell the same tale enough times and it becomes reality. "I'll tell you."

Adam melts away from the door with relief. He plants himself on the bed in a cloud of smoke and waits for me to speak.

It's like this, I hear in my head, although the words don't actually come out. *Years ago, I knew someone who had an aunt working at Roecliffe Children's Home. Turns out that was Miss Eldridge. I met her at a fundraising event and . . .*

"Adam, I . . ." My mouth is dry. I sit down on the desk chair. The cushion is scrunched and lumpy beneath me. I pull it out and hug it to my chest. *I used to work with someone who was brought up in the children's home. She once mentioned Patricia Eldridge's name. That's all. Nothing sinister.*

I dig my fingers into the feathers. My mouth is open, gulping like a goldfish, but nothing comes out. I stare into his eyes. Those colouring-pencil blue eyes leach the lies from me. I am captivated and mesmerised, drowning in the truth as it fights for a voice. I see his sister. Hear her calling out through the years. I am the link between them. If I tell one more tale, they will be lost from each other forever. I take a deep breath. It comes out in slow motion.

"Adam, my father dumped me at Roecliffe Children's Home when I was eight. I lived here for ten years."

A hurricane rushes through me, purging, destroying, cleansing. The noise is deafening, almost preventing what spills out next. "I knew your sister. I was the one who looked after Betsy. I was virtually her mother."

Adam says nothing for twenty minutes. He chain-smokes, lighting one cigarette before the other is out, head cupped in his hands, ash falling to the floor. I see the soul leaking out of him, all the pent-up anger and frustration draining out through the hole I have just made in his life.

I hug the cushion closer, desperate for protection. "No one else knows."

He looks up from the ashtray mug he's clutching between his knees. He coughs — a fake one because he doesn't know what to say.

It's not just about Adam and his sister any more. It's about me wanting to be me. I don't want to lie about my past or think in twists and turns any more. I want to hear the sound of my heart beating inside my own chest. "I'll have to leave Roecliffe," I blurt out, realising the implications. "I can't stay now that I've told you." My hand rises to my mouth, my fingers splaying and pulling at the skin on my cheeks. What have I done?

"I suppose you're going to tell me you'll have to kill me now?" Adam is unduly flippant. "Don't be stupid, Frankie. You're not going anywhere." He stands, knocking over the cup of ash. He opens a cupboard to reveal more books. Tucked between them is a bottle of expensive-looking Scotch and several small shot glasses. "For emergencies. This is one."

I take my measure gratefully. I'm shaking.

352

"So." He sits down again. We are only a foot apart. "Please understand when I tell you that I don't know what to say."

I nod.

"Also understand that I want to know more. Everything."

I nod again. The whisky burns my throat, loosening it, opening it up. Suddenly, it feels as if I am about to vomit up my entire life.

"I want to show you something," I tell him. I can't think of a better way to illustrate the past, at least while I'm still here to do it. He doesn't understand the danger I'm in. "Follow me."

Adam extinguishes his cigarette and opens the small leaded window in his room. I lead him downstairs, through the corridors, through the dining hall and the great hall, down further corridors, up another two flights of stairs and confuse him by doubling back along a passage.

"I've never been in this part of the building," he says from behind.

"Not many people have. I sometimes come up here to fold the laundry. It's quiet. There's space."

"It's cold," Adam comments. He's right. The temperature has dropped by several degrees. We go through a brown painted door and into a room with two tall windows. Boxes and general forgotten rubbish are stacked over to one side, while the other half of the room is taken up by the table I dragged over for folding the sheets on. I also brought in one of the ironing

353

boards and there's an old armchair for when I take a break.

"Looks like you've set up camp." Adam circumnavigates the room.

"Stop right there," I tell him. "Step back a bit."

He squints at me, but does as he's told. "That's where her bed was. The head was under the window. She liked the morning sun on her face. She said it tickled her awake."

Adam turns and spreads his hands against the wall, as if touching the plaster will connect him with his dead sister. "Here? Really?" he asks in a voice that tells me he needs to know everything.

"There's so much more," I say. There's a battle raging in my head. *Be quiet! Get out while you still can!* The other tells me to not stop talking until I fall to the floor, spent, sobbing, empty of all the filth that I've carried around for so long. "Look at this." I rub my hand up and down the door frame. It's not been painted in all these years. If the school gets bigger, they'll strip it all off, redecorate, to accommodate more beds.

"What is it?" Adam bends and stares at the notches in the wood.

"Betsy and me. When she first came here, I was about twelve and she was tiny. Only three or four. These grooves marked our heights back then. I did it to amuse her. The notches going that way are her, and these ones are me. See how she caught up with me as we got older?"

354

Adam is suddenly upright, clinging to me, forcing the breath from me in an embrace that oozes gratitude and sadness. "Frankie, I don't know what to say," he tells me. "This is the closest I have been to her for so long." He crouches by the notches again, running his fingers over the grooved wood.

"I wasn't supposed to have a knife in the bedroom. I got it from the kitchen."

He stares at me again. "This is immense. You telling me this is huge, you realise. What we do now, I don't know."

"There's nothing we can do, Adam. It's over. It's gone." I think of everything else in my life that's gone too, wondering how much I need to involve Adam in that. "It's history."

Adam shakes his head. "But you will tell me everything about her, won't you?" Panic sweeps over him. "You can't dangle the bait then whip it away."

"It's not bait, Adam. It's the truth. Telling it is hard. I don't know what made me say this much." Then I realise it's because I like him. I like him a lot. But I don't tell him this.

He frowns, not understanding. His focus soon turns back to Betsy. "I'll tape everything you say, make notes." He claps his empty hands by his sides. "I need to plan questions and interview —"

"Adam, stop. It's not going to be like that." I reach back my hands to knot my hair — a stress habit — but, as usual, I find it's not there. "I'm serious when I say that I can't stay at Roecliffe. There are things about me you can't know, don't *want* to know. I will help you, really I will, but it has to be on my terms. And I would like to read your book."

Adam nods vigorously. "Of course." He's weighing it all up, pacing himself for the dump of information he's going to get. He knows there'll only be one chance. He wants to get it right. "Come with me," he says solemnly. "I'll get you my computer immediately."

I am alone in my room with Adam's warm laptop resting on my legs. He handed it over as if it was his firstborn child, telling me how to find the file, to read it as quickly as possible. But first things first. I log on to my staff account and waste no time in getting online. I sign in to Afterlife and see that I have a string of messages.

The first one asks when I will be online again. An hour later, *dramaqueen-jojo* messaged me again, wondering where I was. At regular intervals after that, she'd come online looking for me, leaving comments, seeking out her old friend Amanda. Then I click the link that tells me she's sent chocolates. *Thanks*, the message reads. *For being like me.*

I'm halfway through typing a reply, telling her that I'll be around for the rest of the evening, realising that it's already late and she probably won't be up anyway, when her icon flashes live and a message box pops up.

-*Mand*, she says. *finally.*
-*Hello*, I type, abandoning my other words. *How r u?*
-*lol still alive. u?*
-*still alive*, I say, wishing that I was. Kids are resilient, I tell myself.

-i took ur advice. i went to my doc.

-that's good josie, I say.

-jojo, she corrects. I'm jojo now.

She's trying to reinvent herself. -What did the doctor say?

-gonna see a counsellor. a shrink. I'm a screw up thanks to her.

-thanks to who?

-who do u think? my mother.

My fingers freeze, quivering slightly over the keys. There's nothing I can say that will take away her pain.

-how's ur dad?

-obsessed

-with what?

-this man keeps coming to our house.

-who?

-man who buys dads pictures. dad needs a rest.

My chest tightens. -tell me more. Oh God, this can't be happening.

-he paints loads of these stupid pictures 4 this man.

-can't you and your dad go away for a while?

-LOL fat chance.

-why not? I ask.

-dad says he has massive debts to pay.

I frown. Debts? I don't understand. -Josie, I need you to listen to me very carefully. You and your dad have to get away for a while. Tell him to rent a house by the sea. Somewhere nice. He can paint there. It'll do you both good.

He said he'd leave them alone.

-wot u on about?

I hate it that I am remotely pulling strings; still trying to influence shattered lives.

-*When my mum died, that's what me and my dad did. My fingers fly through the lie. Dad took six months off work. We went away. Spent time together. It helped us grieve. It might work for you.*

-*my dads not like that. he barely speaks now. feel like running away on my own.*

"Yes," I reply out loud. "Run away as fast as you can. But please, take your father with you." But she can't hear me. I pray it wasn't all in vain.

-*what if I came to stay with you? she types.*

Then all would be well, I think, forcing myself to type the words, -*you can't.*

CHAPTER
FORTY-FIVE

Later, alone, Nina knew she had to act. It was never going to end. *He'd threatened Josie.* Twenty years in prison didn't change people like him.

Josie was safe in bed. Mick was, of course, working. He'd said angrily that she didn't — couldn't *possibly* — understand. She'd wanted to say exactly the same to him. She'd been down to his studio, to apologise, but he'd locked himself in. "I'll be finished soon," he called through the door. That was hours ago.

In the bedroom, Nina gripped her phone. She toggled through the received calls list to Jane Shelley's number. If I tell her everything — names, dates, facts — she thought, then she'll have to log my call into the system. The names involved in the case would flash a beacon to anyone in the force interested in my whereabouts. *Trust no one*, Mark McCormack had said. *There may be more . . .* How, she wondered, could she have even trusted Mark?

Back then, Nina hadn't understood, couldn't comprehend the depth and breadth of the network being smashed up by the police, all the arrests and convictions nationwide — police, teachers, judges, lawyers, fathers, doctors and brothers. If she had, she might have kept quiet in the first place.

"Hello?" Nina heard the tiny voice coming from the phone in her lap. She hadn't realised she'd dialled Shelley's number. She brought it up to her ear. "Hello?"

"It's Nina," she said quietly. "Nina Kennedy."

A pause, then, "Hi, Nina. How can I help?" There was an experienced patience to her voice, coaxing Nina to spill everything she knew, to fall into the safe arms of the law, except she couldn't be certain that those arms wouldn't creep around her throat.

"I was after some advice."

"Go on."

"Protection." Nina faltered.

"Yes?"

"Is there a department that deals with this sort of thing?"

Nina heard the waterfall of relief as Jane Shelley breathed out. "Of course, Nina. It's what we do."

Nina remained cryptic, but felt she was getting somewhere. "I've had it before. To help me survive, to relocate. It was a long time ago."

"With your current husband?"

"What?" Nina said.

"Was it because of your current partner or someone else?"

"What are you talking about?" Nina's voice rang tight as a wire.

"The abuse, Nina. You can't live in shame. I'm so glad you've taken the first steps."

360

"No, no, you don't understand."

"Actually, I do," Jane Shelley continued. "I'm going to send round a support officer. Someone who is trained to help you, plan the next steps —"

"Don't send anyone round. He'll kill me!" Nina's heart pounded at the thought.

"Then you need to come and see us. Is there a time when you can —"

"No, no there isn't. I was wrong to call. Please do not log this. Pretend I never rang." Nina fumbled with her phone until she managed to end the call. She buried her head and wept.

Ethan Reacher was an old man. He'd retired from the business only when his body had forced him to quit. Occasionally, even in his eighties, he was called upon for advice by the big studios. Nina had been a favourite of his since the day she'd met him at the workshop. It seemed like a lifetime ago. Taking him at his word, she'd studied hard, got good grades, contacted him after she'd finished college. He was instrumental in helping her establish a name for herself. He held her hand through several movies, allowing her to work alongside him and his team on set.

"You'll never be out of work with my name on your CV," he said. And he'd been right. Nina's reputation floated on having Reacher's name in her past. He'd always been there for advice; only a phone call away. This time, though, Nina had driven all the way to London to visit him. She'd dropped Josie and Nat at a nearby cinema complex with strict instructions not to leave. She was certain she hadn't been followed. It gave her time to talk to Reacher.

"Sounds like a load of cornball to me." He wrung his hands in his lap.

"No, honestly, it's going to be great." Nina knew she sounded unenthusiastic about the fabricated movie she'd told him she was working on. "There's a big budget. They've got some good names, and the script's all finalised."

Reacher's wheelchair wheezed up to the fridge. He pulled out a carton of milk and held it up to Nina. "Want some?"

She shook her head and watched as Ethan poured himself a pint glass full and swigged the lot. "They said that I shouldn't eat fatty food."

"Then why are you drinking full-cream milk?"

"To help things along. You think I like living like this?" He pressed the chair's controls and cruised off, instructing Nina to follow. "It's been done before," he told her. "But they'll keep rehashing the same old same old until the day I die."

Which won't be long at this rate, Nina thought sadly. Reacher coughed as he scanned shelfloads of DVDs. "Up there," he said, pointing. "Pull down *Leap*. There's a scene I want you to watch."

Nina found herself watching the end titles for a low-budget made-for-television adaptation of a little-known novel. "There. You see that?"

Nina shook her head.

"My name in black and white. *Special effects advice Ethan Reacher*." He pointed the remote at the machine and selected a certain scene. "Sued the pants off the bastards for that one. The only advice I offered them was to cut the damn scene entirely unless they could do it properly. If you ain't got no stunt man, then less is more in your suicide scene." Reacher mimicked a fake Hollywood accent.

"There's no stuntman in my movie," she said solemnly. "The . . . the actress insists on doing it herself. For real."

"A woman?" Reacher's interest was kindled. "A bridge, you say? How high?"

Nina swallowed. "About two hundred and fifty feet. Maybe a little more."

Reacher guffawed with laughter. "You're having me on, right?" Nina shook her head. "I want a front-row seat to the premiere then. This is going to be a box-office smash."

Reacher hit play and talked Nina through the scene. He paused and flicked backwards, illustrating over and over how not to create a convincing suicide jump. "That cut was wrong. Did you notice how attention was lost at the crucial moment? How our eye was drawn back to the car when it should have been focusing on the body? The car shot should have come later."

"But can you tell me about the stunt, the equipment, the conditions?" Nina asked. She hadn't come to find out how not to do it, or to learn about camera shots. "How can the actress do this and survive?"

Again, Reacher roared his trademark laugh. Then he became serious and Nina waited for the pearl of wisdom she needed to make this work. "The only truly convincing suicides in this business, Nina honey, are the real ones."

CHAPTER
FORTY-SIX

The last time I saw Betsy alive, it was as if spring had wound its way through her veins. Even though it was November, even though there was a biting wind that sent our toes purple and numb, even though there was nothing at all to look forward to, her heart beat with the lightness of new life. The reason for Betsy's happiness was because of an old piano. I'd convinced Patricia to have several of the caretakers drag it down the corridors from the storeroom where I'd found it.

"It'll keep her amused," I told her.

"Annoy the hell out of me," she replied.

"We can have sing-songs."

"No one can play."

"We could learn," I said.

"You wouldn't practise," she retorted.

I walked off, determined to get that piano in the common room if I had to push it in myself. I knew Betsy would adore it, and I was right. My pestering paid off. Even as Ted and his mate huffed and swore and humped the dusty thing into place, Betsy was fiddling with the keys, fitting each of her fingers above a note, carefully thinking which sound went with another.

Some mighty awful noises came out of the piano at first, but gradually, as Betsy sat patiently on a dining chair that was too low, pressing the yellowed ivory keys with arched fingers, something began to emerge. Unusual renditions of "Mary Had a Little Lamb" and "Oranges and Lemons" spilled from the common room. And strange, doleful versions of "Happy Birthday" in minor-keyed notes. Betsy knew my eighteenth birthday was only a week away, and knew also that I would soon be leaving. She had no comprehension of what that actually meant, and no idea either that I would be taking her away with me. The thought of leaving her behind was abhorrent. Who, I wondered, would be there to comfort her in the mornings?

I had no idea where we would go. I expected to be booted out on to the street the minute the council's funding for me expired. If I was lucky, they'd give me the number of a hostel, perhaps a couple of pounds for the bus, tell me where the job centre was. I was determined that Betsy and I were going to start a new life together.

"Happy birthday . . . de-ar Ay-vaaa . . ." Betsy's brittle voice cracked out a contrasting tune to the one she was actually playing. "Haaapy birthday to you!" she shouted in finale.

Everyone clapped when she'd finished. She turned round, amazed at what she'd done. Her sweet-stained lips tried to mask her delight but couldn't. Teeth that I nagged her to clean sat discoloured in her open mouth.

366

It was pure happiness — raw and unexpected, steaming from the warmth of her heart.

I left her contentedly tracking her fingers up and down every single one of the piano keys. Not all of them played a note, and not many of them were in tune. I'd been sent to fetch logs for the big fireplace. In winter we spent most of our time in the common room, huddled by the hearth, watching kids' shows on the telly after we'd tramped back from where the school bus dropped us off. I was the only one trying for A levels. I wanted to make something of myself.

I humped the big basket down into the basement. The stack of wood I usually took logs from was pretty much down to curls of bark and twigs that were fit only for kindling. I ventured into another cellar chamber where I knew there was a fresh pile of dry wood. The ceiling level drew down, forcing me to press my chin on my chest.

As I passed into the next dark area, I heard the rise and fall of voices above me. I glanced up, catching my face in the cobwebs strung between the joists right above my head. I could see chinks of light running parallel between the floorboards. I was directly underneath a room where two men were talking. The wood muffled their identity.

"It's all ready . . ." I heard one say.

"I'll tell the others," another butted in.

I did the geography in my head. It was confusing, but I reckoned I was beneath Mr Leaby's office, even though I didn't hear the familiar resonant growl that clung to the end of his words. I'd heard it enough times during the Sunday services. I couldn't figure out who was up there, but it didn't matter much. People came and went all the time at Roecliffe; men skulking about the corridors, eyeing us up, making the muscles in my legs go weak.

Loud clicking footsteps drowned out whatever else they said. It was freezing down in the basement. I wanted to fill the basket and to get back to the fire. I smiled to myself at the thought of Betsy's piano playing. I wished I'd discovered it months ago. I wanted to make her happy.

"Later, then," the first voice said again. "Don't be late." Then the bang of a door followed by nothing at all.

Betsy was getting over a cold. Patricia was quite happy for me to nurse her through the night — to blow her snotty nose, to dose her with hot lemon and honey drinks, except we didn't have any honey in the kitchen. I made do with orange squash and sugar with a squirt of Jif lemon. I warmed it in the microwave and sat Betsy on my lap as she drank. She pulled a face as the tartness of it spread around her mouth.

"Drink up," I told her. "It'll make you better."

"Will it stop them coming for me?" she asked.

My shoulders drooped; my eyes screwed up. I tried to keep awake all night to protect her, I really did. Every few breaths I'd sit up in a panic, feeling the space beside me or, if she'd been very brave and slept in her own bed, feeling the mattress next to mine for the length of her warm body. When my hand rested on her skin, I could relax for a while longer. Once, I even bound her wrist to mine with a belt, but in the morning it was on the floor, cut in two pieces. Betsy was lying upside-down in her bed, missing her pyjama bottoms, scarlet welts across her thighs.

"It might," I say.

"If I'm a good girl, will that stop them coming?"

I pinched a tissue round her nose and she blew out.

"You are a good girl," I told her.

"But you never get taken. It's not fair."

She was right. It wasn't fair. "They don't like me," I told her. "I'm not cute like you. I'm too big."

"Did they take you when you weren't big?" she asked.

I nodded, feeling guilty. "Just once." What was it he'd said? *Don't bring her again. She's a menace.*

Betsy pushed against me on my lap — a kitten shaping against its mother. When she'd fallen asleep, I used all my strength to carry her back to my bed. I sat propped up against a folded pillow, squashed against the wall, while Betsy spread out. I fought the need for sleep, holding her hand as she wheezed through her dreams. I stroked her forehead and kissed her hair. I pulled her close with every creak of the floorboards, every whip of a branch against the tall windows of our dormitory, every cry from the boys' rooms, and every missed heartbeat as she fell deeper into sleep.

When I woke up, it was the middle of the night. I don't remember drifting off, only that I must have done for her to be prised from the crook of my arms. The semi-open door sent a corridor of light across my bed, illuminating Betsy's absence; showing me the crumpled sheet where she had been only a short time ago.

I ran my hand over it, just to make sure I wasn't imagining it. The nylon bedclothes crackled with static as they rasped against the mattress. I could still feel Betsy's warmth. She couldn't have been long gone.

In a flash, I was out of bed. Wind and rain lashed against the window above our beds. I pulled on my jeans and scrambled into a sweater. My nightdress hung loose around my thighs. I didn't bother with shoes. I was determined to find Betsy. They wouldn't be taking her this time, not when we were so close to leaving.

Before I crept out of the dormitory — the other girls sleeping soundly in their beds — I glanced back to where I'd last seen Betsy. I reached out and touched her pillow before going off in search of the little girl who had made my life worth living.

CHAPTER
FORTY-SEVEN

He's got it all wrong. Adam makes it sound like a holiday camp. Clean dresses and white socks, trips to the beach, and weekends with parents who never existed.

Award-winning children's home, Roecliffe Hall, has been at the centre of hundreds of children's lives since the nineteen forties. Post-war Britain suffered a deluge of orphans and unwanted pregnancies. Children's homes became overcrowded and poorly run, but one institution stood out from the rest. The sprawling estate of Roecliffe Hall, a Victorian Gothic mansion designed and built during the early nineteenth century, sat derelict for nearly a decade before West Riding County Council took it over and converted it into a refuge for kids where they could be given the love they so needed.

"The love they so needed," I say indignantly. "He doesn't know what he's talking about." I hate the journalistic style Adam uses in his book. I read on as fast as I can, not missing a word, but barely pausing to digest the claptrap he's written.

> Roecliffe Hall Children's Home was staffed by a dedicated and well-trained team of carers. Children idolised the innovative ways of their superiors and flourished under the direction of key players during the later years of the home's history. Reginald Leaby, Patricia Eldridge and Margaret Maddocks were the three main characters instrumental in bringing about the home's later success . . .

Only the thought of Adam's anger stops me chucking his stupid computer out of the window. Why, if he knows he lost his sister at the hands of these monsters, is he portraying the home in such a positive light?

I rest the computer on my bed and stand at my window, staring out above the treetops. I'm high enough to break every bone in my body if I was stupid enough to jump.

Feeling dizzy and nauseous — not just from the height — I sit down at the small dressing table. I don't want to read any more of Adam's book. I stare at myself in the foxed mirror. A stranger stares right back.

The scar on my cheek has knitted to form a raised red welt. It's more shocking now than when it was when fresh. It suggests a knife wound, the claw of a wildcat, a road accident, or a botched operation. I run my finger down its length, noticing the way my cheeks have hollowed out and my eyes dropped back inside ash-coloured rings. I look terrible. An adult version of the child that once lived here. A woman without a family. A grown-up orphan.

Sighing, I drag myself back on to the bed and force myself to scroll through more of Adam's book. From the number of pages, I see it's not so much a book as a long essay. He's clearly been struggling for information, perhaps writing, then rewriting, then deleting his words in frustration. How could anyone ever get such a story right, even if they did know all the facts? I flick forward, stopping a few pages from the end.

No one knows what drove four men to take the life of an innocent nine-year-old girl. Until the discovery of her body, at least eighteen other children had already been killed at Roecliffe Children's Home. Forensic investigations, witness interrogation, and admissions by the guilty prove beyond doubt that for many years the children of Roecliffe suffered degrading torture, abuse, and misery at the hands of the very people they should have been able to trust.

Patricia and Miss Maddocks looked after us to the best of their abilities. But I can't accept that they didn't know what was going on; didn't believe for one minute that Patricia hadn't got an inkling of Chef's intentions when I went to visit him in the kitchen, when once I tried to escape his hands by climbing out through the window. I think back to my ice-cream bribed cooking sessions. How he'd sit me on the worktop, prising his body between my dangling legs, pushing himself against me. A puppy eager to please and a child eager for a treat, for some love, it hadn't seemed so bad back then. The worst that had happened, I thought, was that I got ice cream around my mouth.

There's a knock. I snap shut the lid of the laptop. "Who is it?" I press my ear to the door.

"Frankie, it's me. I need my computer back." Adam's voice is urgent on the other side of the wood. He is the last person I want to face right now.

"But I haven't finished."

"Frankie, just open the door."

Reluctantly, I turn the large key. Before it even clicks into place, Adam has wrenched the brass knob and is pushing his way inside.

"What are you . . .?" I stop. Adam's eyes scan my room and, finally, after what seems like a lengthy prying dance, his gaze settles on the dark lid of his computer.

"It needs work," he says. He reaches for it; tucks it in the safe place under his arm. "I have to speak to more people. Get some things straight." He even looks embarrassed. "There's so much missing." He shakes his head, paces nervously.

"I could help," I reply. "If you like."

He folds himself on to the dressing-table stool. "You haven't read the real draft," he says. I frown, leaning on the door. "I gave you the version I write when I'm feeling detached, as if I was never Betsy's brother, as if we never shared the same parents, or have — *had* — the same blood in our veins."

"So there are two versions?" I'm confused.

374

"Yes."
"Of the same story?"
He nods.
"Can I read the real one?"

CHAPTER
FORTY-EIGHT

Nina had been waiting in the car for Josie for two and a half hours. Did she imagine the shadowy figure as it went up the steps and in through the stage door? Was it really him? Or was her tormented mind playing tricks on her?

She pushed up the sun visor and squinted. She'd been trying to distract herself with work phone calls while she waited for Josie to finish rehearsals. There was no way she was leaving her at the theatre alone. Nina stared at the old bricks, the paint, the metal railings as if he'd left a dirty trail for her to follow.

She chucked her notepad on to the passenger seat. Quick talking and help from Tess had temporarily appeased *Grave's* producer for another couple of days. Her limbs shook as she got out of the car. She had to get Josie out of there.

Nina glanced at her watch. It was twenty to twelve. Josie's first *Chicago* rehearsal was due to finish at midday. Most likely, she'd find her daughter in the green room, chatting excitedly with the rest of the cast, comparing lines, hunting for lost dance shoes. She swore she'd seen him go in — hadn't she? — lurking,

376

waiting to make his move. She shook as she approached the theatre.

Knowing the place as well as she knew her own home, Nina pulled open the stage door and followed the dark corridor down into the belly of the building. Her legs felt weightless, almost incapable of holding her up as she strode on. She heard the familiar banter of the youth theatre group as the excitement of a new show stretched in front of them. She listened at the door.

Dizzy with anticipation, Josie had spent the last six weeks of summer longing for rehearsals to begin. But when, only twenty-four hours ago, Nina had inexplicably forbidden her daughter to take the lead role in the production, insisting she quit the theatre company, giving absolutely no reason other than "things had changed", Josie had broken into a thousand pieces.

"Mum, *please*, don't do this to me. When I act, it's the only time I feel like *me*." From the floor of her bedroom, behind a curtain of matted hair and tears, Josie had pleaded with her mother not to crush her dreams. "Do you know how hard I've worked? How long I've waited to get a part like this?" Josie's pleading was raw and desperate until finally Nina cracked and conceded.

"I just don't understand, Mum," Josie said, still sobbing from the shock, backing cautiously away from her mother, hardly daring to breathe in case she changed her mind again. She limped off to the bathroom to recover from the outburst, wondering if her mother had suffered some kind of breakdown, or one of those mid-life crises that she'd heard her friends go on about. Either way, it was so out of character it was terrifying, and her dad had gone mad too, barring everyone from setting foot in his studio. Alone, confused, shaken, Josie logged on to Afterlife to find solace.

Nina burst through the green-room door, half expecting Josie to be pinned up against the wall by Burnett.

"Mum," Josie gasped. Someone chuckled. "What are you doing in here? We're not finished yet." Josie's indignant look and her mother's crazed expression sent a ripple of laughter through the teenage cast. Josie turned her back on her mother and pretended to riffle through her bag for something.

"Looks like you are," someone quipped.

"Mummy's here," another said. More laughter.

"Josie, it's time to go." Nina's eyes flashed between the other girls as they busied about gathering their belongings. He would be here, somewhere, she was sure. Lurking, hiding, waiting for their backs to be turned, their guard to be down. She could *smell* Burnett's presence. She glanced behind the door. Sweat gathered on her forehead, her top lip, along the length of her back. She felt physically ill.

"Josie, come *now*," she said. She was aware of Josie frowning, of her cheeks flushing red, the snatch of her bag as she whiplashed it over her shoulder. More laughter from the rest of the cast as smart comments rained on their leading lady's premature departure.

"I . . . I have the dentist," Josie said to her friends.

Striding along the corridors, Nina broke into a run. "Hurry up," she said, dragging Josie along by the arm. When they reached the stage door Nina paused, panting with fear and exhaustion. She stared at Josie, reaching into the disbelieving depths of her eyes as the gap between mother and daughter widened. It was an abyss Nina had sworn would never exist. Their relationship would be different to other mums and teens — built on trust, respect, confidence, communication. In the last few days, Nina had seen to it that a wide chasm had cracked the ground their lives were built on; made a mockery of all the values she'd held dear.

"Mum, what's —"

"You just don't get it, do you?" Nina lunged at Josie's shoulders, shaking her at first then pulling her into a painful embrace before opening the door.

"Mum, what's happened to you? I want to call Dad." Josie fumbled for her phone. Her mum was in need of more help than she could give. She was scared; hadn't had to deal with anything this weird before. She dialled home but before it even rang, Nina had swiped the phone off her and snapped it shut.

"We have to get out," she said urgently, blinking as they went outside. She scanned the street for Burnett, expecting to see his angular body bent over her car, cutting the brakes, planting a crude bomb beneath the seat, wiring her life for destruction. Shapes morphed in and out of her vision, teasing her brain into believing he was there, doing all these things, stepping seamlessly back into her life as if he'd never even been away.

"Get in the car," she ordered. Reluctantly, Josie did as she was told. Panic leached from mother to daughter. Josie pulled the seat belt across her body, clicked it in place as her mother crunched the car into reverse.

"Mum, stop it. You're scaring me."

Nina had to get Josie to safety. Her fingers clawed at the steering wheel and her feet shook on the pedals. Then a sudden jolt as she smacked the car against a wall. Nina wrenched herself round, yanking the wheel to opposite lock. As she sped forward, as she forced the car to maximum revs, she swore she saw Burnett standing outside the stage door watching their escape.

"Do you remember," Nina said, her hands shaking round a mug of tea as Laura's fingers stroked channels of calm into her shoulders, "when we all four went out for the first time? You said that Mick was my missing half."

Laura had stopped crying now. Instead, her tears had turned to laughter — an incredulous gutter cry of disbelief that Tom had actually left her. Nina's arrival had served as a timely distraction, except that Nina also appeared in a terrible state. Somehow, as the women swapped woes, each found a measure of solace. But why Nina had insisted on locking both back and front doors, checking the windows and closing all the curtains, Laura had no idea.

"I still think that," she said. She dropped down into the sofa. "You know, I never once thought that about

Tom. That we were two inseparable halves of a whole. You're so lucky, Neen."

She gripped Laura's hand. "I am," she whispered, but instead of providing comfort, it just reminded her of everything she had to lose. "I have a long way to fall. You said it yourself."

Laura nodded, trying to make sense of what Nina was saying. They sat together, working speedily through a bottle of wine while their daughters gossiped upstairs about their distressed mothers. Tom briefly returned home to collect some belongings, chucking clothes angrily down the stairs, comforting Nat when she cried and begged him not to leave.

Nina stared out of the living room window as he drove off. "Whose car is that?" She squinted at the dark green vehicle as it sped off down the street. "I thought Tom drove a silver BMW."

Laura made a disgusted noise. "He did until it was taken off him. Company cutbacks. He's been driving about in that Rover for a couple of weeks now. My heart bleeds for him." She laughed hysterically. "He was annoyed that he didn't get the newest model." Laura laughed again. "Serves him right."

Nina nodded slowly. Then her mobile rang.

Mick moved in with Nina eleven days after the picnic they'd shared on the Downs. "Why wait?" he'd said, and she'd agreed, hating the thought of him living in that trailer park. It made sense. She'd been missing work, too lazy to leave Mick's warm bed to catch the early bus to the city. And Mick needed the extra space for his paintings. Even her tiny bedsit allowed him more room to spread out than his trailer did, although it meant giving up part of the kitchen.

"We'll eat out," he said.

"We don't have any money," Nina replied.

"Then we'll steal."

"We'll be thrown in prison."

"I'd die without you," he said, laying her down amongst the tubes of paint, the sketchbooks, the shoeboxes stuffed with photographs, the remnants of their once separate lives. On the mess, they forgot who they were, left behind the people they'd been just days ago. Nina thought only of who she would become, completing the transformation. From that moment, Mick became as integral to her life as the new colour of her hair, or the unfamiliar name on her chequebook.

A week later, Mick sold two paintings, cementing his belief that Nina was his lucky charm; that he had found her for a reason. "I got sixty quid," he told her proudly. He decided, from that moment on, he would change the way he painted. He was done with his old ways and banished to the past everything that had gone before. He only had to think of Nina when he held a paintbrush and his canvas was filled with the future. That was what he told himself as he stroked the knots of her spine, wondering how he would have survived without this young beauty in his life.

As well as the TV work, Nina had taken on another job making sandwiches three nights a week in a local factory. Mick had added warmth, comfort and purpose to her lonely life. She drank up his presence as if she were quenching a great thirst. Mick was everything she wanted him to be — friend, lover, comedian, playmate, soulmate.

When Josie came into their lives a few years later, Nina believed things would be this good forever. She had forgotten the past. She had stepped out of a horror movie and taken the lead role in a love story all set for the happiest ending ever.

"It's a sad ending." Nina recalled Ethan Reacher's guffaw as she'd tried to sidestep his probing questions about the non-existent film stunts she'd been grilling him on.

"Sad ending?" Laura said, only half listening to what Nina was whispering under her breath. She'd been distracted since the phone call a minute ago, and wasn't making any sense. "Bloody right it's a sad ending," Laura continued when Nina stared vacantly ahead, her skin bleached white. "It's a sodding tragedy, that's what it is."

She snatched wet washing from the machine and picked out several men's shirts, bits of underwear and other items that were clearly Tom's. She dropped them into the pedal bin. "I can't believe he actually *admitted* to having an affair. I suspected as much."

"Don't let him leave," Nina said quietly. She stared straight ahead at the kitchen tiles, vaguely aware of her friend's ranting.

"What?" Laura stopped what she was doing.

"Get him back." Nina was deadly serious. She put a hand on Laura's arm. "If you let him go, that will be it. Over."

"Bloody good job."

"It'll be like he's dead," Nina said. "Do you really want Tom to be dead?" She turned her gaze to Laura, desperately trying to pass on her meaning. "Don't let him die," she whispered before calling out to Josie that it was time to go. She wanted to get back to Mick.

They set off on the short drive home, wheels spinning as they pulled off the gravel. Her head swam with the crazy, mixed-up images of the last few days. She knew that, if Burnett had his way, dying was something she would soon be doing herself.

CHAPTER
FORTY-NINE

-Have you ever felt as if ur life's over?

I crush my head between my palms.

-Yes

-What did you do?

I pause. How can a few words sum it all up?

-I made another one.

-I miss my mum so much. Do u miss urs still?

-Of course, I type. Truth is, I can scarcely remember her. It's odd how our minds become a scrapbook of smells, words, feelings, images. A patchwork of a life long gone.

-Dad won't speak about her. He's moody all the time.

-He's coming to terms with it. Let him grieve in his own way.

-He's different with me now. Cold.

-That's normal after a loss like this. Pretending to be a fifteen-year-old girl is hard when all I want to do is throw the arms of a mother around her.

-But he hasn't been the same with me for a long while. I can hear her small sob, sense the tinge of sadness in her voice because she thinks her daddy doesn't love her any more. When he looks into her eyes, it's me he's going to see. Another message flashes up.

— *When I was little, he loved me so much.*

-*It's your mum he's angry at, not you.* I have no experience of decent fathers to share with her. I leave it at that in case she becomes suspicious. -*Does that man still come to your house?* I have to know.

-*Not for a while,* Josie types.

-*How's school?* I ask, relieved beyond belief. Suddenly, a new icon pops up telling me that *dramaqueen-jojo* has added a new picture to her album. Until now, there was just the tiny image of her next to her name.

I click on it. I hold my breath as the loading bar crawls slowly along the bottom of the window, bringing up a larger version. That same breath leaves my body in a dam burst when a full-size image resolves on the screen. Josie's hair is hacked short and banded with bleached white and purple streaks. Her eyes are ringed with smudges of black, from both eyeliner and exhaustion. She looks nothing like the girl I remember.

-*School sucks. don't go much,* she types. My fingers slip over the keys, repeatedly typing the wrong letters as I try to reply.

-*Why not? U must go to school.*

-*Don't do anything now Mum's dead.*

I can hear her sobbing; feel the weight of her head as it drops to her desk. I can see the soft indent as she curls onto her bed, praying that the days will pass quickly.

-*What have you done to your hair?* It's the wrong thing to say, but the server wouldn't cope with everything I really want to tell her.

-*I want 2 look ugly.* The cursor flashes on the screen.

-*What do you mean?*

-*Then no one will like me. How do u know my hair's changed?*

Something from way back stirs in my mind, that whenever anyone told her what a pretty little girl she was, she pouted and said she wished she was ugly. Even as a teen, she didn't like compliments.

-*It's just different 2 when I knew u. Shorter. That's all.* I pray that this covers my mistake. -*Why wouldn't you want anyone to like you?*

-*Because being loved too much can hurt just as much as being unloved.*

Her reply echoes a thousand times through the internet, spreading like a virus. She tugs on every cell in my body. Stopping myself from going right back to help my daughter is so much harder than leaving her in the first place.

The gash split my cheek. What little sense of reality I possessed had been smashed from my head by the blow. I don't recall exactly when it happened, just that I was left with a wound that refused to close and was a talking point wherever I went, when my aim was to be completely the opposite.

"You should see your GP about that," the pharmacist commented, nodding at my cheek.

"Just the Steri-strips, please. And paracetamol." I held out a five-pound note. My headache had grown worse during the morning.

I'd checked out of the motel before the owner asked any more questions. Blood had soaked on to the lumpy foam pillow during the night and made a mess of the sheets.

"I don't think that will heal without stitches," the pharmacist persisted.

"I'll give these a try." I took the paper bag and my change. I used the rear-view mirror in my car to stick the strips to my face. Before I left the motel, I'd showered, symbolically washing away everything that had gone before this day as well as the congealed blood on my face. For a while the strips held fast. But after an hour's driving, I'd curled over the steering wheel from the pain and the wound strips had peeled off, leaving my skin gaping wide again. I couldn't arrive looking like this. I pulled into a lay-by and stared at myself in the mirror. Who — or what — I wondered, had I become?

I was woken by a banging on the glass. My head rested on the passenger seat and the gear stick pushed up under my ribs. There was a man's face staring at me, but all I could see was *him* — that scrawny face pasted on to the body of an anonymous lorry driver.

"Shift forward a bit, love . . ." He mouthed something about his truck, the mobile café up ahead.

Terrified, I drove off into the night, unsure if I was dreaming or driving or, perhaps, even dead.

Adam agreed to let me read the alternative draft. He left the computer lying warm in my lap but before starting on the crazy assortment of notes and rambling files that he'd opened, I logged in to Afterlife. The strange conversation with Josie had left me more confused than ever.

My daughter doesn't want to be loved.

Now, I am sitting here smarting from the virtual slap in the face she's just given me when she swore and logged off, upset that I'd mentioned her father again. Tears are trickling down my cheeks when Adam comes back to my room. He wraps me up in his arms until I don't feel real, until my anxiety melts someplace else. Adam becomes the antidote to my crumbling future simply because we have one thing in common: the past.

I sob uncontrollably on to his shoulder.

"I haven't read it yet." We stand on the sloping floorboards in my crooked-ceilinged room, him bending his neck because of the cross-beam, and me bending my neck the other way so he can't see my teary face.

He holds me out at arm's length. "There's something else wrong, isn't there?"

I want to pour out my heart to him but I can't. It's too dangerous and I've already said enough.

It's then that I realise what has happened. He'd wrapped his arms around me and I hadn't pushed him away. I'd felt the buckle of his belt and the rigid form of his chest against me. His legs ran the length of mine. I'd caught a trace of his scent and a whiff of his aftershave. I'd even smelled the fabric conditioner on his shirt — all the things that an embrace brings, and I'd noticed as if it was my very first time. As if I was hugging the only man I'd ever loved, as if he was still in my life, as if Adam did not exist.

I break down into tears again, desperate to tell him the truth. I'm not sure if I'm standing or lying crumpled on the floor or spinning around in space. The strong grip under my arms tells me that I am on the floor, knees bent against the knotty boards, palms collecting splinters.

"Frankie, let me help you . . ." His words are gentle as he guides me to the bed. He sits me down and crouches in front of me. "Speak to me. Let me in."

Then we both laugh — me hysterically through the tears, and he because he reaches for a box of tissues but overbalances. He saves himself by grabbing on to something. My leg.

"Sorry," he says awkwardly. Our smiles are brief, dropping away from embarrassment. "I want to talk to you. I've wanted to talk to you properly since you arrived at Roecliffe, but you've done a superb job of shutting me out."

I sniff. I blow my nose. He tries to read my sadness. I shrug, plucking another tissue from the box. "I've had a lot going on."

"Tell me," he demands. He's been so patient, so kind. It hurts to shut him out when I know all he wants is to help me. This is too much to bear on my own.

"I can't," I reply, giving away that there is indeed something to tell.

"Oh, for God's sake, Frankie." He stands and shoves himself against the window sill, arms locked, jaw set. His knuckles are knotted and white, as if he's about to fling something across the room. He swings round. "I don't fucking understand why you've taken a job at the very place you should want to escape from."

He fires more questions, but I don't hear them. Suddenly I want to tell Adam everything. Like me, he is searching for something he can't have: another chance with those you love most.

"I'm here at Roecliffe," I whisper, jumping right in, "because I'm hiding from one of the men who was involved in the death of your sister. He's out of prison now. He found me." Adam is wide-eyed, a statue. "I thought that Roecliffe would be the last place on earth he'd look for me." I swallow. My mouth is dry. "And, in a strange way, I needed to come back. Crazy, I know. It was a big risk." I shrug, push my fingers through my hair. "It was because of me that they were caught. I saw . . . what happened. I told the police. I identified all but one of them." I hang my head in shame, but quickly glance up at Adam again, staring him right in the eye. "The one who actually killed Betsy, the man in the hood, he walked free." The knot of guilt grinds my stomach. "I'm sorry."

And it's then, as Adam pulls me close, that I realise the person I'm really hiding from is myself.

CHAPTER
FIFTY

The horrid room where I'd seen the cameras, the place I believed was the centre of hell, was at the end of the forbidden corridor. I decided to search there first.

They couldn't have her. We were leaving soon.

I ran out of the dormitory. The linoleum-covered floors, the cracked tiles, the painted panels on the walls, the waist-height trails of grubby finger marks, each telling a grim story, flashed past in a blur as I charged on.

I stood outside the dreadful room, breathing heavily yet trying to keep down the vomit as I summoned the courage. I burst right in, not caring what happened, hoping they would take me instead. The room was dark, empty, silent. There was a stink.

"Betsy!" I yelled. Turning, I ran out and legged it down another corridor that splayed out at right angles to the first. Door after door, I banged on them all, and flew down a dog-legged staircase that took me to a different entrance to the basement. I pushed through and found myself in a low-ceilinged chamber stacked with old furniture, barrels, paint cans and machinery. There was yet another door off this chamber but it was locked. I swear I heard a pitiful wail coming from behind it.

Forcing my jellied legs to work, I tore back the way I'd come, dashing to the usual basement entrance. I pummelled my way through the series of doors, lashing out at light switches, straining to hear the wail again. The cry could have been Betsy.

I stopped, listened. All I could hear was my rasping breath entering and leaving the cage of my ribs. It was where I kept all my fears, stored up over the years, and now they were coming out, *pouring* out, in my desperate search for the little girl who had brought meaning to my life. She was like a younger sister to me and I'd let her down.

"Betsy?" I cried. My voice bounced through the chambers, dislodging clouds of dust, ghosts of the past, remnants of fear draped like torn, bloodied clothes over the stacks of rubbish. I was seeing things, imagining a cave of horror, watching the small skeletons crackling and shifting on the floor as I stepped over the bones of children long gone. "Are you here?" I shivered. *It's not real*, I told myself over and over as the horror of what had been going on dawned on me.

Nothing. I couldn't hear the wailing sound now. Perhaps I'd never heard it, or perhaps it was someone else hiding, a balled-up body of fear snivelling in the corner, waiting to be found, waiting to die.

I screamed as a rat ran over my feet. I wasn't wearing any shoes. Convinced that Betsy wasn't in the basement after all, I ran as fast as I could back to ground level.

Roecliffe lay still. The children were asleep. The old clock told me it was quarter to three. A spillage of light came from the office where Patricia sat on night duty, hunched over her desk, praying that no one would disturb her.

"Who's there?" she called out. I froze against the wall, pressing myself into the shadows as she ducked her head out of the office, then shrugged and settled back to her book. She didn't want trouble; didn't want to notice what went on at night.

I saw that the front door was open a crack. Had someone just been through it? My eyes cut through the darkness outside as I ran down the steps, praying that I was on the right track.

Barefoot, I flew across the rough stones, tarmac and cold mud. I ran as if my life depended on it.

Dizzy with fear, I spun round, staggering backwards while staring up at the grey facade of Roecliffe Children's Home towering above me. "I hate you! I hate you!" I screamed over and over at the silent stone. A thousand imaginary faces peered out of the dozens of dark windows, each one laughing at me. I lunged at the air, at the shadows, at the drizzle, and ran on again, tripping over my own terror.

On and on I stumbled, feeling as if I was tearing through a nightmare — one stride forward and three back. My arms flailed like wings. If I could have flown, I would. "Take me instead!" I called out. Spit foamed on my lips. My ears rang from the bitter cold. Blood seeped from the welts on my feet as I tore down the drive that led to the gates of hell. I didn't know where I was going.

I stopped suddenly. There was a light in the woods.

I ran towards it.

Everything familiar became unreal. The trees that we'd charged around, hidden in, climbed, suddenly became monsters with arms reaching out to snatch me.

I kept going.

I trampled the ground where the bluebells lay dormant. *Don't. They're special,* I'd told her as she'd ripped them from the ground. Later, during the sermon, her eyes flashed like coins as she crushed the petals in her palm. Purple confetti fell around our ankles, tumbling across the stone floor.

I charged on, leaping over twigs and branches that had fallen in the recent storms. *I'm coming, I'm coming . . .* I panted, convinced that the light would lead me to Betsy. Somebody was out in the middle of the night. I prayed they would have Betsy safe.

The drizzle turned to pelting rain, stinging my face as I ran. The trees grew closer together the deeper I went, as if they were joining arms to stop me trespassing in a place I wasn't welcome. I focused on the light.

The undergrowth and trees finally cleared into an open space with the chapel at its centre. I slowed down. I didn't want to be seen. I crept round the edge, careful to stay in the shadows. I stared up at the big arched window. Someone was in there and had lit candles — dozens of them lined up along the sills.

"Please be all right, Betsy." She was in the house of God. She had to be safe, didn't she? Or maybe she'd taken herself off there, preferring the comfort of the chapel at night, away from prying hands. "Brave little girl," I mouthed, imagining her curled up on a pew. But until I knew for sure, I had to be careful. It might not be Betsy in there.

A clump of bushes stretched from the wood to the chapel. I crouched, following their path until I reached the dank smell of wet stone. I pressed my hands on to the lichen-covered building and followed the wall. Above me the candlelight drew me on, lighting my way to the front door.

I stopped. If I went that way, I'd be seen instantly.

At the end of the Sunday service, the older ones were taken to the back room for extra Bible lessons. The younger kids remained fidgeting in the pews, singing hymns under Mr Leaby's direction. I knew that other room had several windows and a door leading directly outside. Last time we were there, the catch on one of the windows had jammed and Patricia had cursed. "Damn thing will have to stay open then," she said, and clapped a hand over her mouth.

I crept to the window and reached up, hooking my fingers under the rotten wood. It gave and lifted. As soon as I raised it, my nostrils were filled with a strange scent. The chapel usually smelled of damp and rot and wet books, but now a gentle aroma spiralled out. Someone had lit incense.

I curled my toes into the notches between the bricks, and dug my fingers around the window frame. In a moment, I'd heaved myself up and squeezed through the open pane. The room was completely dark, lit only by a thin horizon of light coming from beneath the door leading to the main chapel.

Silently, I jumped down off the sill. I felt my way around the wall to the door opposite. I kicked something — a chair or a wooden box — and it scraped loudly across the floor. I held my breath, stifling the cry of pain as my bare toe throbbed, waiting for the door to burst open, my head to be whipped back and forth as my shoulders were shaken.

Nothing.

I exhaled and drew up to the door, my feet stepping into the invitation of light. Then I heard the chanting. It was like nothing I'd ever heard before.

I put my hand on the door handle. The altar would be to my left, the congregation pews to my right. My fist shook on the knob, but a tiny brave part of me turned it. Praying it wouldn't make a noise, I eased the door open no more than the breadth of my little finger. To the right, I saw the empty racks of wooden pews that had made our bottoms numb on countless Sundays. I couldn't see anyone.

Driven on by the strange noise — somewhere between monks chanting and old dogs growling — I dared to open the door a little wider. When it was open about the width of my hand, I could just make out the windows and the big old door opposite. There was still no one in sight. I closed my eyes for a second, begging God to protect me.

I daren't open the door any more so I peered through the crack at the hinges. There was a vertical shaft of light — a flickering mass suggesting Christmas, angels, some kind of celebration. I twisted my head sideways, waiting until my eyes adjusted to the brilliant array of candle flames around the altar.

My fist rammed the scream back down my throat. I gagged. I bit the thin bones of my hand to prevent the cry that would give me away.

A naked child was tied to a table with swathes of coloured cloth. It was a girl. The bench was perpendicular to the altar with the toes saluting the cross. The body's short length gave away her young age. Four figures, all dressed in black, loomed over her, one at each side of the table. I couldn't see her face.

Tears filled my eyes. "Please don't be Betsy, please don't be Betsy," I muttered against my fist. I had no idea what was going on. Perhaps it wasn't as awful as it first appeared. There was no struggling. The child was lying still. The candles gave off a warm and homely glow to the usually cold chapel, and the chanting offered some comfort.

I stared in disbelief at the man standing opposite.

I knew who he was.

Mr Tulloch. He'd taught me when I was at the village school. His sandy hair was ginger in the candlelight. His pockmarked skin stretched tight over a good deal of fat. He was the shortest of the four and appeared to be in control of the gathering. He raised his arms and waved them above his head. Suddenly the chanting ceased.

Short staccato bolts of fear left my lungs.

Don't make a noise. Don't make a noise.

Sweat broke out on my face. My hands shook — one still glued to the doorknob, the other rammed in my dry mouth. The skin on my arms and legs crawled and prickled as if insects were clambering all over me.

"Let's get on with it," said one of the others. They walked round the table. Their arms were held out with their palms facing down over the poor wretch on the table.

Another face came into view.

I knew him too.

He was the young man from the village, the one who rode the mowers around the grounds, not much more than a boy himself. His hair was frizzy and his ruddy face was pale and intense. He looked excited. I'd heard the other girls calling out his name as he worked the grounds, teasing and flirting with him. "*Hey, Karl,*" they sang. "*Come and get us.*"

The next face to come into view took my breath away.

Mr Leaby.

He followed in the slow parade, illuminated by the circle of candles around them. The low lighting gave him hollows above his eye sockets instead of underneath. My hands crushed my mouth, twisting away any possibility of making a noise. This was the man in charge of the home, the person responsible for our safety.

Why, then, did he draw out a long knife from beneath the table and pass it to the fourth person in the group?

The final man turned to receive the instrument. I held my breath, ready for the shock of someone else I knew. But when he turned into the candlelight, all I saw was a black hood with pale almonds cut out where his eyes should have been.

It all happened so quickly.

The knife went into her chest vertically. More chanting concealed the brief but piercing shriek. Hot vomit spilled silently down my front as blood poured off the edge of the table. I still couldn't see the child's face. Two small arms flailed sideways and one knee rose involuntarily.

Please, dear God, don't let it be Betsy.

Then stillness as the blade was withdrawn and inserted again, this time in the stomach. The metallic stench of blood seeped across the chapel as the hooded man worked like a surgeon.

Finally, when the child lay quite still, words were exchanged and the four men backed away from the body.

Then I saw her.

My little friend, little Betsy, lay lifeless on the table.

My eyes dizzied in and out of focus, refusing to believe what I was seeing. Her soft hair flowed off the edge of the table. Her sweet face with its wide eyes stared blankly at the ceiling. Blood poured from dark holes in her naked body. Her concave chest held a small puddle, while the crook of her armpits released a thickening river of red.

I stared at her for what seemed like my entire life. From the moment I'd found her waif-like and alone in the corridor to only an hour or so ago when she was warm and safe in bed with me, I replayed every moment of our time together.

Betsy was dead. They had killed her.

I couldn't move.

I saw fresh bruises on her face, her legs, the insides of her thighs. I unconsciously drank in the details of the scene, taking in everything with dreadful clarity — every mole on their faces, the colour of their eyes, their hair, what shoes they wore, the tone of their voices, how long their fingernails were, and the way they grinned and applauded each other for a job well done. I saw them all except for the hooded one.

Then, as I crept backwards, I stumbled, and something crashed to the floor.

The men swooped round. I saw the blood drain from three of their faces, just as it had done from Betsy's limp body.

There was a roar followed by clattering and swearing, shouts of anger, thundering feet.

In slow motion, I turned and fumbled my way back to the window. My shaking hands wrenched it open and I scraped myself through. It slammed shut on my fingers. The men were close behind me, crashing into the back room. They were yelling out, threatening me, ordering me to stop.

I jumped down on to the soft earth outside the chapel. Then I ran.

I looked back once, stumbled, locked eyes with the youngest man: *Karl*.

The woods closed in around me, swallowing me up in branches and thorns and roots and fallen leaves. All I could hear was the sound of my breath as it flooded in and out of my lungs, and the whoosh of blood in my ears as I ran on, one foot after another a thousand times over. Cold mud splattered up my legs; I stumbled on knotty roots rising up from the earth.

I stopped. I glanced back with hands on knees, panting. There was no one there. I'd lost them in the dark woods.

But how could I leave Betsy?

In the distance I heard shrieks undercut by low voices. They were still searching for me. But there was no stampede of footsteps, no chase through the trees. They didn't know which way I'd gone; didn't know the woods as well as I did.

I trembled. They didn't want to leave the body either. *Betsy's body*, I sobbed to myself. I couldn't afford to let it out. Not yet.

What were they going to do with her?

Driven by hatred, and by a loyalty to Betsy that overrode any sense I had left, I crept between the trees and headed back towards the dim light of the chapel. Every step I took matched every controlled breath that entered or left my chest. I listened, I waited, I advanced a foot more. I half expected a hand to come from behind, clamping around my mouth, binding me up next to Betsy in the chapel.

Ahead, I saw the flash of a torch.

I was close. One of them carried a candle. It was the hooded one. I crouched behind a bush, squinting through the scratchy twigs at the scene outside the chapel. They spoke in low voices, occasionally punctuated by a raised voice, an angry yell as they disagreed on something. One of them shoved Mr Leaby. He fell over. I had upset their ritual. They didn't know what to do. They didn't know how much I'd seen. They were fighting among themselves.

Carefully, I held on to every detail of the gruesome scene in my head. Every last feature on those three faces, the colour of every piece of fabric, hair and clothing was printed on my mind. It was a scene I would never forget.

There was more shouting, a scuffle. I wanted to get closer but daren't. One of the men was carrying something. Something pale in the white glare of a torch. Flashing in and out of focus, I followed their jerky passage.

Karl, the one who worked in the grounds, brandished a shovel and began to dig furiously. I heard the ring of metal followed by cursing as he struck a rock. Soil pattered in the night.

"Get her in," one of them said. It was Leaby's voice. The hooded man bent over the hole and allowed Betsy to flop into the earth. An arm and a leg stuck out so he kicked them into the shallow grave.

Karl leaned in and plucked something from the body, holding it up. I couldn't see what it was, but the torchlight bounced off it as if it were metallic.

Then he shovelled the earth back and within minutes all that was left of Betsy was a gentle mound in the blackness of the woods. "We need to go," one of them said. Grabbing the shovel, the candle, a discarded jacket, the four of them walked briskly away from the chapel. With his back to me, the man with the hood dragged the black covering from his head. Then they were lost in the dark.

I stared at the muddy mound. Above it, an oak tree towered. After an hour, perhaps two, certain the men had gone, I crawled towards Betsy on all fours. I was a forest creature, hunting, prowling, searching. When I reached the grave, I pushed my hands into the damp soil. The smell of it lined my nose. The rain had stopped, but fat drops fell from the branches.

I scraped away the soil, slowly at first, but then with desperation, scared that she wouldn't be able to breathe. Panicking, I shovelled the wet earth as fast as I could, eventually catching my nails on something soft, something skin-like only colder.

It was Betsy's shoulder.

I wiped the tears off my face, leaving smears of black soil on my cheeks. I pummelled at the ground, tearing it off her face as I exposed her chest, her neck and, finally, dirty strands of her baby-like hair. In it was a strawberry-shaped hairclip — one of a pair that she always wore.

404

"Betsy, Betsy . . ." I sobbed. My tears fell on her face. Pure white skin beneath a mask of mud, she slept with her dirt-filled eyes open. She stared up into the trees.

I shook her. I kissed her. I wiped the blood off her chest with my pyjamas.

She was gone. Taken from me. Dead.

I pulled the clip from her hair, snagging some strands as it came out. Then I ran. I didn't stop until I reached the village. Exhausted, sobbing, hysterical, bereft, I slammed into the telephone box. I called the police. Enough was enough. After ten years of silence, it was time to tell.

CHAPTER
FIFTY-ONE

Nina stared at her husband, unable to move. She gripped the car keys. "Were you in a fight? Who did this to you?" Her voice shook. She approached him cautiously, as if even her presence might hurt the puffy bruises that sat beneath each eye. Mick's nose was crooked and bloody, quite possibly broken, and his bottom lip was split in two. He sat at the kitchen table looking like the bottom had fallen out of his world.

"Oh my God, Dad. Look at you!" Josie ran up to hug her father, but he kept her at arm's length.

Nina tentatively knelt down beside him. She couldn't stand to think that Burnett had done this to Mick. "Were you in a car accident?" She hadn't noticed any damage on Mick's car when she'd raced back from Laura's with Josie. He'd called to ask when she'd be home, that he'd had an accident. He'd hung up before Nina could ask if he was OK. "Josie, run to the bathroom and fetch some dressings and antiseptic cream."

Mick shook his head and winced. "It's so stupid," he said, trying to smile. He sounded as if he had a mouthful of food. "You wouldn't believe it, but I fell down the stairs." He touched his cheek and grimaced.

"The stairs?" she said incredulously. Perhaps it wasn't Burnett. "I'll get you some ice." Nina rummaged in the freezer and emptied a tray of ice cubes into a plastic bag. She wrapped them in a tea towel and gently held them against Mick's skin. "So how did you manage to fall? Are you sure it was the stairs, Mick? Not a car accident or a . . . a fight with someone?"

Josie yelled out that she couldn't find the items.

"They're in the cabinet," Nina called back.

Mick attempted a laugh, but stopped because of the pain. "If somebody had done this to me, would I be sitting here? Don't you think I'd be at the police station making a complaint?"

Nina nodded. He was right. Mick wasn't the kind of man to let someone get away with violence. "I was trying to move that old chest of drawers out of Josie's room, like you've been asking me to do for ages. I felt bad it had just sat there, in the way. I was dragging it across the landing when my phone rang." Mick moved the ice to the other cheek. "I didn't realise how close to the top of the stairs I was. I leaned back to get the phone from my pocket and wham. Suddenly I was at the bottom with my face smashed against the hall table. I took a battering on the way down too. I can still feel each stair."

"Oh, Mick, how awful." Nina gently embraced her husband. On top of everything else, she couldn't stand to think of him hurt. "Shall I drive you to the hospital for a check-up?"

"No. I'll be fine." Mick stood up.

"Take it easy today. Go and lie down. You might be concussed."

Mick laughed. "OK, I'll tell the elves to finish the paintings, shall I?"

"Mick —"

"You don't get it, do you?" Mick steadied himself on the door frame.

"At least let me fetch your paints so you can work in the kitchen. I want to keep an eye on you." Nina thought her head would explode with worry. "Is the studio locked? Give me the key." She smiled kindly; a special reserve.

"No. I don't want anyone to see it yet. It's not finished." He massaged his temples. "I'll be OK." Shaking his head, Mick turned and left, quietly closing the back door. Nina watched from the window as he disappeared inside his studio.

She stood at the window for an age, thinking about everything that she had to do, *couldn't stand to do*. Finally, when she did move, she went upstairs to Josie, who was still trying to find the dressings for her dad. The chest of drawers, just as Mick had said, was blocking the landing. His mobile phone was lying on the carpet beside it. There were scuff marks on the paintwork. Nina let slip the tiniest sigh of relief that it wasn't Burnett who had hurt her husband.

Nina was searching the internet for items she would need when the house telephone rang. She just managed to intercept Josie, who also dashed to answer it. Josie skulked off, not understanding her mother's odd behaviour. Nina's breath flowed cold into tight lungs when the silent caller hung up after a second or two.

In a panic, she asked Laura if she could drop Josie back at her house. She didn't know what else to do. Nowhere felt safe — nowhere near her, anyway, she concluded. She wondered if a sleepover would be best. Laura didn't hesitate. "If it means I can polish off a bottle of wine in front of trash TV later on without worrying about where they both are, then it suits me."

When Nina dropped Josie off, a hiccupping sob left her throat. She didn't want it to be the last time she saw her daughter. Laura already looked as if she'd downed a bottle of something, the way she spoke in slurs, but the girls hanging out on Afterlife was the least of Nina's worries as she briefed a reluctant Josie to stay indoors whatever happened. At least Laura hadn't noticed the state she was in.

Nina left Laura's house. She had things to take care of.

CHAPTER
FIFTY-TWO

Adam rests his fingertips on the altar and closes his eyes. Darkness fills the chapel with a single slice of light seeping through a gap in one of the boarded-up windows.

"She bloody didn't deserve to die."

"None of them did," I say, wondering what the death count was. "We had our Sunday services here. We thought we were close to God, when really only the devil lived here."

Adam turns and reaches out to me. "Something's brought us together, Frankie." In the half-light, I see him frown. "Perhaps it's Betsy's spirit." He squeezes my hands before letting go, realising what he's doing.

"I don't believe in the afterlife," I tell him bitterly. "There is only one life, however many ways we try to live it." I sit on the edge of a pew. "This is where we used to pray," I say, running my hand over the worn wood. "Look. She did this with a flint that she found on the path."

Adam crouches down next to me, tracing his finger over the crude letter "b" that's inscribed.

"I want the investigation reopened, Frankie. I want the one that did it caught."

I lower my head. He has to know that I tried. "Even when they were . . . when they were . . ."

"Go on."

"When they were burying her in the woods, he was still wearing the hood. After it happened, I replayed the scene a thousand times in my mind, hoping to recall some tiny detail that would be useful to the police. I wanted him caught so badly. I loved Betsy too."

I feel an arm slip round my shoulders. The warmth of another human, the comfort of a body against me — from someone who cares, who *knows* — is immeasurable.

"I was so scared. The anger in me was bigger than the entire world, Adam. Perhaps if I'd got to her sooner, I could have saved her. Or at least been able to identify the one that actually did it, seen him without the hood. It was such a sick ceremony."

"Is that how you saw it? As a ceremony?"

I nod. "The police thought that. I was about to turn eighteen when it happened so I understood most of what they talked about among themselves. They kept going on about paedophiles and how they initiated new members. It was one of the biggest groups in the north of England. It had been based at the children's home for years, but no one ever told."

Adam rests his forehead on my shoulder. "You've lived with this all your life," he says.

"There's not a day goes by that I don't think of her."

"You know what I wish? That I could spend just one day with her."

"If you ever get that wish, then tell me how you did it."

"Oh?"

I look him straight in the eye; the closest I'm ever likely to come to telling anyone. "There are a couple of people I'd like to spend a day with too."

A sudden noise makes us jump. It's Frazer Barnard rapping on the door with his walking cane. He's silhouetted by the light behind as he stands on the threshold, still refusing to come into the chapel. "It's time to lock up," he says nervously, as if something evil will happen if we stay any longer.

I give Adam's arm a brief squeeze. "You take a moment," I tell him. "I'll be outside."

I'm glad to get out, even if it means waiting with the old man from the village. The more local people who see me, the greater the risk of being discovered. I only came out here again for Adam's sake. Frazer rattles the keys like a jailer. "Don't understand all the fuss," he says. "What's done is done."

"Sometimes people need to come to terms with their past," I say, annoyed. "So that they can carry on with their future."

Barnard prods his cane into the ground with one hand, and fiddles with the key fob in the other. That's when I see it. His hand is missing a thumb. I stare like a child gawping at a disfigured person, and when Frazer Barnard sees me looking he quickly thrusts it back into his pocket.

"It's a sea of blue in May," I tell him. "From all the way over there and across to the chapel. God's carpet, we called it." I sweep my hand to show Adam. "Come." I take his arm and lead him on.

It was his idea. He emerged from the chapel red-eyed and didn't say much until Barnard had locked up and walked off back to the village. We stood alone on the lane. I was still reeling from what I'd noticed about Barnard's hand. How many people had missing thumbs? He was the one who had stared in at Lexi's window, but why? I didn't know how to tell Adam; didn't want to believe what it might mean.

"I want to see where she was buried."

He couldn't be serious. "No, Adam. Don't do that to yourself." He walked off, knowing it was somewhere close to the chapel.

Our feet kick through fallen leaves. "Where?" he asks as we approach the dismal building again. It's separated from the rest of the world by yards of barbed wire.

"Over here," I say, veering to the left. "I ran away when they knew I'd been spying on them. But when I got a good safe distance away, I stopped. I couldn't leave her. I wanted to go back. Stupidly, I thought she might still be alive." The trees and undergrowth around us are thick, shrouding us from the daylight. We walk on.

"You were brave," Adam says. His voice is croaky.

"No," I say vehemently. "I was stupid. Stupid to have allowed it to go on for so long." My turn to choke back the tears.

I remember what I saw — the chapel windows lit up from the candlelight, illuminating the ground so they could dig, the shoving, the arguing, the sparks that jumped between them.

"It was over there," I say, pointing to a spot about twenty yards from the chapel door. "Where the ground rises and clears." I turn, hoping he'll want to go now. He takes my hand and leads me on.

"Show me exactly."

"Adam, it's been a long time. The trees, the bushes, they've changed."

"Please," he says, with pain in his eyes.

So I show him, wishing that we were visiting a proper grave, not an empty mound that was probed by a forensics team for days after Betsy was exhumed. "It was here." I draw an imaginary rectangle over the area.

"How can you be so sure?"

"There was already a small graveyard in this area. Can you see that old wall?" I point to a low, crumbling stone wall that outlines the area. It's more eroded now, ivy growing all over it. "It ran around the dozen or so graves that are here. They're all flat stone markers. We used to get told off for jumping on them like stepping stones on our way to chapel." I kick aside the layer of leaves — dry and crispy on top, sludgy beneath. "There. This grave was right next to where . . . where Betsy was . . . put."

Adam is on his knees, pushing his fingers into the dirt. He bows down as if praying, lowering his head until it's resting on the ground.

"Look," I suddenly say. "See this?"

414

Adam sits up and frowns. He's lost in a life that never was.

"It's an oak tree. A baby oak that's set itself right here."

Adam glances around for the parent tree. It's there, a little way to our left; a towering giant keeping watch.

"She liked playing with the acorns in autumn. She would have liked this tree growing here."

Adam nods. We sit on the damp earth, talking, me telling him all about his little sister, and him arranging twigs and stones in the shape of a heart.

She hadn't logged on for two days. It was unusual. Coping with the regular tangles and demands of school life grew more difficult as the term wore on. I had no idea what would happen when Christmas approached, and although it was a way off yet, several of the girls had been discussing their plans for the holidays. I wanted to crawl into a hole for the festive season and hibernate until spring. I couldn't face it.

"Can I use your laptop, please?" Adam was in the staffroom, a place I never usually ventured into unless the terminals were free. So far this morning, every computer in the school had been occupied. There were end-of-term exams to mark, reports to write, and the teachers were busy. But I was desperate to chat with her; desperate to know she was OK. It was the only way to get through the interminable days.

"Sure," he said, standing up. As usual, the laptop was tucked under his arm. "Would you like to go somewhere private? The library?"

I nodded and we walked silently through the school together. We hadn't spoken since our chapel visit, since Adam said a private prayer before leaving the spot where Betsy had been buried. The library was empty apart from two girls hunched over a textbook, and the librarian, who was covering new books at the desk. She smiled at us as we sat at a table.

"We never did go to that art exhibition," Adam says. He nods up at the row of portraits staring down at us. "It'll be over now."

I open up the computer and wait for the internet connection to be made. "I don't think I want to go to an exhibition, Adam."

"I thought you liked art," he says. He enters his password. I notice it begins with the letters b, e and t.

"I do. It's just that . . ." I hesitate. "Someone I once loved was an artist." That's all I will say. *Someone I still love*, I think.

Adam's head draws an arc in the air as he understands. "Old flame?" he asks.

I nod.

"Did it end badly?"

I stare hard at the Google page and hope that Adam won't press for a reply. He's got everything so wrong.

"I'll take that as a yes then."

"I won't be long," I say, glancing up, hoping he will take the hint.

"I have a fourth-form lesson in fifteen minutes." He doesn't budge.

I twist the computer round to face me and bring up the Afterlife website. In a moment, I'm logged in and checking my messages. There's nothing new. I pull up *dramaqueen-jojo's* profile and see that she logged in this morning. My sigh is bigger than I realise.

"Everything OK?" Adam peers round at the screen. "Don't tell me you're into that too. I thought it was just for kids." He laughs and pulls a book off the nearest shelf. He opens it randomly. "You are a mystery, Miss Gerrard. Or perhaps it's Mrs Gerrard?" He eyes me curiously, picking away at my layers until it hurts.

"Miss," I whisper. I shift my chair and pull the computer round further. Then, as if by magic, Josephine logs on. Was she watching, waiting for me to arrive? We've spoken regularly now, and she always initiates a conversation. But this time there's no pop-up window for chatting; no familiar greeting.

Nothing happens.

Conscious of the short time I have, I request a line of chat with her. Her character immediately fades and states that she is offline.

"Odd," I say, clicking on her profile again.

"What is?"

I sigh. I have some explaining to do now, whether I spin him another story or not. It's not normal for a woman of my age to be playing on Afterlife.

Suddenly, another request flashes on to my screen. *Griff is online and wants to be your friend.*

"I . . . I have a friend with a teenage daughter. Let's just say she's had a tough time recently." I stare at the online request, not knowing what to do. "She asked if I could keep an eye on her and we both decided that

417

Afterlife was the best way to find out what was going on in her world."

"You're spying on her?" Adam is incredulous. He slots the book back on to the shelf.

"Not exactly spying." I feel my cheeks redden. I click "accept" and Griff's full profile spreads across my screen.

"So she knows it's you then?" Adam isn't letting up.

I shake my head. It was the wrong story to spin, even though it's almost the truth. I skim Griff's details. Same high school as Josie . . . a year older . . . plays hockey . . .

"Spying, then."

"Yes," I admit. At least it's a diversion.

"And what have you found out?"

"That she's very unhappy. That she has no one to talk to. That she may be in danger." The relief at having spilled this much is immense. "I'm so worried about her, Adam."

-Hi, Griff says. -U a friend of jojo's? I stare blankly at the conversation window.

"Then you need to tell her mother."

"She already knows," I say. "She doesn't know what to do either." I fiddle with the mouse pad, sending the pointer flying across the screen. -Yes, I reply to Griff. "She's an absent parent," I continue, breathlessly close to saying too much.

-I'm worried about her, he continues.

"Is she a pupil here?" Adam asks.

I shake my head. "No."

The computer bleeps an alert, while the bright box on the screen suddenly asks if I want to accept the three-way chat with Josephine and Griff. We both stare at it. My fingers hover over the keys. When Josie clicks "Accept", so do I.

-*Hello, dramaqueen-jojo* types.

-*How r u? I was worried. u seem so sad.* I don't like it that Griff can read our conversation. Adam glances at his watch. He's trying not to look, but I can see he's reading every line too.

-*I am fine, thank you.*

-*Whassup, jo-jo?* Griff butts in.

"That's odd," I say, actually grateful that Adam is here. "She doesn't sound fine."

He leans towards me. "Look. She just said she was."

-*Have u been 2 school?* I ask.

-*Nothing is up at all, Griff.*

This doesn't sound like Josie.

-*And yes, I have been to school,* she replies.

"This isn't the way she normally speaks . . . types," I say. "Her language is different. Too formal."

"You can tell from a few words?"

"And I know that she *hasn't* been going to school. She's been too upset."

-*thought u couldn't face school.*

-*Where are you?* Josephine asks me. *What's your address?*

"This is weird, Adam. I think she might be planning to run away."

"Whoa," he says. "Back up there. I've had enough of teenage girls and their hormonal pursuits for one school year. I don't think I want to hear about another."

I'm careful to keep within the story I have constructed, for Adam's sake. "She believes that I'm an old primary school friend called Amanda." I point to my onscreen name. "She's having such a tough time at home, since her mum . . . left, she said she wanted to come and stay with me. Of course, I told her she couldn't. And now she's asking for my address."

Adam pulls a face, his chin resting on the heel of his hand. He glances between the screen and me, puzzling over each. He is so close I can feel the brush of his breath on my cheek.

"I'd deploy rule number one of safe internet use, if I were you." When I raise my eyebrows, he continues, "Say you don't give out your personal details over the internet. Say your dad would kill you." He pats my head in a fatherly way.

-*Why do u want 2 know?* I type. What if she's in trouble? I think. What if she needs to escape?

-*I would like to visit you.*

"Something's wrong, Adam. This just isn't how she chats online." My mind races, wondering if I can somehow get a cryptic message to Mick, perhaps through Laura, maybe Jane Shelley. I don't know what to do.

Adam stands and stretches. It's been an emotional time for him. He doesn't want to be drawn into my mess. "Class begins in a few minutes."

-*Is that man keeping away?* I ask. I have to know.

-*Which man would that be?*

"Frankie, I don't want to pressure you, but —"

"Just another minute. Please."

-*The man from the gallery*. I can't bring myself to type his name.

I turn to see if Adam's reading over my shoulder, but thankfully he's walked away and is talking to the librarian.

-*He's always at our house these days. He's cute. I think he fancies me.*

My eyes widen at her words. I can't believe what I'm reading.

-*What do u mean?* Dear God, no.

And then, as quickly as she appeared, *dramaqueen-jojo* fades to grey and shows as offline. "No!" I call out. My voice rings through the quiet library. Frantically, I type a message to Griff, to see if he can contact her, go round, anything, but he has disappeared too.

"Are you OK?" Adam reaches for his computer, but I grip on to it.

"Please, just another few minutes. I have to see if she comes back. It's all gone so wrong." Adam sees my sobs before I realise I'm crying.

"Frankie, I need it for a history presentation in class. Can this wait until later?" My head hits the desk and I nod, releasing the laptop.

"Can we meet later? Will you help me?"

The warmth of his hand on my back is all I need to know that he will.

Sylvia comes to take over my PSHE class. "I'm so grateful," I say as I hand her my stack of notes. I'd told her I had a migraine.

"What is it this week?" she asks in the corridor. "Affairs with married men or alcoholism?" She laughs and takes the notes.

"We're still talking about bullying, actually, and when it's right to tell someone."

"Oh," Matron says. "Snitching. They'll love that." And she disappears into the common room.

Adam finds me hovering around the single computer terminal in the staffroom. A male member of staff scrolls down a page. "He's been on eBay for hours," I whisper. Adam gives me a knowing look and taps his laptop.

"Use mine, and then I have a treat in store for you." He winks. "To cheer you up."

In spite of everything, I manage a smile. I don't think there are too many of them left. "Thanks," I reply, taking the laptop. I sit in the corner, as far away as possible from the other staff that come and go, gulping mugs of lukewarm coffee, moaning about their workload, marking books stacked in piles on their knees. When the computer asks for the user password, I type "Betsy" and it immediately lets me in. I glance at Adam and he's staring right back. A small smile crosses the barrier between us, another one deducted from my account.

Dramaqueen-jojo has not been back online since our chat several hours earlier. I linger around the familiar public areas where I've noticed she hangs out, and in the meantime I decide to compose a message to her — the one that I would like to send but in reality cannot.

422

It will sit in the drafts folder, a beacon of the truth; a reminder of what once was.

I look up and stretch. My neck is sore and my fingers ache. The staffroom is empty. I typed six pages and still didn't say everything I wanted. I sign off with a single kiss, one to last a lifetime, and save it in my Afterlife account. I pour the last dregs of coffee from the machine.

"School's out," someone says. I turn and Adam is there as if he has been watching over me all this time.

"Your computer. I'm so sorry." I hand it back.

"I didn't need it. I've been busy." He puts it in his locker and clicks the padlock closed. "And now for your treat," he says. "Come with me."

"What . . .?" Suddenly I'm being led by the hand through the many corridors. We head up the staircases and along the passages that lead towards my room. "Where are we going?" I don't want a treat. He jangles a key and grins. My heart misses a beat. I pull Adam to a halt, gripping his arm. I have to tell him. Even if he'll think I'm crazy. "Did you notice it too, Adam? Frazer Barnard's hand when he was fiddling with the keys?"

He frowns, pulling me on. "Notice what?"

"The thumb on his left hand was missing. Didn't you see?" He's silent. "I didn't see it the first time we met, but while I was waiting for you to come out of the chapel, I saw he didn't have a thumb."

"So?" I see the twitch in Adam's jaw, the mini frown above his eyes. Does he still think I dreamt the whole thing up?

"Don't you get it? He must have been the one staring in through Lexi's window that night. I swear the handprint I saw didn't have a thumb. What do you think he was doing?" He doesn't understand how serious this is. If I've been recognised, it's over.

"Being a dirty old man?" he suggests.

"Exactly," I say, wondering why Adam is being so casual about it. "Should we report him?" My stomach turns. Police, statements, arrests . . . Then all I can think of are threats, fear, running away again.

"Frankie." He stops, blocking the way. "I have never met anyone who worries as much as you do."

"But —"

"You're going to make yourself ill."

"I'm —"

"Just for now, relax. Please? Let's deal with it tomorrow." He sighs, reining in his annoyance.

I nod, thinking how easy it would be to fall into his arms until the pain eased.

"Now come with me." He leads me past my bedroom door and a little further down the sloping corridor. Nothing is straight in this part of the building. "Mr Palmer gave me the key. Said he thought we might like a look. I told him about your interest in the library portraits." Adam wiggles the key in the old lock and eventually it gives. "Geoff said no one's been in here for years, but there's going to be a clear-out. The room's being decorated for more staff accommodation." Adam goes in and flicks on the light. "Ta-da!" he sings, watching for my reaction.

424

It takes a moment to realise what he's done. I laugh, shaking my head in disbelief.

"Champagne, madam?" He goes over to the table, dust motes spinning up off the dirty old floor, and peels back the foil on a bottle of Lanson. He gently releases the cork, pours carefully, and hands me a glass, watching as the bubbles rise to the brim before sinking down again. "Our own private viewing," he says, sweeping his hand around the room.

Spread out, leaning up against the skirting boards, stacked on the window sills, hanging from whatever hooks were in the wall are dozens and dozens of paintings. "Mr Palmer said they've been stashed here for decades. He's been through them all and only a couple were of interest to him. He says there are more in the attic above, although he's not seen those yet. No one's ever bothered to fetch them down." Adam waits for my reaction, pointing up to a hatch in the ceiling. "They're all going off to an auction soon. He told me to help myself to anything I liked."

"I don't know what to say." I sip the champagne.

"Since you wouldn't come to the exhibition with me, I thought this would be second best. Some of them are quite skilful. Others are plain awful. I didn't want to upset you though, when you told me about the man you —"

"You haven't." I walk round the perimeter of the room, smiling at what he's done. Then he whips back a white cloth on the table and a feast of cold food is revealed. "Oh, Adam," I say, quite speechless. His kindness hurts.

"You needed cheering up. And I needed . . ." He falters. "I wanted to spend time with you. Just us."

I frown. "A date?"

"Yes."

"Adam, there's no way I can . . ." I stop. He's holding out a plate of crackers and pâté. "Thank you." I shake my head and take one.

"What do you reckon?" he says, lifting up a frameless canvas. "Impressionist wannabe?"

"It's awful," I say, laughing. "Perhaps a talentless pupil did it." I bite the cracker.

"Nope. These were left here way before the school opened up. Mr Palmer doesn't know where they came from originally. Hoarded over the years."

"That's not bad," I say, pointing at another picture, humouring him, and his odd idea of a date. "I like the sky. It's quite clever the way . . ."

"The way that there are clouds in it?" Adam finishes for me.

"It's terrible, too, isn't it?" I spray laughter.

"It serves you right for not coming to a proper gallery with me."

"OK, OK, I will," I promise. He pours us more champagne.

"And dinner afterwards?"

"Perhaps," I say, meaning no. I could never betray Mick. "What about this one? Would you hang it on your wall?"

"Nope."

"Or this?"

"No way."

426

It goes on, me lifting pictures from the dust, the pair of us laughing at them, as if we could do better ourselves, until we stumble upon a batch of canvases that are clearly more professional than the rest.

Adam cuts some cheese. "Do you like Brie?"

"Thank you. These are actually very good." I eat a grape, staring at the abstract yet somehow very real pictures that Adam has set out beneath the window. "They seem contemporary, ahead of their time. Look, this one's dated."

"Nineteen eighty-three," Adam reads.

"Ancient," I joke, staring at it. The champagne has made me relaxed, but for some reason the tension returns to my neck and shoulders. My head begins to ache.

"Take it," Adam says. "Put it on your bedroom wall. Mr Palmer said we can have what we like. The rest will be disposed of one way or another. Probably in a skip."

I lean the painting up against the table. We look at more pictures, eat the food, and finish the champagne. Later, alone in my bedroom, after I sidestepped what I imagined was going to be an embrace, I straighten the new picture on my wall. I lie on my bed, staring at it, getting lost in the folds of green that make up the countryside scene, marvelling at how the flash of red, the glint of gold suggests the hunt, the baying hounds, the sound of the horn, the terrified fox.

I fall asleep, dropping in and out of a dream, in and out of the picture. I am the fox, being chased relentlessly across the fields by a hooded man. I wake, sweating, shaking, twisting the sheets around me. It's dark. I flick on the light. I get out of bed, throw on some clothes, facing up to what it all means.

I run silently through the school. I need to see Adam. I need to use his computer.

CHAPTER
FIFTY-THREE

She couldn't take much with her. It wasn't as if she was an Egyptian queen and her tomb would be stuffed with possessions for the afterlife. She wasn't sure she'd even have a life in forty-eight hours' time. Nina stared into her dressing-table mirror, wondering who she would become.

The house was strangely calm. Josie and Nat were upstairs attempting to use Nina's sewing machine. She'd been called in to untangle the thread several times already. She stood in the doorway, watching the girls work. Nat was cutting fabric, while Josie joined them together. The sewing session had distracted them from making a trip to the shops, to the cinema, to potential danger. It reminded Nina of herself, how she used to make something out of nothing. *The story of my life*, she thought, going back into her and Mick's bedroom.

She lay on the bed and stared at the ceiling, waiting, going over everything in her head a thousand times, like she would before a play opened. All the props must be put back in their correct places after the previous show. All the make-up checked, all the effects put away and stock reordered. There was no room for error, for a wig gone astray, or an empty bottle of fake blood. Just as now, just as in real life, everything had to be ready and perfect for the finale. She was absolutely terrified.

Nina reached a hand across to Mick's side of the bed. She stroked the empty space. It would be the hardest thing she had ever done. She imagined him lying there, and tried to explain to him in her head. But he rose up from the sheets in a terrible rage, demanding explanations, furious that he'd been kept out of her past.

"But I'm your *husband*," she heard him say, dejected, confused, let down. Then there was Josie — turbulent, beautiful, passionate, demanding. Nina didn't know which would hurt her more, knowing that your mother had been living a lie for her entire life, or being let down so badly that she'd never get over it.

She'd taken the cash from the pot she kept in the utility room cupboard. Her secret Christmas fund. Before Mick's recent success with the galleries, money had been tight. Cautious as ever, Nina had been saving here and there — ten pounds one week, twenty the next. Soon enough, a few hundred pounds had accumulated. It paid for the heap of metal that the dealer called a car.

"Name?" he'd asked, to put on the receipt.

"Davies," Nina had said automatically. "Sarah Davies." He didn't care, and neither did she. She had no intention of registering it. She drove the old wreck away from the garage in a cloud of smoke, and twenty minutes later it was parked in the pre-planned spot she had carefully chosen the day before. Stashed in the boot was a small suitcase containing the clothes and other necessities she had recently purchased, also using the saved-up cash. As each stage of the plan came together, Nina's heart beat a little faster. She knew that very soon she would hardly be able to contain it in her chest.

Mick was in his studio working. It was a good thing, Nina thought, that life was going on as normal around her. Her recent behaviour — nervous, emotional, erratic and suspicious — was a perfect answer to the aftermath that would be filled with questions; the note left, reread a thousand times.

Why? How could she? Did anyone see it coming?

Nina had no idea if her plan would work; only that she had no option left but to try. There was no one to turn to for help — no one that she could trust, anyway, and she didn't want to endanger those she loved any more than she already had.

She consoled herself with the thought that it might not be forever; that somehow if she was clever, she could claw back a shred of what she once had, maybe even return, explain, beg forgiveness. But it would be a long time off yet. Without that thought, Nina would have ended things for real. As it was, the uncertainty of her not surviving anyway hung as fat as the moon above the city. Either way, the only certainty in life now was death.

CHAPTER
FIFTY-FOUR

I broke into a thousand pieces. The receiver dangled on its shiny cord, and, with my knees bent, my back slumped against the glass, I slid down the inside of the telephone box.

The police were coming. I'd told them everything.

Two female officers helped me into their car. They were bright, cheerful, acting as though nothing was wrong, humouring me, even though I knew things would never be the same again. We drove past Roecliffe. "There," I whispered, pointing into the woodland. "In there."

As we went by, I saw a single blue light ticking in the night. Marking the spot I'd described on the phone. They'd found her.

I would never see Betsy again.

The constables spoke in quiet voices, spoke in code on the radio, drove me through the night, glanced at me in the rear-view mirror, and took me to the police station.

They gave me a blanket — brown and itchy, the kind fit for covering the shoulders of criminals, not the shaking bones of a young girl who had just witnessed a murder.

Someone gave me tomato soup in a mug. Clumps of powder stuck to the sides.

"Is there anyone you'd like to call?" a man asked. He wasn't in uniform.

I shook my head. Maybe Patricia, I thought. Or Miss Maddocks. But what if they'd known about this all along? "There's no one I want to call," I said. The soup burned my lips.

Over the next few days, I gave statements until my voice dried up. Every detail of the last ten years of my life at Roecliffe was recorded. I was sent to a foster family. I spent my eighteenth birthday with strangers, and while technically I could no longer rely on the council for care, someone had taken pity on me and allowed me to stay in the warm, comfortable home that had a mother, a father, other children, smiles and soft carpet.

I lay on my bed, staring at the ceiling. My temporary mother sat beside me and I pretended that it was her, my real mother, and she'd been there all along, that this was my family home and life had been filled with happiness.

"I love you, Mum." I said the words that had been missing for so long. She stroked my head, but didn't reply. From somewhere distant, I heard the words, *I love you too.*

There was a line-up. I'd seen them in cop shows on the flickering TV at the children's home, but never thought I'd be the one staring blankly through the one-way glass. It was easy to identify them, yet the hardest thing

I'd ever done. Worse than seeing a dead body, because they were real; they were alive and dangerous. They stared back with unblinking eyes, knowing that I was only feet away even though they couldn't see me. They were rabid dogs and they'd got my scent.

There were three separate line-ups of carefully selected adult men. They wore sweaters, glasses, brown shoes, some had their hair combed back. A couple wore rings and watches, and one was taller than the others. They were normal. They were someone's father or son or brother. They would blend in on the street.

"That one," I said immediately. They'd already made three arrests based on my statement. The line-ups were to officially confirm who I'd seen. Two detectives stood behind me. I knew I was being observed, through the one-way window behind me: them watching me watching them. "Number two."

"Take your time," the detective said.

"I don't need to. It's him." It was easy. I'd seen him pretty much every day during my years at Roecliffe Primary School. The kids liked him; he was popular. He made up stories and let us do our work outside in the summer. "He was one of the men in the chapel. His name is Mr Tulloch."

The next line-up consisted of six middle-aged men. Most wore dark jackets, except the last one who wore a beige coat. "That one," I said, pointing to a grey-haired man in a navy blazer. "Mr Leaby was in the chapel too." I looked away. He'd been in charge of the children's home forever. Hundreds of children had passed through his care. The detectives nodded. I sipped the water they'd put out for me, feeling the veneer around my soul harden as the final group of men were brought in front of the glass screen.

This time, I took a little longer. The youngest of the men I'd witnessed that night was the one who buzzed around the grounds of Roecliffe on his ride-on mower. Some of the older girls had a crush on him, and some of the boys got to sit on his knee as the tractor carved grooves in the massive lawns.

"He was there too," I said. "Number five." I pointed at his scraggy features. "He's called Karl."

I learned, after the trial, that his full name was Karl Burnett. His mother was German. His father was a wife-beater, a drug dealer, a car thief, with a second home behind bars. Growing up in gangland London, Karl had seen the darker side of life. But he wasn't stupid or without ambition. The papers told his story, about how he'd moved away from the scene of his deprived childhood to start a new life in the north. He'd enrolled in college, taken a part-time job with a landscape gardening firm, fallen in with the wrong people; the same people that had haunted the lives of dozens of children at Roecliffe.

There was no fourth line-up. What point was there in showing me a group of men with black hoods on their heads? None of the arrested would talk, spill names; none were up for telling tales. The one who killed Betsy was the one who walked free.

The first threat came two days before the trial began. The three men whose identity I had confirmed were in custody, but there were more of their kind out there. Even though the children's home had been shut down immediately, the kids farmed off to other institutions, some of the sickos continued underground, avoiding police radar. That was what it was all about, a detective told me when I asked. "We're cleaning up all the shit," he said.

It was an anonymous phone call, at my foster home, plainly telling me that I would die if I didn't change my statement and tell the police that I was mistaken about what I'd seen. By that time, it wouldn't have made much difference. Other evidence proved that Leaby, Tulloch and Burnett were guilty of heinous crimes to dozens of children.

Tulloch had confessed during one of his many grillings by the determined detective in charge of the case. He named several others in the ring, but refused to name the hooded one. The police told me they'd got a squealer, that they were going to catch Betsy's killer. Then they found Tulloch hanging in his cell. Someone had given him a belt.

Further arrests followed. Bodies were exhumed from all over the grounds of Roecliffe, the first being Betsy's limp form from her shallow grave. There would be no funeral. Just a medical cremation after forensics had finished with her.

After I was hit by the car, I had a police guard in hospital. "Someone wants you dead," the detective told me. He had a daughter my age, he said. He showed me a crumpled photo stuck inside his wallet. She was dark-haired, like me, but prettier. He would look after me, he promised. Make sure that nothing bad happened again. I didn't like his smile.

It was after the knife attack that I was finally moved from the area to emergency accommodation. I couldn't give them a description — his face was concealed — but he was strong, he smelled of car oil, and he meant me to die. If my foster-father hadn't come in the front door, causing the intruder to flee by the back, the knife would have gone in properly, would have punctured my heart.

"Oh Christ, Ava!" He spilled on to the floor beside me, pressing his hands to my ribs. I wanted to tell him to stop, that it hurt so bad, just to let me bleed, to die, but the air had gone from my lungs.

I woke in hospital surrounded by doctors and police uniforms. Three days later, I was transferred to a private nursing home. They wouldn't tell me where it was, and the female detective who'd accompanied me said I'd been registered under a temporary name.

"Temporary?" I replied, thinking that's how I'd felt my whole life.

"Until you get a new one. There are people who will help you now."

It was lucky, they told me several weeks later, that I didn't have any family. "The witness protection scheme deals with relatives in certain cases, but relocating an entire household has its drawbacks."

Mark McCormack looked different every time I saw him. Perhaps it was his job that made him appear as a casual labourer in jeans and check shirt one day, and a businessman in suit and tie the next. He talked me through the whole process.

"You can choose your own name," he said. It was the only thing I got to decide.

I settled on Nina Brookes because it sounded normal, as if the person it belonged to had had a proper start in life; that she might be studying at college, or popular with a group of friends her own age, or learning to drive, or madly in love. It certainly didn't sound as if she'd been living in a children's home filled with paedophiles for the last ten years. It didn't sound, either, as if she had no idea what she was going to do with the rest of her life.

"We're sending you to Bristol," McCormack told me when the trial was underway. "It's a much bigger deal than we ever anticipated." He was simplifying things for me, I knew, but I didn't want to hear the adult truth; didn't want to know the extent of the horror I'd been living with. "You'll be given a new identity, a new home, enrolled at college if you wish or set up with a job. Funds will be allocated to get you started and I will be checking up on you regularly. I will be your only contact with your old life."

I nodded, frowning, contemplating being a naive teenager one moment and an independent woman the next. Mark had taken me to a burger restaurant, not far from the second foster family I'd been sent to. Like the hospital, they'd been given my temporary name, wondered why I didn't reply straight away when they called me down for food or chatted to me around the dinner table.

"You'll be moving away in one week." He slid some leaflets across the sticky table. "College courses," he said. He was a kind man, today wearing clothes that suggested he was my dad, even though he wasn't old enough — a body warmer, a striped shirt, grey trousers. He had stubble. I liked him. "I have all the documents you'll need for a new start. There's somewhere for you to live, too. The landlady knows you're coming. She has no idea who you are, what you've been through."

All this was happening because Betsy was dead; because of one phone call; because I'd told.

"Will I get some new clothes?" I asked. I flipped through the leaflets and knew immediately what I wanted to study at college. I showed Mark.

"Theatrical make-up it is then," he said, as if the rest of my life was unfolding before us — all apart from one small detail. "There are certain things I can't reveal to you about this case, Ava . . . Nina," he corrected. "I've successfully relocated lots of endangered witnesses during my career, but there are several reasons why things go wrong. Every day of your life, I want you to live by two simple rules."

I was bracing myself for a lifetime of being hunted.

"Firstly, you must trust no one. Absolutely no one. They come from all walks of life. Last week, for instance, a police officer was arrested." He spread his hands incredulously. "He was part of that ring, Nina. We know for a fact they haven't all been caught yet. I am the only person who knows of your new identity. If there is a crisis, it is me you come to. I will give you a telephone number and you must keep it with you at all times."

I nodded, shaking from the inside out.

"Secondly," Mark continued, "you must never, ever return to Roecliffe or its vicinity. Someone will recognise you. Someone will tell someone who will know someone else. You will be in danger immediately. I don't see any need for you to return there, so keep away." He saw my expression, reached a hand across the table. "But you'll be fine. Just live by those rules. Trust no one and don't go back."

I repeated that mantra on the long journey south. I had a suitcase packed with new clothes, and a handbag containing a passport, bank account details, a national insurance number — everything I would need to start again. The only thing Mark McCormack hadn't done was erase the memories. They were the heaviest part of my luggage as I dragged my new life up the stairs to my bedsit.

"At least I won't go hungry," I said, pointing at the fish and chip shop sign below.

Pretending to be a father sending his daughter off to college, Mark introduced me to my landlady. He showed me the bus route I'd need to take each morning. Term had already begun but I was slotted into the course with a credible back story. Soon, I'd made a couple of friends; soon Mark's visits dwindled to every six months until he telephoned to say he wouldn't be visiting again.

"You have my number," he said. "Call if you ever need help." Trust no one and don't go back, he repeated before hanging up.

I felt strangely excited, as if I was stepping onto a West End stage as the leading lady. I could be whoever I wanted and, with every new person I met, I made up a different tale about my past.

Eventually, Nina Brookes took on a life of her own. Eventually, I found happiness and became Nina Kennedy when I met Mick, the man who was to finally take me away from everything I feared. Never before had I felt so safe, so secure, so certain that nothing would harm me ever again.

CHAPTER
FIFTY-FIVE

Nina had never imagined saying goodbye forever. Equally, she'd never once thought that the danger she'd lived with — the same danger that had faded to glorious happiness over the years — would harm anyone's life but her own.

If I don't do this then their lives are over too, she told herself in a moment of doubt. By leaving them, I save them.

The stage was set. The only thing left to do was die.

The day was warm, the air thankfully still. As ever these days, Mick had woken with a face lined from broken sleep and stress.

"Juice?" Nina offered. Mick shook his head, and poured coffee, intending to take it down to the studio.

The glass skidded across the floor and juice sprayed the room.

"What the . . .?" Mick turned abruptly as something flew past his head.

Nina was red, shaking, crying and kicking the kitchen cupboard as she acted. *I'm so sorry*, she screamed in her head. "I can't stand this any more," she wailed, tearing at her hair, sobbing, gouging at her skin with her nails. Mick tensed, shook his head, and went to the studio.

Her skin was clammy beneath the wetsuit. She'd changed in public toilets at the edge of a park. The rubbery legs trailed in the disgusting mess on the floor. Her hands shook as she zipped up. Her face shone with sweat.

Over the top of the wetsuit, she wore a skirt. A special skirt she'd sewn from material Reacher had mentioned was sometimes used in such stunts. It was rigged with parachute cord and two thin flexible poles. If it worked, it might just buy her an ounce more chance; if it didn't, she wouldn't be around for regrets anyway.

She recalled Mick's story from years ago, about the Victorian woman who had survived a fall from the bridge only because her old-fashioned skirt had saved her. She thought about Ethan Reacher's advice, the detail he'd gone into about the dos and don'ts of a similar stunt for her make-believe film. She might just have a chance. She had to hurry and catch the tide before it turned.

Her heart beat an unusual rhythm, stretching the rubber of the suit beneath her top. She bagged the clothes she'd taken off and dumped them in a lay-by rubbish bin. She drove off towards the Clifton suspension bridge without looking back.

Earlier, Josie had been preparing her things for school, grumpily seeking out games kit that had been scattered around her room during the long summer break. Nina held up an inside-out hockey sock that hadn't made it into the wash. Silently, Josie snatched it from her mother, and stalked off, rejecting Nina's embrace.

Mick was painting, of course, stewing from Nina's earlier outburst with the glass. The last time she'd seen him was as he disappeared into his studio, as he'd done a thousand times previously.

She prayed that her behaviour over the last couple of weeks, the harsh words they'd had, the six empty packets of paracetamol she'd left lying on the kitchen worktop, her handbag containing her purse and mobile phone still hanging on the hook in the hall, all pointed to what she needed everyone — including the police, the local papers, *Burnett* — to believe.

That she was dead.

Nina parked on double yellow lines on the approach to the bridge. A dead woman wouldn't care about getting a ticket. She blanked her mind, knowing that if she stopped to think now, she would never go through with it. She left the keys in the ignition and the car door open, wondering how long it would take before it was stolen. A suicidal woman wouldn't have had the wherewithal for security.

Nina ran up to the bridge, her footfalls recognising that each one was a step closer to the finish line. She swallowed, but her throat locked up around a lump of fear. She passed the giant cables that stretched up to the stone towers. Her breathing quickened as she ran over the sandy-coloured stone paving, the spotlights that made a beautiful spectacle at night, the benches

444

where lovers sat to take in the view. On she ran, over the expansion joints and on to the bridge itself, the white lattice railings casting a vague shadow on the paving.

Up ahead, she saw a woman walking, her hair billowing in the wind. Nina pulled a nose-clip from her pocket, wondering what good it would really do. She couldn't look down; couldn't face the brown stretch of flowing water several hundred feet beneath until it wrapped around her body and dragged her under.

She felt sick from the height.

Nina forced her legs to carry her along the bridge footpath, approaching the halfway mark. She thought about each present moment — not the one before, not the one ahead. All she could see was the next step in front of her, and all she could hear was the breath she was taking.

She stopped. She reached for the rail that ran along the white lattice. Glancing up, her body burning from adrenalin, she saw the high stretch of the wires above designed to prevent people doing exactly what she was about to. With immense effort and a strength that she'd not drawn upon for a long time, Nina hauled herself up the lattice and clung on to the wires above.

Somehow, as others before her had managed, she clambered over. The wire gouged her hands. The metal bruised her shins, her shoulders, her face and neck. She didn't care.

A car hooted and someone called out, waving as they sped past. Urging her on.

Nina stood, her hands gripping the wires, her skirt billowing loose around her legs, and finally she looked down.

She stared at the rest of her life.

She knew it would take three seconds to die.

"Wait!" She heard a cry. Nina looked along the bridge. The woman's hand was over her mouth, her eyes, even at that distance, clearly bursting with shock. A fat, uniformed man lumbered towards her from behind the woman, screaming and yelling, shouting out.

Nina looked away. *He* had told her to do it. He had told her that if she died, he wouldn't harm the others, that he would leave her family alone.

She was doing the right thing, wasn't she?

"Look for the bubbles," she whispered. Her final words swept away on the wind.

"It's pitch black down there," Reacher had said. "Follow the bubbles to the surface. Then swim for your life," he told her, laughing. "If you were really going to do it. No one would, though," he said. "Not without equipment."

The river below was as far away as another planet, another life.

Nina stepped off the bridge.

She was right. Three seconds to die, yet it took the rest of her life.

The water sucked her down and everything went black.

CHAPTER
FIFTY-SIX

"Adam, Adam! Wake up. It's me. Frankie." My tap soon turns into an urgent thump on the wood. "Adam. Open up."

I hear a groan. "What?"

"Adam, please open the door. I need your help."

A moment later, the door pulls back and Adam stands there in tracksuit bottoms. His sandy hair is only slightly more dishevelled than usual, and his top half is naked. He wipes his hands down his face and yawns. "What's wrong?" He stands aside and lets me in. "People will talk, you know," he jokes.

"I'm so sorry to wake you." I'm shifting about, from one foot to the other. I pull my robe tightly around me. "Oh God, please help me, Adam. I'm so worried."

"Can't it wait?" he asks, sitting on the bed. He pulls on a grey T-shirt.

"I need to use your computer. It's . . . it's about the girl I told you about. She's in trouble. Really in trouble. I'm certain of it."

"Then why don't you call her mother? It's hardly your problem, or mine for that matter, at this time of night." Adam's head flops back and hits the pillow. "It's three thirty. And help yourself." He waves at the computer.

I sit at the desk and open up the laptop. In a couple of minutes, I'm logged in to Afterlife. Of course, at this time of night, there's no sign of Josephine online. As fast as I can, I go into my email folder. I open up a new message and begin to type. She'll get it next time she logs in.

To: dramaqueen-jojo
Subject: Urgent. Pls read!!
Message: Josie, listen to me. You are in danger and have to get away now. I can't explain this now. Get to Nat's house. Call the police. Go as soon as you get this.

I don't sign off as Amanda. I nearly type "Mum", but the shock of this may stop her acting on the message. I click send.

"Oh God, what have I done?" I say to Adam. He sits up, frowning at me.

"I have no idea. Tell me."

I fling open the small window and lean on the sill, drawing in lungfuls of night air. For a moment, it's calming, as if the darkness holds all the answers and as long as I keep sucking it all up, everything will be OK. I turn abruptly.

"I have to go back," I tell him. My eyes are wide but don't see anything clearly. My nails dig into the wood. How can this be happening?

"For God's sake, go back where?" Adam pours two measures of whisky from his emergency supply. He makes me drink.

"Home," I whisper as the liquid burns my throat. "I have to go home to put an end to this nightmare." I'm an animal, pacing, not making sense of my surroundings. I'm thinking, thinking. Nothing's clear.

"Whoa," Adam says. "You're not going anywhere like this."

"He'll kill her," I sing out in a crazed whimper. "I was mad. Insane to think this would ever work." My fingernails claw down the paintwork. Adam refills my empty glass. "Will you drive me?" My eyes drill into Adam's. "Now?"

"Drive you where?" He puts down his glass.

"Home. Bristol. *Please*." I turn to face him, sobbing, desperation leaking from every part of me. "I did something so crazy it hurts, Adam, and now I have to go back and fix it. Before it's too late."

A pair of stern hands land on my shoulders. "Let me get this straight. You want me to drive you to Bristol in the middle of the night. In my old wreck of a car?"

"At least it goes. Mine won't even start." I bend my cheek on to his forearm. "She's in such danger if I don't get to her. It may be too late already." I'm sobbing, slurping my drink in the hope it will help, even though it doesn't, pulling at Adam's T-shirt. "I'd take a taxi, but I don't have any —"

"Yes," he says quite clearly. He's already putting on a shirt and sweater.

"What?"

"Yes, I'll take you."

"But?"

"Tell me who's in such danger." Adam shrugs into a coat.

"My daughter, Adam. If I don't get to her, my daughter will die."

Adam asks how long I reckon it will take to get to Bristol. I think back to my fraught trip up here weeks ago, punctuated by a couple of nights in a motel, long recovery sleeps in lay-bys, me staring vacantly across fields for hours, hardly able to believe what I'd done.

"Maybe four hours. Perhaps five in this." I tap the dashboard. Adam has already filled up with petrol at an all-night service station. He bought coffee and snacks to keep us going. I can't eat but the coffee keeps my heart beating.

"I always knew you'd be trouble. Right from the start." Adam glances at me as we wait at red traffic lights. We've not even made it to the motorway yet. "Something about you when I first saw you at the pre-term meeting. Something in your eyes. That gash on your cheek. The way you avoided everyone. There was a story to tell, I knew."

"Is that why you're helping me, so you can find out my story?"

I don't care what he thinks. I just want to get home. My fingers curl round the seat belt, gripping the strap, praying it's not too late. I am numb. Unable to face the truth.

"You know mine," he says. "How else will we pass the time?"

I'm silent for a while, but as the motorway stretches ahead, a voice comes from nowhere. It's mine but I don't recognise it. It tells Adam all about Ava, the little girl who so desperately wanted a family, but had her mother taken by illness and lost her father to drink and neglect. How she was dumped at the children's home, how they took children in the night and abused them, how they'd taken *her*.

"But I'm no sob story; no case for sympathy. I'm alive, aren't I? All those kids dead." A woman I don't recognise brushes her hands clean of the past.

"And no one ever said anything?" Adam is incredulous. "About what was going on at the home?"

"We all knew that telling would mean a beating or, worse, that we'd lose the only home we'd ever known." I stare out of the window. It won't be light for a while yet. Other cars stream past us.

Adam wrenches the car into top gear. "Never gone this fast in her before." He pats the steering wheel and smiles at me.

"Except me," I add minutes later, mulling things over. "I told, didn't I? And see where it got me?"

"What was she like, Frankie. Really. Tell me about my sister."

I sigh. Lying about Betsy won't do him any favours. "She didn't speak much, Adam. She was as scared as a mouse when I found her alone down a corridor. They said her last home couldn't cope with her. She used to . . . to mess herself a lot." Adam's fingers tighten round

451

the wheel. "But she was so sparky, so clever. We used to sing together and I'd tell her stories. She was like a little sister to me. She kept me sane." There was a pause, enough for several lorries to pass. "I made her stuff. Clothes and things, because none of us had very much. When someone went . . . when one of the kids went missing, we used to raid their things. It kind of sweetened out their absence. Horrid, wasn't it?"

"Did she ever mention back home? About her family?"

"She said brother a few times. As if she'd had one. As if she had this hazy memory of someone she loved. But apart from that, I knew nothing about her background. The carers didn't either. They were quite happy for me to look after her so they didn't have to." I imagine Betsy snuggled on her brother's lap, like she'd done on mine.

"Thank you," Adam says seriously. "I really mean it. Thank you." He rests a hand on mine, both of our fingers interlocking, woven with the webbing of the seat belt.

I must have dozed off. My neck is sore and my right hand warm, still encased by Adam's. I glance over at him. He stares intently at the road ahead. To our left, a red and orange streak lights up the sky above the horizon.

"Things got really bad," I continue, picking up where I left off. Adam listens. "After I'd identified the three men from the chapel, I was threatened constantly. They would have killed me if I'd not been moved. I got a name change. The whole works. I was a protected witness. Turned out that the few sickos in and around

Roecliffe were just the tip of the iceberg. The network was massive."

"But Betsy's killer walked free."

"Yes," I say sorrowfully.

"So you had a new life."

"It was crazy. A kid in a children's home one minute, then an adult woman with a new name the next."

"What did you do?" Adam reaches for a chocolate bar. I unwrap it for him.

"Went to college, worked hard. I made a few friends, but I'd had it drilled into me so many times about not trusting anyone, not returning to the north, that I was half scared to even open my eyes in the morning."

"That must have been hard."

"Hard, yet strangely exhilarating to have the slate wiped clean. A couple of years later, I met my husband. That's when things really turned around." Adam glances at me, seeing my mood change. "We had a daughter, Josephine. She's fifteen."

"The one we're going to —"

"Yes," I interrupt. "Then, twenty years later, one of the three men I'd identified was released from prison. God knows how he found me. There were crooked cops in the ring, I know that much. One or two were arrested during the months after I was relocated. I followed the story closely in the newspapers. It was big news when they discovered that an inspector was part of a paedophile ring. No doubt there were others that got away. That could be how he found me. They'll all be on the internet now, hanging around places like Afterlife."

The light grows every minute, transforming the shadowy scenery around us into a drab, grey day. Low clouds hang above, mirroring my mood as we head south. A hundred and twenty miles turn into eighty-four and, finally, signs for Bristol take over from those announcing Birmingham.

"What would it take?" I ask. Adam glances over, puzzled. "To make someone forgive you for disappearing so comprehensively from their lives that they believed they'd never see you again?"

He pulls a face. "What, you mean like you were dead?"

"Exactly like that."

He blows out hard. "A damned good reason, I guess."

"And what if that person came back to life? Suddenly appeared from nowhere?"

"Again, I'd want some damned good reasons."

I'm silent for a while then I leap. I just say it. Not trusting anybody, I've decided, doesn't work. "Adam, on the twenty-ninth of August this year, I killed myself."

Adam swerves the car. "What? You tried to commit suicide?"

"I didn't *try*. I *did*." He steadies the car, gripping the wheel with both hands.

"But you're here."

"As far as the rest of the world is concerned, I'm dead. You're the only person who knows Nina Kennedy is still alive."

"Nina Kennedy?" Adam's driving slows, preparing for yet more shock.

"I was originally Nina Brookes when I left the children's home. I took Mick's name when we married."

"So who's Frankie Gerrard?" Adam is taking this in his stride, as if he now expects nothing less than intrigue from me.

"Frankie is the person I became after I killed myself. I faked my own suicide, Adam, so that Karl Burnett, the man who was after me, would leave me and my family alone. He'd threatened me, threatened Josie. He made it quite clear that the only way he'd back off was if I was dead. I had no choice."

Adam thinks, getting things straight in his head. "Why didn't you just call the police? And why didn't you take your family with you? You could have all escaped somewhere, started over together."

"You think I'd not thought of that? You don't know this man. If we all suddenly disappeared, Burnett would have never given up looking for us. But with my suicide note, several witnesses seeing me jump off the bridge, it was pretty conclusive that I was dead. My body was assumed washed away by the tide. Suicide was recorded. A bereft husband and daughter, a few newspaper reports, that was just passable. But not three deaths. We wouldn't have got away with that." I draw breath. "Besides, how could I shatter the lives of those I loved because of my wretched past? They knew nothing about who I once was." I pause, bowing my head. "I couldn't let them down."

"But why Roecliffe Hall? Why go back there?"

"Burnett was hardly likely to show his face there again, not right after he was freed. Anyway, as I told you before, I decided it was the last place he'd think of looking for me. No protected witness with an ounce of sense would go back to the very place they'd run from. I thought I was being clever."

"And what part did the police play in all this?"

I laugh. "None. Apart from some young constable who thought my husband was beating me up. I tried to tell them, without actually telling them, but nothing came of it. I'd been drilled about only trusting the witness protection contact who'd relocated me. Hard as I tried, I couldn't find him."

"Frankie, this is an unbelievable story."

"You think I made it up?"

"Far from it," Adam replies. "It's written all over your face." And he reaches out and strokes the scar on my cheek.

We hit the rush hour in Bristol. It seems a lifetime since I was last in the city where I'd spent twenty years hiding. I give Adam directions, short cuts to navigate our way through the traffic, and eventually we are heading out the other side of the city to the place I once called home. The cold sea air blows in through the broken heater.

I glance at the clock on the dashboard. "She'll be getting up about now." I'm wondering if it's worth going to school first and waiting for her at the gates, rather than cause a fuss at home. She said she'd been going again. "I don't know how to do this, Adam. I've never come back from the dead before."

"Sounds like you're an expert at it. Tell me where to go."

"Home." The word that used to spread warmth in my heart now fills me with dread. "I don't think she's really been going to school." I think back to the odd online conversation we had.

I decide, too, that in case Josie has already seen my message through Afterlife, it would be prudent to call Laura's house and see if she has made it there yet. I ask to borrow Adam's mobile phone and dial. I pray I can change my voice enough to sound like a teenager and pull this off.

Moments later, I'm hanging up, reeling from hearing Laura's voice, from the deceit. "They've not seen her for days, apparently. That's odd in itself. She virtually lived at Nat's place."

"We'll drive to your house first and then go to her school. Does that sound like a plan?"

I nod. We're getting close. My fingers turn numb. My mouth is dry and I'm dizzy from trying to think what to say to the daughter I betrayed. "Hurry," I say as, when I close my eyes, the truth lashes out from the blackness.

CHAPTER
FIFTY-SEVEN

An entire season missed. The trees are blackened skeletons, as if after a terrible fire. The lush front gardens in my memory are wilted and rotting, fallen for autumn and winter. The occasional house has baskets of dead summer flowers still dangling outside the front door. But only my house has the complete package of death for a facade.

"It looks awful. Drive on," I say, breathless with fear that someone will spot me. I have the sun visor down, a woollen hat of Adam's pulled low over my face. It looks as if gypsies have camped in the front garden. The curtains are closed. Rubbish everywhere. What's going on?

Adam does as he is told and drives on past number eighteen. He stops at the end of the street, waiting for me to tell him left or right. "Can you turn round? I want another look."

As we cruise past again, I recognise one of the neighbours walking with her toddler. On her way to playgroup, no doubt. Nothing much changes, I realise. Life goes on. "Why does it look as if no one even lives there?"

"Maybe they're still in bed. Shall I park?"

"No! Go up this way. There are some shops. It won't look odd if we park there. We can walk back."

Adam does as I suggest and soon we are leaning against the steaming bonnet of his ancient car.

"I should call her." Adam passes me his phone again. I dial but it rings out. "Perhaps they left early."

"Do you want me to knock at the door? No one knows who I am."

I could hug him, but I don't. Instead, he walks the short distance to my home — a trip I made many times. He returns with a puzzled look on his face. "Could they have gone on holiday?" he asks. "It doesn't look as if anyone's been there for a while. There's post on the mat and six pints of milk at the door. I rang the bell several times. I was going to go around the back, but the side gate was locked."

"It's just stiff," I say, remembering all the little quirks about home that only the inhabitants know; the things that *make* it home.

"I'm going round," I decide. "What if she's there alone, or with *him*, or injured or —"

"What if you stop worrying? If anything was desperately wrong, your husband would have called the police." He takes my arm, but I break off into a run. "Wait," he calls, but it's too late. I'm charging ahead, hammering on my old front door, expecting to see Josie's face through the glass. Will she look older, paler, more womanly?

I ring the bell again. Nothing. Adam follows me to the side gate and helps me shove it open. I'm round the back, calling out, yelling for Josie, praying that she'll hear me.

"What about down there?" Adam suggests, pointing down the garden to Mick's cabin. The grass is knee-high around the wooden structure. The roof covered in dead leaves.

"That's the studio," I say and suddenly, Mick is there, his face at the window, staring at me across the garden with love in his eyes. As suddenly as I saw him, the mirage vanishes — as if he was just paint on canvas wiped away.

I race down to the cabin and cup my hands to the glass. There's no one there, just paintings propped everywhere, occupying every surface, exuding the smell of paint even through the wood.

I turn away, intercepting Adam. "No," I say, breathless. "No one's in there." I steer him away. "We can't go in." I'm dizzy, driven, determined to find Josie. "I don't have a key anyway." I remember how Mick kept it on him at all times.

I run across the lawn — an unkempt bog of weeds, leaves and mud — and go up the steps of the deck. I dash to each of the three windows, staring in, ready to face anything, anyone. "Nothing," I call out to Adam. "It's a mess in there. No one home." I'm panting, not so much from running, but what I might find. "Where *is* she?"

An arm settles on mine. "Just what is it you're expecting, Frankie?" Seeing Adam here, away from Roecliffe, at my house, knowing the link he has to my past — both recent and distant — makes me feel weak.

"I . . . I don't know," I say, faltering over words that want to come out but won't. "There are bad people, very bad people, and I don't want my daughter near any of them." I pull up Adam's arm and steal a look at his watch. "I doubt she'd be at school yet even if she was going. It's too early." I rest my head on the window, and then I see it. Josie's computer on the dining room table — a disconnected mess with a bundle of cables wrapped around it. It's as if she's been bound and gagged herself. Has he taken her? The image of my daughter being held prisoner somewhere makes me want to vomit.

"It was always kept in her room," I say, pulling Adam close for a look. "I don't understand." I rattle the French doors. Locked. "The key. It's hidden under that pot for when Josie forgot to take hers to school." I run over to a line of clay planters and tip the middle one sideways. The key is there and I swipe it up. With shaking hands, I let us inside.

Immediately, we both stop breathing. The smell is overpowering. "Let me go first," Adam says. I know what he's thinking. I can't bear it.

He speeds ahead, cautiously scouting through each room, while I wait in the kitchen terrified of what he might find. The bin is overflowing and there are several other bags of rubbish spilling around the room. Old plates and pans are stacked in the sink, and mugs and old food containers litter every surface. This is not the home I left behind. I imagine Burnett virtually living here, disrespecting everything about my life — including my daughter.

"No one here. Dead or alive, even though it smells like a mortuary." I flinch at the image Adam conjures, that a body could have been in the house for days.

We head for the dining room to take a look at Josie's PC, the only link I've had with her for the last few months. Familiar stickers are peeling off the side of the monitor. The keyboard leans against the tower, the screen crooked and smeared. Wires are bandaged around the stack of dusty equipment.

"Why would it be dumped here? It doesn't make sense." I run a finger over it, as if it might somehow connect me with my daughter; send her a warning message wherever she is. I want to fall to the floor in a heap, but there's no time for regrets.

"Can you connect it up? I need to log in to Afterlife. She might have replied to my message." I wring my hands together; tear my fingers down my cheeks.

Adam's head rolls in an arc of understanding as he realises that it was my own daughter I was keeping tabs on back at Roecliffe. He doesn't pound me with questions. I help him plug in the wires to the computer box and stretch the power cable to the mains plug. All the while we are straining our ears for anyone at the door.

The phone rings.

I clap a hand to my mouth as my own voice cheerily asks the caller to leave a message. There's a click followed by the dial tone as they hang up.

I boot up the computer, impatient at how long it takes to get online. Finally, I am logging in to Afterlife, holding my breath for a reply.

"Look," I whisper. "There's a message from her." All the times I nagged at her about going on the wretched game before school, and now I'm so glad she bothered to log in. I pull up the message and read, Adam leaning over me. His hand crawls on to my shoulder as the truth hits us.

If you want your daughter back, come and get her. She'll soon be following in her mother's footsteps.

"Oh my God, no. He's got her!" I run to the corner of the room and throw up.

I wipe my mouth. Adam supports me as I read the message again, making sure I didn't get it wrong.

"It's time to call the police, Frankie," he tells me. "If your daughter really is in danger, then this is more than we can handle."

"But you don't understand," I cry, reacting the way I've been trained. "If the police know who I am —"

"For God's sake, Frankie, stop." Adam is stern. "I would rather have your permission, but if I don't then I'm making the call anyway. A child's safety is more important than your whereabouts being discovered. He knows you're alive anyway."

He's right. The thought that I am no longer dead makes me wish I was. "How did he find out?" I stare at Adam, remembering the rules. *Trust no one, and don't go back.* I have broken both of them.

"I don't know the answer to that, but if it's true then clearly he . . . or they . . . are using Josie to flush you out."

I slump into a chair. My legs are weak. My stomach twists and cramps. "Adam," I say, staring up at him.

There's a weird, unreal light, making me think none of this is happening. "I can't do this any more." There's a pain across my forehead as it drops on to the table. I don't care. Hot tears rain on to my legs as I sob it all out. I know we have to act, but I have no idea how.

When I look up, Adam is searching for reception on his mobile phone. "Wait. If you're calling the police, then it should be Jane Shelley. She'll help me. She thinks I'm a victim of domestic abuse." I pause at the irony. "It'll get the police involved, but won't alert any other kind of suspicion."

I step over the mess in the living room and go into the hallway. My handbag is still hanging on the hook, but my old mobile phone is missing. It had Shelley's number on it. "Bastards," I yell, thumping my fist on the wall. "I don't know her number. Will you dial the headquarters and ask for her by name? But only her. Leave a message if you have to." Adam nods and makes the call for me.

I stare at the monitor again, re-reading the message. It was sent at six twenty-three this morning, not long after my message. I doubt that Josie has used this computer for a while, so that means he sent the message on another PC. It doesn't help me figure out where they are.

"If they want me," I say to Adam, "then they can have me." I set my status to "online" instead of pretending to be offline. Come and get me, I think, praying that he is watching.

"Frankie, what are you doing? I left an urgent message for Shelley. They said she would call me as

464

soon as her shift started. But I think I should make an emergency call as well, to be safe."

"No!" I say. "Just wait. This will work."

"You think he's going to tell you where Josie is?"

I nod, biting my lip.

"Then what?"

"Then," I say quite seriously, "we're going to go and get her."

CHAPTER
FIFTY-EIGHT

The wait is interminable. At nine forty-five, the house telephone rings again. Adam and I stare at each other as my recorded voice asks the caller to leave a message. "Hello, Mr Kennedy. This is the school secretary here. Just calling to find out where Josephine is again today. The head would like to speak to you urgently, if you could please call school when you get this. Thank you. Bye."

"Where *is* her father?" Adam asks, but suddenly the computer jumps to life and makes a noise. We lean in, our eyes scanning the screen to see what's going on.

"Look, *dramaqueen-jojo* is online. That's her." My hand is poised, shaking, on the mouse.

"Or not," Adam says.

Almost immediately a conversation window appears.
-*hello*

"Be normal," Adam says. "We need to find out where she is."

-*hi*, I type. *How r u?*

-*can't talk long*

-*wot u doing?* I mustn't rush this, but time is running out.

-*Josie?* I type when there's silence. *Where r u?*

466

-i dunno, she says. *somewh sfdn,m*

"What's happened? Look. She's typed rubbish."

"Perhaps her hand slipped," Adam suggests.

Then my lungs swell as the air rushes in and my eyes widen. My body responds faster than my brain. I grip Adam's arm.

"Oh God, no," I cry.

-If you want her alive, do as I say.

I'm nodding, begging him not to hurt my family. I'll do anything. My palms are sweating, my skin tingles cold. Adam slides the keyboard away from me and gently removes the mouse from under my fingers.

-Who is this? Adam types.

-Guess

"Adam, don't play games. You have no idea how serious —"

He snaps a look at me, halting me immediately.

-No

It's clear he doesn't know what he's doing either. "Frankie, pass my phone. I'm calling the bloody police whether you like it or not. Call your husband too."

-No police or she dies.

It's as if he's read our minds. "Adam, help her, please." *Oh God, Oh God, Oh God*, I cry over and over.

-What do you want me to do?

-Die. This time for real.

He thinks it's me typing. We stare at each other. I nod for him to continue.

-Tell me how. Just don't hurt her. All I can see in my head is an image of Josie locked up in a dark room, bound, gagged, terrified.

Adam and I jump as a phone rings — not the house phone, but another one.

-answer it

"Oh shit, he's watching us. He must be." We leap up and follow the 'sound. It's coming from the kitchen. Under a pile of empty takeaway cartons, Adam finds a red mobile phone. The screen flashes "unknown caller". He hands it to me.

"Hello?" My voice doesn't sound like my own.

At first, all I can hear is rustling and footsteps. Then I hear a cry — a female cry — and a muffled order shouted.

"It's Josie. Help me, please! Who's there? Will you help me . . .?" Then sobbing.

"Josie? Josie? Can you hear me?" I look at the screen. The call has ended. "Shit," I say, trying to find the list of received calls. "It was her, Adam. She was hysterical. I have to get to her." Adam takes the phone and presses several buttons.

"Nothing," he says. "No number." We rush back to the computer.

-She's alive. For now, is waiting onscreen.

"We can't just sit here typing and taking calls, Adam. We have to get to her." I'm frantic, unable to comprehend how this has happened. Everything I ever believed has been turned on its head.

"Can you think where she'd be? Where does this creep live?"

"I have no idea." I'm sweating. My fingers tear through my hair.

-*Do it properly this time*, he types. *Or she falls instead. Fifteen minutes.*

Adam turns to me. His eyes are slits. "Where, Frankie? What does he mean?" His voice is urgent now as my mind rattles through the possibilities.

"The bridge," I whisper, taking hold of the computer mouse. "He wants me to jump again."

"Or Josie falls instead," Adam says.

I click in the box and type, -*OK*.

Adam reverses out of the drive. I can't feel my body. I am holding both phones, waiting for either one of them to ring as we speed towards Leigh Woods. "The A369," I whisper. "Follow the signs." I can hardly talk. I'm shaking. "This was never meant to happen." Adam doesn't reply. I know he's thinking, *What did you expect?*

There are roadworks in Abbots Leigh so Adam takes a guess and turns down a side street. Following his nose, we find the main road again just past the jam.

"Please, dear God, don't let our luck run out," I pray.

"It's been ten minutes already." He's pushing the ancient car to its limits. "How much further?"

"Not far," I say. We pass the golf course to our right. "Turn left!" I shriek as we nearly miss Bridge Road. Adam jams on the brakes and lurches the car round. Someone hoots. "Keep going. Keep going." The bridge looms between the trees. I glance at Adam's watch. We are still just within fifteen minutes. We couldn't have done it any faster. I can't stand what we might find.

I don't think about dying.

"I'm going to drive on to the bridge," he says. "It'll take too long to park. If they're there, we should spot them." I nod, watching, waiting, as we approach the massive structure.

The tyres rumble as we cross the expansion joints.

"Where are they? Can you see them?" I'm straining forward, unfastening my seat belt.

Adam looks concerned. "I don't know what they look like."

He drives slowly along the bridge. There are several people walking along, hooded up against the cold wind.

"There!" I scream. "That's them." Two figures are balanced precariously the wrong side of the bridge railings, while another stands squat on the road. "Oh shit, it's Josie up there." I let out a string of sobs. "And that's her father beside her."

Adam stops the car in the middle of the carriageway, about fifty feet from them.

"Slow down," he says as I start to run off. "Let's do this together."

Cars behind us begin hooting. At this, the other man swings round and stares directly at us.

"Who's that?"

"Karl Burnett," I whisper, digging my fingers into Adam's arm as we walk forward cautiously. "He's dangerous." I stare up at Josie teetering on the edge of the bridge. Her face is pale and her eyes are sunken into dark sockets. Her hands are bound behind her back and a grimy rag is gagging her mouth. The only thing stopping her plummeting to her death is her father's hand on her back.

"He's got them both. This is bad, Frankie." Adam pulls the phone from my fingers. "I'm going to call for help."

Josie suddenly wails loudly through the gag — a muffled shriek of disbelief as she sees me. Her face turns ashen and her legs buckle from shock. Mick grabs her arm as she slips.

"It's OK, Josie," I yell up to her. "I'm here. Everything will be OK." I stretch out my arms towards her, desperate to run to her.

"The bloody resurrection itself," Burnett growls, approaching me. A knife blade flicks from nowhere. I shrink back. "Did you think I wouldn't find out about your pathetic con?" Mick tenses behind him, his eyes flashing between us.

"I . . . I . . ." I can't speak.

Adam is on the brink of action, sizing up what's going on. He doesn't realise what he's up against. "Get the girl back over," he yells out to Mick, seeing the opportunity while Burnett is distracted. Bravely, Adam starts off to help them. Burnett moves closer to me, angling the blade at my throat. Everything is in slow motion.

"Adam, no! You don't understand!"

"Stay the fuck where you are or she goes over," Mick says. Every muscle on his face is rigid. He yanks Josie's head back by the hair, shoving his face in hers. He spits something at her.

I scream, but nothing comes out.

The breath floods into me from a reserve I didn't know I had.

"*No!* You bastard," I scream over and over until my voice packs in. Burnett briefly turns away and I take my chance, running towards Mick.

"Fucking get back," he spews across the bridge.

Gone are the deep and rich tones I fell in love with. Mick's new voice nearly kills me as I take it all in, struggling to accept who and what he is. As if I'm staring through someone else's eyes, I watch the hands that used to protect his daughter now roughly manhandling her. She kicks and bites, her head thrashing, her eyes wild. A pitiful wail comes from behind the gag. Futilely, she stamps on her father's foot.

"Keep still, Josie. Stop fighting!" If he lets go of her, she falls.

Adam grabs me. He spins me round by the shoulders. "What's going on, Frankie? You said . . . but he's your husband."

I'm panting. "The painting —"

"You were good cover while it lasted, Nina. What better place to hide than with a protected witness?" Mick laughs. "Until *he* came along." His eyes flick to Burnett.

"Two for the price of one," Burnett chips in. He's looking worried, not knowing who to threaten with the knife. "When the cop tipped me off and informed me of *her* whereabouts finding you married to her was a bonus I hadn't expected. There you were, paintbrush in hand, ready to take orders. Didn't want me to spoil your little love nest, did you?"

Everything goes silent. Nothing is real as I act. Blindly. Coldly.

. . . I'll wake up soon and I won't be charging, hurtling towards the man I've loved and adored for two decades — the man I've had a daughter with — and I'll slip my arm round his neck, pull his mouth on to mine, breathe in the scent of his skin . . .

I dart past Burnett, not knowing what I'm going to do. The knife slashes my arm, but I don't feel any pain. Suddenly the world is upside-down as my head hits the concrete. Everything goes black for a second. Burnett's fist took me down.

"Get her over to me," Mick yells to Burnett.

Several onlookers yell out . . . a woman screams . . . a man calls for them to stop.

"Adam!" There's a sharp pain in my head as I stand. "He's going to kill Josie."

"Hurry!" Mick screams.

"Mick, don't do this. She's your daughter!"

He locks eyes with me. "Show me how much you love her and take her place."

"OK! Stop . . ." I step up to the railings. "Don't you love her too?" All the years flash between us. He doesn't even flinch. "You don't really want to do this, Mick." I'm calm, unable to even cry. "Please don't hurt her. Let her come back over to safety." I wait for the look of compassion, a glimmer of regret, but it doesn't come. He grows even colder. Josie is a single grip from death. She is shaking, whimpering, imploring me with her eyes to help her.

Adam uses the distraction to lunge forward and take a swipe at Burnett. The pair scuffle and fight behind me. It sets Mick off. "Last chance or she falls." He's sweating, desperate, red-faced.

"OK," I scream. "Take me instead." Terrified, I climb up the lattice and over the other side of the wires. I did it once, I can do it again. This time there will be no afterlife; none that I will know about, anyway. No one can survive a fall at low tide. It will be over quickly. "Just get her back to safety. Please." My words are breathy, desperate blasts. I cling on to the rail and wires. My legs are shaking.

Then the sirens, at first a lifetime away, but soon the piercing sound draws close.

"You called the fucking police." Mick's voice wavers. He shifts his grip on Josie, shoving her away. She wobbles. One foot slips. Instinctively, he grips her jacket. Josie's hands are tied — she can't hold on.

"No, no, I didn't call them," I shout back in panic. I can't anger him further. If Adam can't hold Burnett back, they'll have us both off the bridge in seconds. "It must've been one of them." I point back at the crowd that has gathered. Why doesn't someone help us? "Mick, listen to me. Everything can be OK again, can't it? Just get Josie to safety. We can talk about this. You won't have to go to prison. I'll stand by you. We're still a family, right?" The words are bitter.

For a second, there's a glimmer of familiarity in his eyes; a scrap of life. And I think he's about to say

474

something. But then Burnett lunges through the railings, towards Mick now. He's panicking at the approaching sirens. Adam stands up with blood pouring from his nose.

"I'm not fucking going to prison again," Burnett yells at Mick. "You got away with killing that brat in the chapel. It's your turn to serve time."

"I should have killed you too, while I had the chance . . ." Mick's words drop off the bridge like stones.

You got away with killing that brat . . .

The world stands still for what seems like my entire life. The wind whips through my ears high up on the bridge.

"You killed Betsy?" I whisper to Mick, unable to scream any more. I'm dizzy. I can hardly hold on.

Mick stares back at me. The man I knew is gone, replaced by the man who has filled my nightmares for twenty years. I married Betsy's killer. The truth blizzards around me; the beginning of an ice-age. I thought I'd worked it out. But not *this*. Not about Betsy.

I grip the wires, my fingers inching along as I step towards Josie. Then the tears flood my eyes. "Hang on, Josie," I call to her. My body ignites from the pain, from the agony of having everything stripped away, from the knowledge of what I have been living with — *what I have forced my daughter to live with* — all this time. It paralyses me. I'm staring at the monster that has consumed my life, Josie's life, without us even realising.

I wobble on the ledge taking tiny steps to my daughter. I won't let her die.

Suddenly Adam hurls himself at Burnett, dragging him down. They fall in a tumbling mass of punches and kicks. I wince as Adam's head hits the road. Burnett leaps up and races to Mick, lashing out through the railings, trying to knock him off balance.

Mick kicks out. "I'm not going to fucking prison." His grip loosens on Josie as he fights Burnett off. I edge closer.

"You won't go to prison, Mick. Just let me take Josie to safety."

The wind lashes my face. "That's it, nice and slow. Let her come to me."

Suddenly, Burnett dislodges one of Mick's feet. He yells, slipping down a foot or two, both hands struggling for a grip.

Josie is teetering with no one holding her.

"No!" I scream, making a grab for her. Just before she topples backwards, I ram her forward against the metal. My arm locks round her waist, pinning her in place for as long as I have the strength.

Mick clings to the lattice with white knuckles — the only grip he has on the bridge. "It's over, Mick," Burnett says. "It's fucking over."

Then Adam comes from nowhere and, with one almighty swing of his fist, he knocks Burnett to the ground. He's out cold. In two swift leaps, Adam scales the lattice railings. The demented look in his eyes tells me nothing will stop him.

476

"No!" Mick roars. One desperate hand still clamps the railing. His fingertips are white. He stares at me, imploring me to help him as Adam climbs nearer.

Screams and gasps fly from the crowd. Josie's muffled sobs tear at my heart as she shakes with terror. "It's OK, Josie. Don't move, don't look . . ." I know what's coming; I know it has to come. Adam works himself closer to Mick.

"You bastard," he yells, each syllable accompanied by a thud as Adam raises his foot and batters Mick's final hold on life. "*You killed my sister.*"

Mick stares up at me — a moment that speaks of our time together.

Then one final kick from Adam and Mick loses his grip on the bridge.

It takes three seconds to die. I know this.

His body drops to the river bed.

I hold Josie's face against my neck.

Oh God, oh God, oh God . . . My voice repeats on a loop. My limbs are stiff and won't move, but suddenly strong arms are around me, prising Josie from me. My instinct is to keep hold of her, but when I see that it's Adam using his remaining strength to pull her back through the wires, I allow him to do it.

Then another pair of arms lock under mine. Two bystanders haul me to safety. I allow my body to go limp as they get me back on to the bridge. Strangers praise Adam for his bravery, for saving us.

A second later, I have my head pressed against his chest, Josie sandwiched between us. I'm sobbing, but it doesn't sound like me. Through it, I hear Adam's urgent breathing and the noise and scuffle as the police finally reach the scene, spreading through the crowd, herding everyone, unsure who is involved or what's been going on.

Adam guides us away from the railings. He unties the tight knot behind Josie's head. His hands are shaking. Josie launches her arms round my neck. There is a band of raw skin circling her face from the gag. I grab on to her — the only real thing left.

"It's OK, it's OK . . ." We are sobbing on to one another, shaking as one, drowning in temporary relief. "Oh, Adam. I can't stand this. *Mick*. Mick of all people." He's stroking my head, finding the energy from somewhere to tell me it's going to be fine, that we're safe now.

"It was . . . him." I press my face to Adam's neck, so Josie can't hear. How will we ever get over this? My legs go weak and I drop to the pavement. Adam gets taken aside by a detective.

"Oh, Mum." Josie drops down with me, clinging to my side. She has cuts on her cheekbone and forehead. She rubs at her wrists from the tight rope. She's sobbing in short bursts. "He locked me up. Pretended to be me on the computer. Said he was going to . . ." She chokes on her own cries. Another officer comes up to us. "He . . . he said he would kill me if he couldn't get you. Said it served me right for being your daughter."

Across the other side of the bridge, I see that the police have hauled Burnett up off the ground. He staggers, semi-conscious. He's already handcuffed. Adam is telling them what happened.

Someone takes me by the shoulders. I flinch and turn, my senses on fire, but a glance tells me it's WPC Shelley. "Stay calm. You're safe now."

"My *husband* . . ." I say to her in a daze, as if her assumptions were right all along. Shelley has pulled Josie and me close, harbouring us against everything. Ambulance men and women arrive with blankets. I'm sobbing again, unsure if I'm shouting out for real, or if it's guilt banging about in my head; guilt that's already setting a hold on my mind. Guilt that I will have for the rest of my life.

Adam is beside me again. I lean away and vomit. Nothing comes up.

"We've a lot to ask you and your daughter," a detective says. He squats beside me. "Let's go somewhere safe."

I nod, struggling to stand, helping Josie to her feet.

We are taken to an unmarked police car. The three of us, Adam, Josie and I, sit in the back. Around us, officers are clearing the bridge, sealing it off. There's a sudden and welcome silence as we drive away from the chaos. Within twenty minutes, we are led inside the police station. I am empty, bereft, a shell. The only thing keeping my heart beating is my daughter pressed to my side.

In the interview room, I squint at him, recognising his face as it resolves from a distant memory. He's been summoned especially. He takes my hand. "Nina

479

Brookes," he says, breaking out a short smile. "It's been a while. We're going to look after you."

"Last time you said that, I believed you."

"I know. I'm sorry, Nina."

The lines on Mark McCormack's face are deeper, the stomach behind his shirt a little bigger. But generally he's in good shape for a man who's twenty years older than when he last came to my rescue. It's as if I'm eighteen all over again.

"I changed fields, in case you're wondering," he says. "I switched to the paedophile unit. I hunt down images, internet mostly these days. Stop the suppliers. Break up the chains. We've been following a specific line for a while now."

Mark McCormack continues, careful how he spreads out the information, unsure of how close to cracking I am. "You did well, young lady," he says, glancing at Josie. He waits for me to react.

"Josie?" I say. What does Mark McCormack know about Josie?

"There was a call during the night, Nina. An emergency call from a very distressed young woman. Sadly, we didn't get enough details to locate her before the line went dead. Josie was so brave." McCormack stops again, allowing her to take over.

"They took me to some horrid place. It stank. I think it was where that other man lived. It was full of awful paintings." Josie cups her face, as if that will erase what she saw. "They drank too much so I got their phone while they were sleeping." A big breath. "I told the police, Mum. I finally ratted on him." She stares

480

blankly ahead; bled of emotion. This is taking all her strength. "But then that man woke up and knocked the phone from my hand."

"Because of the delicate nature of the call, it was referred to my department," he continues.

"Delicate nature?" I say, not wanting to hear this. I, too, bury my face in my hands. "I only just found out, I swear," I say through my fingers. "He was painting pictures of children . . . awful pictures. He was selling them. He used me. He used *us*." I can't bear to look at Josie. "I was his safe harbour. He was clever."

I turn to Adam, who has stuck by my side since we left the bridge. "It was those pictures in the attic, Adam." I clasp his hand. "That landscape painting you gave me nagged at me all evening until it screamed out what I didn't want to admit." Everything I say is broken; nothing makes sense.

Suddenly Josie claps her hands over her ears "He said that I mustn't tell anyone or he'd get hurt and taken away from me," she whispers. "He said he loved me in a special way. That I was lucky to have a father like him; that other dads didn't love their daughters as much. That's not so wrong, is it, Mum?" Her face searches mine for answers.

Oh God, no. What have I done to my daughter?

I lean over to her, hardly daring to touch her. "He was hurting you all these years, wasn't he?" I whisper, crying. Neither of us needs to say what. We both know.

She hangs her head. There's a tiny nod.

I pull her face to mine, cupping her numb cheeks in my hands.

"You did the right thing to tell, Josie. It's all going to be OK. We can help you." I don't know what to say to her. "Your dad did a bad thing, a very bad thing, but it's not your fault." I have no idea where these words come from. I don't know how I will support her. How can I look at her the same way, knowing what he did to her, knowing that he will always be a part of her? His blood flows through her veins; his genes are in her cells. She has his eyes, that coy twist of a smile when she wants something.

"But you died, Mum," she whispers back. She looks drugged. "You weren't here for me." A frown creeps across her brow. "He kidnapped me. My own dad kidnapped me and tied me up." Josie's voice is as far removed from normality as I have ever heard it. I can hardly stand to look at her, for fear I'll see what he did to her, yet I can't take my eyes off her in case she gets taken from me again.

"I came back," I reply, hating myself for how hopeless that sounds. Acknowledging what she just told me is unbearable, but if I am to help her, I need to be here, to never leave her again. We will face this together. We are both alive. "I'm back for good, Josie. You can tell me everything. I'm not going anywhere again."

CHAPTER
FIFTY-NINE

I have to remind myself where I am.

At Laura's house. Laura my friend. She sits across the table.

Josie is curled up on the sofa, while Nat strokes her head. I list them all over and over, as if mentally checking them off will keep them in my life.

Adam sits beside me, trying to get things straight; trying to piece together an old puzzle.

"I'm going back to finish things in the morning." I'd spent the last twelve hours making statements at the police station. Mark McCormack stayed beside me throughout. Jane Shelley ferried food, drinks, messages. She held my hand.

"I sensed he was trouble," she whispered in the interview room, tapping her nose.

"You never even met him," I said.

"Didn't need to. Your behaviour was enough to tell me something was wrong."

"All these years, and I didn't know. Not a clue." I pull the last tissue from the box. I didn't think there were any more tears, but there are. "He never once hurt me. He was so kind. He was *Mick*."

"Your daughter," Jane Shelley said. "She's talking to police psychologists. They're trained in this kind of thing. While, you know, while things have come to the surface. She's more likely to talk now, to make a statement, than if things bubble under again."

I bruise the inside of my head by shaking it vigorously from left to right.

"Why didn't I see it?" I ask Laura.

If I'm honest with myself, perhaps I did. I just didn't want to notice. I scan through Josie's entire childhood in a flash — how she hated it when people said she was pretty or paid her compliments; how she aggressively avoided physical contact as she grew older; how she defended her privacy fiercely; how self-conscious she was about her developing body; how she'd told me that her father loved her in a special way. And the acting — was it a release for her? A chance to become someone else? Someone normal. Added together, the total makes me feel sick. Individually, spread over an entire life, I can see how these things slipped past unnoticed.

"You can't blame yourself, Nina." Laura wraps her arms around me, knowing it's futile. "It's a question I've often asked myself," she mutters. Her life is filled with bitterness and resentment too, but in the light of me coming back from the dead, she feels somewhat lucky.

"But we *loved* each other. He was meant to protect Josie. We were a family." I spill the coffee Laura has made for me. My hands won't stop shaking. I married a murderer. I married a paedophile. "I had a *child* with him." Internally, I test my love for Josie. It sits tight,

484

firm, an immovable packet in my chest. My heart kicks up when I stare through the door and see her hair spilling over the edge of the sofa. "I've got her back."

"And I've got you back." Laura hugs me tightly. She sobs into my neck. "We had a bloody memorial service and everything." She shoves me roughly then pulls me close again. "I kept saying to Mick I'd sort out your stuff, but he never returned my calls. I wanted to help but he shut me out." Her cheeks are streaked with mascara.

"Thank you, Laura. Thank you for being my dear friend." I blank off the tide of feelings that swell through me every few minutes.

I couldn't sleep. The champagne and the painting hanging on my bedroom wall had knotted crazy dreams around me as tight as the sheet. I needed to speak to Adam. After our session earlier viewing the paintings — his kind attempt at an evening out — I desperately needed to use his computer. I was still in denial; only seeing a fraction of the colossal truth.

I put on my robe and started off down the corridor. I stopped. *There were more in the attic*, he'd said. I had to see them.

Slipping quietly away from my bedroom, I went back to the room where we'd been earlier. Thankfully, Adam had left it unlocked. The table was still littered with the empty plates from the food; the paintings were still propped against the wall, stacked on the sill, lying on their backs and hanging on the walls. I shut the door behind me and flicked on the light. I looked up, relieved that the ceiling was low. I dragged a chair beneath the attic hatch and stood on it, reaching up to shift the board from the hole.

A shower of dust and grit rained on my face. I screwed up my eyes, spitting out the dirt. The board would only shift one way — there was something stopping it. When I reached up with my hand, I felt the cold metal rungs of a loft ladder. I found the rope and pulled it down.

Carefully, I climbed up the steps, wobbling and shaking the higher I got. The air turned cold and musty as I peeked up into the roof space. I could just make out the old light switch on the wall to my left. Clouds of dust motes swirled in the light of the single bulb.

When my eyes adjusted, I saw that the angular space was crammed with boxes and wooden crates. I eased myself up, crawling into the filthy attic.

"More paintings," I said. I tilted forward a stack that leaned against the rough brick of the gable wall. When I flicked through them, my stomach curdled. "Oh Jesus," I said, letting them flop back.

Oil paintings. Watercolours. Sketches. Acrylic on board. Canvas. Stretched paper.

Children. Toddlers. Teens. Boys and girls, their faces turned shyly or grinning directly out of the pictures. Pained expressions lay on howling mouths; clawing fingers; faceless adult bodies. All naked.

They were the most abhorrent things I had ever seen in my life.

I recognised some of the expressionless faces. *Jimmy, Marcus, Heather, Kayleigh* . . .

486

I was going to be sick.

But something about them made me look again.

Holding my breath, I opened another box. This time smaller pictures with a stack of old photographs on top, as if they had been used for reference. They were as shocking as the paintings.

"There," I whispered. The similarity in style had already occurred to me when Adam told me to take the rural scene back to my room. I'd slept on the thought, dreamt about it, had nightmares about it. But there was no signature; nothing to confirm the truth that drilled out of my disbelieving mind. "The scarf," I said, feeling the nausea swell.

In nearly every picture, the subject — the *victim* — was either tied or bound by a swathe of pretty material — beauty and pain. "The same scarf that's in the painting he did of me," I mouthed, remembering the nude that I'd been so flattered by. Purple and red chiffon billowed throughout every picture in the attic, binding the subjects, a sick attempt at softening the vile subject matter as youngsters of all ages had been portrayed with grotesque adult forms hurting them in unimaginable ways. The scarf was his trademark.

On several paintings, there were labels. "One hundred and fifty pounds." He'd sold them, made money from them. Worst of all, he'd been here, at Roecliffe Hall.

I'd spent most of my childhood at the home, in the shadow of paedophiles, while my future husband was painting, profiting from, revolting pictures of kids I knew; kids I grew up with; kids that disappeared. There was no doubt in my mind that this was Mick's work.

I fled the attic in blind disbelief. I ran to the bathroom and doused myself with water. I had to wash it all away. I had to stay calm, collect my thoughts, and get to Josie before something terrible happened to her. I prayed I wasn't too late. I prayed I was wrong about everything.

I dashed to Adam's room. I hammered on his door. He stood there, in the middle of the night, squinting at me, puzzling, wondering. I was sure he could see it written all over my face, even though I wasn't entirely sure I knew what it all meant yet myself.

"But how did Mick find me all those years ago? And how did Burnett find out my new identity?" There's too much to take in, too many questions. I'm not sure I want all of them answered. I remember my wedding. How much Mick said he loved me. How he put a single rose in my hair. "We met by accident."

"My best guess in both cases," Mark McCormack replies, "is a police informant. Sad to say, but it was probably someone in the force who tipped him off. These men are fiercely loyal to each other. Mick following you to Bristol was clever."

I think back to when we met — the painting, my trousers, the wind. How natural it all seemed, how perfectly meshed with fate it was. But he'd planned it all. Watched me. Stalked me. Figured out just how he was going to jigsaw into my life. The safest place for him.

"But how come those paintings were never discovered?" I thump my fists on the table. I'm angry. The water glasses jump. "If the police had done their jobs back then and searched the building properly, the paintings would have been found and maybe the artist apprehended." I dash through an alternative history.

In truth, I know that even if they had found the stash of paintings, locating the perpetrator would have been nearly impossible. It wasn't as if he'd signed any of them. It's just a hopeless wish that — oh God, it hurts to think it — that I'd never married Mick.

"It was a tight circle," McCormack says. The DI sits beside him, a female officer the other side. "We got a couple of names from Tulloch, but then he killed himself. Leaby died of cancer in prison five years ago. I'm trawling back through the case file, but it'll take time. If you think the search of the building was badly handled, you should see the rest of it." He drags his fingers down his face. He looks as if he's been up all night. Like I was, watching over Josie.

"I've worked on one other case similar to this. Further south. About three years ago. The maddening thing was that many of the people involved with the institution knew what was going on at the time."

I gulp water. Roecliffe wasn't unique.

"So why did they keep quiet?"

"Various reasons. Mostly it's because people don't want to rock the boat or face up to the truth. They have their jobs, their lives. The staff at Roecliffe would have lost their incomes if the home was shut down. Telling the police was more than their livelihoods were worth.

489

The eighties weren't known for high employment rates." He breathes out heavily. "Either that or they were part of it themselves."

"So many kids died. They suffered indescribable acts." I'm talking about it, thinking about it in a detached way, as if it wasn't me who lived through it. They've promised me counselling, but I'm not so sure. My priority is for Josie to begin healing. "Will I have to see Burnett in court?"

"That depends," Mark says. His manner is still kind, considerate, but now I see a hard edge around his character. A product of years working in the paedophile unit at Scotland Yard. "On whether you want to testify against him." He eyes me, gauging my reaction. He needs reliable witnesses.

I nod. "Whatever it takes." Already I'm thinking far into the future, to when he's served his time, been released again. I'm running out of lives to live. "And just so you know, I'm Ava now. Ava Atwood. Josie will change her surname too. We'll do it officially." I will not be anyone else ever again. Already there's too much discovering to do; finding out who we really are — me and Josie — what we can become.

"I understand," McCormack replies. "Your cooperation is appreciated."

It dawns on me. "Are there any of them left at Roecliffe, do you think?"

He's nodding before I've finished. "Let's just say we were close. Watching and waiting. Now this has happened, I sent in a team. There have been several arrests in the village and quite a few more throughout

490

the north. Art, if you can call it that, and other images were seized. Websites shut down. There's more to come, I expect."

"That's how Mick and Burnett knew I was still alive," I whisper, hoping Mark can clarify. "Someone in Roecliffe must have recognised me and tipped them off. Then they worked out it was me talking to Josie on Afterlife."

He claps his hands together. "Told you not to go back. Did you listen?"

"Trust no one and don't go back," I say. McCormack's reading a file that his colleague has passed to him.

"Brimley? Does that name mean anything to you?"

I shake my head.

"He received pictures off Burnett. Sold them on." He skims down a list. "Also a Barnard. Frazer Barnard. He's under police guard in hospital. Tried to overdose when he was brought in. Had pocketfuls of diazepam at the ready."

"Him," I say. "It would have been him that tipped off Burnett. He must have recognised me at the chapel." I'm shaking, knowing how close I'd come to one of *them*. How close I'd been most of my life. "One night, there was an intruder. Someone at the school . . ." I trail off. McCormack is lost. I've not reached that part of my story in the statement. There are many days' work left yet.

"We'll continue tomorrow," Mark says. "Go home." He rests a hand on my back when I ask where, exactly, that is.

Adam is waiting for me at Laura's house. "I've got to go," he says. "They need me at work."

"Leave?" I repeat with a tinge of hysteria. He's my friend. I trusted him and it felt right. Amazingly, resiliently, Josie is on the computer with Nat. Their heads are pressed close as they sit on the sofa. Laura insists on Nat using her computer downstairs now. I see the familiar pages of Afterlife glow pink and green in the dark room. "Of course," I say, sighing, resigned, empty. I don't want him to go.

"I called Mr Palmer. The police have already briefed him. He refuses to close school early for the end of term, even though part of it has been sealed off for forensics. He's doing everything he can to help, while keeping the girls safe. He's a good man."

"Typical Mr Palmer," I say, attempting a smile. "*Non scholae sed* . . . or whatever it is."

"The show must go on." He puts on his jacket; jangles his keys.

I think of my show — of the films I was going to work on, taking Chameleon to the next level, of Josie's musical. "Did you speak to Sylvia?" I imagine her wrath at the hundreds of odd socks, the creased skirts, the muddy sports kits.

"She sends her love," Adam assures me. Somehow his hand has settled on my shoulder. It's drawing me close. A last embrace.

Suddenly I am in Adam's arms, my face pressed to his chest, inhaling all that potential, everything that never was — not for a married woman — and all the common history between us.

Adam's history . . . I recall Sylvia's words as we were introduced.

It's true, I live in the past . . . he'd replied.

We're outside. He's beside the car. "I hope it gets you back," I say, patting the roof, meaning the complete opposite. I pray it won't even start. Laura stands in the light of the doorway, Josie and Nat beside her. They wave. Adam embraces me again.

"We'll speak soon. OK?"

That brings on the tears. I nod. Smile as best I can.

He gets in and starts the engine. A cloud of black fumes billows from the exhaust. He winds down the window, faking a cough. "Bye then."

The car moves forward, but, before I know what I'm doing, I've hurled myself into its path. I land on the bonnet.

"Stop!"

The sudden braking sends me sliding off the front and on to the road. Four faces stare down at me.

"Mum, you could've killed yourself!" Josie hugs me.

I stand up. "I'm fine," I say. "Josie, get your things."

"What things?"

"Anything. Your coat. Whatever you need for the rest of your life." I turn to Adam. He is shaken and pale. "We're coming with you," I tell him.

"What?"

"Don't trust anyone and don't go back," I say. Josie is beside me wearing her coat, her shoes, hugging her arms round her body. She doesn't want to risk being left behind again. "So I'm trusting *you*, Adam Kingsley, and we are going *back* to Roecliffe." I bundle Josie into the car. "I have a job to do, and Josie needs a school to go to." I hug a speechless Laura, then Nat. "You can see her on Afterlife," I say to the shocked girl. "And come up in the holidays." It's all so easy.

"Josie?" Nat circles the car and leans in at the window. "Are you really going?"

For a second, Josie looks pained. "I want to be with my mum. If she's going, then I am too." She smiles weakly. "Everything's horrid anyway." The girls hold hands and Josie allows Nat to open the car door and wrap her arms round her. The embrace is long and tender — the promise of lasting friendship, of holidays together, of chats online, of phone calls and letters.

"Look after Griff for me." Josie wipes away a tear.

"I'll sit next to him at lunch every day and make sure no one else talks to him." The girls laugh. "Did you see that he's changed his room on Afterlife again. He's gone all pink. He told me last week that he's getting in touch with his feminine side."

Josie rolls her eyes and eases Nat out of the car. She blows her a kiss.

A moment later, I'm sitting beside Adam. "Go on then. Drive us home."

He frowns, glancing sideways at me. "But the investigation? What about the police?"

"I'm not under arrest. I'll still help them. They can come and find me. Laura will tell them where I've gone. Just drive, Adam." Momentarily, I cover my face

494

with my hands. If what I'm doing is wrong, why does it feel so right? "Please."

Adam stares, nods, then drives, coaxing the old car along the motorway as we head north to Yorkshire — sometimes sitting silently, watching as cities turn to countryside, and sometimes the three of us chattering excitedly, our words tumbling over each other until at last we pull down the long drive to the school.

From behind I feel the tentative fingers of my daughter creep along my shoulder. I reach back and hold her hand, feeling her grip tighten as she gets the first glimpse of Roecliffe Hall. Her eyes flick over the other girls in uniform as Adam parks the car. Her pupils widen. She licks her lips. "Don't be scared," I tell her. Don't be scared, I tell myself.

Seven Months Later

On the way to Mr Palmer's office, I pass by the IT room. Several girls are hunched over computers, heads down, biting lips, nibbling nails. One of them is my daughter. "Hey."

She turns at the sound of my voice. Her cheeks redden. She looks good in the green uniform — checks, a starched blouse, jade-coloured blazer. Josie fits in as if she has been here all her life. She lifts her hand in a lazy wave then returns to the screen. She takes notes from a website about animals.

"He's not back until morning," Bernice says. She plucks the letter from my fingers and puts it in the headmaster's pigeonhole behind her desk. "I'll see he gets it." There's another letter already on the wooden shelf; the one Adam wrote earlier.

"Thanks," I say, and walk briskly down the corridors to continue sorting games kits.

Adam is waiting for me, leaning against the wall with a newspaper spread out between his hands. "More today," he says, holding up the relevant page. I turn away. I can't look. "They're back at the gates again."

I shake my head. "It's not good for the girls." Fourteen pupils have already been removed from the school by worried parents. Police guards to keep the journalists and tourists out of the school have been in place since the story broke a few months back. The only reprieve was while the case was waiting to go to court. Eight further men arrested for possessing child pornography; one of them Burnett who was charged with kidnap and selling indecent images of children. All refused bail.

Children's Home Horror. Kid-Pic Monster Arrested. Paedo Dad Dead.

Some of the stories were blatantly wrong; some were painfully true, like the one with the headline: *Woman Falls For Pervert.*

"Did you do it?" Adam asks. Curiosity has got the better of me and I'm skimming the latest article. A picture of Burnett shows him being led into an armoured police vehicle after the guilty on all counts verdict was delivered yesterday.

"Sorry?"

"Did you deliver the letter?"

"Oh. Yes."

Adam slips a hand round my waist and it soon becomes an embrace. The newspaper drops to the floor between us.

"How soon?" Sylvia asks. She looks tired. She fields phone calls every day from concerned parents, convincing them that their daughters are safe, that the council-run children's home of years ago has nothing to do with Roecliffe Hall Independent School. "You're the best assistant I've ever had."

I hug her. She smells of laundry powder and cigarettes. "Soon," I say. "Next week if Mr Palmer agrees to let us go before the end of term."

"Us?" she says.

"Adam, too. We're going away. The three of us." I bow my head as if that will make it easier for her to accept.

"Are you two . . ."

"Oh no. It's nothing like that." In my head I scream, *Yes it is!* "We're just friends. We want the same thing." A quiet life far away from here.

"Where will you go?" Sylvia asks. Her hands are on her hips, her elbows jutting, her eyebrows raised high.

"Australia." Something swirls in my stomach. It will be good for Josie. She's excited. We want to be on the other side of the world. "Nice and hot."

Since I returned to Roecliffe, I've chatted to Sylvia about everything that happened but she knows I don't want to talk about it in detail. She's been watchful of me, careful if someone asks for me on the telephone. She's briefed the receptionists not to let anyone past front desk if unexpected visitors come calling. She's been my mother, my protector. She understands.

"Don't be paranoid, Sylvia," I told her, one of my hands wrapping round two of her bony ones. "I have to live. I can't hide any more." I sighed. "They're all behind bars now."

"I won't have anyone hurt you," she said. "Besides, there's no one as good at ironing as you." She laughed, probably knowing all along that I wouldn't stay, that Roecliffe bled misery into my head at night. Josie, thankfully, blustered on, but seeing her skittle down the corridors, curl up in the dorm at night, zig-zag around the sports field was becoming too much to bear, just too familiar.

When Adam said he was going home, back to Australia, that he'd been offered Head of History at a school in Brisbane, I told him I was going with him. I clapped my hand over my mouth.

"It's a long way," he said, smiling, curious, looking as if he still hadn't figured out an ounce of me. "And there are evil spiders and it's bloody hot. Besides, you don't have a visa." He play-punched me.

"I'm serious, Adam." I looked up at him. I was shivering. It was freezing in the dining room. "I thought that coming back to Roecliffe would be the answer."

"You had to find out for yourself." Then he took out his Rizla papers and rolled one without any tobacco. He bent it into a circle and passed it to me. "Marry me," he said as if he was asking me to pass the salt. "I want to take care of you . . . And Josie."

"OK," I said, slipping the circle of paper on to my finger. Then we both laughed, and after that I fell against his shoulder and cried for an hour.

"These were hers," I say, holding out the hairclips. When my house was finally sold last week, I fetched the last of our personal belongings. I had several thousand pounds' worth of make-up and effects to collect that would be needed for my new business in Australia.

Adam takes the clips. He twists them between his fingers. "All that's left of her," he says. "I think I remember her wearing them." He shoves them deep inside his pocket. He's told me he won't ever come back to England. Not now he knows. We're marking the spot with another tree, hoping the little birch will push up under the canopy of oak. Betsy has no other grave. She was cremated anonymously when the police were done with her.

"She loved the flowers," I tell him. Clumps of bluebells shine azure around us. Summer sun spatters through the leafy spread above. It's as if we're paddling in a lake. "For Betsy," I say, plucking a handful of stems and laying them at the base of the little tree. Adam nods in agreement.

Mr Palmer is waiting for us, hovering behind the receptionist's desk as we bluster back into school. Adam was telling me about the rainforest in Queensland; about the amazing birds. He gasps as he sees the clock. "I'm late for class," he calls, speeding off, but Mr Palmer stands in his way and herds us both into the photocopying room.

"A quick word," he says, flicking on the light. Adam is agitated, unhappy about his timekeeping.

"Yes, Mr Palmer," I say, knowing it is about our letters.

"I wanted to let you know that I accept your resignations." His face is blank, pallid, tired. "I understand completely," he says.

500

The poor man has been through more than a head teacher should have to cope with these last few months. Instead of running the school, he's been fielding the press, and police forensics teams have taken over various parts of the building. Once the journalists found out he was a local man, they tried but failed to prove a past link with him and Tulloch. The story would have been huge.

In the meantime, Mr Palmer insisted the school function as normally as possible. Some classrooms have been relocated to mobile buildings in the grounds. "I wish you luck with your new ventures. There will be a formal letter to you both. Mr Kingsley, you will be released from your two-year contract early. Miss Gerrard, we will all miss you. The girls especially warmed to you." He nods; unfolds his arms as if letting us go.

"Thank you, Mr Palmer," Adam says and excuses himself.

"It's been a gruelling few months," I say.

Mr Palmer flicks off the light. "You can leave as soon as you wish," he says through the darkness.

I am staring out through the window beside the old front door. Josie sits on the window seat with her hands splayed out on the glass. "It's not fair," she says. "It'll be winter all over again."

"Except winter in Queensland isn't like winter here, silly." We're both staring down the long drive, waiting for the taxi to arrive. It's hard not to see myself where Josie sits, all those years ago, praying that the next time

I opened my eyes I'd see my father's Granada sailing towards me.

"Taxi's been held up." Adam drags the last of our bags into the hallway. "Fifteen minutes."

Josie groans and slides off the seat. "This is boring," she grumbles, wandering off.

"Don't go too far," I tell her. I latch myself to Adam's arm. It's tense from carrying the bags. "Should I be doing this?" I ask, although really I am asking myself. "This whole Australia thing."

Adam laughs. "The lifestyle's good. With the proceeds from your house sale, you'll be able to buy something very comfortable."

"We," I say, producing the paper ring from my pocket.

"Crazy woman." And he kisses me.

"Betsy used to sit here and wait for me to come back from school," I tell him. I'm dizzy from the depth of him. I glance at my watch. "I'd better track down Josie. She's probably disturbing lessons and hugging all her friends again." I've already said my goodbyes, making Sylvia promise not to wave me off at the door. I want to slip away unnoticed.

I set off down the corridors, quietly calling out her name. I swear she went this way. "*Josie.*" I turn left and walk briskly past a row of leaded windows facing out on to the old courtyard. "Josie Atwood, where have you got to?" There's no sign of her.

I peer through the glass-topped door of a classroom and hear French verbs being recited. She isn't in there. "Maybe she went down here," I say, heading towards the IT room. "She might be sending an email before she leaves." I glance at my watch again, aware that the taxi will be hooting for us at any moment. I give up and turn back, deciding to try the other corridor leading off the main one.

"Jo-*sie*," I sing out. There's no reply. Most of the rooms along here are either storerooms or offices used by different heads of departments. I fling open a door and a pile of hockey sticks collapses out. I gather them up and stuff them back behind the door. "Where are you, Josie Atwood?" Her new name still sounds odd. Two more doors are locked and then I go right into an office, interrupting Mr Dixie who is standing there, holding his mobile phone out in front of him.

But he's not calling anyone.

"Oh, I'm sorry," I say. I'm about to leave when I see the girl. A year seven girl. Her face is red. Mr Dixie snaps the phone shut and sits down behind his desk. The girl tucks in her blouse.

"Sorry," I whisper, backing away. I'm suddenly freezing cold. "S . . . sorry."

"No problem. Harriet was just leaving. Weren't you?" He eyes the girl. She runs out of the room.

"I'm going," I say, terrified, not knowing how to contain the pot of fear that's boiling inside me all over again. "I'm going too."

The walls are closing in on me. The school bell sounds and suddenly the corridors are filled with the chatter and footsteps of teenage girls. I run as fast as I can back to the hall.

"Josie," I shout, charging towards Adam. My face is burning; tears sting my eyes. I have to get out of this place.

"She's here, Frankie. Calm down. She just went to the loo." Adam has his arm around my daughter's shoulders. "Cab's here," he says. "Everyone got everything?"

I'm panting, trying to breathe normally. Hiding my face, I gather up as many bags as I can manage. Between us, we lug them out to the taxi. "Skipton station, please," Adam says when we are all belted in. "Frankie?" he asks, turning round to grin at me, but halting when he sees I'm upset. "What's the matter?" He hasn't got used to my real name yet.

"I'm fine," I tell him. I stare out of the back window, watching the diminishing sight of Roecliffe Hall as I leave for the very last time. "They're like cancer," I whisper, thinking of my mother. A liver tumour spread to her bones, her lymph glands. "You can never get them all out."

"What are you on about, Mum?" Josie has been naming as many Australian animals as she can think of with Adam. *Echidna*, someone squeals.

"Who's got cancer?" Adam asks. He chucks Josie a packet of mints. "You've forgotten a koala," Adam tells her.

There's more excited banter as I pull a notepad out of my bag. I begin to write. My hand shakes as we bump along to the station.

I feel queasy. I don't have an envelope. As we pull up to the dropoff point, I rip up the note and let it fall into the gutter as we get out. I don't know what to do.

It's raining and Adam sends us inside while he loads a trolley. "Mum, what's wrong? You've been really weird since we left school." Josie links her arm with mine. "Aren't you excited?"

"I've been trying to forget everything."

"You'll be OK when we get to Australia. It's what we need, Mum."

I give her a squeeze.

"I still don't know," I whisper to Adam as he joins us in the queue. "If telling was the right thing to do."

He doesn't answer; simply holds on to me as we trundle through the countryside to King's Cross station; plays cards with Josie when she's bored; fetches us hot chocolate and sandwiches from the buffet carriage.

Four hours later we're checking our bags in at Heathrow for an evening flight. Josie yawns. "Not long now," Adam says. "It's an adventure."

There's a man sitting next to me at the departure gate using his laptop computer. He's looking at photographs of kids — some on the beach, some at a party, some taken at the park. He pauses on one in particular, a little girl of about four or five standing completely naked in a paddling pool. Someone is squirting a hose at her. She is red with laughter. The man stares long and hard, smiles to himself and then shuts the lid, patting it. He makes a call, talking in a silly voice, grinning fondly, blowing kisses down the phone, telling someone night-night, that he loves her.

"Adam, I'll be right back," I say. Josie's eyes have closed and she doesn't notice me leave.

I push enough coins into the payphone. I pull out the card from my purse and dial the number. At this time of night he won't be there, but I know he regularly checks voicemail.

"This is a message for Mark McCormack," I say clearly, anonymously, and I tell him what I saw in Mr Dixie's office. It might be nothing. But I can't risk it.

"Done," I say, when Adam asks where I've been. "It's all done. Over. I can't do any more." I snatch up my bag, my jacket. I glance around at the other passengers.

"I wondered where you'd gone," he says. "They've just called our flight."

I lean against Adam and drop a kiss on my tired daughter's head. We shuffle forward in the queue to board. As we hand over our boarding passes, step through into the tunnel leading to the plane, I take a last glance over my shoulder, saying a silent prayer. There's a young family behind us, an old couple. I sigh and briefly close my eyes. No one is watching us leave.

Also available in ISIS Large Print:

Unspoken

Sam Hayes

A mother with a secret: Mary Marshall would do anything for her daughter Julia. A devoted grandmother, she's always been the rock her family can rely on. Until now. Mary has a past Julia knows nothing about, and it's come back to haunt her . . .

A husband on his knees: Murray French is walking a tightrope. A solicitor struggling with an alcohol problem, he's about to lose his wife Julia, and his children, to another man. Someone successful, someone they deserve. Someone who's everything he's not. Can he ever get his family back?

A woman in danger: just when Julia Marshall thinks life is starting to turn around, she stumbles upon the brutalised body of a girl she teaches. And as the terrible present starts to shed light on her mother's past, Julia realises her family's nightmare is only just beginning . . .

ISBN 978-0-7531-8242-0 (hb)
ISBN 978-0-7531-8243-7 (pb)

Blood Ties

Sam Hayes

Harrowing, shocking, impossible to forget . . .

January 1992. A baby girl is left alone for a moment. Long enough for a mother to dash into a shop. Long enough for a child to be taken.

Thirteen years later, solicitor Robert Knight is delighted that his stepdaughter has won a place at a prestigious London school for the gifted. The only puzzle is his wife Erin's reaction. Why is she so reluctant to let Ruby go?

As Erin grows more evasive, Robert can't help but feel she has something to hide, and when he stumbles across some mysterious letters, he discovers she has been lying to him. Somewhere in his wife's past lies a shocking secret — one that threatens to destroy everything . . .

ISBN 978-0-7531-7932-1 (hb)
ISBN 978-0-7531-7933-8 (pb)

ISIS publish a wide range of books in large print, from fiction to biography. Any suggestions for books you would like to see in large print or audio are always welcome. Please send to the Editorial Department at:

ISIS Publishing Limited
7 Centremead
Osney Mead
Oxford OX2 0ES

A full list of titles is available free of charge from:

Ulverscroft Large Print Books Limited

(UK)
The Green
Bradgate Road, Anstey
Leicester LE7 7FU
Tel: (0116) 236 4325

(Australia)
P.O. Box 314
St Leonards
NSW 1590
Tel: (02) 9436 2622

(USA)
P.O. Box 1230
West Seneca
N.Y. 14224-1230
Tel: (716) 674 4270

(Canada)
P.O. Box 80038
Burlington
Ontario L7L 6B1
Tel: (905) 637 8734

(New Zealand)
P.O. Box 456
Feilding
Tel: (06) 323 6828

Details of **ISIS** complete and unabridged audio books are also available from these offices. Alternatively, contact your local library for details of their collection of **ISIS** large print and unabridged audio books.